SPEED
THE DAWN

Also by Philip Donlay

The Donovan Nash Novels

Seconds to Midnight

Pegasus Down

Aftershock

Deadly Echoes

Zero Separation

Code Black

Category Five

SPEED
THE DAWN

A DONOVAN NASH NOVEL

PHILIP DONLAY

OCEANVIEW ◖ PUBLISHING

ISBN 978-1-60809-230-7

Published in the United States of America by Oceanview Publishing
Sarasota, Florida
www.oceanviewpub.com

10 9 8 7 6 5 4 3 2 1

PRINTED IN THE UNITED STATES OF AMERICA

For my son, Patrick

ACKNOWLEDGMENTS

FIRST AND FOREMOST, I want to offer my deepest gratitude to all of the brave first responders everywhere—the few among us who run toward the danger instead of away.

I want to extend my profound thanks to my family and longtime friends. You always help keep me pointed in the right direction. To my parents, Cliff and Janet; as well as to my brother, Chris; and son, Patrick—thank you. To Bo Lewis, Kerry Leep, Scott Erickson, Pamela Sue Martin, Nancy Gilson, Brian Bellmont, Phil High, and Mike Orindgreff: You've all played a bigger part in the completion of this book than you'll ever know.

I'd also like to thank my agent, Kimberley Cameron, and her team of talented professionals. Then, of course, there are the people who shed light on subjects well beyond my expertise. Dr. Philip Sidell and his entire staff, thanks for being there for me. And, as always, Dr. D. P. Lyle, you're the best. Jason Forthofer, Dr. Richard Blomberg, Thomas Humann, Victoria Dilliott, Samantha Fischer, Jeff Frye, David Ivester, Maddee James, Pat Frovarp, and Vicki Harlander: You are all amazing, and I'm the first to admit that I couldn't do what I do without your efforts. To Oceanview Publishing, the people who turn my words into books—I am forever thankful.

And finally, heartfelt thanks go out to all of my thousands of brothers and sisters around the world, who, like me, battle Ankylosing Spondylitis and the associated nightmares that come with this fearsome disease. You inspire me each and every day to keep fighting and move forward.

SPEED
THE DAWN

CHAPTER ONE

DR. LAUREN MCKENNA looked up from her tablet as an intense white light shot past the window of the Gulfstream. Lauren squinted as another burning object fragmented under the tremendous forces of high speed and friction, creating hundreds, if not thousands, of small separate hazards racing downward.

The noise came all at once, like a sudden hailstorm. Instantly, hundreds of small pinholes opened in the ceiling. Lauren gripped the seat as the Gulfstream shuddered. She turned away from the window to shield her eyes from the brightness. In the aisle toward the cockpit, her friend Montero spilled coffee as she went to the floor. Lauren looked beyond Montero. Someone in the cockpit cried out in pain. Rick, the first officer, was recoiling in his seat as if he'd been shot. Lauren's ears popped, and from somewhere above her, she heard air rushing from the cabin. She felt the first sharp sting of terror claw at her self-control.

Lauren glanced at the screen mounted on the bulkhead. The Gulfstream was descending out of thirty-five-thousand feet, seventy-five miles east of their destination of Monterey, California. Outside the large oval window, another bright white light fell from above. Spots from the harsh light danced in her vision. She followed the meteors all the way to the ground, expecting them to vaporize well before they struck the earth, but the shockwaves expanded outward as they impacted the desert below. Stunned,

Lauren watched more glowing debris slam into the ground, and when she looked upward, there were more clusters entering the atmosphere high above them.

This meteor shower was happening faster than Lauren could process. Disbelief turned into fear as more glowing meteors continued to rain down out of the late afternoon sky, careening earthward.

Lauren threw off her seat belt and raced for the cockpit. The pressure leaks sounded louder. Her anxiety escalated as she wondered why the oxygen masks hadn't dropped. She reached Montero, scared that her friend had been hit. "Montero, are you okay?"

"What in the hell happened?" Montero reached out to Lauren for support as she pulled herself to her feet.

"Are you two okay?" Michael Ross called out from the cockpit. He took a quick glance over his shoulder. "Hang on," he said. "We're going to make an emergency descent."

"What can we do?" Lauren asked. "Do we need masks?"

"No, the hull has been breached, but it's a slow decompression. I'll have us down below ten thousand feet before we need the masks."

Strapped into the right seat, Rick thrashed against his injuries. He grimaced in pain and pulled his arms tightly around his midsection. Blood soaked his shirt and one leg of his trousers. He looked up at Lauren, tried to speak, but what came out sounded more like a strenuous groan. "What happened to us?"

"A meteor shower," Lauren said as she heard the engines change pitch as Michael maneuvered the damaged Gulfstream into an even steeper descent.

"Lauren, you and Montero go back and sit down," Michael said. "This could get rough. When you're back there, I need both of you to assess any damage to the plane. Come back once we're level and bring the first-aid kit for Rick."

Montero stepped aft, peering out the front cabin window, then turned to Lauren. "Tell Michael, both wings are leaking fuel."

"We're leaking fuel," Lauren said.

"I heard, now get strapped in," Michael said.

Lauren used her hands to steady herself as she followed Montero to the rear of the plane where they buckled themselves tightly in their seats.

Montero was right about the fuel. When Lauren looked out her window, she saw tiny streams of mist billowing off the upper surface of the wing. Jet fuel was vaporizing as it escaped the tanks. Ahead of them, the sky was aglow as dozens of huge clusters streaked toward the ground. To her surprise and confusion, contrails crisscrossed the horizon. She spotted different trajectories in play, debris falling at different rates and directions, as if some sort of cosmic chaos had been unleashed. Of all the meteor reentries she'd studied, she'd never seen or read about anything like this.

A deafening boom filled the cabin. Lauren flinched, her ears popped, and she felt the reverberation from the explosion in her chest. She frantically searched out the window, looking for any sign the Gulfstream was coming apart around them. Streaking across the sky well above them was an object far larger than all the others. Burning debris was falling away as it hurtled beyond the haze and clouds that marked the horizon. A flash of pure white light momentarily filled the sky and then it was gone, leaving only a vast contrail across the heavens.

Montero gripped the armrest of her seat. "Lauren, what was that? What's happening to us? Was that sound from the airplane?"

"It was the sonic boom from a big meteor, which just passed over the top of us and hit somewhere far to the west."

"How far?" Montero asked.

"I couldn't tell. The meteor vanished into the haze. I'm hoping it hit well out to sea. The second Michael levels off, we're going up front to help Rick. Could you tell what happened to him—where he was hit?"

"I was standing at the galley, talking to both of them when there was that awful noise. Dozens of holes appeared in the roof like we'd been hit by a twelve gauge. All I saw was that Rick got hit in the back, near the right shoulder," Montero said. "There may be more."

"With the speed those objects were traveling, whatever hit him most likely went straight through," Lauren said. "We'll have to work fast to try to stop the bleeding."

"I'll be right behind you," Montero said, the hard expression in her eyes marking her determination. "I'll grab the medical kit and be ready. You're the better doctor."

Lauren felt Michael begin to flatten out the descent. She unbuckled her seat belt and ran forward with Montero trailing. Reaching the cockpit, she touched Michael's shoulder. "We're still leaking fuel out of both wings, not a big leak, just a bunch of small ones," she said. As she spoke, she saw that most of the instrument displays had gone dark.

"It's okay," Michael said. "We have enough fuel to get on the ground."

Lauren reached for Rick's wrist and felt for a pulse. He was strapped into his seat, chin resting on his chest. Mercifully, he'd lost consciousness. She looked up and studied the holes in the ceiling of the airplane. It didn't take much to imagine the fragments, no larger than a BB, traveling at thousands of miles per hour punching through the aluminum skin of the Gulfstream. Lauren leaned over to find Rick's wounds and heard the distinct crackle of electrical wires shorting above her. The acrid smell of burnt insulation quickly filled the air, and a dozen circuit breakers popped, followed seconds later by several more. A loud bell sounded, and Lauren saw red warning lights on the instrument panel. Michael gripped the controls tightly as he began to react to this new emergency. She knew enough to understand that the bell meant there was a fire in one of the engines. Michael's hands flew around the cockpit as he silenced the warning bell and began the process of shutting down the engine. Once the procedure was finished, he fired the first of two fire extinguishers.

When Lauren found the entry wound on Rick's shoulder, she began feeling for the exit wound.

The red light stayed on, and Michael pushed the button to release the second fire bottle and waited.

In the confines of the cramped cockpit, Lauren located the larger exit wound. Alarmed at the amount of blood soaking Rick's shirt, she clamped her hand over the wound, hoping to staunch the flow.

When she looked over to Michael, his eyes were glued to the instrument panel. The red light remained on. They were still burning.

CHAPTER TWO

DONOVAN NASH LEANED against the railing of a second-story balcony at the Monterey Bay Aquarium and took in the beauty. It was first time he'd been alone all day. He inhaled the marine air and listened to the gentle crash of the waves as he gazed out at the Pacific Ocean. In all of his travels, the Monterey Peninsula, and Pebble Beach in particular, had been one of his favorite places, so much so he once lived here. He'd been gone for twenty-five years, though some of the memories had never dulled. He sifted through his distant past, and pictured, as he always did, the ways his world had once crumbled around him. Pebble Beach wasn't far from where he stood, and it marked the place where everything came apart. As he pictured his former home, the man he used to be, he was powerless to hold off the flood of memories.

He was born Robert Huntington III, heir to the family oil business. His idyllic childhood ended when he was fourteen years old, when his parents died in a boating disaster, a sinking that spared only Robert. His godfather was a family friend, William VanGelder, and under William's tutelage, Robert began the task of education and refinement that would prepare him for his destiny. On his twenty-first birthday he inherited billions, becoming one of the ten richest men in the world, and he took the helm of Huntington Oil. He worked hard, and played even harder. Robert was a charismatic mix of JFK Jr. and Howard Hughes. His ever-expanding world eventually brought him face-to-face with the wildly famous environmentalist Meredith Barnes, and the unlikely pair fell in love.

The evening Meredith said yes and put on his engagement ring was easily the best moment of Robert's life. Six weeks later, Meredith was dead. She'd been kidnapped and shot, and Robert was the target of the investigation. Though quickly cleared of any wrongdoing, he was vilified. The world believed he'd used his money and influence to escape punishment for his crime. His business enemies used the resulting media frenzy to cripple him, his integrity, his work, and his entire life began to unravel. As Robert recoiled, he felt helpless, wounded like never before. Initially, he left California and flew to Virginia to stay at an old family estate that few knew existed. But eventually, he returned to Monterey and took refuge in the Pebble Beach house he had shared with Meredith. His grief and despair slowly devoured him. William discovered him lying in his mansion, unshaven, grieving the death of Meredith, caught in a vicious cycle of endless sorrow, drinking, and taking pills.

William had asked him if he'd thought about ending his life. Without hesitating, Robert admitted that he had. In a matter of weeks, William laid out the plans for Robert's death, and together they orchestrated the plane crash that killed Robert Huntington. Around the world, people cheered the death of the man they considered a billionaire murderer. Rumors swirled about Robert's guilt in killing Meredith. It didn't take long for conspiracy theorists to paint Robert as the cause of any death that may have given Huntington Oil more power. It was an undeserved label forever connected to Robert Huntington.

He'd always remember the crisp fall day, months later, in the Swiss Alps when he first stepped into the sunshine as Donovan Nash. Thanks to William's efforts, his wealth still intact, Donovan was sober, twenty pounds lighter, and with his appearance surgically altered, he boarded a private jet and flew to London to start his life over. In retrospect, his biggest surprise was that he and William had managed to maintain the deception. Other than the two of them, only eight other people in the world knew that Robert Huntington had never died.

As the images faded, his thoughts shifted to the present. He was having a birthday in a few days, turning fifty-three. He was in good shape, and his wife, Lauren, told him he could easily pass for a man in his forties. Despite a little more gray hair, he contemplated being another year older, and decided he was content, and for the moment at least, he wouldn't change a thing, back then or today. He and Lauren were happily married and were parents of a remarkable seven-year-old daughter, Abigail. Donovan often explained to others that his daughter was a highly inquisitive wild child, a perfect mixture of her parents. Like her mother, Abigail was intelligent, and it never took her long to solve a puzzle or understand the nuances of a new game. She was also fearless, regardless of the activity, be it riding horses, catching snakes and frogs at the farm, climbing trees, or going flying with her dad. Abigail had a constant thirst for knowledge and adventure, and she read constantly. Though perhaps his daughter's greatest achievement was turning Donovan into her coconspirator. She was Daddy's little girl, and at times, Donovan inwardly cringed at the thought of Abigail becoming a teenager.

The latest Eco-Watch ship, the *Howard Buckley*, cruised majestically just outside the harbor. With its sleek design and clean lines, this magnificent ship was one of Donovan's proudest achievements. Members of the Monterey Bay Aquarium's Board of Directors had just finished touring the ship. Tomorrow would mark the official launch of the joint venture between Eco-Watch and the Monterey Bay Aquarium. The collaboration put the state-of-the-art *Buckley* into the hands of some of the world's leading oceanographers.

Fifteen years ago, Donovan had first envisioned Eco-Watch. From those early dreams, he'd created a reality that far surpassed his expectations. As Director of Operations, he'd presided over the activities that made Eco-Watch the world's premier private environmental research organization, operating two highly modified Gulfstream jets, multiple helicopters, and three oceangoing science ships. With a nearly unlimited budget, he'd assembled the best minds in the industry to work on the planet's most pressing environmental problems. Eco-Watch's mission statement was simple. Streamline the time it took ideas to reach the field and be tested. Private meant no red tape, and that was Eco-Watch's specialty.

A wistful smile came to Donovan's face. The new ship, the *Howard "Buck" Buckley*, was named after a friend and colleague whose untimely death had hit everyone at Eco-Watch hard. The ship was Donovan's way to try and give back to the former Navy SEAL who had done so much for not only Eco-Watch, but for the extended Eco-Watch family. Donovan missed Buck intensely. He'd been more than a friend, more like a part of the family. Lauren and Abigail loved him, as did most everyone else he encountered. As an employee, Donovan missed Buck's quiet, determined attitude and the infectious energy he shared with everyone he met.

The *Buckley* represented the culmination of years of planning and building. The ship was designed around the latest cutting-edge technology in marine research. Ice capable, the research vessel was just over four hundred feet long. In addition to a crew of thirty, the *Buckley* was outfitted to carry sixty scientists for two months with a range of nineteen thousand miles, and could easily make headway against ice up to a meter thick. With climate change undeniably under way, the first changes in Earth's ecosystems were taking place in the polar oceans, and the *Buckley* would be the ship that would take the scientists to the front lines.

Donovan glanced around the vacant landing, then at his watch. It was a little after five p.m. and the aquarium was closing. He briefly wondered where Shannon had gone. The last he'd seen, she was with the chef in charge of tomorrow evening's reception dinner. She was somewhere close, as she knew as well as he did that they needed to leave shortly to get to the airport to rendezvous with William VanGelder, the chairman of the board of Eco-Watch, and Donovan's oldest and closest friend. William had spent the afternoon playing golf at Cyprus Point with one of Eco-Watch's largest donors and would meet up with Donovan and Shannon to greet the inbound Eco-Watch Gulfstream. Once everyone arrived, they would all be helicoptered out to the *Buckley*.

William wore many hats. For over fifty years, his unparalleled business savvy, combined with his keen intellect, allowed him to rise to the pinnacles of Wall Street power. Known as a formidable behind-the-scenes power broker on both sides of the Beltway, he eventually made the transition to active member of Washington's political elite. In addition to his role at Eco-Watch, he was also a special envoy with the State Department. Although he was seventy-seven years old, William had the exuberance of someone half his age. Donovan loved William like a father and looked forward to having him at tomorrow's event.

"There you are," Shannon said as she pushed through the heavy glass doors. "I'm not intruding, am I?"

Donovan smiled at her perfect timing. He'd met Shannon three years earlier, shortly after Buck's death. She and Buck had been romantically involved, though she didn't talk much about their relationship. Buck had been notorious for keeping his private life private, and everyone respected his wishes. Only under the most tragic of circumstances had Donovan gotten to know Shannon, and discovered that she was smart and talented, though perhaps a little on the quiet side. Donovan wondered if she were always that way or only when she was around him.

Shannon was medium height and slender, a gifted athlete who grew up in the Bitterroot Mountains of Montana. She'd gone to school to become a mental health therapist and then combined her analytical skills with her artistic talent. She used art therapy in a myriad of ways to reach out and help troubled and damaged people, focusing mostly on veterans with PTSD. She was in her early thirties. She had straight brown hair that hung below her shoulders, and her deep-blue eyes were framed by bangs. Although she was attractive, with the hardship she'd endured over Buck's death, she always seemed a bit subdued, as if on the verge of a smile that just didn't quite materialize.

"It's such a beautiful ship," Shannon said as she joined Donovan at the railing.

"It really is. I think this is the first time I've had a chance to be alone and just admire what we built."

"Again, I can't thank you enough for allowing me to be a part of the ceremony," Shannon said. "It means a great deal to me to send the *Buckley* off in good hands. I think Buck would have approved."

"I'm happy you're here."

"I think about him all the time. I miss him. When I picture the ship, it helps. I feel that, in a way, he's still out there, at least in spirit, doing good things for people." Shannon sighed and then changed the subject. "Speaking of people, I was hoping you'd give me a final rundown of everyone I'm going to meet when the airplane lands, and then again, when we get out to the ship. I'm still trying to put names with faces and how they all connect back to Buck."

"My pleasure. It's pretty simple. You've already met William."

"Of course—he's quite the charmer, isn't he? You two seem very close."

"I've known William for years. He was a friend of the family, and when I graduated from college, we began a professional relationship, as well as maintained our friendship. He's part of the family. My daughter Abigail calls him Grandpa, and everyone, especially William, is happy with that job description."

"It shows. So, on the jet coming out today is Michael, your wife, Lauren, and Montero, right? Plus another pilot—you said his name is Rick?"

"Yes, you met Lauren at the funeral."

"I do remember her. She's a doctor, right?"

"She has a PhD in Earth Science and is a consultant to the Defense Intelligence Agency. She and Buck were close. He saved her more than once—and my daughter, too. I hope you and Lauren get a chance to visit over the next two days."

"I'd like that," Shannon said. "Buck didn't talk much about the jobs, but he did tell me about some of the people. I know he thought highly of Eco-Watch."

Donovan felt the sting of losing Buck. He'd known the weekend was going to be emotional, and with long-practiced effort, he gathered himself and buried his feelings to be dealt with later. "Janie is the helicopter pilot on the *Buckley*. She's Australian, and though I'm not a big fan of helicopters, she's one of the best pilots I've been around. If I have to be on one, Janie is who I want flying the thing. She'll be taking us back and forth from the ship to the aquarium. Michael is my right-hand man at Eco-Watch, and I couldn't do the job without him. He's the glue that makes everything we do stick together and work like it's supposed to. He's a former Navy pilot, so he and Buck got along great, of course. Michael is rarely serious—you'll love him, I promise."

"I remember him. He's like a younger version of William— outgoing and charming. I didn't know if Janie was going to make it here or not. Last time I spoke to her, she was still based on the other West Coast Eco-Watch ship."

"*The Pacific Titan*," Donovan said. "She and Buck were such good friends, so when she requested immediate assignment to the *Buckley*, I gave it to her."

"Janie and I are friends, and you're right, they were close. Right after the helicopter crash in Alaska, when Janie hurt her shoulder, Buck was sidelined, as well, with his injuries. She was recovering in Australia, Buck wasn't sleeping well, and the time zone difference allowed them to speak on the phone a great deal. I got to know her when she returned to the States to wait for delivery of the new helicopter. I love that girl. She is so nice. Best of all, there's a wild Australian ranch girl underneath her cool demeanor. Growing up in Montana, I swear, it's like we're sisters. Which brings us to Veronica Montero. I gather she's a different animal altogether?"

"That she is." Donovan smiled. "Oh, and by the way, never use her first name. She hates it. Just call her Montero like the rest of us. She's an acquired taste. She and I didn't hit it off straightaway, but eventually our relationship evolved into respect, and finally, friendship. She's one of my favorite people. She and Lauren are the best of friends. In fact, it was Lauren who reached out to Montero after she'd left the FBI. And Abigail calls her Aunt Veronica. She's the only person allowed to say that name out loud."

"Janie and I talked about what happened in Guatemala. I guess Montero did some work behind the scenes."

Donovan once again sensed Shannon's pain—Guatemala was where Buck had died. Donovan had been there. He could relive the details second by second. Buck was beside him. A moment later, he was gone forever.

"I don't know much about Montero other than her work at the FBI, when she stopped terrorists about to commit an atrocity in

Washington, DC," Shannon said. "I was living there then. She saved so many lives, including mine. She's famous, larger than life, but I'm not sure Buck ever met her. What I do know is that she was on the cover of every magazine that mattered. I watched as she testified before the Senate anti-terrorism committee. She was on television for weeks. I thought she was kind of a rock star."

"She still gets treated that way, especially by anyone in law enforcement. It's uncanny how many people know her name, what she did, even though she's changed almost every detail of her life."

"So, she up and quit the FBI?"

"She didn't like what her life had become. After the FBI exposed her, made her the poster child for the war on terrorism, she was unable to do the kind of fieldwork she loved. Her skill set, while different than Buck's, is good for Eco-Watch. As for meeting Buck, I think they crossed paths after the terrorist attack, when she and I were in the hospital recovering from our injuries. I got the impression later on that Buck wasn't a huge fan of all her publicity."

"He wouldn't have been," Shannon said as she shook her head. "Buck hated that stuff. I think they teach them humility at SEAL training. Every Special Forces guy I know is that way. They do the job, they go home. It's a culture the military builds. I find that the Special Forces guys are the hardest for me to reach in therapy. They integrate so fully into their job, and much of what they do gets buried so deep, they don't even realize it's there."

"It is a culture unto itself," Donovan said. "I know people in the community, and you're right. Training and dedication are everything. I'm glad there are people like you who can help them."

"Who else am I going to meet?" Shannon asked, changing the subject again.

"You'll meet Rick, who's been flying with Eco-Watch for several years now. Good pilot, nice guy. He didn't know Buck, but I can promise you that everyone on staff, whether they've been with us from the beginning or started last week, knows about Buck and the contributions he made. There will always be a ship in our fleet named the *Buckley*."

Shannon started to reply when Donovan's phone pinged. He looked at the screen and saw a text message from William:

I'm on the 17th tee, and just learned I'm without a ride to the airport. Can you swing by and pick me up?

"Change of plans," Donovan said as he returned William's text, telling him they were on their way. "We need to leave now. We're going to Pebble Beach to pick up William at Cypress Point Golf Course. We'll head to the airport from there."

Shannon started toward the door and then abruptly stopped, reaching out for the railing as if to steady herself.

Donovan felt the vibration coming up from his feet at the same time he heard what sounded like thunder. He snapped his head skyward and spotted a cluster of glowing burning objects streaking down from above. Moments later he heard and felt the impact. More objects hurtled toward the ground and hit just on the other side of the aquarium. He couldn't see the result of the multiple impacts, but he knew enough to realize that each one would spark a fire.

"What's happening?" Shannon flinched at each new explosion.

Donovan grabbed her by the wrist, and they ran toward a fortified concrete overhang and pressed themselves against the wall. "A meteor shower, I think. Though I've never seen so much debris reach the ground."

A massive detonation shook the building, and Donovan felt his chest reverberate from the shock wave of a sonic boom. He threw his arms around Shannon and knelt to make them a smaller target for what was coming. Despite the pressure building in his ears, he heard a deep rumbling sound that pummeled them both. The sky above them lit up, and Donovan held up his hand to try and block out the intense brightness. He was stunned as a huge, white-hot meteor sizzled across the sky and hit somewhere just over the horizon. Still seeing spots and swallowing against the ringing in his ears, a shock wave rolled in from the open ocean. Pieces of concrete sheared off the building, peppering Donovan's head and back. The sound of shattering glass mixed with the distant sound of car alarms and the panicked screams of people beyond his sight were all he could hear. More meteors whistled down from above, plunging into Monterey Bay and throwing up geysers of water as the superheated elements exploded upon contact with the cold Pacific Ocean.

Diesel smoke poured from the *Buckley's* stacks and water boiled from the stern as the ship accelerated and turned hard out to sea. Donovan was momentarily confused as to why the *Buckley* would leave, until the reason registered, and he pulled Shannon to her feet.

"What are we doing?" she asked, confused.

"We have to move."

"Why?"

"Because there's a tsunami coming."

CHAPTER THREE

"DAMN IT!" MICHAEL'S eyes were locked on the instrument panel. "The engine is still burning. Keep working on Rick. We're flying, but we're in trouble. I have to get us on the ground. Now."

Lauren tried to visualize the trajectory of whatever hit Rick. She figured the object came in high and slightly from behind him. She'd found the entrance and exit wound in his shoulder and arm, but when she'd moved his arm aside, she discovered a second entry wound in his right thigh, and as she thought she would, an exit wound, along with an expanding pool of blood underneath.

"I've got the first-aid kit. What do you need?" Montero knelt behind Lauren and opened the red carry bag.

"Gauze, lots of it." Lauren used both hands to quickly rip open Rick's shirt to expose the entry wound on his shoulder.

"Here." Montero handed up a handful of gauze.

"I need more," Lauren called to Montero. She pressed hard against the shoulder wound. "Give me twice as much for the exit wound, and then I'll need some tape."

They worked fast, and once the bleeding on Rick's right arm and side had slowed, Lauren hooked her finger inside the hole in his trousers. Using all of her strength, she tore apart the material to expose the second entry wound in his thigh close to the knee. Then she reached under Rick's leg and found the exit wound. Meantime, Montero kept ripping open packages of gauze from the first-aid kit and presenting them to Lauren, who slid them into position and pressed them against the wounds.

"Now what?" Montero said.

"Look for a tourniquet. Something for his thigh. We need to stop the bleeding there."

Lauren kept pressing Rick's thigh wound as hard as she could.

Michael, still focused on flying the plane, diverted his attention to ask, "How is he doing?"

"At first I thought he was hit multiple times," Lauren said. "But now I think a single fragment came in high and hit him in the shoulder, exited his arm, and then went clear through his thigh. He's lost a lot of blood."

Montero handed Lauren a strap with a buckle attached. Lauren loosened Rick's seat belt to create some slack in his harness. She pulled the tourniquet underneath his wounded thigh, positioned it just above the wound, snapped it together, and cinched it as tight as possible. When she checked under the gauze, Lauren was relieved the bleeding had slowed.

Michael was next. He'd been nicked in the scalp and a small notch of his right earlobe was gone. The wound didn't look serious, but both lacerations were bleeding.

"Is my ear still there?" Michael said with a grimace.

"Don't squirm," Lauren said as she gently touched his ear to inspect the wound.

"Ouch, damn it, that hurts." Michael jerked away. "It's my earlobe, isn't it? I'm disfigured now, aren't I?"

"It's nothing a big earring won't hide," Montero said as she handed Lauren a small section of gauze and some tape.

"Thanks," Michael said. "Maybe I could get a matching nose ring as well?"

Lauren had always loved Michael's humor, and she found herself momentarily caught between a smile and tears. If Michael could fire off a joke while flying a burning Gulfstream, then maybe it wasn't the end of the world. Michael was one of the most resilient men Lauren had ever met, and over the years, Donovan had reiterated that Michael was one of the best pilots he'd ever seen. But at this moment, Michael looked worried as he alternately looked out the windshield, searching, and then turned his attention back to the partially operating instrument panel.

"What can I do?" Lauren asked.

Michael turned toward her. "What few instruments I have tell me the engine is still burning. Salinas is dead ahead. I wanted to land there, but there's a fire midfield, blocking the runways. Monterey is just beyond."

Lauren looked at what lay out in front of them. The Salinas airport was just off the nose. A blackened oblong crater bisected the runway all the way to the ramp, where a string of parked planes, vehicles, and buildings lay destroyed and burning. Farther ahead, she spotted Monterey. Dark smoke rose from a dozen or more distinct sections of the city, with more smoke climbing into the sky to the south. Intermittent flashes told her that the fires were no doubt spreading, feeding and growing, as they consumed everything flammable.

"How long until we're down?" Lauren asked.

"Less than ten minutes," Michael replied. "I need you to secure Rick as best you can."

Lauren started tucking Rick's hands underneath his shoulder straps to keep them from flying around at touchdown. Montero zipped up the first-aid kit and stowed it in the forward closet. Michael gave both women a quick nod of approval. Rick was as secure as they could make him. Lauren made one more check of his wound. The tourniquet seemed to be working.

"I've got this," Michael said. "Get to the back, and don't get out of your seats until we've come to a complete stop. I'm not kidding.

I don't know if the gear or flaps are going to come down. This could get ugly in a hurry."

Lauren leaned in and kissed him on the cheek. Michael was doing what he did best. She trailed Montero to the rearmost seats and strapped in tightly. Lauren was doing her best to control her fear. As they descended, Lauren started smelling the smoke billowing from multiple points near the airport. She saw flames reaching high above the houses and buildings, curling and flaring brighter as they expanded and intensified. She heard the landing gear swing into place, though she had no idea if it was down and locked. She memorized the emergency exits and dug her fingers a little farther into her seat.

"The gear sounded normal, right?" Montero asked.

"We're going to be fine. We've got Michael being Michael, and he's going to get us on the ground in one piece," Lauren said as she braced herself, helpless to do anything about her fight or flight impulse but sit and wait for the wheels to touch.

The Gulfstream rode through the low-level turbulence and drew closer to the ground. Lauren's legs quivered with exertion as she braced her feet for impact. Michael brought the remaining engine to idle, and a glimpse of the runway appeared beneath the wing. She held her breath as the main gear touched the runway. She waited, almost anticipating the sound of screeching metal, or the muffled explosion of blown tires. Instead, she felt her seat belt dig into her abdomen as Michael leaned heavily on the Gulfstream's brakes.

Out her window, Lauren could see only about a hundred yards in the smoke as they rolled out past the main terminal. Parked near a doorway sat a destroyed commuter jet, its right wing collapsed at the root. Smoke billowed from the terminal itself, but the absence of firefighters or ramp workers told her that everyone had evacuated. Through the smoke, Lauren caught sight of the control tower perched on a small hill. At least two of the large glass windows had been shattered, and she saw no evidence of movement inside the cab.

Michael taxied the Gulfstream to an empty section of ramp at the Monterey Jet Center, swung the jet around, stopped abruptly, and shut down the remaining engine.

Lauren threw off her seat belt, and with Montero right behind her, ran to open the main cabin door and lowered the steps. As the stairs swung outward, Lauren could see sheets of flame dancing skyward just beyond the airport perimeter. Massive pillars of black smoke boiled up, nearly obscuring the sun. She tried to push aside thoughts of herself, and instead, she focused on what was supposed to unfold after they arrived. The plan was for Donovan, William, and Shannon to be waiting, and then Janie, the *Buckley*'s helicopter pilot, would shuttle everyone out to the ship for a private Eco-Watch dinner. From what she could see, there was no Janie, no William, and no Donovan.

"I'm shutting everything down," Michael called over his shoulder. "Lauren, I need you to help me with Rick. Montero, you make a quick check of the airplane, especially the left engine. Try and see if anything is still burning."

Lauren waited as the stairs extended and then slid into place. As the whine of the right engine spooled down, Montero bolted down the steps. A gentle breeze brought in the sound of a civil defense siren in the distance, and Lauren envisioned a new and deadly threat. Lauren turned toward the cockpit. "Michael, how high above sea level are we?"

Michael had already pulled himself out of his seat and was unbuckling Rick's harness. "Two hundred feet or so, why?"

"I hear a tsunami warning." Lauren's voice wavered as she said the words aloud, and Michael's expression told her he was thinking the same thing. Two hundred feet was safe, but the aquarium was at sea level.

"I can't see any obvious flames or smoke coming from the engine or the airplane," Montero called out from the top of the stairs. "There's burn marks all down the fuselage on the left side. The paint has bubbled, some has even been peeled away. There's still fuel leaking from the wings, but not like before."

"This is one messed-up airplane. I'm just glad we're on the ground," Michael said to Lauren, and then shifted his attention toward Montero. "We're bringing Rick out. Do you see any emergency vehicles at all, anywhere?"

"No, nothing, it's like the entire airport has been evacuated," Montero said.

"I guess meteors falling from the sky will do that," Michael mumbled as he flexed his legs and slid his hands under Rick's arms in preparation to move the unconscious pilot. "Lauren, when I get him to the entryway, I'm going to set him down. Then I want you to check and make sure his tourniquet is still tight."

"I'm ready," Lauren said as the rhythmic sound of thumping rotor blades reached them both. She and Michael looked out the cockpit windows and spotted the low-flying helicopter. Lauren recognized the Eco-Watch Bell 412 as it came in directly overhead, banked sharply, its rotors biting into the air as it swung around in preparation for landing.

"Our ride just showed up. Let's go!" Michael shouted to be heard above the noise from the helicopter. He lifted and pulled Rick out of the blood-soaked chair, eased him the short distance to the aisle near the door, and carefully set him down.

Lauren checked the tourniquet and his pulse, and despite what appeared to be a great deal of blood loss, Rick's pulse was steady. "Everything's good," she told Michael.

"See if you can take his feet. Once we're down the airstair, the three of us can carry him to the chopper."

Lauren nodded her understanding and hurried down the airstair as the helicopter descended the last few inches and lightly touched its skids to the tarmac. Janie Kincaid was clearly visible behind the controls. Lauren waited, and when the cabin door didn't slide open, her hopes plummeted. There was no one in the cabin; Donovan hadn't showed up as planned.

Michael, with Rick cradled in his arms, negotiated the stairs while Lauren protected the tourniquet. Once on the ramp, and with Montero's help, the three of them carried Rick to the idling helicopter. Janie had unfastened her harness, moved to the cabin, and slid the door open from the inside.

"I'm going to close up the Gulfstream, then we're leaving," Michael called out once they laid Rick down on the floor. "Try and secure him as best you can."

"Have you heard anything from Donovan, William, and Shannon?" Lauren asked Janie above the noise of the helicopter.

"Nothing. I tried to call both him and William, but the phones are out. All I get is a busy signal," Janie said as she shook her head. "We'll get Rick to a hospital and then I'll come back for them. This place is absolute chaos. They could be anywhere, but he knows to come here."

After Michael tossed chocks under the nose tires and closed the Gulfstream's door, he ran toward the helicopter. Lauren climbed into the cabin and sat on the floor near Rick. Montero was next, and Michael jumped in behind them.

"Janie! Get us out of here," Michael said as he sat heavily.

"The area hospitals are out of the question. The last thing we want to do is land in the middle of some triage situation at an overrun local hospital," Janie said over her shoulder as she began the quick process of spooling up the turbine engines to flight speed. "I think we should fly straight to a hospital in the Bay Area. Everything I've heard from air traffic control indicates the worst of the destruction is south of San Jose."

"Do it!" Michael said and slid the door shut as Janie lifted the 412 off the ground, pivoted hard, and accelerated northward. "Janie, I can't tell you how happy I am you stuck around. All the radios aboard the Gulfstream were damaged. Did you hear me calling?"

"No," Janie replied. "The tower knew you were inbound. They relayed the information to me just before they lost power. When the airliner at the gate caught fire, the entire terminal was evacuated. I diverted north and waited, not knowing if you were going to land or not. I finally swung south for a look, just as you were touching down."

"Do you have any idea where the big meteor came down?" Lauren asked Janie.

"From what I could tell, it hit out to sea, well beyond the coast. You're the scientist, what's happened? How can we have a meteor shower like this and no one know about it in advance?"

"It's not just a meteor shower, though you're right, it did sneak up on us, just like the meteors that struck Russia in 2013, and again in 2016. In my estimation, this meteor was bigger than those two put together. I also saw objects falling at different angles and speeds. That's not typical behavior for a meteor. There's something more going on here besides a rogue meteor shower."

"Before I lost communication, several airliners reported being hit," Michael said. "Could those aircraft have been the other burning debris you saw?"

"I don't think so. The random objects I spotted were high up in the atmosphere, well above any commercial aircraft," Lauren said.

"Do we know if the *Buckley* suffered any damage?" Montero asked Janie.

"Yes, but Captain Pittman said it seemed minor. At the first sign of the meteor, he wisely headed the *Buckley* out toward the open ocean at flank speed," Janie said as she pursed her lips. "Everything happened so fast."

Michael gestured out the left side of the helicopter. "Look."

Lauren straightened so she could see where Michael pointed. Janie was flying over the community of Seaside, just inland of the shoreline. Out to sea, Lauren spotted a ship she recognized as the *Buckley*. Beyond, a column of dark smoke rose from something too far away to identify.

"Here it comes," Michael said. "The tsunami."

Lauren shifted her gaze to Highway 1, clearly visible from the helicopter, and then to the shoreline and the receding water level. Lauren watched as the initial pulse from the meteor's impact raced inland. The energy powered in from the open ocean at nearly five hundred miles per hour and slowed as it met resistance near shore. Friction with the sea floor began slowing the wave, and as a result, the faster water began to build up and rise, creating a larger wave, that when it finally broke, surged inland with unstoppable force.

Lauren wanted to turn away but couldn't. Safely removed from the violence below, she watched the certain destruction of everything the wave touched. Hundreds of vehicles on Highway 1 were swept away in an instant, tumbling helplessly in the turbulent water. Other cars on higher stretches of road survived the onslaught and then set off a cascade effect of collisions as drivers panicked. The tsunami caved in the walls of a shopping center, pushing cars, trucks, and large debris through the walls of a Walmart, and picked up even more wreckage in the process. Lauren looked northward up the beach. The wave went as far as she could see, and obliterated nearly everything for hundreds of yards inland. Below them, cars, buses, and tons of wreckage swirled in eddies created between buildings. The seawater was dirty brown, a muddy froth created by the tremendous forces at play. Lauren knew that inside the tsunami's footprint, there would be very few survivors, and when the water finally receded, many would never be found. Lauren glanced at her watch and noted the time. A second wave could arrive in as little as five minutes, and it could easily be even bigger.

With the sun dropping lower toward the horizon, they continued flying toward San Jose, leaving Monterey behind to burn. Lauren closed her eyes at the enormity of everything she'd just witnessed. She sent up a silent prayer that her daughter, Abigail, was safe in Virginia with Lauren's mother, and that her husband, Donovan, was hopefully safe somewhere in Monterey. Her eyes clouded with tears at the thought of Donovan and William, and the possibility of never seeing them again. Overwhelmed, and feeling helpless at all the death and destruction she'd just witnessed, Lauren looked at her hands, still covered in Rick's blood. She closed her eyes, fought the tears, and summoned all of the strength she had to maintain control.

CHAPTER FOUR

DONOVAN, WITH SHANNON right behind him, raced down the stairs, running as fast as they could to the exit level. They encountered aquarium employees shouting back and forth about a tsunami and what needed to be done to secure the building. Two people ran to release the otters and seals, while another bolted to set the birds free from their exhibit.

The fire alarm sprang to life and its blaring warning echoed through the cavernous main hall. As Donovan and Shannon rounded the last corner, he had his first unobstructed view outside. Through the massive glass entrance was Cannery Row and the town of Pacific Grove. All he could see were panicked people, and just beyond, smoke and fire. He came to a stop and put out his arm to slow Shannon.

"Oh, dear God," Shannon said as her hand shot to her mouth.

The entire roadway was jammed with vehicles and pedestrians. Across the street, dozens of cars were burning, as were two wooden buildings. Drivers did whatever they could to push past vehicles that had been abandoned, ignoring any sense of order as they honked and lurched forward in what Donovan could only describe as blind panic. Through the black smoke, he glanced up the street that led up the hill away from the beach. The chaos looked to be even worse as frantic people jumped the curbs with their cars, pedestrians scattered, or were hit, and a bicyclist was tossed helplessly into the air.

The instant a car made any progress, more cars would try to funnel into the perceived opening. Terrorized people were doing whatever they could to escape the area. In the distance, Donovan heard the first warble of a civil defense siren warning of the impending tsunami. He and Shannon both watched as people on foot stopped, listened, and then began to run with renewed abandon.

"Our chances are better if we try to ride it out here," Donovan said as he pictured all the different places he'd toured throughout the day. "This way."

As they ran, Donovan pulled out his cell phone and speed-dialed William, only to get a busy signal. He thumbed through his directory, found Janie's number, and waited anxiously until it, too, went to a busy tone. They pounded up the first flight of stairs to the second floor, which looked vacant, the fire alarm louder.

"Where are we going?" Shannon said as Donovan led the way.

"Up one more flight. We have to get to the kelp forest overlook. I was there earlier—it's at least three floors up."

"There!" Shannon pointed to a marked stairwell.

Donovan, breathing hard, reached the last step and pushed out into the evening air, ran to the railing, and looked to find that they now had a partial view of Pacific Grove gently rising from behind the aquarium. The chaos they'd seen from ground level was amplified by their new vantage point. Through the billowing smoke from multiple nearby fires, Donovan could see traffic mired in gridlock. People were abandoning vehicles, yelling, running wildly, adding to the confusion. There were bodies lying in the street, and he turned away, sickened by the blind fear of the mindless stampede.

"Donovan, you'd better come see this," Shannon called over her shoulder.

He went to the seaward railing where Shannon was standing and looked out over the water. In the distance, the *Buckley* rose out of a trough, bow high, the hull pointed skyward against a massive wave. The ship seemed to hover momentarily at the crest, as if faltering, and then eased over and crashed down the backside creating an explosion of white spray that covered the entire superstructure.

"The tsunami is almost here," Shannon said as she gripped the iron railing with both hands.

Donovan watched as the *Buckley* came back into view, sloughing off the sea in huge sheets as it continued its charge toward the deep ocean. Three stories below where they stood, the water in the tidal pool began to draw back, exposing natural rocks as well as the concrete footings of the aquarium. With alarming quickness, the ocean raced away from the shore and exposed a vast stretch of the seafloor. Donovan watched as a wave formed, gathering momentum as it powered toward the shore.

"We need to get away from the edge and hold on!" Donovan shouted above the growing roar of the tsunami. Donovan anchored himself where the railing bolted into the concrete, and motioned for Shannon to do the same. He saw the fear and determination in Shannon's face as together they clutched the railing.

Shannon turned away as the tsunami seemed to slow and then begin to climb. With no idea how high the water was going to reach, Donovan linked a protective arm around her waist just as the wave broke. The intense crack as tons of seawater slammed into the aquarium was deafening. The wave shot upward and powerful geysers of frigid seawater exploded skyward. Donovan kept his grip on both Shannon and the railing as heavy sheets of cold seawater cascaded down from above, threatening to sweep them both from their perch. The concrete beneath his feet shuddered and vibrated, driving them both to their knees. Donovan tried to open his eyes against the water, but was helpless to see anything as the spray from the tsunami obscured the world in every direction.

"We can't stay here. We might not have much time before the next wave," Donovan said above the roar of the wave and its destruction. Adding to the apocalyptic feel of the scene, the tsunami siren warbled in the distance. As the mist from the initial impact settled, Donovan looked down the shoreline and watched a tall red and white antenna snap free of its guy wires and topple out of sight. Half a dozen buildings crumbled and began to collapse. Structures he knew had stood for decades surrendered, tilted, and failed before the onslaught from the ocean. Donovan looked at Shannon, and from her horrified expression, he guessed she'd seen what he'd seen, all of it, including the doomed people on the rooftops of the failed structures. The aquarium had shuddered and shook during the worst of the pounding, but was still standing.

Donovan looked over the railing and studied the rush of water still pouring in from the sea.

"We can't go down," Shannon said as she took in the scene. "There's no way; that's just crazy."

Donovan turned and surveyed the roofline behind them. "What about up?" He used both hands to test the railing and make sure it was still secured, and then turned toward Shannon who was also looking upward, studying their options.

"Climb up on the top rail. I'll give you a boost the rest of the way," Shannon said. "Once you're in place, I'll climb the railing, and you can help pull me up."

"Really?" Donavan eyed the roof suspiciously. "Are you sure?"

"Gymnastics as a kid," Shannon said. "It's all about leverage and momentum."

Donovan nodded and climbed the railing, then put one foot into Shannon's hands and felt her provide a surprisingly effective springboard to reach upward and grip the edge of the eave. He used his motion to swing a leg on top of the sloped roof and he pulled himself up to a point where he could roll his entire body on top of the metal roof. Seconds later, using an air vent to anchor his leg, he reached out to Shannon.

She climbed until she was standing on the top of the railing, using one hand to steady herself. She reached up, and she and Donovan were able to brush fingertips.

"Hang on!" Donovan yelled as he inched toward the edge into a better position. When he reached again, they were able to lock themselves hand to wrist.

"Perfect. On three!" Shannon called upward. "I'm going to push outward, and you swing me up and over the roofline."

Donovan looked down at her and their eyes met. She nodded with a mixture of determination and trust. As the countdown hit three, she launched herself off the railing and Donovan felt her weight. He lifted and swung her along her upward trajectory. He exhaled in relief as she rolled onto the roof, and he pulled her toward him until they were both lying firmly in place.

Shannon sprang to her feet and then crouched to balance herself on the pitch of the roof while she waited for Donovan.

Donovan stood to his full height and took a second to scan the roof. The path they needed to take traversed multiple peaks that rose from the roof of the complex. From this height, he could see large clusters of flames devouring entire sections of Pacific Grove, and not far away, a full city block roared as it burned. Beyond, fires dotted the entire horizon, and on the other side of the initial flames was nothing but dense smoke. Standing on one of the remaining high spots on Cannery Row, Donovan had no idea how they were going to escape, let alone reach William. He looked out over the ocean and spotted the *Buckley*. The white-and-red ship vanished, which told him they were still fighting swells and that more surges were inbound.

"Which way?" Shannon asked.

"We'll work our way to the smokestacks." Donovan pointed in the direction he had in mind. "That will take us as far away from the beach as possible. Then we'll have to think about getting down to ground level."

"I'm right behind you," Shannon said.

Donovan kept his eyes on his footing as he began to jog up one slope and then down the other side. They quickly reached the section where three smokestacks rose up from below. He climbed onto the next level of roofing, turned, and helped Shannon do the same, and then he moved quickly along the peak, using his outstretched arms for balance. Another small climb put them on their last leg across the roof of the aquarium.

"The tree next to the building. It's perfect," Shannon said as she stopped next to Donovan. "And look, I think the water is starting to recede."

Donovan was counting on the fact that the terrain rose fairly fast in this section of Pacific Grove. Three blocks inland the inertia of the first wave had stopped, leaving a clearly defined boundary of debris to mark the maximum surge point before the water surrendered to gravity. What Shannon was seeing was the beginning of the flow back downhill into the ocean. Directly below them, brown water still swirled at or near the tops of the stalled and abandoned cars.

"How do we do this?" Shannon asked. "What if we use the roofs of the cars as a sidewalk of sorts? Look, we could get all the way to the next block before we had to swim."

Donovan traced the route she'd described, but as he did, the retreating water dislodged one of the mostly submerged vehicles, which slammed it into another car and started a chain of minor collisions dissolving any plans of immediate escape. "We need to sit here a little longer and let the water level drop. If we try to make it up the hill to dry land right now, we'll run into the same panicked mob as before." Donovan could hear a distant combination of yelling, screaming, and car horns. The chaos was every bit as deadly as a tsunami.

"What if the next wave comes and we're still up here? Can the building absorb a second pounding?"

"I don't know, but I'd rather be up here than down there," Donovan said, and realized it was a bit ironic that he was preaching the art of patience.

"What are the chances Janie shows up in the helicopter to rescue us?"

"Virtually zero," Donovan said, keeping his eye on the diminishing water level. "The Gulfstream most certainly diverted out of this mess. With no way for Janie to know exactly where any of us are, it would have been too dangerous for her to fly into the heart of the meteor storm hoping to spot us. I'm sure she diverted somewhere safe as well."

"So, no helicopter?"

"It's just you and me."

"Okay, Buck told me once you were pretty capable, for a civilian."

"I hope he's right. What else did he say?"

"That he wasn't sure who was more impatient, you or me."

"That's not really a compliment to either one of us," Donovan said.

"At least we won't sit around wringing our hands."

"Probably not," Donovan said as he glanced at the water level again, startled by how quickly the street looked to be draining. "It's time to go, but we need to be cautious. I can still hear some stragglers out there, but from what it sounds like, people are making their way toward downtown Monterey. We need to get to Pebble

Beach, which is in the opposite direction, so it'll be unlikely we have to deal with anyone at this point."

Shannon was the first to step from the metal roof to a thick branch of the tree. From there she descended quickly until she was only a few feet above the dark water. Donovan eased himself down and stopped one branch above her and pushed away the leaves until he could see the trailing edge of the water rushing toward them. From wading in streams while fly fishing, he knew the power of moving water against a stationary object. He eyed a car he had a clean look at, and when the water finally dipped below the axle, he called out for Shannon to go. He climbed down after her into the cold water and slogged away from the tree.

Taking powerful strides, Donovan moved uphill through the torrent, with Shannon following, her hand gripping the back of his jacket. Using the surrounding buildings as breakwaters, they moved out of the fastest water and began to walk perpendicular to the flow until reaching a pedestrian walkway. They went up a flight of steps that acted like a miniature waterfall, and finally reached water's edge. Donovan got his bearings, and they turned left and began to run toward the garage where they'd parked their car. The entrance was open, and as they rounded the corner onto the main level of the structure, they stopped.

"Oh dear God," Shannon said.

Donovan, too, was shocked at the devastation. The tsunami had powered in through openings on the seaward side of the building and mangled cars into unrecognizable chunks of metal. He maneuvered toward the valet window and found the door and glass broken. The body of one of the uniformed attendants was facedown in the dirty water.

"What happened?" Shannon said as she waded toward the board where the valet hung the keys. "It's almost empty, but there are still cars here."

"My guess is people panicked before the wave hit. They grabbed keys and started pushing buttons; the first car that lit up, they took and fled."

Shannon felt around on the floor and from under the dirty water pulled up several key rings. None of them belonged to the SUV Donovan had rented. "I guess we could try the same thing. Go up one level and see if we get lucky."

Donovan cocked his head as a new sound rose above the noise from dripping water. It was a dull roar and it was getting louder. "Shannon, there's another wave coming! Run!"

They burst out of the darkened garage, Donovan crossed the street, and moving as fast as they could, raced toward higher ground. A second wall of debris climbed the terrain behind them. Straight ahead was a two-story brick building and on the side was a metal fire escape. Donovan kept his legs pumping, though his lungs burned, as he leaped onto the trunk of a parked car. He stopped for a moment to make sure Shannon made the jump as well, and then he took two steps, leaped into space, and seized the bottom rung of the ladder. It didn't budge. Hanging by the crook of his arm, he turned and motioned Shannon to follow. She took one step backward, then charged forward and flung herself toward him. Donovan caught her and pulled her into him just as the car beneath them was swept away by the thunderous surge.

CHAPTER FIVE

JANIE FLEW NORTHWARD and navigated inland, away from the coast and the carnage created by the tsunami. Lauren opened her eyes at the turn, silently thanked Janie, then lowered her head again. The scope of events seemed beyond comprehension. The scientific part of her brain fully understood that planetary bodies have been impacting and shaping the Earth for millions of years. Now here she was, at ground zero of perhaps the biggest Earth-altering event in centuries. All around her, people were hurt and dying. Her horror and revulsion began to grow—as did her fear. She placed her hand on Rick's wrist and tried to rein in her thoughts and narrow her focus by concentrating on his pulse, one beat at a time, willing the young man to survive.

The fact that she didn't know Donovan's location nearly gutted her. Was he at the aquarium, the hotel, with William, or any one of a hundred places in between? Days earlier, as he'd explained his itinerary to her, she'd been half-listening as she helped Abigail pack for Grandma's house. As the founder of Eco-Watch, Donovan had flown out early with William, who was the chairman of the board, to tend to the details for the *Buckley* handover ceremony. William was going to meet with an Eco-Watch donor, and at some point, Buck's former girlfriend Shannon was to arrive, and after everything was set for the reception, they were all going to meet at the airport. The reality that she didn't even know where to begin searching for her husband made her nauseous. Lauren's anxiety increased when she realized it was early enough on the East Coast for Abigail to be aware of what was happening in Monterey. Lauren would call as soon as possible, though at the moment, she had no idea what she'd tell their daughter.

Lauren felt someone touch her arm. She opened her eyes and realized that her thoughts of Donovan and Abigail had drawn tears. Montero had reached out to comfort her.

"Are you okay?" Montero asked.

Lauren nodded that she was, though she knew she was far from it, but there was nothing Montero, or anyone else, could do for her right now. She was touched by Montero's gesture. After Buck's death, Donovan had hired former FBI agent Montero to take his place as Director of Security. While Montero wasn't the highly trained soldier Buck had been, on more than one occasion, Lauren had seen Montero take the advantage because no one expects the biggest threat in a situation to be the attractive woman suddenly holding a Glock. Montero was exceedingly attractive yet downplayed her looks. She'd dyed her blond hair black, and rarely smiled in an effort not to stand out while she was working. Lauren had wondered if this weekend, with the emphasis on Buck, would be difficult for Montero.

"Due to other inbound medevac flights, we're being instructed to fly to the Stanford Medical Center," Janie reported. "ETA is six minutes. We'll be met at the helipad, but we'll have to vacate immediately, as they expect other medevac choppers."

"Michael, you need to get off here with Rick," Montero said. "Get looked at by a doctor."

"Janie," Lauren said. "Can we drop Rick and Michael, and then fly straight back to the Monterey airport? Maybe Donovan and the others are there by now."

"I've already tried to get permission. Air Traffic Control shut me down. As of a few minutes ago, everything west of the Mississippi River is a no-fly zone. All aircraft are grounded, except recognized emergency response flights, Cal Fire aircraft, or certified medevac helicopters. We don't fall into any of those categories. They gave us two options: We can land at an airport in the Bay Area until the situation changes, or if we want, they'll give us a special clearance out to the *Buckley*."

"That's crazy." Michael sounded both angry and upset. "We've got a perfectly good helicopter and are willing to help, and they ground us? I say we do whatever we want. We'll say we're sorry later."

Lauren silently commended Michael's outburst. "I suggest we go to the San Jose airport and regroup. I need to talk to Calvin at the Defense Intelligence Agency and get a grip on the scope of what's happening. Maybe I can pull some strings through Washington, DC, channels and get us permission to fly."

"What do you mean *happening*?" Montero asked Lauren. "Hasn't it all happened?"

"I doubt it." Lauren shook her head. "I've been thinking about what I saw earlier from the Gulfstream. There were all these different objects entering the Earth's atmosphere at different angles. There's a theory called the Kessler Effect that deals with the sheer numbers of satellites and other pieces of space junk in low Earth orbit. I think the meteor collided with man-made objects, which in turn broke up the meteor, and introduced wild variations in the reentry profiles of every object involved. We've seen the worst, but debris is still up there with deteriorating orbits."

"So, there could be more space junk coming down?" Michael asked. "Stuff that hasn't entered the atmosphere yet?"

"If I'm right, then yes," Lauren said. "At last count, there were roughly twenty-three thousand objects in orbit. Some as small as two inches with very little weight, all the way up to the nine-hundred twenty-five-thousand-pound International Space Station. If any of the objects have their trajectories compromised, it's only a matter of time before orbital decay brings them down."

Janie descended and swung the helicopter around to face into the prevailing wind as she prepared to land. Lauren could see people on the ground waiting to whisk Rick inside. The second the skids touched, Michael slid open the door, and medical personnel swarmed around Rick and quickly transferred him to their gurney.

Michael hugged Lauren and said, "I'll be in touch. Go find them." Then he jumped out and closed the door.

Janie waited until everyone was clear before she lifted the helicopter into the sky, banked to the east, and set a course for the San Jose airport.

As Lauren looked off to her right, at the way they'd just come, she was stunned. The sun, moving lower toward the horizon, cast an eerie orange hue against an enormous curtain of smoke in the distance. She knew that Monterey was a little over fifty miles away, but all she could see in that direction was smoke. After all the damage she'd witnessed, there was only one agonizing question. Were her husband and any of the other people she cared about still alive?

Five minutes later, Janie slowed the helicopter and made a straight-in approach to the private aircraft area at the San Jose Airport. Janie followed the hand signals of the Pacific Jet Center ground personnel as she guided the 412 to a landing spot at the outer edge of the ramp.

Lauren felt the bump that told her they were on the ground. Montero opened the helicopter's side door and jumped to the ground. Lauren fell in behind her as they ducked and headed toward the entrance of the Jet Center. All around them were dozens of parked corporate jets, yet the only noise or movement was from the Eco-Watch helicopter. She stopped and scanned the terminal. The gates were all full, and the outer portions of the ramp were stacked with stationary airliners. Everything had been grounded— no airplanes were taking off or landing. It reminded her of the hours after 9/11.

CHAPTER SIX

"Do you have a good grip on the ladder?" Donovan called to Shannon as their feet dangled just above the rushing water.

"Yes! But I need to go higher."

"Can you get around me?" Donovan said.

Shannon got a foot firmly on the bottom rung and climbed upward.

Donovan pulled himself up after her, his breathing coming in labored gasps, a sharp pain radiating in his side. Above him, Shannon crouched on a small second-floor landing, trying to open the window.

"Turn away," Donovan said as he joined her. He pulled off his left shoe, and used the heel to shatter the glass. After clearing the shards from the frame, he slid his shoe back on and eased inside the opening. Once his eyes adjusted to the darkness, he understood they'd broken into what looked like a storage room. He helped Shannon inside, and they walked across a creaking wood floor. Once through the door, there was a long hallway that led to a stairwell down to the main level. They descended halfway into what turned out to be a partially flooded tavern.

Shannon pointed toward the door that led outside. "It looks as if the water has already started to recede."

"We're further up the hill and there's more slope, so the runoff would be quicker," Donovan said. "I'm going to wade over to the bar and get close enough to the windows to see what's happening outside."

"I'm right behind you." Shannon put her hand on his shoulder as they carefully moved down the remaining steps.

The cold water came up just short of his waist, an uncomfortable reminder that the Pacific Ocean temperature this time of year was somewhere in the mid-fifties. Donovan pushed away floating wooden chairs and headed toward the bar. When he reached the sturdy structure, he flexed his knees, pushed off, and turned until he sat on the edge. Shannon did the same, and then quickly stood to get her legs out of the water. She stomped her feet to coax back the circulation.

Donovan stood as well and found there was just enough headroom to move around, though he had to navigate around the light fixtures. Walking on the bar toward the front of the establishment, they'd get a better view outside. Out the window, he saw water coursing back down the incline toward the sea. Across the street, several doors down, three buildings were on fire, flames licking out the windows and black smoke twisting and billowing into the sky.

"What now?" Shannon asked.

"We need to find a car and figure out a way to get to Pebble Beach. I need to make sure William made it out, because if he didn't, he's still there."

"How far away are we talking?"

"On a normal day, no more than a twenty-minute drive. Today, who knows?"

"Then what?"

"We get someplace safe, wherever that might be, and eventually make contact with the outside world. At some point in the near future, we arrive on board the *Buckley*."

"Wow, you sure made that sound easy," Shannon said. "Are you kidding? Has it struck you as odd that there's a major fire burning outside, and there's not a single siren sounding in the distance other than that incessant tsunami warning? I mean, the tsunami has hit twice, I think they can turn the damn thing off now! Where are the police, the fire department, the National Guard? There are dead people floating in the street. Don't you think there should be someone doing something about that? Have you seen a single cop since all of this started? Have you?"

"Feel better?" Donovan asked when she paused to take a breath. He knew all about the effects of stress and adrenaline. Shannon needed to vent, get it out, for her sake.

"This is just so frustrating." Shannon hung her head, seemingly to collect herself. "This golf course, is it one of those right next to the ocean? If William was still there, what are the chances he's—we were almost killed, how can you stand there and be so damned calm?"

Donovan held out his right hand; it was shaking. "I might be a little calmer than you on the outside, but I'm just as angry and frustrated by what's happened as you are. I saw the dead people. It's a complete catastrophe out there. You have every right to be upset. As for William, the course weaves along the shore near some cliffs. I think there's a reasonable chance he could have escaped the worst. Which is why I have to go."

"Oh my God, it all happened so fast. There was no warning, no nothing. People panicked—like a human stampede. The people standing on top of the building as it collapsed—they never had a chance."

"Pebble Beach is far less populated than Cannery Row. You know, Buck told me once that there is never an absence of fear in these situations, and those who manage that fear the best are likely to be the survivors. I always remembered those words because I think he was right."

At the mention of Buck, Shannon's shoulders slumped and she crossed her arms in front or her and began to shake, tears rolling down her cheeks. "He'd be furious if he could see me unraveling like this. I'm supposed to be his rough and tumble girl from the mountains of Montana, not some crybaby."

"I say you get a pass on any character judgments after being rained on by meteorites and then being thrashed by a tsunami. From where I stand, you were great. You never hesitated, you got us on the roof of the aquarium, and from there we made it here. Considering the number of people who didn't survive, I'd say we did okay."

"God, I could use a drink." Shannon held out her hands. They were shaking worse than Donovan's.

"We'll have that drink once we're on the *Buckley*. Maybe more than one," Donovan said, relieved that she'd moved through the initial shock and was once again focused on survival. He sat down on the bar and slid down into the water, which was now mid-thigh. "If we can make it two or three more blocks up the hill, we'll have put the tsunami behind us. Then we can start our search for a car that hasn't been underwater."

Shannon ignored Donovan's offered hand as she slipped into the water. He opened the front door and led the way out onto the sidewalk. Another building was burning farther up the hill, the smoke starting to block the sunlight, casting a surreal glow over the scene. Donovan glanced to the west toward the setting sun and understood that it was going to get dark fast.

"We need to move away from the fires," he said. "Let's cross the street and then go one block over and see if we can get up the hill that way."

As they pushed through the water, dodging the floating debris, Donovan kept glancing up into the sky. Shannon was right. He hadn't heard any emergency vehicles. He expected there would be helicopters or airplanes aloft, but there was nothing but empty sky. He wondered where Lauren was and how he was going to get word to her that he was safe. He thought of his daughter, Abigail, whom he loved more than words, and how close he'd been to bringing her on this trip. Thankfully, there was an equestrian event that she desperately wanted to attend, and Lauren's mom stepped in to watch his daughter back home in Virginia.

"This street looks good," Shannon said as they came to an intersection.

Donovan shook off his thoughts of what might have been and glanced up and down the block. To their left, between them and the ocean, cars and tons of wooden wreckage blockaded the street, leaving a clear boundary where the tsunami had run out of energy. In the other direction was a quiet, tree-lined road that led up the hill. Wordlessly, they made the right turn, and when they reached the next intersection, Donovan spotted the familiar sign. The business he'd hoped to find intact was still there, and he allowed himself a tiny smile.

CHAPTER SEVEN

"Dr. McKenna?" A tall man in a suit walked out of the sliding glass doors of Pacific Jet Center and headed in their direction.

Lauren slowed, as did Montero. The man was clean-cut, in that certain way that identified him as law enforcement, not what Lauren wanted to deal with right now.

"Dr. McKenna, I'm Fredrick Price, Homeland Security. I was advised to be on the lookout for an Eco-Watch helicopter, and that hopefully, you'd be on board. I have a message for you to contact a Mr. Calvin Reynolds at the Defense Intelligence Agency. Follow me. You're supposed to call him the second you land."

Lauren held her position and allowed Price to walk away without her.

"Mr. Price," Montero said. "Dr. McKenna will be the one who will organize her priorities, not you."

Price stopped and turned. "Ms. Montero? I was briefed that you were part of the Eco-Watch team now. It's nice to finally meet you."

"I'm Director of Security for Eco-Watch, and we have concerns that demand our immediate attention."

Price remained undeterred. "Look, I'm just trying to help the few people we have in there trying to piece together what's happened. We have a full-blown disaster in the making. Many of our satellites are down, and the few we can reach belong to the

Department of Defense. Dr. McKenna, you're DOD, not Eco-Watch, and we need you. There's a makeshift operations center being set up in one of the Jet Center's conference rooms. Will you at least come with me and talk to these people and see if you can help them?"

"I'll do that after I get cleaned up, if you'll do something for me," Lauren said.

"I'll try."

"I need to work around the no-fly zone."

"That specific order came from Washington, but I'll see what I can do. This way, Dr. McKenna." As they entered the main lobby, he gestured for her to follow him down a carpeted hallway. "The washroom is the second door on the right. The conference room is further down the hallway."

Lauren walked out of the ladies room, relieved to have cleaned the blood from her hands. She pushed into the conference room, and it instantly felt like a familiar setting. Though not the modern nerve center she had at the Defense Intelligence Agency, this room reminded her of any number of field offices she'd worked out of all around the world. In the middle, two tables were pushed together to accommodate dozens of large paper charts. To her right, a large map of the United States covered one wall. On the opposite side, two tables were buried with computer monitors, servers, printers, and at least four multi-line phones. What she didn't understand was the lack of people. One man, youngish, with thinning blond hair and glasses, sat in front of one of the computer screens, furiously typing in short staccato bursts. The other occupant was an older, heavyset man dressed in a suit and tie. He looked to be in his late forties with wavy salt and pepper hair and a closely trimmed beard gone gray. Intelligent blue eyes gave him an intrinsic warmth, offset by the concerned expression etched on his face. When he spotted her, he quickly ended a call on his cell phone.

"I'm Ernest Rincon, Cal Fire Deputy Director of Fire Protection Programs. You must be Dr. McKenna with the Defense Intelligence Agency? I know you by reputation only, but I'm awfully glad you're here."

Lauren instantly liked the man. He seemed unaffected by political posturing and gave her a welcoming smile. She shook his outstretched hand. "Where is everyone else? I know a little about fighting fires, and it isn't usually by two people in a conference room at the local airport."

"You're right," Rincon said as he nodded. "My office and staff are in Sacramento. I was on my way back from a business trip in Seattle when everything happened. The plane landed here, and Agent Price brought me over here from the terminal to start making phone calls. As we learned how widespread the damage was, Pacific Jet Center set us up with what they had on hand. The forward fire base is assembling at a point closer to Monterey. I'm hoping to join them there as soon as possible."

"Mr. Rincon, I might be able to help you with that. Plus, I've just seen firsthand some of the meteor damage done near Salinas and Monterey. We also witnessed the initial surge of the tsunami from Monterey to Santa Cruz."

"We have no real-time intelligence coming out of the Monterey Peninsula right now, and haven't since the initial impacts. All power and communication is out. What can you tell me about the tsunami, and what's the condition of the Monterey airport?"

"I need to reach Calvin Reynolds at DIA headquarters. Homeland Security said he's looking for me. Can you help me do that? If I can have a phone, a map of the area, and a pen and paper, I'll be able to give you a proper briefing on much more than what I've seen."

Rincon turned to the young man seated at the computer. "Alan, can you find Dr. McKenna an office with a phone, as well as everything else she needs?"

"Yes, sir." Alan shot to his feet.

"Mr. Rincon, I wouldn't count on the viability of the Monterey airport for much longer. What I can tell you now is that there were large fires near the airport perimeter. The terminal building is unusable and the control tower appeared damaged. Also, as we flew in over the Salinas airport, we saw that the runways had been hit and there were dozens of small aircraft burning."

"I know about the Salinas airport." Rincon stroked his beard as he thought. "The tsunami damage you witnessed—was the surge strong enough to take out Highway One north of Monterey and Seaside?"

"Yes, a sizeable section of the road is completely unusable," Lauren said.

"How far inland did the tsunami travel?" Rincon asked.

"I saw it compromise the highway, flood a shopping area, and sweep up hundreds of cars and trucks, pushing them into an industrial park. It also breached the banks of an existing lake, which extended its reach inland. The biggest surge was north of Seaside, in what looked like a floodplain connected to a river."

"I know the area. There are two watersheds that empty into the Bay; one is near the power plant at Moss Landing."

"Nuclear?" Lauren asked.

"Thankfully, no, though it does burn natural gas."

"Dr. McKenna," Alan called from the doorway. "I have an office set up for you."

"Thank you. I'll be right there," Lauren called out. She turned back to Rincon. "I'll find you after I make my calls."

Lauren followed Alan to a private office. He handed her a bottle of water as she sat down and spread out a map of the Monterey Peninsula, arranged her paper, and then dialed Calvin's direct line. "Calvin, it's Lauren."

"Oh, dear God, Lauren, finally," Calvin said as a greeting. "I've been worried sick. I heard the Gulfstream you were in lost radio contact, then disappeared from San Francisco's radar. I couldn't help but imagine the worst. Where are you?"

"I'm fine, Calvin, I really am. I'm at the San Jose airport." Lauren appreciated his concern. They'd been friends since her days at MIT. He managed to convince her to join the Defense Intelligence Agency as a civilian contractor, and she'd never regretted working for him. She loved Calvin like a father. "I'm alive, thanks for worrying."

"I tried calling Donovan, but I couldn't reach him either. He's out on the *Buckley,* isn't he?"

"No, we're not sure exactly where he is." Lauren didn't want to get too far into the subject. Each time she thought about Donovan, her emotional control seemed to dwindle. "Calvin, I have to tell you, this is a complete shit show here. Tell me everything that's happened."

"You've only witnessed a fraction of the complete event, and it's worse than you know," Calvin said. "We never saw this meteor coming. The initial collisions with multiple Earth-orbiting satellites was our first warning we were about to be hit. The impacts started a cascade event, which served to break the meteor into dozens of pieces. So, naturally, along with the meteor, we also have man-made space debris entering the atmosphere. The loss of our orbital assets is adding to our problems. We've tracked impacts from Idaho all the way out into the Pacific Ocean—hundreds of them, maybe thousands. From the data I've seen, Monterey Peninsula is the hardest hit."

"A large section of meteor impacted off the coast and spawned a tsunami," Lauren said. "Is the worst of it over? How many more satellites have deteriorating orbits?"

"We're still trying to assess the scope of the space debris that may or may not reenter the atmosphere."

"Calvin, these people are in trouble. The debris falling from space didn't just start fires, the objects blew huge craters when they hit, so the damage goes far underground. We've had a tsunami wipe out a major evacuation route. Hundreds of fires are burning. Monterey, Oceanside, and Pacific Grove are virtually gone, burning out of control, and from what I saw firsthand, all essential services are gone."

"I know, I've already spoken with the Pentagon. This thing is big and going to get far worse before it gets better."

"Meaning?"

"We're losing command of many of our satellites. Not only are we going to be without the data and services they provide, we have no idea where they're going to come down once their orbits deteriorate."

"So there could be more impacts, more fires?" Lauren asked.

"We have no way to know."

"So, the answer is yes."

"Just promise me one thing."

"What's that?"

"If the situation gets out of control, you'll fly out to the *Buckley*, and leave the area."

"I will, and thanks again for looking out for me," Lauren said, though in her heart, she couldn't imagine sailing away without Donovan and the others.

"I know the odds are small that you'll actually do it, but thanks for allowing me to indulge in a little overprotectiveness. If something ever happened to you, I'd never forgive myself," Calvin said.

"I'll be careful, I promise."

"I can work with that, though I have to go," Calvin said. "Keep me posted, and I'll do the same."

Lauren hung up, then collected herself as she dialed her mother's phone number.

"Hello."

"Mom, it's me. How are things going?"

"We're fine. Abigail is in the den curled up watching a movie, but at last glance, she'd fallen asleep."

"Let her sleep." Lauren ached to talk to her daughter and searched for the right words to say to her mother. "There's been a disaster in the Monterey Peninsula, a meteor strike. I'm fine, but I haven't heard from Donovan or William since I arrived."

"Oh, Lauren, we had no idea. We haven't had the news on since dinner. Where are you now? How are you doing? What can I do to help?"

"Abigail doesn't need to hear about this tonight. By morning maybe I'll have heard from Donovan. Either way, I'll call before you and Abigail leave for the equestrian center. In the meantime, you might get up to speed on events. You know how Abigail is. Once she hears the news report, she's going to start asking questions."

"Believe me, I know. Can I call you back on this number?"

"No, it's a borrowed phone," Lauren said. "You can try my cell, but the power is out all over the place. Leave me a message, and I'll get it at some point. As always, you have Calvin's number if there's anything urgent."

"We'll be fine, but please, promise me you'll get somewhere safe and take care of yourself."

"I will," Lauren said. "I love you, and I'll talk to you soon."

The instant she hung up the phone she took a deep breath, finished her water, and then began to hone Calvin's data down into information Rincon and Cal Fire could use. Lauren replayed Calvin's words as she headed for the conference room, trying to get a full grasp on the scope of events. Thousands of impacts, space-based platforms in disarray, and the possibility of more meteors. Rincon wasn't going to like what she had to say.

CHAPTER EIGHT

THE AUTO BODY repair shop was tucked back from the road, nearly hidden from view by larger buildings. Donovan had spotted the sign, and now he and Shannon were standing in front of the locked office. They walked to the side, where a chain-link fence topped with barbed wire cordoned off the back lot filled with wrecked cars awaiting their turn at redemption.

Donovan studied the enclosure and decided on the best place to scale the fence.

"Here, let me," Shannon said, and before Donovan had a foothold, Shannon effortlessly climbed to where the chain link met the barbed wire. "Toss me your jacket."

Donovan underhanded the soaked garment and Shannon caught it. She spread it over the barbs and crawled to the other side. She eyed her landing area and dropped softly to the ground.

"Two cars in." Donovan motioned. "The red BMW 325 with the smashed rear end—see if there's a tool kit attached to the inside of the trunk lid."

"I have it!" Shannon called. "There's not much here besides a screwdriver, a pair of pliers, and some wrenches."

"Okay," Donovan said. "See if you can pull up the carpet. There will be a piece of fiberboard beneath that."

"Is this what you want?" Shannon held up a tire iron and raised her head out of the trunk.

"Bring everything," Donovan said. They now had their way inside the shop.

Shannon handed Donovan the tools through the fence.

"Wait here. I'll be right back," Donovan said. He hurried to the front of the building, planted his left foot, and swung the tire iron against the front door. The thick safety glass spider-webbed outward, and with the second blow, the glass exploded inward and an alarm sounded. Donovan stepped into the waiting room and, with one more swing of the tire iron, stripped the plastic alarm control from the wall. The alarm went silent as the batteries rolled across the office floor.

As Donovan headed through the garage to let Shannon inside, he quickly assessed the cars in the bays. The first was disassembled, a Mercedes. There was a Porsche 911 that looked ready. Another vehicle, a Toyota Roadster, needed two rear quarter panels, tires, and paint. The last vehicle was a Ford F-250 pickup. He reached the door, slid the heavy bolt, and pushed it open to allow Shannon access.

"I'm not sure which cars run," Donovan called out over his shoulder as he returned to the office. He spotted several clipboards with keys clipped to the paperwork and started there. He found the information on the truck, and though he had trouble reading the handwriting, he could make out that it was waiting for the correct paint so they could shoot the right front quarter panel and finish the job. Donovan noted the name of the owner, then gripped the keys in his hand. He stopped as he noticed a leather jacket draped on the back of the desk chair. He tried it on, and though it was a little big, it would do.

"I don't think any of these are finished except the 911, but that's too small," Shannon said as he pushed through the door into the shop. "Nice jacket."

"At least it's dry." Donovan pushed the button on the key fob, and the throaty engine inside the jet-black F-250 erupted to life. He walked around the idling truck and noticed the hood of the Ford was taped off in preparation for painting. He ripped away the paper and discovered a large welded tubular bumper. He silently thanked the owner for his taste in trucks. And then shut off the engine. "Perfect. It's not supposed to be ready until next Thursday, so the owner won't be trying to use it as an escape vehicle."

"So, just like that," Shannon asked. "We take it and drive off?"

"Not exactly. There is the problem of this door." Donovan examined the garage door and the electric motor that would typically open it at the touch of a button. He pressed the button, and as he expected, with no power, the door remained motionless. He spotted a three-foot-long, inch-thick steel bar that was flattened and sharpened at one end, with a yellow grooved handle at the other.

"What's that?"

"This is one serious pry bar," Donovan said, testing its weight in his hands. "I think I'll borrow this. Let's get out of here."

Shannon climbed into the passenger's seat and strapped herself in tight.

Donovan made a quick check to make sure the floor was clear of anything he might run over as they left, then once again started the truck. He was happy to find that there was a little over a half tank of gas. There were no warning lights, so he adjusted the seat, fastened his seat belt, gripped the wheel, and stepped on the gas. The sound of bending metal echoed through the high-ceilinged shop as the heavy bumper caved in the garage door and ripped it off of its tracks. The screech of tortured steel continued as the Ford lurched into the parking lot. Surprised that the airbags hadn't gone off, Donovan slammed on the brakes and what was left of the destroyed door slid off the truck.

Donovan backed up, spun the wheel, and drove the Ford out of the lot and headed south. He knew Monterey Peninsula well enough to know the major thoroughfares, and he intended to avoid them. They'd work the side roads to try to reach the Pacific Grove gate into Pebble Beach. Donovan felt exhilarated—they were finally in motion and headed to find William.

Shannon turned on the radio, and once she discovered that there were no FM stations to be found, she switched to AM. The scanner stopped. A computerized voice was midsentence announcing evacuation routes.

"... *normal programming to bring you this urgent tsunami warning in effect for the coast of California. All coastal residents should immediately move to higher ground and away from all harbors and inlets. Those seeing unusual wave activity may have only a few minutes before tsunami arrival and should evacuate immediately. Homes and small buildings are not designed to withstand tsunami impact. Do not stay in these structures. All residents in the area should be alert for further instructions. This tsunami warning is based on visual confirmation of meteorite impact in the Pacific Ocean off the coast of Monterey California at 5:25 p.m., Pacific Daylight Time. The impact could be powerful enough to trigger multiple large waves. Coastal residents should seek higher ground. Tsunamis can be dangerous waves that are not survivable. Wave heights are amplified by irregular shorelines and are difficult to predict and remain a threat for hours after the initial surge. Do not return to evacuated areas until the all clear is given by the proper local authorities.*"

"Yeah, no kidding," Shannon muttered as the message began to repeat, so she searched for more information. Seconds later she found another station.

"*Monterey County Sheriff's office has ordered the immediate mandatory evacuation of the following municipalities in Monterey*

County; Carmel, Carmel Valley, Monterey, Pacific Grove, Pebble Beach, and Seaside. Some roadways are impassable, and all residents are directed to use Highway 68 toward Salinas. Highway 1, north of Monterey, is closed. Highway 1, south of Carmel Highlands, is closed. Uniformed officers are in place to direct traffic. This is not a test; Monterey California Sheriff's office has ordered the immediate evacuation of the following—"

Shannon turned off the radio, sat back in her seat, and pressed her palms against both eyes. "I can't believe this is happening. A mass evacuation—it's just like the street outside the aquarium, only on a far larger scale. Dear God, how many more people are going to die?"

"We're not headed that way," Donovan said. "The evacuation problems should ease dramatically by the time we make our own way out of here."

"Is that because right this second, we're headed back towards the ocean that already tried to kill us twice today?"

"I'd rather take a chance being near the ocean than to be stuck in traffic with fires burning everywhere. The way we'll survive is to keep as many options open as we can," Donovan said as he was forced to slow by a group of burning buildings and downed power lines that blocked their path. His earlier elation at being in motion evaporated as he pictured the evacuation routes in use—against the number of people he guessed lived in the Monterey Peninsula. Shannon was right. What was taking place in the Monterey Peninsula was chaos of the highest order, and all Donovan could think of was Lauren—and hope that she and everyone else aboard the Eco-Watch Gulfstream were someplace far away and safe.

CHAPTER NINE

"LAUREN, THERE YOU are. I think you'd better come and take a look at this," Montero said.

Lauren turned at the sound of Montero's voice and saw her standing in front of a large computer monitor. As Lauren crossed the room, she spotted a screen saver on another computer showing a bright red Boeing 747, a huge 944 painted on its tail, dropping water on a fire. She hoped that somewhere, there were about a hundred 747s just like 944 waiting to go to work. Rincon, the Cal Fire guy, was sitting in a chair operating a mouse.

"Mr. Rincon," Lauren said. "What exactly are you looking at here?"

"This is as good a place to start as any," Rincon said as he rose from the chair and offered his seat to Lauren. "Please, Dr. McKenna, call me Ernie."

"Thanks, Ernie, I'm Lauren." She sat and leaned forward for the optimum view of the screen. "Where did this image come from?"

"This is Homeland Security's first estimation of the damage inflicted by today's events," Ernie said. "The yellow areas are probable meteor strikes. The green indicates suspected strikes from man-made objects."

Lauren methodically broke down the display. First, she focused on the yellow marks only. They began near Idaho Falls, Idaho, and stretched southwestward across Nevada, and finally ended well offshore of Monterey. The initial impacts in Idaho and Nevada were scattered, and mostly in low population areas—Lauren didn't anticipate great damage or loss of life in those states. Just west of the California border, the sporadic impacts increased and formed clusters that ran well out to sea. In the Monterey Peninsula, the yellow marks were grouped together until it was impossible to count the individual strikes.

Lauren shifted her focus to the green marks. While the yellow marks held tight to a hundred-mile-wide swath across the country, the man-made objects had come down in nearly every state west of the Mississippi River. The meteor had held a constant trajectory, but the satellites in Earth-orbit could have been traveling in polar orbits, equatorial orbits, or anything in between. Their course, disrupted by either the meteors or the ensuing collisions with other man-made space debris, created random headings and they ended up wherever their inertia took them. An estimation of the number of man-made impacts quickly escalated into the hundreds.

"What are the purple marks?" Montero asked. "And these red areas?"

"Purple indicates unconfirmed impacts." Ernie shifted his weight as if uneasy. "As you know, the entire West Coast is wired to detect any seismic activity. A meteor, or crippled satellite, sends a ripple through the Earth's crust when it hits, which the seismic array records and sends to the United States Geological Survey, which in turn sends their data to Homeland Security. These are all thought to be points of impact."

There were three times as many purple notations than green or yellow, and Lauren tried to imagine the damage inflicted.

"The red areas are all of the known fires," Ernie continued. "These depictions mark the point of ignition, not how far the fires have spread."

"Ernie," Lauren asked, "can I zoom in on specific fires?"

"Sure," Ernie said.

Lauren moved the mouse until the pointer hovered over Monterey, and she clicked it until she had what she wanted. The area from Carmel Valley, north to Salinas, was peppered with multicolored spots. Monterey was pockmarked by impacts, most of them resulting in a fire.

"None of the fires in the Monterey Peninsula are contained," Ernie said. "I'm told we're having trouble getting men and equipment into the area to start fighting them."

"What air assets are available?" Lauren asked, knowing that Cal Fire had numerous bases with both aerial tankers and helicopters at the ready.

"We're working on it." Ernie sighed. "But it's not safe. Until we get word that the meteors have stopped dropping, they're grounded. Which leaves us with our surface equipment only, and the preliminary reports are we've lost nearly twenty percent of our firefighting capability from direct damage inflicted by the meteors. Our response vehicles are meeting resistance from the outflow of civilian evacuations. Plus it's getting dark, which complicates the entire process."

"The Defense Intelligence Agency informed me that this is one time we might need to sit and wait a little bit before we act, "Lauren said. "There are more impacts coming."

"How long are we talking? I mean, how will we know when it's finally safe?"

"My boss said he'd get you the information the second he does. What can you tell me about the status of the population?" Lauren spoke without taking her eyes off the screen, overwhelmed by the amount of real estate already destroyed by impact or fire. The thought that Donovan was down there somewhere caused her stomach to roil.

"All that seems to have worked in our favor was the tsunami warning. People dropped what they were doing and started heading to higher ground," Ernie said. "The downside is that the entire grid is down. No electricity, no phones, cell or otherwise. In addition to the FAA no-fly rule, Homeland Security has implemented a restricted area over the entire Monterey Peninsula in an effort to keep the airspace free from interference from civilian aviation. From past experiences, media helicopters and drones have been a problem."

"They always are," Lauren said as she shook her head.

"He still has plenty of escape routes," Montero said as if reading Lauren's mind.

"You have someone on the ground in Monterey?" Ernie asked.

"My husband, Donovan Nash, but I think we should stay focused on the big picture. He'll find his way out." Lauren said the words but guessed that neither Ernie nor Montero were buying her act.

"Mr. Rincon . . . Ernie," Montero said as she held out her hand. "I'm Ms. Montero, the Director of Security for Eco-Watch. Donovan Nash is the executive director. His well-being can only be in everyone's best interest. We already have assets in the area, obviously our helicopter, plus our new research ship, the *Buckley*. I'd like to head back to the original rendezvous point we had with Mr. Nash, as he may be there now, waiting."

"I can't authorize that," Ernie replied as he shook her hand. "I'm sorry."

"Okay, how about this. You just said you have very little information and you wanted to get to the forward fire base," Lauren said. "You come with us, we're an official flight. You can survey the areas you want to see firsthand, and on the way, we stop at the Monterey airport."

"If we do this," Ernie said, holding up an index finger for emphasis, "we come straight back here the moment I say we do. Dr.

McKenna, you will then remain as my liaison with the Department of Defense, to help us understand what these fires are doing."

"You have a deal," Lauren said and saw Montero already headed for the door to find Janie.

"How long do you think it'll be until we're ready to depart?" Ernie asked.

"If I know Montero and Janie, you'll be airborne inside fifteen minutes."

"I need to notify Agent Price," Ernie said. "He needs to clear our departure with the FAA."

Lauren stepped aside as Ernie looked at his phone and thumbed through e-mails or texts. She watched as he stopped and read one twice. His expression shifted, and his face seemed to drain of color. He seemingly collected himself and then he dialed a number on his cell phone. She heard him begin talking to Agent Price. The conversation took less than thirty seconds.

"Okay, Price says we're good to go." Ernie grabbed a Cal Fire windbreaker and pulled it on. "I appreciate this. More than anything else, I want to take a look at the current fires as well as the evacuation routes."

"Ernie." Lauren made no effort to move. "What is it you're not telling us?"

"I've just been told that Highway 1 is officially closed north of Seaside, which gives us only one viable exit out of Monterey. We're diverting our ground assets to ensure the evacuation route stays open, and they've already converted all lanes to handle the outbound traffic, but the evacuation process is slow."

"Those are facts," Lauren said. "What is it you're not telling me?"

"Water mains have been compromised. Emergency services are evacuating. It's going to be dark soon, and we're in full retreat. What makes matters worse is, at night, the fear level rises. People trying to escape are going to see actual flames that they couldn't see during the day. Traffic is moving, but if a full-scale panic ensues, everything will change. Add the possibility of looters, and complete chaos can quickly sweep over any remaining civilians. There's no law enforcement in the area. All official vehicles have been recalled to help keep traffic moving."

"There are also going to be more meteors visible in the night sky; we haven't seen the last of them," Lauren said.

"I didn't even think about that." Ernie pursed his lips and shook his head at the thought. "One of the worst things I've ever seen as a fireman was a nightclub blaze. The place wasn't up to code, the building was overcrowded, and the fire exits were locked. The fire happened fast and people panicked. Most of them were crushed and trampled before the smoke and flames ever reached them— but not all. I helped unstack the victims piled up against exits that wouldn't open. Imagine that scenario, except it's not a building, it's an entire city."

CHAPTER TEN

"I saw something just above the trees," Shannon said, leaning forward and pointing upwards through the windshield of the truck.

"What was it?" Donovan's eyes darted from the road to the sky, searching through the smoke.

"I think it was a helicopter—headed the same way we are."

Donovan rolled down his window and listened. All he heard was the thrumming of the tires on the pavement. He slowed until he could hear the distinct thumping of a helicopter's rotor blades.

"There!" Shannon pointed lower on the horizon.

Donovan spotted the helicopter. A white Bell Jet Ranger. He accelerated and the F-250 roared down the street until he had to slow down where a group of homes were engulfed in flames, which forced him to turn away from the heat. He zigzagged through the residential neighborhood in an effort to spot the helicopter again as flames licked upward in heated spirals, glowing embers drifting well above the trees. The smoke was getting thicker, and the light was fading. Cinders bounced off the metal and glass of the truck. All around them, cedar shake roofs, dried grass, and landscaping began to burn.

"I lost it," Shannon said.

Donovan switched on the truck's headlights. They passed wrecked cars abandoned in intersections, yet he didn't see a single soul, and even more distressing, still didn't see or hear a single emergency vehicle—just fire, smoke, and destruction. He continued to adjust his route, driving as fast as he dared down the curved roads fighting the heavy smoke. Debris littered the road, flames consumed entire blocks. Houses, trees, utility poles, everything was burning in the relentless path of the fires. Downed power lines hung inert. There was no electricity. Donovan flinched when a house a block away exploded and sent fiery wreckage tumbling high into the air. Unlike a forest fire, an urban fire fed off of so many other sources. Natural gas, automobile fuel, stored paint, virtually everything except ceramic and concrete would burn, and sometimes hotter than a simple wood blaze. All around them, he continued to hear the rumble of explosions.

"Where are we going? Do you see the helicopter?" Shannon asked as Donovan made an abrupt turn, and they headed down a different street.

"We have to be out in the open for anyone to see us." Donovan searched in vain through the canopy of mature trees for what little sky he could see. "I'm headed for the beach. Years ago, I spent time in Monterey, long before I joined Eco-Watch. It's coming back to me in bits and pieces."

"There!" Shannon shouted as an object flashed low on the horizon.

Donovan couldn't look. He'd spotted a street name he recognized and made a sharp right turn. They skirted a fire by pulling up over the curb and cutting through the scattered trees and brush of a deserted lot. The speeding Ford came down hard on the other side, but Donovan was now on a street that would take him where he wanted to go. He held his breath and rounded a corner and exhaled a silent thanks as he spotted the gate that led into Pebble Beach.

They roared past the abandoned guard shack, and Donovan pressed harder now that he knew exactly where he wanted to go.

"I see it," Shannon said excitedly. "Look, they're hovering. We can catch them!"

Donovan spotted the Jet Ranger. Channel 10 was painted in large letters on the fuselage. He cranked the steering wheel hard over, and the Ford's tires screeched as he made the turn onto 17 Mile Drive and barreled toward The Inn at Spanish Bay. Still obscured by the trees, he saw intermittent flashes of the chopper through the trees. He accelerated even faster. Ahead lay a section of road that split two fairways. They'd be clear of the trees, out in the open. He drove as fast as he could, his eyes locked on the road. They were close enough that he could hear the beating blades of the hovering chopper.

Donovan made the turn on Old 17 Mile Drive and sped from the trees. The setting sun caused him to squint and blink against the brightness. He reached up to pull down the visor, and in doing so, he spotted another airborne object. Coming fast down the beach was a low-flying personal drone. Four feet across with six separate rotors, its course remained steady as if the drone pilot was following the shoreline.

Donovan slammed on the brakes, bringing the truck to a stop. He jumped out and hit the ground running, waving frantically, trying to get the attention of the helicopter crew. He watched with stunned disbelief, as neither aircraft took evasive action. The drone slammed into the Jet Ranger's tail rotor, and splintered metal and plastic flew upward into the main rotor arc.

"Oh, God, no!" Shannon screamed.

The crippled helicopter twisted and turned as it plunged downward. The fuselage hit the ground on its side, and the sickening sound of crumpling metal carried across the grass. The uncontained blades threw hunks of grass and sod into the sky. The ruptured fuel tank exploded, and a large ball of flame boiled upward as the wreckage scattered and settled. The heat from the fire caused

Donovan to turn away with the certain knowledge that no one could have survived the crash.

He staggered back to the truck. As he slid behind the wheel, Shannon was staring at the scene, unblinking, her eyes brimming with tears that rolled down her face. She turned toward him and shook her head in obvious disbelief.

"There's nothing we can do." Donovan put the truck in gear.

"Someone will see the smoke and come, won't they?" Shannon said as she used the back of her hand to wipe at her tears.

"Look at the horizon, it's just more smoke."

"Don't aircraft have locator beacons or something?"

"Yes, but there has to be someone in a position to do something about it, and we've seen no evidence that anyone is coming."

"We were so close." Shannon slumped.

Donovan accelerated down the road, giving the fiercely burning helicopter a wide berth. Once they were past the wreckage, they both saw what the Channel 10 chopper had been fixated on. A yacht was sitting upright on the soaked fairway, placed there by the tsunami. Continuing on, Donovan let Shannon work out her growing disbelief in silence. He hadn't gone far when he plowed through the first pool of standing water, then another, which was even deeper. He slowed and stopped on an uneven section of the road that was above water. Squinting into the sun, he surveyed 17 Mile Drive. It was the fastest route to Cyprus Point, but all he saw was the setting sun glint off the pools of standing water. As far as he could see, 17 Mile Drive was mostly underwater or covered with mounds of sand and kelp.

He turned and looked back into the hills, at the smoke pouring from scorched neighborhoods, and he knew he had no choice.

"What are we going to do now?" Shannon asked.

Donovan put the truck in four-wheel drive, and cranked the steering wheel hard to the left. "To every golfer in the world, we're about to do the unthinkable," Donovan said as he powered through the shallow, water-filled ditch, and when they popped up onto a fairway of the Monterey Peninsula Country Club, he gunned the Ford and headed uphill. On the pristine grass, free from tree limbs, burning houses, and downed power lines, the Ford quickly reached fifty miles per hour. At the sound of the truck, a startled coyote ran for cover. Donovan watched it flee in his rearview mirror and ignored the chunks of grass and dirt flung upward by the all-terrain tires.

CHAPTER ELEVEN

LAUREN SAT NEXT to a window on the right side of the helicopter and fastened her seat belt. Montero sat next to her, and Janie went through the engine start checklist as Ernie took a window seat on the left side of the helicopter.

"Okay, this is what I know right now," Montero said as Janie started the first engine and the turbine began to spool up. "I spoke with Michael. Rick is in surgery. The doctors were encouraging, but guarded. I asked him if he had his injuries looked after, and he said he didn't want to talk about it, so I'm assuming the answer is yes."

Lauren heard the second engine start and accelerate until both turbines were spinning the heavy rotor in preparation for liftoff. Janie called out for everyone to plug in a headset so they could communicate. Moments later, everyone checked in loud and clear and Lauren watched Janie do her familiar scan outside the chopper, clearing the area before takeoff.

"Here we go," Janie announced and then they lifted straight up, pivoted ninety degrees, and began to accelerate southward.

As soon as they lifted free of the hangars and other buildings, Lauren could see the sun still above the horizon in the west, though toward the Monterey Peninsula, all she found was a wall of dirty black smoke.

Montero nudged Lauren and passed her the cell phone to show her a text:

Ms. Montero,

We have received the proper authorization, and as soon as possible, we will attempt to locate the vehicle rented by Mr. Donovan Nash from our Monterey, California, airport location. Due to scattered satellite outages, this may take some time. We appreciate your patience.

Sincerely,
Bethany Daniels
Customer Service, Prestige Rentals

Lauren nodded her approval and returned Montero's phone. Then she checked her own. There were several missed calls she already knew about, but nothing from Donovan or William.

"Once we cross the Santa Cruz Mountains, I'll be taking us lower as we approach Monterey. The smoke might create some visibility problems." Janie's voice carried through the intercom. "Air Traffic Control has reported unauthorized media helicopters in the area, and the radar coverage is sketchy with all of the power outages, so everyone keep an eye out."

Lauren's ears popped as they climbed. She put away her phone and began to scan the sky and ground on her side of the helicopter. They topped the highest peak and Lauren looked out over the Pacific Ocean—usually a breathtaking sight, but at this moment, she felt the press of the waning daylight wear on her already tattered nerves. The sun glowed orange through the dense smoke, and she calculated that there was only an hour of useful daylight remaining.

"I just got an update on the civil evacuations," Ernie said. "Full-scale evacuations are under way. Thank God it's Saturday, so we don't have the schools to worry about. Priority has been given to hospitals, assisted living facilities, and detention centers. Buses have been pulled into service, and many of the Monterey area military personnel are assisting. Critically ill or disabled individuals are being airlifted out by a combination of civilian medevac as well as law enforcement helicopters."

"Do you know if the governor has called in the National Guard yet?" Lauren asked.

"Even if he has, those assets won't typically be made available for twenty-four to thirty-six hours. I'm sure it'll happen, but not within a time frame that helps us now."

"What about Carmel?" Montero asked. "Do we know about those residents?"

"Carmel was lucky," Ernie continued. "As far as we know, they avoided any direct meteor hits. The majority of people reacted to the tsunami warning, and local authorities were able to direct everyone out of the city. We're hoping for very few casualties in Carmel as well as most of Carmel Valley."

"Pebble Beach?" Lauren asked.

"No power, multiple meteor impacts, roughly the same level of damage as Pacific Grove. We can only hope their higher elevation, and fewer people, means fewer tsunami casualties."

As they neared the shore, Lauren began to survey the tsunami damage. It looked as if the surge had reached inland beyond the initial thousand yards she'd estimated earlier.

"Lauren, do you think there was a second wave?" Janie said over the intercom. "The damage looks to be further inland than before."

"That's the Salinas River." Ernie pointed to the area where Highway 1 was completely submerged. "The elevation of the flood plain doesn't rise very fast. It looks like the surge traveled inland for miles."

"Yes, there would have been a second wave, typically larger than the first, maybe even a third. Look at how much water is just now streaming back toward the ocean." Lauren wished she had an idea of the mass of the meteorite that had plunged into the ocean off-shore. Depending on the disruptions to the water column when the meteor finally settled onto the ocean floor, there could easily be more tsunamis of unknown strength on their way.

The wreckage below was complete—buildings ripped apart, streets flooded and clogged with debris. Lauren tried to shut off everything but her scientific brain. They were flying low enough to spot individual bodies floating in the carnage, and despite traveling at 150 mph, their speed didn't lessen the reality. She turned her attention out to sea, and as Janie made the turn inland, Lauren was able to see the Monterey harbor. Almost nothing remained of the marina.

A massive pile of ships was stacked on the beach and strewn well into downtown. Most were buckled and broken, smashed against the buildings. She didn't see a single vessel still afloat. Fisherman's Pier, which housed dozens of restaurants and gift shops, had collapsed. Not a single structure remained, just the twisted remnants of plumbing fixtures. The center section of the pier was split in two from a large fishing vessel flung by the surge, its superstructure smashed by the force of the tsunami. With the angle of the sun, Lauren could see a thick sheen of fuel oil coating the water inside the marina and trailing out into the ocean.

The one miracle seemed to be wharf number two, the older commercial pier that jutted out into the water and then bent slightly to protect the ships moored within the marina. The working pier of Monterey's fishing fleet, it, too, was stripped clean of buildings by the powerful waves, but it still stood on its pilings, and seemed mostly intact. Lauren strained to spot Cannery Row and the aquarium, but a combination of low altitude and smoke made it impossible.

When Janie leveled the helicopter and slowed, Lauren spotted the wall of tangled wreckage that marked the inland boundary of the tsunami's surge. It was well short of the airport. Below them, she saw their abandoned Gulfstream was still parked where Michael had left it after they landed. She leaned closer to the window and frantically scanned the apron, looking for any sign of Donovan. She could feel the collective frustration in the cabin as Janie made one complete circle and continued on. The terminal looked gutted by the fire that still burned inside. Black soot scarred the building, and smoke swirled and joined a larger fire just outside the airport perimeter. Janie swung in a wide arc, putting considerable distance between the helicopter and the flames leaping skyward. Just beyond the airport, Lauren spotted Highway 68. It looked like a long, narrow parking lot filled with vehicles.

"We have a problem." Ernie looked up from his phone. "Highway 68, east of here, is the main evacuation route. We have an overturned vehicle and it's blocking two lanes near a bridge. Tow trucks are mired in traffic, at least an hour away. I need to take a look."

"Where exactly is this place?" Janie asked.

"Follow the highway," Ernie said.

"Roger that. Everyone hold on," Janie announced.

As the helicopter flew through some heavy smoke, they were buffeted by rough air. Lauren gripped the seat until it passed, knowing that the rising air created by the fire had caused the turbulence.

Janie raced along the traffic-choked road, until they came to the accident scene. She slowed, and then banked around the wreck. Lauren could see the overturned vehicle, a blue SUV. Cars were stuck, and with the guardrails along the bridge, there was no space for traffic to pass, or for anyone to push the damaged SUV out of the way. Janie slowed the 412 to a hover, and then made a slow circle around the wreckage.

Janie keyed the intercom. "Anyone have a guess at how much a Subaru Outback weighs?"

"Hang on. This close to Salinas, I have a signal on my phone," Montero said. "I'll have that for you shortly."

"Ernie," Janie said. "I can hoist two tons. Do you have any experience at Cal Fire rigging a sling load?"

"You bet. I trust you have the hook and release mechanism?" Ernie asked.

"Yeah, it's coiled up in the baggage compartment," Janie replied.

"I got it." Montero looked up from her phone. "The Outback has a curb weight ranging from thirty-four hundred to thirty-six hundred pounds."

"I'm going to set us down, and we'll rig up." Janie scanned the ground for a place to land. Satisfied with her selection, she started to descend toward a flat spot in a field not far from the road. The skids settled into the grass, and Ernie slid open the door. Janie brought the engines to idle, and the rotor spun harmlessly overhead, only a barely perceptible swishing sound coming from the blades.

From what Lauren understood about the process, there was a hook mechanism that attached to a mount beneath the 412. A cable then ran down to another hook that would securely clamp itself to the straps supporting the cargo. She watched as Ernie and Janie crawled beneath the helicopter to install the cable. Moments later, Janie brushed the dirt from her flight suit and climbed back inside the cockpit.

"I'll meet you at the Subaru," Ernie said.

"You know the drill," Janie called out. "If it's too heavy or starts swinging, I jettison the load."

"I've seen it happen," Ernie said. "Be careful."

Out the side window, Lauren watched Ernie sprint for the Subaru.

"Son of a bitch!" Montero cried out as her head snapped up from her phone and she turned and scanned the long row of vehicles stuck in traffic.

"What happened?" Lauren said, turning to find what Montero had seen.

"Donovan's rental car is back there a little ways. It's a gray Chevy Tahoe. If he'd have seen us land, he'd be here by now. Let me out!" Montero said as she unsnapped her seat belt and went for the side door.

"Wait!" Lauren called out to her. "What are you going to do?"

"My job," Montero said. "You guys take care of that Subaru; I'm going to go have a little chat with whoever is driving Donovan's rental."

"Do you need any help?" Lauren asked.

"No, I'm good." Montero's eyes narrowed with anger as she jumped to the ground and closed the door.

As she headed for the road, Lauren saw Montero double-check her Glock.

"Ernie was quick with it and had a bit of success. He says he's ready." Janie gestured toward the Subaru and Ernie.

Lauren could see Ernie standing on top of the wrecked SUV holding what appeared to be heavy-duty canvas straps high over his head.

"Here we go." Janie spooled up both engines to their familiar takeoff crescendo.

Lauren kept her eye on Montero as the former FBI agent walked briskly down the narrow shoulder in search of the Tahoe.

Janie lifted off and neatly brought the 412 into a hover above the Subaru, watching the events below through the bubble window next to her seat. "We're all hooked up and good to go," Janie announced.

Lauren couldn't see anything that happened straight below the helicopter, but down the road she saw Montero step up to a gray SUV, her Glock in hand but hidden behind her. An instant later, she was on the ground, and the Tahoe had pulled off the highway throwing dirt and sand high into the air. The SUV negotiated the ditch, nearly tipping over, then hit the bottom, spun its tires and fishtailed, then climbed up the other side. The driver of the Tahoe negotiated the incline, careened through a fence, and sped away, mowing crops as he raced down the middle of the field.

"What in the hell happened?" Janie yelled as she caught sight of the fleeing SUV. "Where's Montero?"

"Those people are driving Donovan's rental. Montero went to talk to them," Lauren said squinting through the dust to find Montero on her feet running after the SUV. "Montero's okay, but we're going to lose them."

"No, we're not," Janie said as she cleared the bridge, the Subaru slowly twisting at the end of the cable.

Lauren hung on as Janie banked the 412, swinging the helicopter around and accelerating on a heading to intercept the SUV. Within seconds, the 412 roared over the fleeing SUV. The moment Janie released the weight of the Subaru, she threw the now unburdened helicopter into a steep bank, and Lauren watched the Subaru drop. When it hit, a cloud of dirt exploded upward, nearly obscuring the scene. Janie cranked the helicopter steeper as the Subaru seemed to break apart and fly into a dozen separate pieces, the wheels and tires bouncing in crazy directions from the pancaked blue body. An instant later, the fleeing SUV plowed into what was left of the Subaru and came to an abrupt stop.

Janie pumped a gloved fist and glanced back at Lauren, smiling. "Bad day to be a Subaru, aye?"

Below them, Montero was in a dead run. She went to the driver's door, opened it, yanked a man out, and threw him hard to the ground. With one foot on the back of his neck, she pointed her Glock inside the SUV. Two other men piled out of the Tahoe, hands in the air, and lay down in a neat row next to the driver.

Janie touched down forty yards from the wrecked vehicles, and Lauren climbed out of the helicopter and ran toward Montero.

CHAPTER TWELVE

"Go!" Shannon screamed as a tree lining the narrow fairway crashed to the ground, showering the truck with burning branches that shattered upon impact. Donovan stepped on the gas and the F-250 lurched forward and blew through a swarm of glowing embers, each piece pinging off the windshield before bouncing away. Above them, the forest canopy was on fire. Flames whirled and spread in all directions. Just to his right, through the trees, he spotted the sun glint off the ocean. Silhouetted against the water, he saw a small herd of deer racing through the trees.

Donovan made a snap decision and peeled off the fairway. Shannon grabbed a handhold as he weaved the F-250 between the trunks of towering trees, racing through patches of burning pine needles. He held the wheel tight as they careened out of the trees onto another fairway. They sped downhill in the dwindling light, and Donovan slammed on the brakes to bring the truck to a stop just at the edge of a crater.

He put the truck in park, slid out, and walked to the edge. The crater was maybe ten feet deep and thirty feet in diameter. He saw only dirt and sand at the bottom. Shannon stepped out of the cab, but instead of walking toward him, she headed for an overturned maintenance cart lying in the rough. When Donovan saw her sink to her knees and bury her face in her hands, he began to sprint toward her. As he neared, great wrenching screams erupted from her chest and carried across the empty golf course.

Donovan slowed as he spotted the body trapped beneath the cart. The man looked to be in his twenties; a massive chest wound indicated that the end had been quick. Donovan knelt close to Shannon, and put an arm around her shoulders. He steadied her as she fought for tortured gasps of air.

"It's so senseless and random. He's wearing a wedding band. Somewhere out there is a woman. She's worried about him and he's never coming home. Why!" Shannon screamed at the heavens and sobbed as her words poured out. "I listen to what my PTSD patients tell me, about what they experienced, the helplessness. I know about the deals they make with God to make it all stop. I can't breathe. I need everything to slow down. I want the destruction and the horror, to somehow go away. When we made it to the golf course, away from the fires, I thought it would end. I saw this man lying underneath the cart. For a second, I thought he was alive. I hoped we could help him. We haven't seen a single person today we could do anything for. When I saw he was dead, it just all hit me at once."

"Stopping here was the first relatively safe, calm moment we've had since we saw the first meteor," Donovan said. "We haven't had any time to contemplate what we've seen today. We need to accept the fact that neither one of us will ever be the same. But we need to keep moving forward. Our job is to survive. There will be time to try to pick up the pieces later."

Shannon made no effort to move as she continued to sob.

"See that spit of land at the bottom of this hill?" Donovan pointed as she raised her head to look.

"I see it."

"That's where we're going. It's not far. If William is still there, we'll find him and get out of here. We need to go before it's completely dark." Donovan put out a hand to help her to her feet.

"What if we don't find him?" Shannon said. "What will we do then?"

"Then I can safely assume that he got out, and that we didn't leave him here to die," Donovan said. "Once we know, I'll get you out of here. I promise."

Donovan walked Shannon to the truck and climbed behind the wheel. Shannon sat and stared out the side window. He put the Ford into gear and continued down the hill toward Cyprus Point. Donovan studied their surroundings. If his calculations were correct, the next fairway marked their first intersection with the front nine of Cyrus Point. Donovan sped toward the Pacific, turned golden by the smoky sunset. The 17th hole bordered the rugged rocky coast that ran south. There wasn't much smoke coming from Cyprus Point, and all he hoped was that if William was still on the course when the wave hit, the elevation was high enough to have protected him from the tsunami.

Donovan cut hard across the parking lot of the clubhouse and headed down a fairway that would take him to the ocean. "Keep your eyes open, it's getting dark. He and his caddy could be anywhere."

Donovan honked the horn as he slowed. He located the switch to the light bar in the grill and lit up a wide swath of the rolling grass of the 18th hole. When he came to the 17th green, he rolled down his window, honked the horn again, and carefully drove around the putting surface and then began the slow drive down the 17th fairway.

"William almost always hooked the ball to the left on this hole. That puts him along the tree line to our right."

Off to their left was the steep cliff that went all the way down to the ocean, and Donovan could hear the waves crash against the rocks below. He spotted something shiny at the same time Shannon pointed.

Closing the distance, Donovan saw the reflection off the shaft of a solitary pitching wedge lying on the fairway. He stopped, jumped out, and as he drew closer, he began to feel the first flush of raw fear.

Off to his left, in the rough, he recognized a mangled golf bag bent against the trunk of a tree. The bag looked like William's.

"William!" Donovan yelled as he hurried for the tree, searching for anything, a movement, a sound, something that would tell him his mentor was still alive. The sopping wet grass told him the wave of the tsunami had surged up and over the cliff onto the fairway. Behind him, headlights swept across the trees as Shannon repositioned the truck, flooding the long shadows with light. He broke out in a run as he reached for the rough, yelling for William. He stooped below the branches, and ten paces away, next to the crushed golf bag, he spotted colors that didn't belong in nature. Pale yellow trousers and a blue pullover.

William was lying on his stomach. The heavy strap of the golf bag had been pulled around the trunk of the tree and looped under William's belt. His head was canted just far enough to the side for Donovan to see that his eyes weren't open. He took two steps and then dropped to his knees and brushed the pine needles and grass from William's face. Tears pushed to the surface of Donovan's eyes as he whispered, "No, no, no." He pressed his fingers into William's neck and found nothing, then he dug deeper into the slack flesh and finally felt what he was searching for. A pulse. William was still alive.

CHAPTER THIRTEEN

LAUREN ARRIVED AT the wrecked Tahoe just in time to hear Montero issue her first set of orders to the man who'd been driving. She'd rolled him over, and he was now lying on his back next to his two accomplices.

"When I pull the barrel of this gun out from under your chin, you're going to start talking, and it better be the truth. If not, I'll pull the trigger and move on to your friend. Do you understand?"

Montero was instantly rewarded with a wide-eyed nod.

Lauren saw the fury in Montero's eyes. It was a look Lauren had only seen once or twice. Each time it startled her.

"Where did you steal this vehicle?" Montero said as she pressed her gun barrel against the trembling man's forehead.

"A parking lot near the aquarium."

"How did you get the keys?"

"They were in the office, it was crazy, everyone was fighting over them. We all grabbed keys and started pushing buttons. This one started."

Lauren walked closer to the Tahoe; both doors on the driver's side were still open. As she peeked inside, she saw a strap of some kind sticking out from under the seat. As she pulled it out, she realized it was a purse. Upon closer inspection, there were several purses, and inside one of them were half a dozen men's wallets. The last item she came across was Donovan's briefcase. Lauren held up the evidence for Montero to see.

"When did you leave the aquarium? What time?" Montero asked.

"When that damn meteor came down and the tsunami siren went off."

"If you were in such a big hurry to leave, when did you find time to grab purses and wallets?"

"We don't know nothing about that."

Montero held up her free palm and turned her head to the side as if she was about to pull the trigger, and wanted to deflect the inevitable mess. The man began to thrash, and Lauren saw a wet spot form and spread out from the crotch of his jeans.

"Them people was already dead," he called out with his eyes wide, his lips trembling.

"Here's my advice for all three of you," Montero said calmly, but her tone left no doubt as to her level of intent. "If my friends who rented this vehicle turn up dead, you'd better plead for the police to keep you in jail for the rest of your miserable lives. The day you walk free is the day you'd better start looking over your shoulder for me."

"Drop the gun!" a highway patrolman yelled as he stopped ten feet away, his service weapon drawn and pointed at Montero.

Montero set aside her Glock and raised her hands and placed them behind her head. "Officer, I'm former FBI agent Veronica Montero. This is a rental car, and these men stole it from our colleague. They also have stolen purses and wallets in their possession. I placed them under citizen's arrest."

"Dear God, you're *the* Agent Montero?" The trooper lowered his weapon and tipped the brim of his hat in a gesture of respect.

"That's me." Montero nodded and lowered her hands.

"I'm Dr. Lauren McKenna, with the Defense Intelligence Agency."

Ernie was breathing heavily when he finally approached the group. The trooper turned and held up his hand for Ernie to slow his approach.

"This is Mr. Rincon with Cal Fire," Montero said. "He can vouch that we're on a mission of some importance, and the only reason we're even here was to alleviate the traffic obstruction. These carjackers were a bonus."

"Yes," Ernie said as he caught his breath. "They're with me."

On the road, traffic was moving again, and on impulse, Lauren waved. Her action resulted in a chorus of honking, waving drivers, showing their appreciation for being under way again.

The trooper glanced at Lauren and then turned back to Montero. "I'll take these men into custody. If I need a written report on this later, can I count on you to provide me with one?"

"You bet," Montero replied and handed the trooper a business card. "Now if you'll excuse us, we need to go."

Lauren held her husband's briefcase as if it were her own.

Montero reached down for her Glock, and as she did, she leaned closer to the man she'd terrorized. "Don't forget what we talked about."

Four minutes later, with streams of cars all honking and waving as they passed by, Janie brought the power up on the helicopter and lifted off.

"Are you okay?" Lauren asked Montero.

"Sure, why?" Montero answered as if startled by the question. "Oh, those guys. I saw the trooper coming, and knew I didn't have much time to extract the truth. That tactic is usually pretty effective, especially when there's more than one of them."

"Really, so you can just turn that rage on and off?"

"It's never actually turned off," Montero said as if she were sharing common knowledge. "I just control how much people get to see."

Lauren wasn't sure how much to believe, though a part of her understood that her friend might be telling the truth.

"Nice grab with the briefcase," Montero said. "I was afraid the trooper would want it as evidence."

"Ernie, exactly where are we going now?" Janie asked via intercom.

"Straight east—I want to get a look at Highway 101, and then we'll head west to the fire base."

As Janie was banking the helicopter around in a wide turn, a huge flash lit up the entire western horizon. Through the smoke and haze toward the ocean, the light flickered twice and then went dark.

"What the hell was that?" Montero asked.

"Forget the highway," Ernie said. "Turn toward the ocean. I need to know what just blew."

Janie kept the turn coming around as a shock wave buffeted the helicopter. She kept the 412 steady and raced toward the point where they'd seen the explosion. In the dark of the smoke-induced twilight, they flew in silence until they saw the flames.

"We just flew over this part of Seaside earlier, and it wasn't burning," Janie said. "Now it looks like a straight line through town is on fire."

"Ernie, look," Lauren said as they approached the devastation. "That wasn't a meteor. What caused that?"

"A gas main," Ernie said as he turned from the window. "It's not supposed to happen. There are check valves that close, sectioning off the pipe and the contents. Even if it's ignited at street level, it should just burn off the remaining gas aboveground and then go out. I don't understand. Janie, you'd better get us out over the water. We'll be safer out there."

Lauren sat back and thought of Ernie's earlier description of a huge theatre fire. All she could do was hope that Seaside had already evacuated due to the tsunami, and the gas explosion didn't kill anyone.

"They're moving the fire base further north," Ernie reported as he listened to reports streaming in from the earpiece of his handheld radio. "Janie, I need to get back to San Jose. All senior emergency services officials are going to rendezvous at the airport."

Lauren felt her phone vibrate in her pocket, and a quick glance told her it was Michael. She pulled off her headset and answered.

"Lauren, it's Michael, can you hear me? Where are you?"

"I can barely hear you. I'm in the helicopter," Lauren said.

"I think I saw him," Michael said. "I think I saw Donovan on television. I was watching news coverage, and the studio cut to a live shot from their news helicopter just before they lost the feed. I swear I saw him, waving his arms."

"What station? Where are you now?" Lauren had a million questions—and just as many doubts.

"It was Channel 10, that's all I know. I tried calling them, but I keep getting a busy signal. In fact, I'm surprised I reached you. Right this moment, I'm standing next to an empty helipad. The same one where you guys dropped me off earlier. How soon can you pick me up?"

"Janie," Lauren shouted above the rotor noise. "Flying time to Stanford Hospital?"

"Twenty minutes."

"We'll be there in twenty minutes. Michael, how certain are you of this?" Lauren needed to hear a number, something she could latch onto and process. She counted on Michael to give her the unvarnished truth.

"In reality, maybe fifty percent," Michael said. "I only watched it once, but, Lauren, the instant I saw the guy, I shot up out of my seat and yelled at the television. My gut tells me it's him."

"We're coming as fast as we can." Lauren ended the call and then pressed the phone against her chest and closed her eyes and tried to control her soaring hopes.

"What's happened?" Montero asked.

Lauren slipped her headset back on. "Okay, everyone. That was Michael. He's still at the hospital. He was watching a live TV feed from a news helicopter, and swears he saw Donovan, alive. The feed was lost, but we have a station, Channel 10. We're going to get Michael and then drop Ernie at the San Jose airport."

"Once we land at San Jose, I want to top off the fuel tanks," Janie said.

"Where's Channel 10 located?" Montero said and began typing into her phone.

"Channel 10 will be waiting when we land," Ernie said. "I've already been alerted that there's a media presence starting to gather outside the Pacific Jet Center."

"Perfect," Lauren said and then put her hand over her microphone and leaned toward Ernie. "How bad is the situation now, with a fire base in retreat?"

"Bad. I'll know more when I get all the updates on the ground. I hope you're not thinking of going back down into the fire, at night?"

"If I know where my husband is, and that he's still alive, then, yes. If it was your family, what would you do?"

"Firefighters are my family, and I know for a fact that dozens of my brothers and sisters are missing. This could be the single biggest loss of life event in Cal Fire history. My job, and yours, is to use our positions to try to save the population. Or to put it another way, you and I need to help everyone get out of the burning nightclub."

CHAPTER FOURTEEN

"WILLIAM, I NEED you to talk to me." Donovan was afraid to move his friend without knowing what his injuries might be.

"Oh God," Shannon said as she arrived at Donovan's side. "Is he alive?"

"Yes, but I don't want to move him yet."

"His foot." Shannon put her hand over her mouth and pointed to William's right golf shoe.

Donovan saw the blood-soaked sock and the peculiar angle of his golf shoe. He crawled on his hands and knees until he could lean over, and with two hands, ease up William's pant leg. In the light from the headlights, he saw the whitish bone protruding from William's sock. Trying to be as delicate as possible, Donovan attempted to examine the wound by widening the hole in the sock. William let out a cry of pain and blindly reached out with his right arm.

"William, can you hear me?" Shannon said as she put her hand on his cheek. "It's Shannon and Donovan. We're here."

William tried to talk, but a cough drowned out his words, and he spit out some grass and water.

"I know about your ankle," Donovan said. "Can you tell me where else it hurts?"

"I think—" William struggled to find his voice, coughed again, and then opened his eyes. "I think my left elbow might be broken."

"Okay," Donovan said to Shannon. "I'm going to support William and keep him steady while you unbuckle the strap holding him to the tree. Once we've done that, we're going to put together a splint and then try to move him out of here. William, are you ready?"

William nodded and used his good arm to wipe his mouth.

"Was the strap your idea?" Donovan asked as he reached under William's waist.

"I knew that with my bad hip I couldn't outrun the tsunami. My cleats allowed me to get up this tree, but the second outgoing surge was too much. A floating log caught my ankle. I hurt my elbow when I fell trying to get down."

"Climbing the tree was the one thing that saved your life. You're lying on your elbow, so I'll take your word that it's broken. Your ankle is definitely broken. Other than all of that, how was the golf?"

William let out an involuntary chuckle, which quickly turned into a groan.

Shannon loosened the heavy buckle and slowly fed the strap under William's belt until he was free of the trunk. Donovan eased him down until William was lying flat on the ground.

"I'll go find something to use as a splint." Shannon hurried toward the truck.

"I'm sorry it took me so long to get here," Donovan said. "Where's your caddy? Where's Senator Evans and his caddy?"

"I don't think they survived. They were still running when the wave arrived." William's eyes took in his surroundings. "What time is it? I think I must have blacked out."

"You've been out for a while. I'm going to very gently remove your shoe. If it's too painful, let me know." Donovan untied the laces and loosened the tongue as much as possible. He tried to stabilize the foot below the break and began to slide the shoe off of the blood-soaked sock. William's sharp intake of breath told Donovan what he already knew. With a final pull, Donovan finished with the shoe and grimaced as William pounded his good fist into the ground in pain.

"I think this might work." Shannon laid down one of the rubber floor mats from the truck.

"Nice," Donovan said and then tried to think about the proper first aid for a compound fracture. "Look in the pocket of his golf bag for a folded towel. He usually keeps a spare."

"Here. It's wet." Shannon handed the folded towel to Donovan. She unsnapped the used towel still clipped to the bag, found a clean spot, and used the damp material to wipe William's face.

"I'm going to use the towel as a compress, then we'll engineer a splint." Donovan swallowed hard, and careful not to touch the bone, he pulled apart the sock and exposed the wound and quickly pressed the towel against the worst of the bleeding.

"I'm having a little trouble getting a full breath," William said between shallow breaths. "I need to try and turn onto my back."

"You got it." Donovan moved from William's ankle to his torso. "Shannon, we're going to roll him in the direction of the incline. When we start, can you try to ease his leg while I turn him?"

"I will," Shannon said. "Don't forget his elbow."

"I've got it." Donovan leaned down toward William. "Are you ready? Are you sure your neck and back are okay?"

"Just get it over with."

Donovan nodded at Shannon and lifted William's shoulders, and accompanied with a sharp intake of air, and a string of profanities, they turned and rested William on his back. "William, it's done, can you breathe better?" The silence brought Donovan's eyes to William's face where he saw a grimace mixed with tears.

William gasped and moaned. His breathing was shallow. He shook his head side to side as he fought each wave of pain.

"We need to get this splint finished and get him out of here," Donovan said as he grabbed the rubber mat.

"Where do we start?"

"We fold the mat a couple of times until it's U-shaped, then we use it to cradle his leg without the rubber touching the broken bone," Donovan said. "After we position the splint, we'll need to find something to secure it in place."

Shannon unfolded the towel she'd used to wipe William's face. "If we rip this into strips, we can use one on his ankle and the other above the break. We may have to improvise, but I think we can use the bag's shoulder strap to secure the rubber mat further up his leg."

"I like it," Donovan said and looked at William who had closed his eyes.

Shannon knelt next to Donovan, and together they worked to maneuver the mat into place.

Shannon tied the makeshift splint with strips of the towel, while Donovan held William's leg steady. When she finished with the larger strap, she leaned back to examine their work. They'd created a semirigid support around William's leg.

"Okay, that's not bad," Donovan said. "William, are you hanging in there?"

William managed a strained groan.

"We have to get him to a hospital," Shannon said.

"Can you back the truck up as close as you can?"

Donovan watched her go, thankful that her energy seemed entirely focused on the one survivor they had seen all day that she could actually help. Shannon turned the truck around in a half circle, and then inched backwards to where William lay. She jumped from the cab and lowered the tailgate.

"Okay, buddy," Donovan said to William. "This is going to hurt, but we're going to move you to the bed of the truck, nice and gentle. It'll be quick, I promise."

Donovan waited until Shannon was in position to support William's leg. He told William to support his injured elbow with his good hand. Once everything was set, Donovan went down on one knee and slid his arms under William. Counting on his fear and adrenaline to accomplish what he needed to do, he lifted his friend off the ground. Ignoring the protests from every joint in his body, Donovan staggered upright, swayed, and then walked as carefully as he could toward the taillights.

Trying his best to ignore William's cries of pain, Donovan set William on the tailgate while Shannon steadied his legs. Donovan climbed up into the bed and pulled William inside the bed until he was all the way forward. He pulled off his leather coat, folded it, and laid it under William's head. "Shannon, close the tailgate and drive us out of here."

Shannon ran around to the driver's side, stepped on the side runner, and turned toward Donovan. "I'm not sure which way to go."

"Follow our tracks to the left. I'll help you navigate. Though, I think we might have a different problem."

"What?"

"The evacuation—it would include hospitals, wouldn't it?"

CHAPTER FIFTEEN

THE HELICOPTER'S LANDING light illuminated Michael, who stood well away from the center of the hospital's helipad. Lauren felt the skids touch at about the same time as Montero yanked open the door. Michael piled in, and Montero closed the door as Janie lifted off the pad and climbed away. The entire operation took less than fifteen seconds.

"Any news about Rick's condition?" Lauren asked as Michael buckled his seat belt.

"I was able to speak briefly with the surgeon," Michael said. "Rick was lucky. Thanks to you two, the blood loss wasn't an issue. He said he was able to reconnect everything that was damaged. He explained to me that the wounds were about the same as a small caliber bullet, through and through, so there wasn't massive tissue damage. Rick will recover."

"And you?" Montero said, gesturing at the wad of gauze that covered half of Michael's right ear. "Did you get a stud or a hoop?"

"Hey, I got a meteor through my earlobe, so that's not even funny. Though my wife asked me the exact same thing," Michael said with an irritated smile. "She told me I could borrow some of her earrings while I decided on my new look."

"Guys," Janie said over the intercom. "Take a look to the south. San Jose Tower says we're about to have more objects enter the atmosphere. They said the estimated impact point should be well out to sea, roughly eighty miles southwest of our position."

Lauren dimmed the cabin lights and studied the sky. The first object rushed toward the ground, burning white-hot before it winked out against the distant horizon. Seconds later, at least ten other objects burst into view, burned brightly, and changed to a deep red glow from the smoke before vanishing. Putting her science aside for a moment, she thought of Ernie's words, about the crowded nightclub, and how easy it was to incite panic and confusion. All she could do with those thoughts was hope that the majority of people were away from the fires, maybe even indoors where the meteors would pass unseen.

Janie brought the helicopter in over the Pacific Jet ramp, and set down in the same spot as before. The one difference Lauren could see from when they departed were the television cameras being trained on the Eco-Watch helicopter from what used to be a half-empty parking lot. Beyond the fence, she spotted the microwave towers reaching up from the equipment vehicles.

"I think everyone should get inside as quickly as possible," Montero said, uneasy at the scene of dozens of unknown people crowding against a fence. "I'm going to stay out here with Janie and help get the helicopter refueled. We'll be in as soon as we're finished."

Michael slid the door open and he and Ernie jumped to the ramp and then helped Lauren out. The three of them put their heads down against the cameras and hurried to the door.

"Lauren," Ernie said. "Can you get me an update from your people in Washington?"

"I'll see what I can do." Lauren checked her phone for the time. It was late in Washington, but considering the day's events, Calvin would still be there.

"I'll be right back," Michael said, and they stepped through the glass doors into the lounge of Pacific Jet.

"What are you doing?" Lauren asked.

"I'm going to find someone from Channel 10. Want to come?"

"I have to touch base with Calvin. If there's anything I need to know, come and get me, regardless of what I'm doing."

"Will do."

Ernie went straight toward the converted conference room, and Lauren turned down the hallway to the office she'd used before and was relieved it was empty. She closed the door behind her, sat down in the chair, leaned back, and took three deep breaths to try and uncoil from the stress. She told herself that Donovan was nothing if not a survivor. She could let Michael and Montero handle the quickly changing landscape surrounding them, and as Ernie so aptly said, Lauren needed to focus on her expertise. She picked up the phone and punched in Calvin's direct line.

"Deputy Director Reynolds."

"Calvin, it's Lauren. I'm back on the ground at the San Jose airport. Cal Fire wants an update."

"Lauren, what do you mean back on the ground?"

"I'm fine, we were out in the helicopter doing some reconnaissance with Cal Fire. First question though, do you know if anyone besides television stations record what goes out on the air? Say a live feed from a helicopter. Does anyone we know monitor that stuff?"

"The NSA doesn't, at least not domestically. The FCC is who you need to talk to, but good luck, it's Saturday night, why?"

"It's just a question that came up," Lauren said, deciding that Calvin was in no position to help, and he'd only worry even more about her than he already did. "We'll look into it at this end. Never mind, back to business. What can I pass on to Cal Fire?"

"We just processed the latest intel taken of the meteor's debris field. There is some good high-resolution infrared imagery that might be useful. I'll e-mail you the packet."

"E-mail is fine," Lauren said as she moved the mouse on the desk and the monitor sprang to life. "What about the International Space Station or any of the larger platforms like Hubble? Did they take any hits?"

"No, not so far," Calvin said. "If you were just out flying, did you by chance see the latest barrage of reentries?"

"I did. The objects were pretty far south and looked to be breaking up. Were they meteors or man-made?"

"A mixture of both. They were tracked from reentry all the way into the Pacific Ocean. What's significant is that collection of wreckage included GOES 15. GOES 16 isn't responding."

GOES stood for Geo Stationary Environmental Satellite, and Lauren knew they were the backbone of the weather forecasting for the northern hemisphere. As far as weather forecasting tools, they'd just taken a huge hit. "What about GOES 12? Can you retask it to give us the coverage we need?"

"We can, but no one will take it out of its current orbit for fear that it'll be disabled by the rogue debris we have up there right now."

"What about our allies?" Lauren asked. "Can we piggyback off of their weather satellites until a GOES can be repositioned?"

"We're working on that."

"When you can, pull up the latest data from any orbital platform, and send it to me so I can compare it with the data everyone here is using. I have no idea where Cal Fire or the Forest Service is getting their meteorological updates."

"Will do. I also just spoke to the Pentagon about our military assets in the immediate area. We already know that most of the War College in Monterey is damaged or destroyed. Coast Guard personnel have been evacuated as their vessels in port were destroyed by the tsunami. Both bases were evacuated quickly and the occupants have joined forces with local EMS to assist in civilian evacuations.

The Pentagon wants six-, twelve-, and twenty-four-hour situation reports of the areas affected by the fire. I told them you were on scene and would take care of that personally."

"Do you want me to go through you or contact the Pentagon directly?"

"They have more staff than we do, so go ahead and contact General Curtis directly, and copy me on the correspondence."

"Will do," Lauren said.

"Before I go. Donovan? William? Any word?"

"I'm trying not to think about that right now. If I hear something, I'll be sure and let you know." Lauren hated what she'd said the second the words left her lips, and she blew out a heavy sigh. "Calvin, I'm sorry. I hope you understand. I'm not brushing you off. I've seen what's happening here, and I can only describe it as a complete disaster. I can't focus on them right now, or I promise, I'll completely unravel. I'm hoping that if I concentrate on the big picture, and try to help as many people as I can, Donovan, Shannon, and William will be among them."

"You're right, that's exactly what you should be doing," Calvin said. "And Lauren, if it were me out there, you're the one I'd want searching for answers."

"Thank you." Lauren said good-bye and disconnected the call. She clicked through the computer screens until she accessed the DIA website, which would let her open her e-mail. Moments later she had the file and began sifting through the data Calvin had sent.

She skimmed the first few pages, noting the first impact craters in Utah, then sporadic clusters through Utah, Nevada, and finally into California. It quickly became obvious that the satellites that initiated the meteor's breakup did humanity a favor. Instead of one concentrated point of impact, the energy was dispersed over half of

North America. As bad as things were, Earth had dodged a bullet and ended up with just a flesh wound.

When she came to the high-resolution images of the Monterey Peninsula, she glanced at the printer to her left. A green light promised that it was warmed up and ready to go. Lauren knew better than to flood bureaucrats with too much information, so she selected five of the best images and sent them to the printer. The infrared data was the most damning. Because the cities were without power, they were essentially dark, so each glowing spot was a point of ignition.

"Lauren," Montero said from the open doorway. "We found Channel 10. You need to come now."

Lauren logged out of the computer, snatched the still warm pages from the printer tray, and followed Montero down the hallway. She stopped at the conference room door, knocked, and stepped inside. Ernie was standing over a large-scale map spread out on two tables. There were four other men in the room with him. Lauren ignored them and went straight toward Ernie.

"Gentleman," Ernie said. "This is Dr. Lauren McKenna, an Earth Science consultant with the Defense Intelligence Agency."

"Ernie, here's the latest high-resolution images of the entire Monterey Peninsula. Number five is the one you'll be most interested in, as it's an infrared picture of everything burning. I'm needed somewhere else at the moment. The information is straightforward, and I'll check back to answer any questions." Lauren turned smartly and headed toward Montero.

"Dr. McKenna," Ernie called after her. "Thank you. I trust you're not leaving the premises?"

Lauren shot a questioning look at Montero, who in turn addressed the men. "She's not going far. We need her to examine some aerial footage. We'll be back shortly."

As they crossed the lobby and proceeded through the glass doors that led outside, Lauren couldn't stand the suspense any longer. "Tell me. Is it him?"

"Slow down. We located a technician from Channel 10, and Michael and I persuaded him to try to find the feed. I thought we should all see it together. Hopefully, he'll have it up and ready to roll by the time we get to the van."

Lauren and Montero wound through several parked cars until they came to a van sporting decals announcing that it belonged to Channel 10, the Bay Area's News Leader. Michael was crouched just inside the rear sliding door, and he reached out to help Lauren climb inside. Montero went last. All three of them gathered around a young man with curly red hair who was sitting behind a console. Lauren's excitement plummeted when she saw that the screens in the panel were smaller than the ones used on a common tablet.

"This is Joshua—he's the cameraman-slash-engineer on this van," Michael said.

"We don't have a great deal of time," Lauren said to Joshua. "Can you please roll the tape?"

"Sure." Joshua reached for a switch on the panel and pressed a button.

Lauren moved closer as a destroyed yacht materialized on the small screen. Her eyes danced around furiously as she tried to take in every detail. As the image stabilized, the camera angle panned right to left along the superstructure of the boat when in the upper left-hand part of the screen, a blurred object shot into the frame. Moments later, the camera swung to the left revealing a man waving his arms. Lauren's breath caught in her chest and then the screen went black.

"Can you play it again and freeze the final image?" Lauren refused to look at the others as she exhaled slowly and tried to ignore the blood vessel pounding in her neck. Three more times she watched the scene unfold, and each time she tried with every fiber of hope to convince herself that the man was her husband, but she couldn't. There looked to be someone in the passenger seat of the truck, but the glare from the sun washed them out. Lauren turned to Michael and Montero. "I honestly don't know. The man is standing in the long shadow cast by the helicopter. Khaki pants, a dark-colored shirt that I can't tell if it's black, dark green, or navy blue. Then there's the leather jacket, which I don't recognize at all and makes him look larger than Donovan."

"I know what you're saying," Michael said. "But what was your gut instinct the first time you saw the tape?"

"Same as you," Lauren said as she shrugged. "Though, I was anticipating it being Donovan, so I'm not sure that proves anything."

"Montero," Michael said. "What do you think? Is there a definitive answer here?"

"No," Montero said. "We all know how unreliable an eyewitness is at the scene of a crime or an accident. We see the man on the tape for less than three seconds, and none of us can identify him as Donovan. In fact, as Lauren pointed out, if we look at the truck and the jacket, there's more evidence that it's not Donovan."

"If I had to make a decision based on this, I'd say no," Lauren said. "What it does tell me, though, is that there are survivors out there."

CHAPTER SIXTEEN

SHANNON SLOWED WHEN the Spanish-style clubhouse came into sight. She leaned out the open side window toward Donovan. "Where do you want me to go?"

"I have an idea. Go around front to the parking lot," Donovan said as he tried to determine what condition the building was in. He kept one hand under William's head as a cushion while Shannon rounded the 18th green and pulled onto the pavement. She swung the Ford into an arc and stopped with the truck's high beams aimed at the front door. "I'm thinking we go in and find some pillows and blankets, maybe some bottled water to make things more comfortable for William."

"Stay here, I'll be right back," Shannon called out as she slipped out of the cab, jogged up to the door, and pushed inside. Donovan was startled when she came out moments later holding something in her arms and running as fast as she could.

"There's a gas leak—it smells like rotten eggs in there." She called out as she tossed Donovan a large section of heavy material and scrambled back behind the wheel and drove away.

Donovan spotted the hooks that ran along one edge of the fabric and realized that Shannon had walked in, smelled gas, yanked down the closest set of drapes, and ran. He did his best to cover William, if nothing else to try to protect him from the wind swirling through the bed of the pickup. As Shannon approached 17

Mile Drive, he tapped on the rear glass and signaled her to turn right. As she swung out and accelerated, he focused on the rough ride, and how to keep William stable. As she negotiated each curve, Donovan swore under his breath and knew that this was a bad idea. They needed to stop someplace safe and reassess how best to care for William.

"Shannon," Donovan called out and motioned for her to stop the truck.

"What's wrong?" she asked.

"This isn't working. We're both getting thrown around back here." As he spoke, he spotted several points of light on the hill above the road.

Shannon turned as well and saw what Donovan had seen. "Houses with lights. Not everyone evacuated."

"Make the next left turn and drive up the hill. The first house we come to with electricity, pull in the driveway, and honk the horn."

Donovan felt them climbing and was relieved the road didn't have as many sharp curves as 17 Mile Drive. He felt Shannon slow and then make a right turn. With his limited view out of the front of the truck, Donovan saw what he guessed was her destination. A house, all lit up, sat just ahead. She made the turn into the driveway and pulled up to the massive front door. Twin matching chandeliers hung down from the towering eaves that protected visitors from inclement weather. Shannon blew the horn on the truck and then switched off the engine.

Donovan looked around to see if anyone was responding to their arrival.

"The day is starting to look up," Shannon said as she stepped out of the truck and stood for a moment, as if taking in the entire dwelling. "Wow."

"Check the door and see if it's locked," Donovan said as he lowered himself out of the bed of the truck.

Shannon pushed and pulled on the handle, as well as rang the doorbell, which triggered a chorus of bells inside. "I don't think anyone is home. Which window do we break?"

Donovan grabbed the pry bar he'd taken from the body shop and followed a brick sidewalk around the garage, through a gate, until it finally spilled out onto a massive patio. A swimming pool glistened blue from underwater lights, and somewhere on the treed property Donovan heard the muffled roar of a generator.

Shannon walked to a large sliding glass door and peered inside. "I don't see a soul."

He gripped the pry bar and using the flattened end punched a hole in the glass. He repeated the process until he could reach in and unlock the door, sliding it open effortlessly. He listened for an alarm, but there was only silence. Even if there was a silent alarm, no one was going to respond.

They stepped inside and Donovan worked his way through the house to the entryway foyer where he unlocked the double doors and hurried down the steps to the F-250. Donovan climbed into the bed of the truck, set the pry bar aside, and kneeled next to William.

"What if we find a mattress and pulled it down here for him to ride on," Shannon asked. "Would that work?"

"I thought about that, but even if we make it to a hospital, I'm afraid it would be evacuated. Then we've gained nothing."

"Do you have any idea how far away the nearest hospital is?"

"I remember seeing signs on the highway when we came back from dinner last night in Carmel." Donovan, as he'd done for twenty-five years, lied and was vague about anything having to do with his past as Robert Huntington. In reality, he knew exactly where the closest hospital was located.

"What are you saying?" Shannon asked. "That we stop here and wait for help to arrive? That'll be tomorrow at the earliest."

"No, I'm saying we stop here for now, quit beating William up in the back of a pickup truck, and I go and see if I can find help. I'll try to get to the hospital. If anyone's there, I'll come back with help or an ambulance."

"That makes sense," Shannon said. "What if we move him to one of the chaise lounges from the pool area? We could roll him inside. It has an adjustable back, and wheels. We could clean him up, keep a closer eye on him, and he'd be much more comfortable."

"Great idea," Donovan said. "It would almost be like a gurney."

"I'll go get one." Shannon hurried down the sidewalk and vanished in the darkness as she headed for the pool.

Donovan put his palm on William's forehead, and it reminded him of when he was a teenager, just after his parents died, and he went to live with William. It had been a hard time for Donovan. He missed his parents horribly, and he often felt abandoned, cast aside. When he was sick, William always took great care of him, and even if he didn't have a fever, the feel of his hand was always reassuring, and made him feel protected.

Donovan had William to thank for so much, and what Donovan needed more than anything was to make sure he did everything in his power to make sure William survived. He heard the squeaky wheels of the chaise lounge as Shannon came into view, pushing it around the corner of the house toward the truck.

"We're going to get you off this metal onto some cushions," Donovan explained. Together, using the drapes as a combination hammock and stretcher, he and Shannon were able to slide William to the tailgate, and then Donovan gently lowered him onto the chaise lounge. A long groan slipped from William's lips as Shannon stabilized his shattered ankle and arranged his injured elbow onto his chest. Donovan covered him with the curtain and together he and Shannon wheeled him around to the back of the house. With William supported by the cushions, it was a simple task to pull the wheeled chaise up the steps into the kitchen.

In the bright light, Donovan winced at the scratches on William's face and hands. The inside of his wrists especially were rubbed raw from his efforts to hold on to the tree trunk to keep from being swept away. The golf towel wrapped around his ankle was almost completely saturated with blood and needed to be replaced.

"I'm going to go see if I can find a first-aid kit," Shannon said as Donovan continued to examine William's wounds.

"A proper blanket and some pillows would be good as well," Donovan said to Shannon as he spotted a butcher block on the counter holding a pair of scissors among the knives. "Hand me those scissors, will you? I need to get a look at his elbow."

Shannon passed them to Donovan. "Do you need me to stay for this?"

"I've got it," Donovan said as he snipped a small opening in William's pullover.

"I'll be back as fast as I can." Shannon started to leave, hesitated, turned, and waited until Donovan looked up at her. "Earlier, I'm sorry about my, you know, meltdown. It won't happen again. I was just caught off-guard, and a little overwhelmed."

"You're human," Donovan said. "As long as you keep getting up and pushing forward, you and I are fine."

"Thank you," Shannon said, then turned and walked from the room.

Donovan focused his attention on William and was surprised to find that he seemed to be squinting against the light, trying to comprehend his surroundings.

"William," Donovan said. "How are you doing?"

"Oh God, it hurts," William said quietly, straining to form the words.

"We're going to get you comfortable, okay? Do you want something to drink?"

William nodded.

Donovan eyed a bottle of water in the nearly empty refrigerator, twisted off the cap, knelt, and helped William take a sip. When he'd had enough, Donovan set the bottle aside and picked up the scissors to continue cutting William's sweater at the elbow.

"This is my favorite Argyle sweater," William managed to whisper.

"I'll buy you a new one," Donovan said as he opened enough material to finally expose William's broken elbow.

"What do you see?"

"Your elbow is definitely swollen, so it could very well be broken. I'm going to leave it the way it is until someone can take an X-ray."

"I gather we can't call 911?" William managed to say as he closed his eyes.

"Oh, we can call, there's just nobody at the other end." Donovan pulled the curtain up over William's arms to keep him warm.

"How bad is it out there?" William asked.

"There are fires burning in Pacific Grove, Monterey, and Pebble Beach. All of the power is out, no cell phones or landlines, no emergency vehicles. We caught part of a radio broadcast about evacuation routes. I think between the tsunami and the fires, the entire area has been evacuated."

"What about Lauren and the others?"

"I have no idea," Donovan said. "I'm assuming they diverted somewhere safe and are stuck on the ground. It's dark outside, plus the smoke and fires would make it difficult, if not impossible, for Janie to fly any kind of search-and-rescue mission. They also don't have any idea where we are, so, for the moment, we'll have to orchestrate our own rescue."

"I heard you talking to Shannon," William said. "Is she okay?"

"She's a little rattled, but she'll be fine. It's been a tough day. My immediate concern is you. We don't know if the area hospitals are open or have already been evacuated. Driving from point A to point B has proved problematic with all the fires. Plus, bouncing you around in the back of a pickup isn't doing you any good. My thinking is to wait here until I can venture out and find help. Best scenario is that I'll bring the right people back here to help you. If I can't, I'll come back, and we'll wait it out until morning. Once the sun comes up, someone will find us."

"Okay, I found a few things," Shannon called out as she bounded into the kitchen with her hands full. "Not much in the way of first-aid supplies. This house is virtually empty of personal items, but there were lots of towels, blankets, and pillowcases. I figure we can improvise some bandages, and maybe make William a sling for his elbow."

"Good work." Donovan took a stack of towels and set them down on the chaise lounge near William's feet.

"William, you're awake," Shannon said with more than a trace of surprise in her voice as she knelt down next to him. "How do you feel?"

"Not great. I do need to thank you for helping find me."

The sky outside flickered as bright as daylight, and Shannon visibly jumped as explosions rumbled and echoed through the hills. By the time Donovan reached the window, the last of the meteors were breaking up and had vanished below the tops of the trees.

"How close?" Shannon asked as her body trembled.

"Not close at all," Donovan said to Shannon. "Those meteors impacted far out to sea. Why don't we focus on getting William as comfortable as possible, and then we'll talk about making a run for the nearest hospital."

CHAPTER SEVENTEEN

LAUREN STEPPED OUT of the close quarters inside the news van and took a few moments to take in some fresh air. She was angry with herself that she'd put so much faith in the man in the video being Donovan. She'd allowed her hopes to soar, when in fact, she knew better than to start on that particular roller-coaster ride.

Having collected herself, Lauren hurried back inside the Jet Center. As she neared the conference room, she heard what sounded like angry raised voices. She pushed open the door, and Ernie, plus three other men, stopped talking.

"Dr. McKenna," Ernie said. "Welcome back. You're just in time to hear what FEMA has in mind, as well as the US Forest Service."

An older, stocky man with short gray hair came toward Lauren, and held out his hand. "Dr. McKenna, I'm Joseph Guerra. I'm with FEMA. I've heard a great deal about you over the years. It's a pleasure to meet you in person."

"Mr. Guerra, thank you." She shook Guerra's outstretched hand and then waved at the others.

"I'm James Reston," said a tall man who stood where he was and raised his hand in greeting. "I'm with the United States Forest Service."

"Mr. Reston," Lauren said and returned his wave.

"I'm Paul Frantz, Monterey County Emergency Services," said the third.

"Mr. Frantz," Lauren replied as she took stock. Of all the men, Guerra had his tie knotted firmly, his shirt crisp with razor-sharp creases. A good four inches shorter than anyone else in the room, Guerra's body language seemed poised to push his agenda.

"Please, join us," Ernie said. "We were having a bit of a disagreement about the proper course of action."

She went to the table. There was a map of Monterey County, and next to it was the infrared image Lauren had dropped off earlier. "Okay. What's going on?"

"We at FEMA were considering the best place to set up an evacuee center," Guerra said. "Salinas is the logical choice, but I'm being told I'm getting in the way."

Ernie jumped into the conversation. "An urban fire of this magnitude is virtually impossible to stop. I'm not sure we can stop it from reaching Salinas—there's simply too much fuel from the extended drought combined with all of the man-made accelerants. I don't want to have to try to evacuate those people yet again."

"Mr. Frantz," Lauren said before Guerra from FEMA could start talking, "I represent the military interests in the area, and from what I've seen already, the governor will, if he hasn't already, request the National Guard to be called up to help fight the fire. Keeping that in mind, in terms of logistics, what's the current state of emergency services in the Monterey Peninsula? How many people have been evacuated, and where can we put these people so they're not in the way?"

"We believe that the cities of Carmel, Carmel Valley, Pebble Beach, Pacific Grove, Monterey, and Seaside at this moment are nearly ninety percent evacuated. I can confirm that all hospitals, nursing homes, and assisted-living communities have been evacuated, as have all of the detention centers and jails. Traffic on Route 68, where we've focused all of our efforts to keep open, has dropped considerably in the last hour. If it were my decision, the evacuees should be moved another thirty miles north of Salinas, so as not to interfere with the logistics of Cal Fire, the military, or the Forest Service."

"What's the status of the firefighting efforts?" Lauren directed her question at Ernie, as well as Reston, with the Forest Service.

"Our firefighters aren't making a dent in this fire. It's too dangerous, and we've pulled back. We're waiting for more reinforcements from the Forest Service. The aircraft can't fight fires at night, so we're preparing for a big push at sunrise," Ernie said.

"Reinforcements being?" Lauren asked.

"We're assembling all available aerial tankers to start a systematic pattern of fire retardant disbursement in key areas starting at first light," Reston said. "We'll have five very heavy tankers at our disposal. They'll be operating out of Sacramento."

"Mr. Reston, when you say very heavy tankers, what exactly are you referring to?" Lauren asked.

"There are three DC-10 airliners that have been converted to fight fires, plus two 747s."

Lauren turned to Ernie. "What are the Cal Fire assets?"

"We've got helicopters, smaller tankers, and observation aircraft being mobilized from all over the state. The helicopters are especially flexible. We're going to base some at the Hollister airport with our twin engine tanker aircraft. We're also using the Salinas airport as an assembly point for emergency service workers. It's close to the only road in and out of Monterey. Tomorrow is going to be a long day of fighting fires, and we need the evacuees out of the way."

"Salinas is the most cost-effective place for FEMA to begin serving the needs of the displaced and homeless," Guerra said.

"Gentleman, with the situation being what it is, with all of the lives at stake, I think we need to agree that budget concerns should be the least of our worries," Lauren said quietly but firmly as she picked up the infrared image of the fires. "Let's get back to the big picture. How many of these fires can you stop by noon tomorrow?"

"Considering the equipment and manpower we'll have working by then, maybe eight percent, maybe ten," Reston said. He looked at Ernie, who nodded his head in agreement.

"The cities you mentioned earlier in Monterey County," Lauren said. "Will you be able to save them when the tankers start their work?"

"Very few, if any," Reston said.

"How many people do you think are still at risk?" Lauren asked.

"Without accurate casualty figures, that question is impossible to answer," Frantz said. "My position remains the same. There have been losses today, there will be more losses tonight, as well as to-morrow, but we have to pull back. Every engine company is fighting a losing battle."

"The forest service is going to be taxed as well just to keep the current evacuation routes open," Reston added. "As Ernie pointed out earlier, years of drought conditions make for a big, fast-burning fire."

"So, gentleman . . ." Lauren looked around the room. "It is your considered opinion that the nature and ferocity of the fires burning right now will consume the Monterey, Seaside, Pacific Grove, and Pebble Beach communities on the Monterey Peninsula?"

"Yes," came the unanimous reply.

"I have a report to give the Pentagon," Lauren said. "This is an extraordinary event, and as your liaison to the military, and by de-fault, the White House, let me help you. I can make things happen. Is there anything Washington can provide that would change what is happening here?"

"Men and equipment," Ernie said. "A fire can be slowed by the aerial tankers, but men on the ground finally put it out."

Lauren looked at Frantz. "You mentioned casualty figures. Any estimates?"

"Nothing official at this time."

"Off the record?" Lauren asked.

"We have models for disasters such as earthquakes and tsunamis, and the initial casualty rate is typically somewhere between six to ten percent of the population. This means we could have ten thousand victims already. Add in the fires, and that number could easily double."

"I've got some phone calls to make," Lauren said, staggered at the number of possible fatalities. "Mr. Guerra, from what I've just heard, I think it would be wise for FEMA to keep the evacuees moving north, and that will be my recommendation to my superiors in Washington. I'm going to urge the Pentagon to expedite the mobilization of National Guard units from all available resources. You'll get your men and equipment, but from a personal observation, I know there are people out there hiding, terrified, thinking and praying you're coming to the rescue. They're counting on you. Do the best you can, gentleman. I'm going to get us some help."

Lauren walked out of the room. The lobby area was nearly deserted, then she spotted Janie sitting in a chair, studying a chart.

"I can't hear them anymore," Janie said as Lauren came closer. "Sounds like you calmed them down."

"I hope so," Lauren said as she sat down on a sofa that allowed her to face Janie. "How are you doing?"

"I'm hanging in there, considering the day we've had." Janie set aside the chart. "The bigger question is how are you doing?"

"I don't know how to feel." Lauren pressed her fingers to her temples. "He should have been there; he's never late."

"I know, but if there's no way for them to reach us, we just have to wait. He knows we're here."

"You know me. I want information. I need to know if my husband is still alive."

"Donovan gave me some advice when he hired me, and it's stayed with me because it's how people in high-risk jobs need to think. He told me to hope for the best, and plan for the worst. I know it sounds a bit simplified, and at the time, he intended it as an approach to being an Eco-Watch pilot, but it works for damned near everything."

"I've heard him say that before; he even says it to Abigail." Lauren was unprepared for the avalanche of grief that welled up at the thought of their daughter. Tears blurred her vision.

She felt Janie move next to her on the sofa. "What can I do?" Janie asked softly.

Lauren shook her head and fought to regain her composure, but the harder she tried to keep it together, the deeper she spun out of control. Struggling for quick gasps of air, she rose unsteadily to her feet and headed toward the door and the darkness beyond.

Janie walked with her through the door that led to the ramp. Lauren felt the night air hit her face as she leaned against the side of the building. With Janie standing silently beside her, Lauren's gasps became measured breaths, and slowly she gathered in her tattered emotions and wiped at her tears.

"If you'll be okay for a second, I'll run in and find some tissues," Janie offered.

Lauren nodded, and as Janie hurried off, she managed to open her eyes, breathe more evenly, and take in her surroundings. The darkness and the eerie silence of the usually busy airport served to focus the enormity of the day's events. Lauren's tenuous grasp of her control wobbled as she thought of the predicted fatalities. The scientist in her fought back, and she tried to tell herself that Donovan had a 90 percent chance of survival. Her argument dissolved with one simple question—where was he?

"Lauren?" Michael said softly as he approached.

She sniffed, wiped her eyes, turned, and saw that he was holding a box of tissues. She took several, and drew in a deep breath.

"Janie said you were out here." Michael leaned against the wall next to her. "She had a call from the *Buckley*. I told her I'd come out here and be with you. You know, I'm fighting it, too."

"We saw the evacuations—there were families, kids. If they could make it out, where is he? Where's William? Even after those idiots stole his car, he'd be able to find another, right?"

"I'm playing the same 'what if' game you are," Michael said. "It's not what we should be doing. At first light, Montero and I will start searching for them."

"Is that what Montero is saying? Or are you just trying to make me feel better?"

"To be honest"—Michael lowered his voice and leaned in a little closer—"Montero's wired a little different than normal people. You and I might take a private moment to shed a few tears. Its nature's way to release the stress. We don't stay there for long, and then we keep doing our job. If you ask me, right now, I think Montero's brain is about to explode. I've never seen her so intense. We'll go at first light, following Montero's plan."

"Thank you," Lauren said, a hint of a smile toying with the edges of her mouth as she momentarily imagined the former FBI agent's brain actually exploding. She squeezed Michael's hand. He was a Godsend, spinning a little humor, even at Montero's expense.

Montero blew through the sliding glass doors and spotted Michael and Lauren. "Thank God! Finally."

"What is it?" Michael asked.

Montero held up her phone. "We couldn't identify Donovan because of the shadow from the helicopter, but the person sitting in the truck is Shannon. It's them, the two of them—Donovan's alive."

CHAPTER EIGHTEEN

DONOVAN CONSIDERED THE supplies they'd gathered. A collection of towels and pillowcases, bottled water, and a pair of scissors. Not much. There were no personal effects in this house, no photographs, no clothes, just furniture, towels, linens, and kitchen utensils. The house was either for sale or a rental.

"I'm ready when you are," William said, his voice strained, his eyes open, fixed on the ceiling.

"I'll be as careful as I can," Donovan said. "I want to remove the wrappings we put on at the golf course, rinse the wound with bottled water, and put on fresh bandages."

"Good plan," Shannon said. "William, you're going to be fine."

With the scissors, Donovan cut through the bloody bindings. Despite taking care, Donovan couldn't help but jostle the ankle. William sucked in air through clinched teeth and squeezed his eyes shut. Donovan kept cutting. Once the towels were removed, Shannon helped him remove the rubber mat.

William let out a groan of agony as Donovan peeled away the last golf towel, exposing the ankle and the protruding bone.

"The worst is over." Shannon used both of her hands to hold William's clenched fingers. "You're doing great. In fact, the wound doesn't look nearly as bad in the light."

Donovan shot Shannon a look of skepticism. In the glare of the kitchen light, the blood, combined with the bone jutting out into space, was one of the worst bone injuries Donovan had ever seen. He opened the first bottle of water and tipped the bottle and poured a smooth flow to rinse out the gash. He struggled to push William's agonizing groans from his mind as he emptied the first container. Grass and other bits of debris flooded out onto the floor. Donovan opened a second bottle and continued to irrigate the wound. He then began to lay clean towels over the ankle as gently as possible. He took the pillowcases, folded them lengthwise, and bound them snugly. Shannon splashed water on the mat to wash away old blood. Then they placed the rubber splint back into place. Donovan tied everything securely. He leaned back and examined his work, convinced the field dressing was as good as they could get it under the circumstances. It would hold up for now, but he genuinely hoped he wouldn't have to move William. In his nearly four decades with the man, he'd never seen him in such pain, and he truly feared for his friend's life.

"William," Shannon said. "Focus on your breathing. In through your nose. Out through your mouth. Slow and easy. In and out."

"One more little detail, William, and I promise you'll feel better." Donovan held up a pillowcase and folded it into a triangle. He lifted William's injured elbow, arranged the fabric so as to cradle the entire elbow and forearm. He adjusted the angle of William's elbow in reference to his torso and tied the knot to complete the sling. "There, we're finished. How are you holding up?"

William nodded, his chest still rising and falling as his breathing began to slow, though the strain etched on his lined face spoke volumes as to the level of pain he was enduring.

"I'm heading to the hospital," Donovan said. "I'll get you out of here as fast as I can."

"You both go," William said, his eyelids closing. He pulled his hand from Shannon's grasp and reached for Donovan. "Son, if you can't get back here for me, you two need to keep going."

"We're all getting out of this together," Donovan said as he patted William's hand. The combination of pain, stress, and exhaustion was taking its toll, and William closed his eyes. With his fingers on the pulse in William's wrist, Donovan felt his friend's heart rate slow as he drifted into sleep. He covered William's arm with the blanket and turned toward Shannon. "I need to go."

"First, come and look at something I found." Shannon stood. "It might help."

Donovan stayed close as she climbed the stairwell that led to the second floor. She led him up the stairs, down a hall, into a room, and then up a spiral staircase to a cupola.

Shannon pushed open the door into the octagon-shaped room. Cushioned seats lined half the wall space, and positioned against another wall was a telescope aimed out a window. Had the sky not been filled with smoke, Donovan knew the view would have been spectacular. As it was, only a few blocks away, he could see several distinct homes on fire. In the distance, the smoke reduced the individual fires to a mere glow in the darkness. As he turned, he realized he could take in the full three hundred sixty degrees of horizon. To the west, the ocean was black, with no sign of lights at all. As he turned toward the east, the scene looked like one solid fire. As he continued to pivot, he noticed that to the southeast, toward Carmel, there was no glow at all.

"Which way is the hospital?" Shannon asked. "Do you think we can make our way there?"

"Maybe even better." Donovan pointed outward. "Not far in that direction is a gate leading from Pebble Beach into Carmel. From Carmel, it's a straight shot out to Highway 68, the evacuation route we heard about on the radio."

"A way out? Are you kidding me?" Shannon said.

"I'll go to the hospital," Donovan said as he took one last look, turned, and started down the stairs. "It'll be safer if you stay here with William."

"You're not leaving me here," Shannon said as she caught up with him.

"It's a thirty-minute round trip. You'll be fine. If the road is passable, I'll come back for you and William, and we'll go." Donovan hurried to the staircase that would take him down to the first floor when Shannon reached out and grabbed his arm.

"You heard what William said. What if you don't come back? Then what? I have no idea where I am. There are no cars in the garage and no way for me to help William on my own. You're not leaving me behind. We've come this far together, and we're not stopping now."

Donovan assessed her words, the fear behind them, and he understood that, under the circumstances, she was probably right. "You're right, but we need to hurry."

"Okay, then." Shannon nodded for emphasis.

Together, they checked on William one more time. Shannon put a bottle of water within his reach should he wake up thirsty. They went out the front door, and Donovan slid into the cab and fired up the Ford. As he threw on the headlights, he could see that the smoke was thicker than when they'd arrived.

"Hang on," Shannon said as she jumped from the cab and vanished inside the house. Moments later she reemerged carrying two pillowcases.

"What are those for?" Donovan asked.

"I don't know about you." Shannon folded one lengthwise and then test-fit it around her head until it covered both her mouth and nose. "But I'm tired of breathing in smoke."

He drove down the hill until they made a left turn onto 17 Mile Drive. As the road wound through the forest, he saw damage to their right that he couldn't explain. Trees were toppled, power lines draped across the road from snapped electric poles. A car's rear reflectors shone from beneath the branches of an immense tree.

"What happened here?" Shannon asked as she, too, saw the destruction.

Donovan tried to piece together where they were, and when he spotted a landmark through the smoke, he understood what had happened. "Up ahead is the Lodge at Pebble Beach. The damage here must have been inflicted by the tsunami. The ocean isn't very far."

"Wait. What's that?" Shannon said as she pointed and strained to see in the other direction.

Donovan stepped on the brakes as their headlights swept across a paddock holding several horses. Without a second thought, he turned the wheel and used the heavy front end of the Ford to pressure the latch on the wooden gate until it splintered and swung open on its hinges. He backed up, rolled down the window, and whistled loudly. One by one, in single file, the horses, keeping a cautious distance from the truck, streamed out of the corral, and pounded off into the darkness.

"My daughter would never forgive me if I didn't free them," Donovan said as he closed his window, turned the wheel, and proceeded toward the Carmel gate.

"How old is she?"

"Abigail is seven, and she controls my entire world. I almost brought her on the trip. I'm so glad she's safe at home."

"Even if she were here, you'd make her feel safe. She's a lucky girl."

They continued on in silence, but when Donovan made the hard right turn, his hopes plummeted. The headlights illuminated an RV lying on its side, the crumpled structure splayed across both lanes of the road. Torn metal and mangled bicycles, still locked to their rack, intermingled with the branches and trunk of a massive tree. The RV was dark and silent as Donovan put the Ford into park and stepped out of the cab.

He called out as he climbed across the wreckage to peer through the broken windshield into the cab. He found it empty. He felt the hood. The metal was cool to the touch. He called out several more times. No reply.

"Did they get out?" Shannon asked when he returned.

"There wasn't anyone in the cab. Whatever happened here took place earlier. I didn't see evidence that anyone was hurt."

"Is there a way around the wreck?"

"No," Donovan said as he began the task of turning the truck around.

"What now?"

"I think we need to try to make it to the hospital from here."

"Which way is it?" Shannon asked. "When we were back at the house, could you see any fires in that direction?"

"Yes, there were flames, but mostly smoke, so there's no way to tell what's burning and what isn't. We have to go find out for ourselves."

Shannon nodded in agreement as Donovan accelerated up the hill. He turned on 17 Mile Drive and momentarily reached forty miles per hour before he had to slow down in heavy smoke. His eyes burned as he kept them fixed on the white stripes marking the road. Shannon tied the pillowcase around her head and covered her mouth and nose. She held the wheel while he did the same.

Breathing easier, but with watery eyes, Donovan slowed as he spotted flames off to the left. As they passed through the trees, they could see a row of at least four homes, all in various stages of burning to the ground. He could feel the heat from the fire on his face and he turned away and continued to drive. They burst from the dense smoke into a clear area, and Donovan brought the Ford to a stop and rolled down his window to get to the less contaminated air. He used the pillowcase to wipe away his tears, and after several more restorative breaths, he replaced the mask, stepped on the gas, and within minutes, they were again shrouded in smoke.

The makeshift masks were a godsend. On both sides of the road, trees burned in clusters; ash and flaming sparks drifted down and showered the metal of the truck. Donovan was forced to slow as they reached two burned-out cars, their charred shells billowing thick black smoke.

"How much longer?" Shannon asked, raising her voice to be heard through the mask.

They'd passed a blue hospital sign only a few minutes ago. All other landmarks were obscured by smoke until they passed the empty guard shacks that marked the end of 17 Mile Drive. In the distance, flames climbed and danced from the roof and windows of what he guessed was an outlying medical building. On the other side, illuminated by the fire, were the white walls of the hospital.

"That's it!" Shannon said as she removed her mask. "We made it!"

Donovan pulled down his mask and followed the signs toward the emergency room. His hopes dwindled as he spotted empty parking lots. As he wheeled to the emergency room doors, he saw there were no lights coming from inside the building.

"Oh no," Shannon said as she slumped at their discovery.

Donovan silently eyed the building. He put the truck into park, opened the door, and stepped to the ground. He reached into the bed, grabbed the pry bar, and headed toward the door.

CHAPTER NINETEEN

"HERE, LOOK AT the image on my phone," Montero said. "I called in a favor at the Bureau, and they used some advanced computer filtering to eliminate the glare on the truck's windshield. Facial recognition identified the woman as Shannon, so it follows that the man is Donovan."

Lauren examined the computer-enhanced image and the woman was indeed Shannon, her large eyes and bangs clearly visible. "Just because this is Shannon doesn't mean that the man is Donovan. She could be with anyone, and then there's William. Where is he?"

"We don't have all the answers, but we have a lead we need to pursue," Montero said.

"Are there coordinates with the image?" Michael asked. "Channel 10 should know where this was shot."

"No, the data stream that broadcasts the latitude and longitude was either malfunctioning or damaged," Montero said. "Let's think this through. Donovan's rental car was stolen from a garage near the aquarium just before the tsunami hit. He found another vehicle and ended up at an unknown beach, post-tsunami, a shoreline with a wrecked yacht, with perhaps a crashed helicopter nearby."

"Usually, given the time that's elapsed, the variables of his current position would be enormous," Michael said to Lauren. "Except the roads on the Peninsula are a complete mess. His options are limited."

"What about the emergency distress beacons?" Montero said, the excitement rising in her voice. "Not just one, but two. A ship that size might have a marine emergency transmitter, as does a helicopter, if it crashed. Can we pinpoint the position from those?"

Lauren shook her head. "Doubtful. They're all satellite based. Even if the orbital platform is undamaged, the accuracy is maybe one to three miles. Plus, the number of Maydays in progress has probably overwhelmed the satellite's receptors. I've seen it happen—an earthquake will set off all the aircraft locator beacons along the fault line and the computers can't process all the data and become unreliable."

"So we need to eyeball sections of the coastline where the waves could have deposited a yacht the size of the one in the video," Montero kept pressing. "We can do that from the helicopter at night. Maybe Donovan would still be close enough to hear us and make himself known."

"Even if we could pinpoint the spot, to do that we'd have to risk all of our lives, plus Janie's, to search via helicopter, violating a no-fly order." Lauren wiped the last tears from her eyes and balled up the tissue in her hand. "And we would have accomplished what, exactly? All we'll know is where Donovan was hours ago. It does nothing to tell us where he is now. I think we wait until daylight, unless we know for sure where they are. Otherwise the risks to everyone are just too great."

"Did you just bring up rules?" Michael said to Lauren. "I mean, look who you're talking to. Have you never met us?"

"No, she's right." Montero snatched a tissue from the box in Michael's hand and dabbed at her eyes. "I'm sorry, I'm clutching at straws. It's so hard to sit here when they're out there somewhere."

"Guys!" Janie called out as she came outside. "I just got off the phone with the *Buckley*. They're pulling the crew off a sinking containership and they have an injured sailor who needs immediate medical attention."

"Are we going?" Michael asked. "We're not exactly equipped for trauma patients."

"Captain Pittman understands, as does the captain of the sinking vessel, but the Coast Guard has their hands full with tsunami victims. We can get there faster than anyone else, which makes us all this guy has. I've been precleared for the flight, but I need someone to go with me in case we have to use the hoist."

"That's me," Michael said as he leaned in and kissed Lauren on the cheek. "Go do your science thing. He's out there somewhere and he'll survive until help arrives."

Lauren loved the words, but the rumble of doubt still shook her faith. Michael and Janie headed off toward the helicopter, and Lauren looked at Montero. "Thank you for being here and for caring. You're exactly who I want trying to figure this out, though right now I need to talk to the Pentagon."

"Let's go see if the office you used earlier is available," Montero said.

"How far out is the *Buckley*?" Lauren said as she stopped short of the door.

"Janie said they'd be overhead thirty minutes after liftoff. Why?"

"I've changed my mind," Lauren said as the prospect of being surrounded by friends sounded infinitely better than hanging out at the San Jose airport. "I'll call the Pentagon from the *Buckley*. I don't want to deal with the minute by minute individual concerns of Cal Fire, the Forest Service, or FEMA. I'll let General Curtis brief me, and then I can relay what I know from the ship."

"Let's go." Montero put two fingers to her mouth and whistled loudly across the ramp to get Michael's and Janie's attention.

"Can you drop me on the *Buckley*?" Lauren called out as they drew closer.

"Sure," Janie said. "Climb aboard and strap in. We'll be out of here in a few minutes."

Lauren and Montero did as they were instructed, and with practiced ease slipped on their headsets. Michael was outside making sure the rotors were clear, and at his signal, Janie turned on the exterior lights and quickly, but systematically, fired up both turbine engines. Michael gave Janie a thumbs-up and climbed into the cabin. As he positioned his headset and cinched his harness, Janie lifted the helicopter off the ground and hover-taxied out away from the surrounding buildings and parked airplanes. Once clear, she climbed higher, pivoted the helicopter crisply, and banked to a direct heading for the *Buckley*.

"I'm going to take us up and over the Santa Cruz Mountains. That'll give us a straight shot out to the *Buckley*. Everyone needs to put on a floatation device before we coast out," Janie announced calmly over the intercom. "We'll be there in twenty-eight minutes."

Lauren watched the carpet of lights from San Jose pass below them as they flew toward the ocean. Once they crossed the mountains, she could see down the coast toward Monterey. At first, there was only darkness, but she finally picked out a sliver of orange. To the untrained eye, the light looked like the glow from a distant city, not a series of raging fires. She compared the size of the glow she was seeing to the infrared images she'd given Ernie and the others. Lauren did the math and realized that an urban section, roughly the same size as the entire District of Columbia, was burning out of control on the Monterey Peninsula. As they roared out to sea, Lauren double-checked her life vest and studied the fires until they receded in the distance.

"I can see the *Buckley*," Michael said. "Wow—and what's left of the containership."

Off the nose of the helicopter, Lauren saw the *Buckley*. High-intensity lights were trained on the listing superstructure of a far larger ship. She pulled a pair of binoculars from their pouch and trained them on the distant scene. The containership was going down by the bow and listing nearly twenty degrees to port. Scattered in the sea were dozens of containers that must have broken free as the bow sank.

"Janie, do we know where the wounded sailor is yet?" Lauren asked as she handed the binoculars to Montero.

"He's on the stern of the containership," Janie said. "Reports are he's unconscious, but still alive. The *Buckley* says he's on a stretcher, and they've rigged a harness for us to attach to the hoist."

Lauren kept her eyes on the two ships, as Janie sped toward the scene. Michael pulled on a helmet and checked the intercom with Janie. He swung his arms into a sturdy canvas harness, buckled himself in firmly, and then hooked a lifeline to the ceiling that would keep him from falling out of the helicopter if he lost his footing. He uncoiled the hoist control and laid it out so it was ready.

"I'm secured, hoist checklist complete," Michael transmitted to Janie. "Let me know when we reach door speed."

"Will do. We're coming in fast, so be ready."

Lauren held her breath as both the sinking containership and the *Buckley* seemed to fill the windshield. Montero was furiously buckling herself into a safety harness identical to Michael's. Multiple search lights on board the *Buckley* illuminated the stern of the containership. Janie flew closer, and as they reached a point directly above the *Buckley*, she made a tight turn overhead and began to bleed off their speed to arrive precisely over the sinking ship. From her vantage point, Lauren saw the name of the ship painted on the stern—it was the *Olympia*.

"Cleared to open the door," Janie said, slowing and adding the helicopter's bright lights to the scene as she maneuvered the 412 into a hover.

Cool wind from the open door swirled and buffeted the inside of the cabin. Below them, Lauren spotted the injured man on the stretcher, and on each side were men wearing Eco-Watch wetsuits as well as flotation devices. An Eco-Watch runabout was holding position just off the starboard side, away from several shipping containers bobbing in the gentle swell. Michael, the control box in his hands, began to pay out the cable from the hoist pod mounted above and outside the cabin door.

Janie inched the helicopter into position directly above the wounded sailor, and Lauren lost sight of what was happening below. Montero, her own harness finally secured, was leaning as far out the door as she could. She signaled Lauren to come and sit next to her. Lauren unbuckled and changed seats while listening through the intercom. Michael, Janie, and the two Eco-Watch crewmen who had boarded the *Olympia* from one of the *Buckley*'s runabouts were discussing the situation. From her new vantage point, she could see far more of what was happening below.

"Ten more feet, hold it steady." Michael ran the line downward, giving Janie status reports as she held the helicopter's position. "Six feet. You're drifting slightly to the left."

"Correcting," Janie replied.

"Three feet, steady, looking good," Michael said. "They've got the hook. They're attaching the payload. Stand by."

"Roger," Janie said.

"The stretcher is secured. We've got an all-clear signal from the crew on deck," Michael said. "Pulling up the slack and commencing hoist."

"Michael, what's happening?" Montero called as she braced herself against the side of the helicopter.

Lauren watched in disbelief as the deck of the *Olympia* tilted steeply to port. The stern dropped lower in the water. The Eco-Watch crewmen on deck tumbled aside, and, despite efforts to catch themselves, they both crashed into the railing and were flung overboard. The helicopter staggered as the winch seemed to grind to a halt and jerk the 412 downward.

"Janie," Michael yelled. "The cable is fouled!"

Illuminated by the *Buckley*'s lights, Lauren tracked the cable from the hoist, down to the deck, where the stretcher was entangled in the railing as the ship began to slip further beneath the waves. She felt Janie pivot the helicopter and descend.

"Michael, stand clear. I'm cutting the cable," Janie said through the intercom.

Severed by explosive squibs, Lauren watched the cable drop from the winch housing. The lifeline to the injured sailor below twisted as it dropped into the ocean.

"Janie," Michael radioed as he gripped an overhead handhold and stepped out onto the skid. "I can still reach him before the ship goes under."

Without hesitating, Janie maneuvered the 412 downward to place Michael within reach of the stretcher. Montero stepped out next to Michael, and Lauren held on as her limited view outside filled with the stern of the *Olympia*. Cable cutters in hand, Michael reached out and began snapping through the tangled metal line as Montero gripped the litter and began pulling.

"I can't hold him; the blankets are soaked. Even if you get him free, I'm afraid he'll sink," Montero said to Michael as she produced a knife and began slicing the fabric straps securing the wounded man to the rescue basket.

"You've got ten seconds before I have to climb us out of here," Janie said.

Lauren saw Montero's knife flash repeatedly. Michael moved closer and crouched, bracing himself. From how his legs and back flexed, she knew he had the sailor.

"We have him!" Montero called out to Janie.

Lauren felt the helicopter rise, and she watched as both Montero and Michael strained against the injured man's weight as the ship slipped beneath the waves.

"Is he on board?" Janie asked as she held the 412 in a steady hover, despite the growing froth, bubbles, and debris released from the *Olympia*.

"Almost," Michael said as he and Montero struggled to pull the soaking-wet man up and into the cabin.

Lauren unbuckled, crouched, and added her strength to the effort. Working in unison, all three of them pulled the unconscious seaman aboard. Michael was about to close the door when a single shipping container, freed from the submerged deck of the *Olympia*, erupted from the dark water next to them.

Janie slammed the controls in an effort to try to avoid the freight car–sized object as it bobbed vertically before it began to fall on its side. Lauren felt the impacts and saw the shower of sparks as the helicopter's rotor blades slashed three-foot-long slices into the metal of the container before it tipped over in an explosion of seawater.

Severe vibrations instantly racked the helicopter, and Lauren, terrified, braced for the crash. The helicopter banked, and just as quickly banked in the opposite direction as Janie fought to level off. The noise from the vibrations set off by the damaged rotor blades was deafening. The shaking was severe enough that it felt as if the machine was on the verge of tearing itself apart.

"*Buckley*, Mayday, Mayday! Severe rotor damage," Janie radioed as she fought to control the damaged helicopter. "We may have to ditch."

Lauren spotted more containers pushing to the surface and crashing into others already floating in the ocean. In the midst of the debris field, the *Buckley* was coming fast, impacting containers, battering and crushing them with its ice-capable hull before rolling them out of the way. The *Buckley* steamed straight for them, the helipad bathed in light.

CHAPTER TWENTY

DONOVAN PUNCHED THE hardened steel of the pry bar into the lower panel of the glass door. It made a quiet pop, and when he leveraged the bar against the handle, the safety glass cracked into hundreds of pieces and collapsed harmlessly to the floor. He ducked inside the deserted building and spotted the sign pointing to the emergency room.

"I'm right behind you," Shannon said as she hurried to catch him.

Donovan pushed into the emergency room. The only light was coming from the battery-powered emergency lights. He pulled open a partition to a disheveled bay. There was no bed. Wiring from a monitor was tangled on the floor. The next room was clean and ready for business. A waist-high cabinet was pushed against one wall. He saw it was on wheels and pulled it out to position it under a light. He started at the top, and sifted through the drawer and found what he needed most, a penlight. He clicked it on and continued searching.

When Shannon returned, he was stuffing items into his pockets. "What have you found?"

"Basic first-aid stuff: gloves, rolls of gauze, scissors, tape, and elastic bandage," Donovan said. "We may have to redo William's leg, and this time we'll have the supplies."

"I checked the phones and computers, nothing works," Shannon said. "You keep searching, I'll be right back."

Donovan continued his search, rifling through more items. He grabbed a packet of intravenous needles. Next to it were clear plastic packages of tubing. He was about to stuff them in his pocket when Shannon reappeared. She snapped open a plastic trash bag and held it toward him. He emptied his pockets into the bag and continued. He collected more gauze and tape, as well as betadine wipes, and threw them in the bag.

"He needs antibiotics," Shannon said.

"I know, plus there have to be splints around here somewhere."

"Take this." Shannon handed him the plastic bag.

Donovan nodded, walked into the next trauma room, where he spotted another six-drawer cabinet on wheels. He pulled open the first drawer and discovered duplicates of what he'd already seen in the other cart.

"I found where they kept the drugs—it's empty," Shannon said from across the room. "They must have cleaned it out as they left. I did see a map of the place—there's a pharmacy, as well as an operating room just upstairs. I'll go check them out and be right back."

"Make it fast." Donovan handed her the penlight. "I'll take this stuff out to the truck, and then make one last pass through the emergency room for anything else I can find."

Donovan lifted the plastic bag into the cab and set it between the seats. The smoke was growing worse, the glow to the west more intense. He turned and hurried back to the emergency room where he stopped and tried to think of what else he might need to help William. He walked to the nurse's station, and there was just enough light for him to see they must have left in a hurry. Papers were scattered, clipboards and pens strewn on the floor, desk drawers partially opened. Donovan tried to understand the reason for the chaos, but couldn't. It reminded him more of a place that had been ransacked than evacuated. As the thought formed, he heard a faint scream echo in the darkness.

Donovan ran to the emergency room, snatched the pry bar he'd leaned against the wall, and, using the emergency lights for guidance, climbed the stairs. He ran as fast as he could down the hallway, and heard another cry, this one more of a wail, enough to give him a bearing. He spotted the sign for the south pavilion. Just beyond were the operating rooms.

He slowed as he listened. Then he heard a man's voice: "I didn't hear you, baby."

Donovan rounded the corner and saw two men, their backs to him. One was big and fat, his trousers hung low, and a ponytail dangled down from under his headband. The other guy was much thinner and wore a stocking cap pulled down over bushy black hair. Shannon's face was pressed into the wall. Both men had their hands on her.

Noiselessly, Donovan swept in from behind, and swinging the heavy pry bar like a baseball bat, connected with the fat man. The metal impacted the shoulder with enough force to cave it in, and an unseen knife clattered to the floor. As the man yelled in pain and staggered sideways, Donovan shoved him into his buddy. With both men off balance, Donovan shifted his weight and brought the pry bar over his head and swung downward, aiming for the second man's collarbone. Using all his strength, he hit his intended target squarely. Bones snapped and the man dropped to his knees, screaming. The fat man rolling on the floor thrashed wildly as he struggled to grasp the butt of a pistol in a shoulder holster. With a sweeping arc, Donovan used the steel bar against the fat man's jaw. A muffled popping noise coincided with the fat man's eyes rolling up in their sockets. His big body sagged, and he collapsed sideways onto the floor and went still. Donovan reached down and snatched the pistol.

Shannon pushed away from the wall and stepped around to face the man in the stocking cap. He was on his knees, groaning, using his good arm to support his shattered collarbone while trying to get his feet under him to stand.

Shannon moved aside as Donovan stepped in and brought his knee straight into the bridge of his nose. The man went limp and crumpled in a heap.

"We need to go. There're more of them," Shannon said as she leaned down, picked up a canvas backpack off the floor, and threw it over her shoulder. "These two were stealing drugs from the operating room, and I gather the others are trying to break into the pharmacy."

Donovan checked the gun he'd taken, a 9mm Beretta. There was a round in the chamber and the magazine held fifteen. They began to run down the hallway that would take them back to the truck. As they reached the top of the stairs, Donovan heard shouting. They ducked through the shattered door and sprinted the final distance and climbed into the truck.

"They're coming!" Shannon cried out as she pointed down the truck's hood toward the glass doors.

Donovan slammed his door shut, cranked the ignition, threw on the headlights, and switched on the high beams. In the intense light, he spotted a man with long red hair pulled into a messy ponytail. There was a pistol in one hand, and the other shielded his eyes from the lights.

As Donovan threw the truck into gear, the man raised the weapon. Donovan slammed his foot to the floor and the truck lurched forward. Accelerating, he saw the barrel flash and heard the bullet hit the metal grill. Clenching his teeth, Donovan held the truck steady as the F-250 exploded through the glass and aluminum and charged into the foyer of the hospital. The man was late trying to move out of the way, and the grill caught his hip, tossing him screaming into the air. He landed back-first on the reception desk. His wails ended as his body went limp, the pistol dropping to the floor. Donovan braked hard, put the truck in reverse, and the truck tires screeched on the glossy floor as he gunned the engine. He backed all the way out through the destroyed entrance, and once they were clear of the building, he spun the wheel, pulled the gear shift into drive, and accelerated. In the rearview mirror, he saw three more men arrive at the destroyed door. One man ignored the downed man and stood in the light facing Donovan. He was broad-chested, wearing a sleeveless t-shirt with tattoos covering his exposed skin. His shaved head sat on a thick neck, and he raised an arm, and with an empty hand, mimicked pulling the trigger of a pistol.

Donovan understood the gesture. He and Shannon had just started a war.

CHAPTER TWENTY-ONE

"THE *BUCKLEY*'S COMING!" Lauren yelled just as the helicopter began a steep descent.

Janie banked the damaged helicopter toward the ship. Lauren could see the controls shaking violently in her hands. Montero had one arm around a seat support, the other trying to hold the injured sailor in position on the floor. Lauren reached out to help Montero as the *Buckley*'s bridge filled the windshield. The superstructure towered above them as Janie brought the crippled helicopter into a momentary hover above the helipad just before the skids touched down hard. Janie throttled back to reduce the vibrations, but it wasn't until she shut down both engines and pulled on the rotor brake to slow the blades that the 412 stopped shaking.

"Everyone out!" Janie called out as she continued flipping the switches to fully shut down the 412.

Crewmen surrounded the helicopter, and a medic climbed into the open door nearest Michael. Behind Lauren, the other door was opened from outside, and a crewman reached out for her. Once on the deck, Lauren and Montero were escorted toward the closest hatchway. Lauren stopped and turned as medical personnel converged near the door to help with the injured man from the *Olympia*. Michael and Janie were already out of the helicopter, and Lauren could see the drained but determined expression on Janie's face.

"Is everyone okay?" Janie asked as she drew near.

"We're good," Lauren said. "That was a hell of a landing."

"I just about got us killed out there," Janie said through pursed lips as she shook her head at the thought.

"What happened surprised the hell out of all of us, but you handled it," Michael said. "The good news is, we didn't crash."

"Oh, we were well on our way to being in a crash. All that stopped that from happening was the *Buckley* got in our way."

"I say the *Buckley* gets an assist, then," Montero said as she peeled off her personal flotation device and handed it to a crewman.

"How long do you think until the helicopter can be fixed?" Lauren said as she removed her PFD as well and crossed her arms in an attempt to hide the fact that her body had begun to shake.

Janie clicked on her flashlight and aimed it upwards at the tip of one of the four rotor blades. Instead of a smooth metal tip, the steel was ripped and distorted. A string of mumbled swear words came from her lips and then she looked straight at her passengers. "The tip of this blade is trash."

Lauren looked over at the next blade, and even without the flashlight, she could see that it, too, was damaged.

"They all are," Michael said.

"The rotor caps are stainless steel," Janie said, sweeping her light to illuminate each tip. "Look, that one is missing the cap altogether, which is what set up such a severe vibration. I'm surprised at least one of the blades didn't come apart."

An officer burst from the hatchway and stopped when he spotted Montero.

"Are you okay?" he asked her and then looked at Lauren and the others. "Is anyone injured?"

"I think we're fine," Montero said.

"Dr. McKenna, I'm first mate Ethan Wiley. If none of you require medical attention, the captain has requested you join him on the bridge."

"Janie and I need to check out the rest of the helicopter," Michael said. "Though I'm pretty sure we're not flying out of here anytime soon."

"No chance." Janie shook her head. "This thing needs to be taken to a shop on dry land, have four new blades installed, and a small army of technicians to check out the rest of the machine."

"We'll be on the bridge," Montero said to Michael and Janie, as she stepped through the hatchway and made her way with Lauren down the passageway. "Ethan, Dr. McKenna will need a computer, and a voice link with the Pentagon."

"I'll take care of it right away," Ethan said.

As they rode the elevator up to bridge level, Lauren's thoughts turned to Captain Ryan Pittman, a man she'd known for years. He was a retired Navy officer and lifelong mariner. He and Donovan had formed a lasting friendship during the design and construction of Eco-Watch Marine. Whenever business brought Ryan to Virginia, he always had dinner with them. Lauren loved listening to Ryan's stories; they gave her a glimpse into the marine side of Eco-Watch. When the elevator opened onto the bridge, Ethan moved aside to allow Lauren to step out first. She breathed in the new ship smell and took in the entire bridge.

"Lauren," Ryan said warmly, reaching out to give her a hug. "I apologize for the circumstances, but welcome aboard the *Buckley*."

"Ryan, it's good to see you," Lauren said, returning the quick hug.

"Ms. Montero," Ryan said.

"Captain," Montero said with a nod. "Can you give us a situation report? Janie mentioned you took damage during the initial meteor barrage."

"We took a hit to our primary radar array—several holes were discovered in the antenna. It'll be an easy fix once we're ashore. In the meantime, we have no radar. There's also a single hole in the aft deck—it's about the diameter of a ping-pong ball. We traced its trajectory, and it went through multiple decks before it seemingly vaporized. No appreciable damage was detected."

"It could have been far worse," Montero said.

"We've moved away from the debris field created by the sinking ship. Twenty-eight men from the *Olympia* are safely aboard the *Buckley*. I'm waiting to hear the status of the injured seaman you brought aboard. There's a commercial salvage tug steaming this way from Oakland. They'll take over the oil spill response, as well as secure the floating containers. Several Navy vessels that were inbound to San Diego have now been diverted to the area and ordered to assist. The tug should arrive midmorning, the Navy ships around noon. Other ships should be on scene by late tomorrow."

All of Lauren's earlier visits to the *Buckley* had been in broad daylight. She hadn't ever been on the bridge at night and was mesmerized as always by a design that was as sleek and modern as the exterior. Her late father had served in the Navy. She loved his stories and always felt closer to him when she set foot on a ship.

Located just under the heavily angled forward windows, the main control panel wrapped around in a semicircle. Two crewmen were standing side by side, quietly talking into headsets. They were separated by a console that ran aft. Ship's controls for the throttles and thrusters were located within reach of either man. Rows of screens glowed in the darkness. Electrical schematics told of engine and system status. At the end of the console, two larger instrument displays were canted so they could easily be seen from the elevated captain's chair, and off to the side was a chart table. On either side of the compartment were hatchways that led outside to an observation deck that wrapped around the leading edge of the bridge.

"What happened to damage the *Olympia* to the point it sank like that?" Montero asked.

"She took multiple impacts forward, and judging by how fast she took on water, their captain estimated that the meteors went all the way through the ship and came out the keel. When we arrived, she was already listing ten degrees and taking water over the bow."

Lauren slipped past Montero, stepped through an open hatch out to the exterior observation deck, and looked down toward the bow and the helicopter pad. Two crewmen steadied a ladder, as both Janie and Michael closely inspected the damage to the rotor blade. Already, a high-powered bank of lights had been erected to provide illumination. Lauren had great affection for the efficient, highly structured environment aboard ship. These men and women worked and lived together, sometimes for months at a time. She knew that just below the casual manner in which they operated was a highly trained professional, handpicked for duty aboard the Eco-Watch flagship. The same sense of camaraderie was one of the reasons she loved working for Calvin and the Defense Intelligence Agency. The loyalty and high level of professionalism were very similar.

Overhead, she took in the few stars she could see through gaps in the clouds drifting above. As she watched, a furrow came to her brow. She turned until she located Polaris, and once again tracked the movement of the clouds against a north reference. Her mind raced with the implications of what she was seeing, and she rushed back inside the bridge.

"Lauren, what's wrong?" Montero asked, instantly on alert.

"We have another problem," Lauren said, pressing her temples as if contemplating the unimaginable. "I need a computer and a phone."

CHAPTER TWENTY-TWO

"I SEE LIGHTS," Shannon said as she looked up from the Ford's side mirror, and turned toward Donovan. "They're coming."

"How many?" Donovan asked

"I only see one car." Shannon spun to get a better look out the rear window. "No, wait. It's not a car, it looks like motorcycles, three of them."

"Do you have any idea how many men there were inside the hospital?"

"I only saw the guys you saw," Shannon said as she slid on her makeshift mask.

"Hold the wheel," Donovan said as he, too, secured his mask against the dense smoke to come.

"How are we going to fight a motorcycle gang?" Shannon asked as she turned the wheel back over to Donovan.

"They're not a gang. They didn't have any colors. They're just criminals looting a hospital for drugs," Donovan said. "We don't want to fight them. We just need to put some distance between them and us. The last thing we can afford to do is lead them back to William."

Shannon recoiled and ducked as the glass in the rear window exploded inward.

Donovan winced as the pieces of safety glass bounced off the side of his face and pelted the dashboard, which now sported a single bullet hole. In the mirror, he saw three motorcycles roaring out of the smoke, coming fast, and far closer than he would have calculated. He stepped on the gas, and the Ford began to accelerate.

Donovan sped down the winding road, wind and smoke swirling in the cab along with the distinctive roar from the powerful motorcycles. Donovan understood he had no chance of fending off multiple motorcycle riders who were willing to open fire at will. Ahead and to the right was the cluster of four burning homes they'd passed earlier. The smoke and ash twisted upward, and the fire looked alive as red-hot embers climbed into the sky.

"Hang on," Donovan called out just before they plunged into the thick smoke. He guided the Ford into a tight turn, and they bounced off the main road down an unpaved side road. Donovan braked hard, made another quick turn, and switched off the lights. Without hesitation, he jumped from the cab, drew the pistol he'd taken, and ran to the back of the truck. Invisible in the thick smoke, he listened as the motorcycles, following the paved road, roared past.

His exposed skin was peppered by the drifting embers from the nearby fires. Small collateral fires began to flare in the pine needles that covered the forest floor. His eyes burned and filled with tears as he found his pry bar, and with two quick swings demolished the brake lights. Instead of tossing the pry bar back into the bed, he slid it behind the driver's seat, tucked the pistol he'd taken into the pocket of his leather jacket, and climbed back in the cab.

"What was that about?" Shannon asked.

"Our brake lights are nothing but a homing beacon for these guys. I fixed the problem."

Donovan searched the darkness that surrounded them, put the Ford into gear, and with the headlights extinguished, he backed the truck toward the main road.

"Listen." Shannon cocked her head. "I hear them."

Donovan nodded and tried to pinpoint the direction and distance.

"They're coming," Shannon said, her voice wavering with fear.

"It only sounds like a single motorcycle. I think they split up to find us," Donovan said. He gunned the truck up to the edge of the pavement and stopped. From around the corner, the beam from the motorcycle's single headlight filtered through the trees. Donovan judged the speed of the motorcycle and then stepped on the gas pedal and swung the black F-250 onto the road until it blocked both lanes. The driver swerved and dumped the bike, sliding in a shower of sparks to keep from hitting the truck at full speed.

The motorcycle tangled with the Ford's heavy front bumper. The impact shook the truck, and Donovan threw on the headlights in time to see the motorcycle bounce off the pavement and catapult into the air, shedding parts. Donovan stepped to the ground just as the battered, denim-clad motorcyclist pulled himself to his feet, staggered backward, and then pulled a long knife from his boot.

Pistol held firmly in his right hand, Donovan sidestepped the first wild swing of the knife and stepped in and used the weight of the gun to maximize the punch to the man's jaw, dropping him to his knees. The knife fell from his hand, and he swayed as Donovan threw another punch, though before Donovan could deliver another, the man collapsed to the pavement.

Perplexed, Donovan knelt cautiously and lifted up the unconscious man's goggles. Next, he removed the bandana that covered his mouth and nose. The biker looked to be in his mid-twenties. Thin-faced, almost gaunt with a stringy, tangled beard. Tattoos crept above the collar of his jacket, and Donovan spotted the top part of a swastika.

Shannon walked from the cab and knelt. In the harsh light of the headlights, she examined the man, too. She spotted a pistol on the ground, which she picked up but then dropped the second she saw the steel covered in blood.

Donovan frowned and reached down to the biker's neck and felt for a pulse. There wasn't one, but there was a pool of blood spreading out from an unseen injury to his back.

"He's dead, isn't he?" Shannon stood to distance herself from the corpse.

"Yes, but I'm not sure why." Donovan lifted the man up on his side. The thin material of his jean jacket did little to protect him as he slid. Near his lower back Donovan caught sight of something protruding from what was left of a shredded t-shirt. "He caught something in his back, a branch, or a piece of metal off his bike when he dumped it. He's gone."

"We should get his body off the road," Shannon said, her voice on the verge of panic.

"He's far enough to the side no one will run over him. Someone will find him in the morning." Donovan untied the handkerchief from around the man's neck and used it to wipe the blood off the gun Shannon had found. It was a .357 caliber revolver. Donovan handed it to her. "I trust you know how to shoot?"

Shannon made a face and nodded. "Buck taught me, so yes, in theory I'm deadly when it comes to paper targets." She slid the pistol into her pocket. Somewhere in the smoke, the unmistakable sound of a motorcycle engine drifted in on the wind.

"We need to go." They got back into the truck. Donovan backed up, avoiding motorcycle parts lying in the road, and drove away.

Donovan went as far as he could without headlights, using the muted orange light from the park lights to slowly maneuver to where the thick smoke began to end. He killed all the lights when they finally emerged, peeled off his mask, rolled down the window, and listened. Smoke hugged the ground, turning the sky into a formless opaque dome. Sparks spiraled and flew everywhere, and the glow of multiple fires dotted what Donovan guessed was the horizon.

"It looks like the aftermath of a war." Shannon took a tentative breath without her mask, testing the air. "I want to thank you for getting me out of there."

Donovan nodded and then held up his hand to cut off Shannon. Off to his left, he caught the staccato rumble of a distant motorcycle. A few moments later, in the opposite direction, he heard the same sound. "They're looking for us."

"We're the only ones out here, and there aren't that many roads. We won't be hard to find," Shannon said.

"I agree." Donovan switched on the headlights, stepped on the gas, and allowed the Ford to lurch forward, quickly gaining speed. He dodged some of the bigger branches that had fallen and ignored the smaller ones. He coaxed the truck toward the destination he had in mind. He rounded a big right turn, braked heavily, sped down a narrow tree-lined driveway, shut off all the lights, and slowed as he pulled out from under the trees onto a broad expanse of grass. He brought the truck to a stop and switched off the engine. Not far away in the darkness was the house where Robert Huntington once lived with Meredith Barnes. For a moment, Donovan felt like a ghost drifting past, an apparition from long ago wandering in the smoke.

"Where are we?" Shannon whispered in the darkness.

"We're on the back nine of the Pebble Beach golf course."

"You sure know your way around this place," Shannon said.

Donovan ignored the statement. "Once we let our eyes fully adjust to the darkness, we'll be able to use the maintenance roads to navigate without lights. We'll pick a fire in the distance, and head for it, like using a star to navigate at night. They won't be able to find us."

"Is that how you fly at night?" Shannon asked,

"Not anymore, but a long time ago, when I was a young man, it's how I flew. I didn't have the high-tech picture tube instruments or onboard computers. Back then, I flew using a flashlight, holding a paper chart on my knee. My instructor called it basic airmanship."

"How long have you been flying?"

"A long time. I started taking lessons when I was sixteen. Got my license when I was seventeen."

"Buck told me once he could tell when someone was in their element, and he said you were definitely in your element in the cockpit of an airplane. He also mentioned you were equally out of your element at sea."

"He's right," Donovan said as he picked out a fire on a distant hill, started the engine, eased the Ford into gear, and let the truck creep down the single lane road that ringed the golf course. "I don't like being out on the ocean, and I never will."

Going slowly at first, Donovan focused on his distant beacon and the subtle difference in the color between the asphalt and the grass. As his eyes fully acclimated to the darkness, he was able to go faster, and they wound around the back nine until he spotted the clubhouse. With the famous 18th green on his left, Donovan knew that he'd just run out of golf course. He rounded a corner that would put him on a public street and stopped. Together they listened but heard only the crashing of the waves and the faint roar of a nearby fire.

"How close are we to the house?" Shannon asked.

"A mile, maybe a little more. The problem is we need to use public streets. I'll need the headlights."

"We have the flashlight we took from the hospital. Can we use it to make our way instead of the headlights?"

"If you're talking about the small penlight, then no, I doubt that it would work," Donovan said.

Shannon dug around in their garbage bag, until she pulled out a simple plastic, D-cell flashlight. She cupped the lens with her palm and switched it on. The red glow leaking from the edges told them it worked. She turned it off and handed it to him.

Donovan clicked on the flashlight and allowed the beam to play out ahead of the truck until he zeroed in on a combination of grip, field of illumination, and maneuverability that would allow him to sweep the light back and forth as well as drive. He pulled out onto a side road, and then took a hard left onto 17 Mile Drive.

As fast as he could, concentrating on the disk of light provided by the flashlight, Donovan drove until he found a street that would take them up the hill, away from the ocean. He felt like there were more homes ablaze than earlier, and he felt a tightness form deep in his stomach. William was helpless to flee if the house began to burn. At the thought, he drove faster.

Donovan sped around a corner; the road ahead was clear of any fires. With the pavement free of debris, he kicked the truck up even faster. Through the scattered trees, he spotted lights coming from a modern house set back from the street. Up the illuminated driveway, he caught sight of two motorcycles parked near the garage. Both riders turned as Donovan sped past, but one man caught Donovan's attention—it was the same guy from the hospital, the bald one who pulled the trigger on an imaginary gun. Only this time, he leveled an actual gun and fired.

CHAPTER TWENTY-THREE

"CALVIN, WE HAVE to talk," Lauren said the second he answered his phone. She was seated at the chart table on the bridge of the *Buckley*, scribbling furiously on a pad while pulling up data on the computer monitor.

"Lauren, where are you?"

"I'm aboard the *Buckley*," Lauren said. "Calvin, I'm looking at the latest weather for this entire region, but it's hours old. Do you have any updates?"

"We're working on that," Calvin said. "You already know about the GOES platforms, but now we've lost two of our DMPS reconnaissance assets. Lauren, we're struggling to collect any data at all."

Lauren pondered the ramifications of losing two of the Department of Defense Meteorological Program Satellites. The DMPS was the DOD dedicated space-based weather data she'd used for years. She visualized the other arrays that might still be operational. "What about the satellites the Russians and Chinese have in polar orbit? Can we get any real-time information from them?"

"What specific information are you asking for? The Air Force has tasked a reconnaissance Global Hawk drone out of Beale Air Force Base to monitor the fire situation. It was on its way to Guam, but they turned it around, and it should be overhead before first light. I can send you the latest aerial assessment of the Monterey Peninsula fires. It was taken by a Cal Fire spotter plane, and it sums up the fire situation if that's the data you're after."

"Yes, of course. Though I think we've got a bigger problem brewing that will completely change the fire situation. I'm thirty miles offshore of Monterey, and the winds aloft are coming from the south, southwest. Calvin, I think Tropical Storm Evangeline has changed track, and the area of low pressure is headed north."

"The last track update we had showed that after Evangeline coasted out over the Pacific near Guadalajara, Mexico, she headed on the usual northwestern track out to sea."

"Calvin, that's not what I'm seeing. The low has drifted north, and while the usual cool sea surface temperatures normally dissipate what's left of the storm, we don't have the usual sea temperatures. I'm not saying she could grow stronger, but she could stay a tropical storm, which means the winds could easily be in the fifty to sixty miles per hour range. I have a theory that we could see those winds here in California, inside of a few hours."

"I know you well enough to realize you've already done the math. How bad could this get?"

"Eastern Pacific tropical storms impacting California are nothing new, but what is new is the powerful El Nino that has set up off the coast. The warmer water could keep the low pressure rotating far longer than usual. Because of the data blackout, I'm not sure where the center of the tropical storm is located, or what the current track is, or what the wind speeds might be. Just using the old data, and allowing for the change in trajectory I fear has taken place, the outermost reaches of Evangeline's influence could see sustained winds over forty miles per hour, with much stronger gusts. Mix that with an out-of-control fire, and therein lies the potential for a disaster of epic proportions."

"Explain."

"From what I'm told, right now, even with the winds at less than ten miles per hour, we lose Monterey, Pebble Beach, Seaside, and Pacific Grove."

"And if the winds reach forty miles per hour?"

"I think we could see a fire that has the potential to race unchecked all the way to San Jose, and then perhaps keep moving and destroy the entire city of San Francisco."

"That's impossible," Calvin said almost in a whisper.

"Trust me, it's very possible, though I don't think the windy conditions will arrive for at least another few hours, and we both know how much can change with the weather in that time. What we need are rudimentary images of the tropical storm, sea state, anything to give us an idea of wind direction and velocity. If there are any aircraft or even ships out there, they could give us current surface condition reports."

"I'll get that process started," Calvin said. "What else?"

"I'd push the Pentagon to immediately mobilize any and all troops to work in coordination with Cal Fire and other agencies to find a way to minimize the damage this combination of wind and fire might inflict. I'd also strongly suggest they begin the evacuation of all vital military assets sitting in the potential path of this fire. Ships, aircraft, men, and equipment—start moving everything."

"In your opinion, and I'm talking about worst scenario," Calvin said, "how long does it take a fire like you've suggested to burn from Monterey to San Jose?"

"Once the winds begin—and understand there are far more variables than my expertise can provide—my rough calculations say the fire, if unchecked, could reach San Jose in ten hours or less. And, Calvin, it will be huge by the time it arrives."

"Lauren, I want you to remain on the *Buckley*. I'll need instant access to you, and being out to sea is the safest place for you right now. Do I have your word?"

"I'm not going anywhere." Lauren didn't bother to mention she couldn't, with the helicopter out of service. "I do want to pull in the experts at Cal Fire as well as the Forest Service. They need to know what we know, plus they have the brain trust to fully understand what can and can't happen. We need answers if we're going to contain this fire here in the Monterey Peninsula."

"Do it," Calvin said. "I'll call you after I talk to the Pentagon. Take care of yourself."

Calvin hung up, and Lauren pocketed her phone and spun in her chair to find Montero, Michael, and Ryan standing nearby. The alarmed expressions on their faces told her they'd heard her conversation with Calvin, and each understood the dire predictions she'd made.

"Is this for real?" Montero said. "The fire could reach San Francisco?"

"Yes. Montero, show me where we can find a cup of coffee. It's going to be a long night."

"This just keeps getting worse," Michael said. "Janie's been on the phone about the helicopter. I'm going to go see what she knows."

"The coffee is this way, follow me." Montero led the way off the bridge, down a passageway and into a ready room with a table, a coffee maker, and a small refrigerator.

Lauren poured herself a cup and then faced Montero. "I need to ask a favor."

"Name it," Montero said.

"Is there anything else we can do to try to find Donovan? If he's still alive, waiting somewhere for the sun to come up, it might be too late."

"I've been thinking about that as well. I've talked to Ethan about taking a boat ashore, but he pointed out that with all the debris in the water, plus the current and surf, it would be far too dangerous. With the helicopter grounded, our options drop to near zero. I'm sorry—if I knew what to do, I'd already be doing it."

"Thanks," Lauren said as she took a sip of coffee. "I had to ask. This fire is on the edge of becoming an even bigger disaster, and I don't know if there is anything we can do to stop its progress. To be honest, I'm scared."

"I know. We all are."

CHAPTER TWENTY-FOUR

AN INSTANT BEFORE the muzzle flash, Donovan jammed the gas pedal to the floor. The Ford lunged forward. He glanced over his shoulder as another round was fired, but a bend in the road blocked his view. He maneuvered through another turn, and drove the F-250 up the hill into a forested area. He reached a small clearing, cranked hard on the steering wheel, and spun the rear end around until the truck now pointed back the way they'd come. He shut off the engine and rolled down the window. The distinctive sound of two motorcycle engines drew closer. He could see the headlights as they passed right to left, moving fast, and it didn't take long for the sound to fade in the distance.

Donovan cranked the ignition and allowed the truck to roll quietly down the slope. All the while, intent on the one sound he didn't want to hear. What he did hear was the thump of distant explosions mixed with the dull roar coming off the fires. He reached the pavement, pulled out onto the street, and accelerated.

"How long?" Shannon asked.

"Five minutes." Donovan glanced in the mirrors and extinguished the headlights as he approached an intersection. He slowed, listened, and out there in the darkness, he heard the percussive rumble of two motorcycles as they pounded closer.

"Where are they?" Shannon twisted in her seat, trying to locate the threat.

Donovan sped through the intersection. He caught sight of headlights to his left and heard the roar of motorcycles. Their destination was just up the street, and through the smoke, the lights from the house made it easy to spot. In a flash, Donovan understood what the motorcyclists were doing. They were systematically searching the houses that were lit up. A new sense of urgency shot through him. As the driveway approached, he braked hard, swung the wheel into the turn, and powered up the drive through the open gate. Just missing the pool, he pointed the truck at the landscaped bushes used to camouflage the generator. He turned off the truck's headlights just before they hit.

The weight and inertia of the truck, coupled with the heavy steel bumper, demolished the generator. The steady hum of the engine vanished as it flew apart, leaving the house entirely dark. Donovan brought the truck to a halt. He and Shannon listened as the throaty roar of the motorcycles cruised down the street and receded in the distance.

"I don't know if I can do this," Shannon said, holding the pistol. "Buck and I talked at length. I'm not sure I'm the kind of person who can point a gun at someone and pull the trigger."

"Then put the thing away. People holding guns tend to get shot."

"You take it." Shannon held the pistol out to Donovan.

He wedged the pistol above the sun visor, shut off the engine, and stepped outside.

"Hurry, get your things." He grabbed the flashlight and the trash bag he'd filled at the hospital and ran toward the sliding door that led inside. Once inside the darkened house, Donovan clicked on the flashlight.

In the kitchen, William lay on the floor, thrashing helplessly. Blood from his ankle streaked the tile. Cries of pain filled the room as he tried in vain to pull himself up onto the chaise.

"Oh God." Shannon's hand shot to her mouth.

Donovan rushed to his side, set aside the flashlight, then knelt and wrapped William up in his arms. "It's okay, I've got you."

"You're here," William uttered between ragged gasps of air as he blinked at the light. "Help me."

Donovan kept William from moving, his heart breaking at the terrible pain he was enduring. "Shannon, get the drugs, now."

Shannon sat the backpack down and unzipped the flap. Using the flashlight, she grabbed a handful of vials and several sterile packs of syringes and laid them on the floor.

"What are they?" Donovan asked.

"There's several. Some are fentanyl, a few propofol, but mostly morphine," Shannon answered. "The packages are the syringes and needles."

"I say we start with the morphine. I'm assuming one vial is one dose?"

Shannon handed the light to Donovan and ripped apart a package. "A vial is ten milligrams." She attached a needle to the barrel of the syringe, held the vial upside down, inserted the needle, and emptied the small container. Without hesitation, she stuck the needle in William's thigh and pushed the plunger all the way down.

Donovan could feel William's muscles begin to relax. His eyes softened and far less agony marred his face.

"Where are we?" William asked.

"We're in Pebble Beach," Donovan said. "How much do you remember?"

"I was on the golf course. Everyone ran."

Shannon grabbed a bottle of water from the refrigerator, twisted off the cap, and knelt next to Donovan to let William take a sip, then another, until he turned his head away.

"I remember it getting dark, and all I could think about was the mistake I made. I'm so sorry," William said as his eyes filled and tears trickled down his lined face. "I should never have allowed you to go through with what we did. I couldn't bear how much pain you were in."

Donovan tilted his head in confusion. William's drug-induced train of thought made no sense. "It's okay, we've got you. You're going to be fine. The drugs are going to take away your pain."

"You would have survived. Robert Huntington was strong, but I got in your way. I'm so sorry." William's words became slurred. "We didn't need to kill you. We could have proven them all wrong. I failed you. Please forgive me."

Shannon's eyes grew large, and Donovan felt his nerve endings begin to buzz, trapped between William and Shannon. All he could do was sit, helpless against the words spilling from William. Not only was he distressed at what Shannon was hearing, he was horrified that William had carried around his regret for decades.

"We know you didn't kill Meredith," William said in a whisper. "I'm so sorry I robbed you of your life."

William was fading fast, his eyes blinking slowly as he tried to focus. Donovan was shocked by the words and couldn't help but briefly wonder what his life would have been like in William's version. There was no debate. Donovan was exactly where he wanted to be. William finally closed his eyes and was out, but the damage was done.

Shannon went to the refrigerator, pulled out a bottle of water, and drank most of it in one prolonged swallow. When she'd finished, she handed one to Donovan.

"Let's get William back up on the chaise. We need to change the dressing on his ankle."

"No wonder you know Pebble Beach so well," Shannon said, her arms crossed across her chest.

"Help me take care of William, and then we'll talk." Donovan needed time to gather his thoughts. He hadn't had to face the reality of his secret becoming public for years. At this moment, he had to add one more to the very short list of people who knew he had once been Robert Huntington.

Together they lifted William back onto the chaise lounge. Shannon used a towel to wipe up the blood on the floor. She pulled out the last two water bottles and set them down.

Donovan unfolded and spread out a clean towel at the foot of the chaise lounge and dumped the medical supplies from the plastic bag they'd loaded at the hospital. He took a moment to turn every package right side up and sort them by category.

"Are you thinking about trying to push the bone back into place?"

"No, I'm afraid we'd make matters worse. For the moment, his toes are pink and warm, so the blood is flowing to his foot. I say we just rewrap the ankle and leave the rest for a doctor." Donovan handed the penlight back to Shannon.

"I found an ankle splint in the emergency room." Shannon rifled through the pile of medical supplies. "Maybe we can use it to replace the truck's mat."

"Nice," Donovan said as she ripped open the plastic and held the adjustable splint above William's ankle, eyeing the fit. "We might have to modify the straps, but this could work."

Shannon set the splint aside, grabbed a pair of surgical scissors, and ripped them free from the packaging. She handed them to Donovan, but didn't make eye contact.

Donovan understood she was trying to absorb a great deal of information. He took the scissors and began to cut away at the earlier bandage. He peeled off layer after layer, until he reached the final clump of dressings, which he gently removed and tossed aside. So far, William hadn't so much as flinched. Blood oozed from the opening, and the skin at the edge of the wound looked as if it were starting to darken. He twisted the cap off one of the water bottles and poured most of it over the wound, saving the last for himself. The single swallow felt good on his dry throat. He repeated the process, and then used a clean towel to absorb the water on William's foot and ankle.

"Here's the antibiotic ointment." Shannon handed him a tube with the top already removed.

Donovan squeezed out some of the contents and had an idea. "Unwrap some of the gauze pads, and hand them to me one at a time."

Shannon placed the penlight on William's thigh with the light aimed at the supplies. "Do you want the biggest ones or the medium-sized ones?"

"Medium," Donovan said, and applied the antibiotic directly to the first gauze square, and then pressed it onto the wound, listening carefully for any response from William. There was none. Once Donovan had the wound covered, he asked for the large pads and covered the wound with another layer and then finished with several strips of white tape to hold everything in place. He leaned back, stretching his neck from side to side.

"Much better. Now, what about this?" Shannon picked up the plastic splint and held it above William's ankle.

Donovan calculated the dimensions and selected a roll of elastic bandage. "I'm thinking we wrap the ankle to provide some padding, and then we position the splint, and use Velcro straps to hold it in place."

Working quickly, Donovan and Shannon fit the elastic bandage underneath William's ankle, foot, and calf, until all the gauze was covered and secured. The entire time, William lay still with his eyes closed. The long shadows, cast by the penlight distorting his features, made him look older, almost otherworldly, like he'd already passed away.

When she and Donovan finished, Shannon stood and went to the sink, and with the last of the water pressure, rinsed the blood from her hands. She turned until she made eye contact with Donovan. "It's true. William wasn't making anything up. You're him."

Donovan heard the low rumble the same time Shannon did. She snapped off the penlight. Donovan rose to his feet and moved through the darkened hallway until he could see out the front window. The two motorcycles, headlights ablaze, cruised slowly down the street. He could see the riders, their heads turning, surveying each house as they rolled past. The bald man with the tattoos looked straight up the driveway, and for the briefest of moments, though Donovan knew he was impossible to spot, he felt like they were zeroed in on each other in the darkness, readying for a fight.

CHAPTER TWENTY-FIVE

LAUREN DIALED ERNIE'S cell phone and waited for him to answer. She was back on the bridge, standing, leaning over to study the details of an aeronautical chart Montero had retrieved from the helicopter. She ran her finger along the shoreline of Pebble Beach and then beyond, wondering where Donovan could have taken refuge.

"Deputy Director Rincon."

"Ernie, it's Lauren. We need to talk."

"You're damn right we do. Where in the hell are you?"

"I'm out on the Eco-Watch ship, the *Buckley*." Lauren ignored Ernie's understandable anger at her disappearance. The playing field was changing rapidly and the men in San Jose only had part of the picture. "Are you someplace you can talk?"

"Hang on a second," Ernie said. "Give me time to walk down the hall to the office you were using earlier."

Lauren heard a door shut and Ernie exhale. "Ernie, I'm sorry I bolted like that. The helicopter was called in for a rescue, and I needed to leave. To be honest, the chaos there with all of the politics and posturing was less than productive. Plus, I needed a place where I have unlimited use of the latest communications equipment. This ship provides me with all of that."

"I get it," Ernie said with a sigh. "If I could get out in the field, I would. We keep getting bits and pieces of what's happening in Monterey, and none of it is good. Several volunteer crews, including some K-9 units, have gone into the city trying to locate survivors and establish usable routes that EMS crews can utilize at first light. We haven't found much, mostly victims who for whatever reasons didn't evacuate. Besides fire and carbon monoxide, the bigger problem with urban fires is the high levels of poisonous gases that some materials give off as they burn. Hydrogen cyanide, sulphur dioxide as well as phosgene are formed when certain household products, such as plastics, PVC pipe, and vinyl are burned. These gases don't dissipate outward like gases from forest fires—they can linger and build up in structures, form deadly pockets where you don't expect them. We had to pull all the units out—it's just too dangerous right now."

"I think you need to start pulling everyone back," Lauren said. She'd been around Ernie long enough to know that his firefighter mentality pushed him to get in there and fight the fire and save the people. It was a mind-set that existed in everyone who fought fires, a necessity that allowed a unique group of people to run toward the fire instead of away. "I'm waiting for data to confirm my theory, but I think we're only hours away from a significant change in the meteorological conditions."

"What kind of a change?"

"High winds out of the southwest."

"No way. We just looked at the forecast while we planned our air and ground attacks for first thing in the morning."

"Check the time and date of those forecasts. There haven't been any updates because two of the GOES satellites are down. We're trying to pull in observations from other agencies, foreign governments, any hard data we can get our hands on. Right now, the downside is it's the middle of the night, on a weekend, and while we don't have visual confirmation yet, there are signs that the remnants of a tropical storm have veered north, and the low-pressure area is going to impact our area."

"Evangeline?" Ernie said, as what Lauren was telling him clicked.

"Yes, though I'm surprised you know what I'm talking about. People in California rarely pay any attention to the tropical storms that sweep across Mexico."

"I have some good friends who are seasoned boaters. They were planning a fishing trip down south and they invited me, but said they were waiting and watching the tropical storm before they made any final decisions."

"Ernie, based on rough calculations at my end, we could see winds start to pick up in less than two hours, and they'll continue to build over the next twelve hours."

"What kind of velocities are we talking about?"

"Too soon to tell." Lauren glanced down at the legal pad where she'd made her early calculations. The two numbers she'd circled were easy to spot. "I predict the winds will reach forty miles an hour, with gusts possibly as high as sixty miles per hour."

"That's it, then," Ernie said as if the air had been forced from his lungs. "If we have as much as twenty-mile-per-hour winds fanning these flames, we're going to lose the entire peninsula."

"What if we get the winds I'm talking about?" Lauren asked, wanting to hear the answer directly from Ernie.

"There are so many variables. Offhand, I say we lose Salinas, and if we don't hold it there . . ." Ernie paused as he fully imagined the enormity of the situation. "It could burn all the way to San Jose. Maybe consume the entire Bay Area."

"We agree, then," Lauren said. "The Pentagon is already aware of what is happening. People are starting to work on this, but you and I are at ground zero, and they'll be coming to us for answers. I'll do what I can to provide the meteorological data. You figure out how to fight this fire."

"We're going to need some expert input on fire behavior," Ernie said. "I need to call a colleague in Montana. He works at the Forest

Service Fire laboratory. I'll call you back when I have him on the line. Give me ten minutes."

"I'll be here," Lauren said. She disconnected the call and dug into her phone to see if the latest images from Calvin had arrived. She searched for what she was looking for, opened the file, and began to scroll through the various pictures of Monterey, using her fingers to enlarge the area. The images were still too small for her to make any determinations. She sat down at the console and brought up Calvin's e-mail on the large high-definition screen. As the image filled the screen, Lauren minimized it, clicked through her inbox, and saw the earlier images Calvin had sent hours ago, just after the initial meteor event. She felt Ryan slide from his captain's chair and move in next to her as she brought up both images and arranged them side by side. She looked up at him. "I know they're different formats, but they're both taken of the same Monterey fires. Tell me what you see."

Ryan used the tip of his pen as a pointer. "These individual fires have obviously joined together, small clusters have become larger clusters, and each actively burning sector seems to be growing larger, though the fires aren't moving in the same direction."

"Exactly—the winds are light and variable," Lauren said as she enlarged both images. "But there's something else."

Ryan leaned in and studied the screen.

"The smoke," Lauren said. "When the fires began, the smoke was being pushed by a slight breeze from the west, less than five knots. Now look—the wind at the outer edges of the field of view shows the clouds shifting from a southerly wind. See this—the sharp gradient in the cloud direction. It's evidence of a strong midlevel shear. Evangeline is coming, and she's bringing her winds."

"What can the *Buckley* do?" Ryan asked.

Lauren pondered the question before she answered. "Is there an update on the helicopter?"

"I don't think so," Ryan said as he stepped away and began speaking into a handheld radio.

Lauren's phone lit up indicating a call, but she didn't recognize the number. "Dr. McKenna."

"Lauren, it's Ernie. I have Dr. Adam Harrison, with the Forest Service Fire Lab, on the phone. Dr. Harrison, meet Dr. Lauren McKenna with the Defense Intelligence Agency."

"Dr. McKenna, nice to meet you," Dr. Harrison said. "I'm just now processing the data Ernie sent me. Can you tell me more about this wind event you're expecting?"

"First of all, to simplify this, call me Lauren. Adam, there is an earlier infrared image I gave to Ernie, taken not long after the initial event. Do you have that in front of you?"

"Let me pull it up," Adam said. "Ah yes, there it is."

As Lauren waited for Adam to examine both images, she tested the cup of coffee she'd poured earlier. It was lukewarm and she set it aside. Moments later, a crewman set a fresh cup down and stepped away.

"Okay, the first feature of note is the fact that the vectors are not the same," Adam said. "Not all of the burning clusters are moving in the same direction."

"I saw that as well," Lauren said as her eyes were pulled to the aeronautical map from the helicopter. She'd spotted a detail that instantly nibbled at her subconscious. She pulled the chart closer, put her finger on Monterey, and oriented it to match the perspective of the two images on the screen. The contour lines and elevation changes were what had registered. All of the computer images were flat, one dimensional, but the people who flew were always interested in the terrain.

"In a low-wind situation like we have now," Adam replied, "the local geography, available fuel, and even the rising energy from the fires themselves are the driving factors in the direction of the burns. What we have now are localized updrafts. The intense fire is drawing in air at ground level, much like a chimney. The ambient air temperatures, plus the contours of the surrounding terrain, are dictating the direction the fires move. All of this changes if there is even a slight shift in the direction and velocity of the surface winds. What changes do you think we can expect?"

"Within two hours, I predict winds from the southwest at twenty knots, intensifying to winds steady at thirty knots, with higher gusts. I expect these conditions to continue for twelve hours before beginning to subside."

"It won't matter if it's twenty or fifty knots," Adam said. "If you're right, these fires are going to explode out of control and race northward. The mountains in Big Sur will act like a funnel, and as the wind pushes through the valleys, the air will accelerate. The total effect is that I'd expect to see surface winds downrange of the mountains reach sixty to seventy knots. We can't fight that; no one can."

"Gentlemen," Lauren said. "Is there anything we can do to stop, or even slow down, this fire?"

"We should start setting backfires," Ernie said. "If we can burn enough of the available fuel ahead of the fire, it might serve to slow it down when the winds start to pick up."

"I would start there," Adam said. "Let me get to the lab and see what type of models the program generates. Ernie, it might make sense to fall back and think about setting a second barrier of backburns. I'd also start evacuations downwind, the sooner the better. Lauren, the more weather updates we have, the more accurate the simulations."

"Thanks, Adam," Ernie said. "We'll be in touch."

"Lauren," Adam said. "Can you explain how this happened? A single meteor hurtling through space has a single vector. Everything travels in a straight line. I'm unclear as to what actually took place. According to these images, there's no natural explanation for the impact pattern."

"Have you ever heard of the Kessler effect?"

"No, I don't believe I have."

"It's a theory that deals with the sheer number of objects in low Earth orbit. I think the meteor impacted dozens, if not hundreds, of satellites, came apart, and set off a domino effect. The man-made objects careened out of their orbits and were pulled to Earth, thus creating the chaos you're referring to. We're lucky it happened the way it did. Had the meteor remained intact, we could have been looking at an extinction-level event."

"Dear God," Adam said. "I had no idea."

"We still have to stop what's happened. Ernie, will you make sure we all have each other's phone numbers? We have work to do. I'll keep you in the loop." Lauren ended the call and studied the map before her, and pictured the corridor from Monterey to San Jose. The lowlands to the west were bordered on the east side by higher terrain. It wasn't difficult to visualize a wall of fire pushed by gale-force winds racing up the valley toward San Francisco Bay.

CHAPTER TWENTY-SIX

DONOVAN CONCENTRATED ON listening. In the distance, the distinctive sound of the motorcycles ebbed and flowed in the night. He wondered if the two remaining men were ransacking empty houses or focusing only on trying to find him and Shannon.

Standing next to Donovan, Shannon made no effort to mask her fear. "It's worse when they stop, and I don't know where they are."

"Yeah, I don't like this either. How about we roll William into the living room and wait there. It might be more comfortable, plus we can watch the street while we talk."

Together they rolled the chaise into the front room and positioned William where they could attend to him from either side of the makeshift gurney.

"I like this better," Shannon said as she checked that the front door was locked.

"Sit." Donovan motioned to a cushioned chair and took the one across from it. He leaned back and rubbed his tired eyes.

Shannon sat, hands in her lap, thumbs making anxious circles around each other.

"I'm not going to insult your intelligence and deny what we both heard in there," Donovan said, deciding damage control was best served by the truth. "It's been a long time, and I'm not interested in explaining the details of my past tonight."

"I agree. This isn't the time or place, and you don't need to explain anything," Shannon said. "I do have to say, this is so surreal. When I was in graduate school, I wrote my thesis on clinical observations and treatments of delayed PTSD events. Boring, I know, but I used you—or Robert Huntington—as one of my subjects. I probably know more about Robert than I do Donovan Nash."

"You would have had to gather your data from the public record," Donovan said, growing more uncomfortable with the conversation. "Much has been written by people who flat out got it wrong. Be careful with what you think you know."

"In my research, I refused to delve into your tabloid exploits. Instead, I focused on your first and greatest trauma—the death of your parents. I argued that event was like the lighting of a very long fuse. When you lost Meredith, and for the record, I never believed for a second you were involved in her murder, the earlier trauma caught up with you and ignited the long buried explosive stress. You, like so many others, committed suicide. Or, as I now understand, your version of suicide. My paper illuminated multiple examples of how small variables could serve to avert a catastrophic ending. For people with PTSD, it's rarely a single event that ends them."

"I dealt with my issues in a way that made sense to me, and I survived."

"You're one of the lucky ones." Shannon lowered her head. "I'm sorry. I didn't mean to go all therapist on you. I, of all people, understand the difficulties you've faced, and what you've accomplished is remarkable. Buck didn't know about your past, but he was equally impressed with Eco-Watch, and especially you as a person. It's why he joined your team. He felt strongly enough about what you were doing to give his life for the mission. That speaks volumes."

Donovan blinked at the surprise tears forming in his eyes, then wiped them away.

"Am I right that Eco-Watch is your creation, a sort of living shrine to Meredith and her life as an environmentalist trying to save the planet?"

Donovan nodded, not sure he could trust his voice.

"I think that gives Buck's death even more meaning."

"There are only a handful of people who know my secret," Donovan said while clearing his throat. "I refer to all of them as a family. Through Buck, you're already part of the family, and I hope you stay that way."

"That's a discussion for later," Shannon said.

"I agree. Now, I need to go out and move the truck out of the bushes in the backyard. When it comes time to leave, I want it ready and pointed in the right direction. I'll be right back." Donovan was anxious to break away from the emotional conversation. He slid through the kitchen door and out onto the patio. This close to the cold Pacific Ocean, the nights were usually cool, but tonight the warm air seemed thick and cloying. The smoke particles instantly burned his eyes, and he could feel the harshness in his throat.

The truck was where he had left it, and after he started the engine, he turned the wheel hard to the left and inched forward in the darkness. He maneuvered the Ford until it was parked just outside the sliding glass door. If they needed to leave, it was a quick turn through the wooden fence and down the driveway. He put the transmission into park and killed the engine. As an afterthought, he switched on the AM radio but found only static. He shut everything off, and as he walked toward the house, he stopped and felt the rough hole in the metal where the radio antenna should have been. It seemed at some point he'd managed to rip it off the truck.

In the kitchen, Donovan slowed at the sound of Shannon's voice. He rounded the hallway toward the living room, and as he drew closer, he realized Shannon was praying.

"As always, Lord, we trust in you to protect us from danger, and in your wisdom, we pray that you'll speed the dawn. Amen."

"Amen," Donovan said quietly so as not to startle her. "That was nice."

"It was a prayer Buck taught me," Shannon said as she brushed her hair back behind her ear. "I first heard it at a funeral for one of Buck's friends. The family had asked Buck to say a few words, and he ended his eulogy with that prayer. He told me later that when he was a little boy, he was afraid of the dark. He wanted to be brave for his mom and dad, but when the lights went out at night, the sounds of the house would seize him. His mother taught him that prayer, and he told me it helped. I memorized it, thinking one day I might teach it to our children."

Donovan remained silent. Shannon was dealing with the death of a loved one. It was a loss he was familiar with, and there were no words.

"Listen," Shannon said as she snapped her head toward the street.

Donovan, too, heard the motorcycle. From the sound, he could tell it was just one machine. The biker gunned the engine and accelerated straight up the driveway. Both Donovan and Shannon ducked away from the headlights as the motorcycle stopped just beyond the door. The rider revved the engine twice and then shut it down.

"Put your hands above your head!" a deep voice called out from behind them.

Startled, Donovan wheeled around and in the dim glow from the fires burning outside saw the bald man standing in the living room. He'd used his friend as a diversion and snuck in through the kitchen. His sawed-off shotgun was leveled at them.

CHAPTER TWENTY-SEVEN

LAUREN FELT AS if the walls of the bridge were pushing in on her. She stood at the forward bridge windows and spotted Michael and the others still gathered around the damaged helicopter.

"Good idea," Ryan said as he turned toward Lauren. "You need to stretch, get some fresh air. You've been sitting there for a long time staring at those maps."

"I'm charging my phone," Lauren said. "It's almost dead."

"Leave your phone with me. I'll see that it gets charged. Here, take a radio. I'll call you if we need you."

Lauren nodded, checked the radio, and made her way to the elevator that would take her down to the helicopter pad. As she neared the bow, she was more aware of the pitching deck under her feet than earlier. She swung open a hatchway and squinted away the brightness from the halogen lights pointed down on the damaged rotor blades.

"Lauren," Michael called out. He peeled off his life jacket and helped Lauren put it on. "What about you?" Lauren asked as they walked toward Janie.

"Someone will bring me one."

"Where's Montero? I thought she was down here."

"She was." Michael looked around the deck to no avail. "I saw her talking with the first mate, Ethan Wiley. They were discussing the need for current weather information, but I didn't see them leave."

Lauren stepped to the side as a crewman handed Michael a life jacket. High above her, Janie and another crewman stood on separate ladders, measuring and discussing the twisted metal at the end of a rotor blade. She looked at Michael. "How bad is it?"

"Not good," Michael said. "I've been on the phone with a helicopter repair outfit in Oakland. They're the nearest factory-approved repair shop. I sent pictures of the damage, and without hesitation, the engineer said all four blades needed to be replaced, and whatever we do, don't start the engines as the vibration we experienced earlier could have stressed not only the blades, but the rotor mast, the mounts, and transmission as well."

"If we had the blades flown out here, could we make the swap at sea?"

"No, the process is more complex than that. His suggestion was to sail to Oakland and have the helicopter lifted by crane from the deck of the *Buckley*. He offered to arrange transportation to their facility and calculated the downtime shouldn't be more than a week, though it could be longer if they discovered additional damage. I said we'd get back with him. Oh, and I left out the part that there was a possibility that a massive fire was going to beat us to Oakland."

Lauren looked over and saw the smallest trace of a grin on his face. She found his sarcasm comforting. If Michael could kid around, then all wasn't lost. "Okay, the helicopter is out of the picture. Let's say we get a signal from Donovan, hell, a signal from anyone on the shore. Is there anything the *Buckley* can do to facilitate a rescue?"

"No." Michael motioned toward the disabled helicopter. "I mean we have a couple of runabouts aboard, but as sturdy as they are, they're not equipped to pick their way through all of the junk left in the water after a tsunami. You need to impress on all your contacts that what's needed are rescue helicopters. I'm hoping any survivors, Donovan included, will make themselves known at first light, and the helicopters can pull them out."

"I'll work on that," Lauren said. "Part of the problem is that as soon as there's enough light, Cal Fire and the Forest Service are going to launch a small air force of aerial firefighters to suppress the fire. They need an empty sky to operate unencumbered. I'll see if I can suggest a fixed corridor where helicopters can operate."

"I like that plan," Michael said. "Have Cal Fire draw up multiple pathways, so if fire operations shut down one, they can open another."

"Good idea." Lauren felt a surge of energy at the thought of doing something positive. "I'm still trying to put together a complete look at all the meteorological variables. Our weather gathering system took a real beating today."

"Heads up!" shouted a crewman standing near the helicopter.

Lauren saw Janie lunge to the side to try to catch a dropped flashlight. Michael started toward her as Janie's ladder began to tip. A crewman reached out and steadied her as the light shattered on the deck.

"Janie," Michael called out. "Get down from there—the rotor blades are junk."

Three crewmen were converging to help Janie climb down from her lofty perch. Once she was firmly on the deck, she walked to Lauren and Michael.

"Janie, you're acting like the damaged rotor blades are your fault. Quit taking it personally," Michael said. "The last thing we need is for you, or anyone else, to get hurt."

"Easy for you to say." Janie shook her head in exasperation. "You didn't fly the bloody machine into a shipping container."

"I once crashed an Eco-Watch Gulfstream jet," Michael said to Janie. "Then, if you remember, there was the time I destroyed a thirty-million-dollar experimental drone, on purpose. Now relax, these things happen."

"I just feel so helpless with my wings clipped," Janie said. "I mean, what the hell am I good for if my damned chopper is busted?"

"Speaking as another pilot with clipped wings, you help where you can," Michael said. "We all do whatever it takes to help Lauren and the crew aboard the *Buckley*."

"Is that an order?" Janie asked. "I'd really like to focus on getting the helicopter flying."

"You know I hate orders," Michael said. "I will, however, insist that Captain Pittman put you to work in the crew mess. You need to forget about the helicopter and do something constructive, like peel potatoes. Which is what you'll be doing if you won't give the dead helicopter a rest."

Lauren watched the tension momentarily leave Janie's face, as if she were picturing Michael making good on his threat.

"I'd like for you to take a break; sit down and do some planning," Michael said. "Once the fire bombers start flying at first light, it would be nice to have some helicopter-friendly corridors for Cal Fire to consider. Hopefully they'll allow nonmilitary air ambulance assets into the area. Reach out to Cal Fire flight operations and see if they need our help."

Lauren pointed toward the shore and the thick boiling smoke illuminated by the unseen flames below. "To bring you both up to date, there's not much in the way of wind right now, so Cal Fire and the Forest Service are starting a series of backburns to try and rob the fire of fuel as it starts moving. The winds are going to pick up considerably, and once they start blowing, the fire is going to grow—we just don't know by how much. If I were going to plan helicopter evacuation routes, I'd make them out over the water."

"That makes sense," Janie said. "What assets will be joining us off-shore? Are we going to have the Coast Guard or the Navy to assist?"

"Eventually, though not in the time frame we need." Lauren shook her head and bit her lip at the thought of the coming nightmare.

"He'll find a way to get out," Michael said. "Donovan's clever like that. He knows the *Buckley* is offshore. It's maybe the only thing he knows for sure. We just have to pay attention and then react."

"Dr. McKenna." Ryan's voice crackled from the handheld radio. "Lauren, you have an urgent call. Repeat, you have an urgent call. Do you copy?"

"On my way," Lauren said into the radio as she looked up toward the darkened windows of the bridge. She ran down the passageway and stepped into the elevator. The second the doors opened on the bridge level, she hurried down the corridor. As she stepped onto the bridge, Ryan pointed to the chart table where her phone, plugged into a charger, waited.

"Lauren, it's Adam from the fire lab."

"Adam, I didn't expect to hear from you so quickly."

"It's Missoula, Montana, in the middle of the night. My commute was all of ten minutes," Adam said. "So, I've plugged some of your preliminary data into the computer model. I need to talk with you before I report back to fire command."

"Okay," Lauren sat down. "What can I do?"

"I ran the simulation three times. I used the wind direction and the theoretical velocities you gave me earlier. Have there been any changes or updates to that information?"

"No, we're still working on that," Lauren said as Montero and Ethan burst onto the bridge. Montero came straight for Lauren, a sheet of paper in her hand. "Adam, hang on a second."

"Lauren, we have the current weather at six different points out to sea," Montero said as she set the information in front of Lauren. "The list starts close to shore, and works westward from our position."

Lauren recognized seven sets of coordinates, followed with the wind direction, velocity, temperature, and sea state. Her eyes shot to the wind speed. Not a single reporting point showed less than twenty-five knots. "Where did this come from? Some of these co-ordinates are pretty far out to sea."

"It was Ethan's idea," Montero said. "He started calling ships with a request for the current weather. The *Buckley's* radio only has so much range, but each ship we contacted, in turn, made the same outward request. We finally ran out of ships, but not before we reached a commercial vessel nearly three hundred miles offshore."

Lauren stood and pulled up a nautical chart of the Pacific Ocean. She quickly marked each ship's coordinates, then penciled in the wind direction and velocity.

"Adam, I'm sorry for the delay," Lauren said. "I just received some real-time weather observations. The low-pressure area seems to be farther east than anticipated. Right now, less than fifty miles off-shore of Monterey, we have reports of winds from one nine zero de-grees at twenty-five knots. The direction holds fairly steady, though three hundred miles west of Monterey, the winds progressively build to forty-five knots."

"Oh, dear God," Adam said. "You know, I made a phone call on the drive in, and spoke to an old friend of mine who lives in London. He went to MIT, same as you, and he knew of you and your work."

"Adam, get to the point. What does my past have to do with this?"

"He told me to trust you, and that your problem-solving abilities were considerable. He also confirmed that you're with the Defense Intelligence Agency. Which brings me to my question: How famil-iar are you with Dresden, Germany, during World War II?"

"Are you talking about the firebombing?" Lauren asked cautiously.

"Yes, Churchill's raid, which created the fire tornadoes that killed as many as two hundred fifty thousand people."

"I know the history. What does that have to do with the Monterey Peninsula?"

"The computer models put the exact same conditions into play. We have the wind, mass ignition, plus the irregular terrain, which will cause the initial rotation. They'll start small, less than a hundred feet tall, maybe ten feet across. But if the winds reach thirty knots, we could see rotating giants, a hundred yards across and a thousand feet tall. As you know, the wind near the center of the vortex reaches enormous speeds, drawing in and depleting the oxygen in all directions. Then, of course, there's the heat. Like a giant bellows, the temperatures can reach fifteen hundred degrees centigrade."

From classified DIA files, Lauren knew far more about the history of the Dresden raid and the eventual bombing of Tokyo, Japan, than most. The Dresden raid, and subsequent fire whirls, were an experiment in destroying cities while using just enough incendiary bombs to put an organized system of fire tornadoes into motion. Armed with the knowledge of what took place in Germany, Japan was the next target. Incendiary bombs dropped from B-29s onto Tokyo created walls of spinning fire, which approached one hundred miles per hour. The temperatures were estimated to have reached well over a thousand degrees centigrade. Everything flammable was consumed, flesh ignited, or melted—piles of bodies were fused together in the aftermath. The carnage in Tokyo was worse than the combined effects of the atomic bombs dropped on Hiroshima and Nagasaki. Lauren shuddered at the reality of what a fire that size could do to an unprepared population.

"Lauren, are you still there?" Adam asked.

"Yes," Lauren said as she once again looked at the data Ethan and Montero had collected and did more calculations in her head. "You need to call fire command and tell them what you've discovered. Tell them we spoke—and it's not a question of if the winds are coming—they are coming. We'll have twenty-five-knot winds within the hour."

CHAPTER TWENTY-EIGHT

Donovan raised his hands as the second man kicked his way in through the front door, pistol at the ready. A broad smile broke out on his face as he spotted Shannon.

"Search them!" the bald man called out as he switched on a flashlight and held the beam on Donovan. The shotgun pressed against his shoulder was aimed at Donavan's forehead. "Who are you?"

"We're trapped by the fire, just like you," Donovan said as rough hands patted him down and removed his wallet and gun. "I needed medical supplies for my friend. Take the drugs and go."

"I asked you who you are."

"I'm Donovan Nash. Who are you?"

"That's what his driver's license says," the second man said as he read from Donovan's open wallet and then handed it to the bald man. "He's from Virginia. This looks like Hector's gun."

"Where are the keys to the truck?"

"They're in it," Donovan said without breaking eye contact with the bald man. Beside him, the second man turned his attention to Shannon.

"Who's the old man?" the bald man asked. The beam of his flashlight lit up William's face.

"He's my friend. He was injured in the tsunami." Donovan spoke as he subtly shifted his weight to his right leg.

"How about some light over here," the man standing next to Shannon said.

The instant the bald man broke eye contact and turned the flashlight toward Shannon, Donovan lunged forward, slapping aside the barrels of the shotgun. He shoved the bald man sideways, pushing him off balance.

The shotgun roared and the muzzle flashed as a dozen holes appeared in the ceiling. Shannon screamed as Donovan turned, put his head down, and powered toward the second man who was swinging his pistol to shoot. Wrapping his arms around him, Donovan kept his momentum going until they both careened over the sofa and crashed through the picture window, hitting the ground outside.

Donovan heard a groan as all the air was forced from the man's lungs. With the biker breaking his fall, Donovan was able to pull the pistol from his hand and quickly rolled to face the shattered window, the pistol up and aimed, ready to return fire.

"Donovan!" Shannon screamed from somewhere back in the house.

Donovan jumped to his feet and felt a crack of pain from his left knee as he put weight on his foot. He staggered to his right, nearly falling, as he made his way toward the driveway that would take him around the house. He heard the engine of the Ford roar to life. Donovan limped toward the gate. The truck, headlights burning brightly, rounded the corner, and headed straight for him.

A muzzle flash erupted from the passenger window, and Donovan realized the bald guy was on the passenger side. Another flash, and he felt his left leg begin to collapse beneath him. He lunged out of the way as the truck, still accelerating, passed only inches from his legs.

Donovan hit the ground on his left side. He ignored the pain as he turned and took aim at the bald head just visible through the back window. The distinct flash from a weapon illuminated the inside of the truck, and the Ford swerved hard across the front lawn and went out of sight. Before Donovan could move, he heard the sound of a crash, and then the air was silent.

Against an avalanche of pain, Donovan struggled to rise. His left pant leg was soaked with blood. He pulled himself up using his right leg and hopped, jumped, half-limped to the corner of the house. One glance told Donovan what had happened. The Ford had been driven into the trunk of a large tree in the front yard. The passenger door was open. Donovan raised his weapon. He was aware of the sound of footsteps, coming his way, moving in the shadows close to the house.

The first shot Donovan fired hit the biker low in the abdomen, and in that fraction of a second, Donovan saw that it wasn't the bald man, it was the other guy, the one he'd taken through the window. Donovan fired two more shots, the muzzle flashes acting like strobe lights, and Donovan watched as the man took both rounds in the center of the chest and crumpled forward from the waist, a knife slipping from his hand. A fourth and final flash, and the man stumbled and hit the ground face-first. As Donovan hopped closer, the man exhaled his last breath and lay motionless.

"Donovan?" Shannon called out.

He snapped his head toward the truck as Shannon stumbled from the driver's side, before collapsing to the ground. Several houses away, a motorcycle engine popped to life and Donovan heard it fade rapidly in the distance as the bald man fled. Donovan rushed to the Ford. The driver's-side door was open, and the interior light illuminated a semicircle on the lawn. Shannon was lying on her back. His fear spiked when he saw blood spattered on her face and shoulder. He dropped to his good knee and began to brush her hair from her face. "Shannon, I'm here. You're bleeding. Where are you hurt? Talk to me."

She opened her eyes, pulled in a slow, careful breath, and spoke in a raspy whisper. "I don't know. The airbag hit me," Shannon said through a string of groans, interspersed with profanities. She reached up and touched the burns on her face.

Donovan could see no other blood on her clothes. "I saw a gun go off inside the cab. What happened? Did he shoot you?"

"I shot him." Shannon rolled on her side and started to stand. "I remembered the gun you tucked above the sun visor, and it only took me about two seconds to remember everything Buck ever taught me at the range."

"I'm glad you changed your mind. Where did you hit him?"

"Arm, I think. He cried out, grabbed for the gun, and then we hit the tree." Shannon held out her hand, waiting for Donovan to pull her to her feet.

"I've been shot," Donovan said. "Can you help me up?"

"Donovan!" Shannon spotted his leg. She stood and leaned against the truck bed, reached out a hand, and pulled until Donovan, too, was up on both feet.

"We need to get out of here. Does this thing still run?" Donovan asked.

Shannon gingerly climbed behind the wheel, and seconds later, the engine fired and settled into its usual low rumble. Donovan hopped around to the rear and lowered the tailgate, and then pulled himself into the bed. "Back us up to the house."

Shannon eased the F-250 away from the tree and reversed slowly until the truck was back on the driveway, and then she shut off the engine.

Donovan slid to the ground just as Shannon came around. She stopped to look at the body lying near the driveway.

"Is he dead?"

"Yes," Donovan said.

Shannon helped Donovan up the steps. Once inside, he sat heavily on the floor near William.

"Is he okay?" Shannon asked Donovan.

"I don't know. I need some light." Donovan collected a flashlight from the floor and switched it on. He felt William's pulse. No change. He checked William's ankle and his toes. Still warm and pink. As he turned the light toward Shannon, he could see reddish blotches on her face, burns from the rapidly expanding airbag. The skin around her eyes looked swollen as well. Blood splatter reached down from her neck to her shoulder.

"Storming the house like they did, they'd been looking for us, hadn't they? They were going to kill us."

"Yes." Donovan remembered the leer in the second man's eyes when he looked at Shannon; he guessed she wasn't going to die quickly.

"How did you know that going out the window would work?" Shannon asked as she gathered up their scattered medical supplies and piled them close to the backpack full of drugs.

"I didn't." Donovan shrugged. "They spent a great deal of time and effort to find us. My guess is they wanted retribution for what we did to their friends. I'm so sorry I let you be taken. I was ready to kill the bald guy. I expected him to be standing in the window once I went through the glass and landed. Never once did I expect him to take you and run. Did he say anything to you?"

"Once you went out into the darkness, he grabbed my arm and yanked me toward the kitchen. He said you were crazy, he'd deal with you later, and that he was taking me as insurance."

"Again, I put you at risk and I'm sorry."

"Don't be. They were animals. We both know what they were going to do to me." Shannon said the words with anger, but as she picked up a pair of scissors they'd taken from the emergency room, silent tears began to run down her cheeks. With shaking hands, she cut away the material of Donovan's trousers. Wiping her eyes, she ripped open a package of gauze and cleaned the blood from his thigh.

Donovan could see there was a long furrow on the side of his leg, a near miss. He was lucky. A direct hit from the sawed-off shotgun would have taken off his leg above the knee.

Donovan grimaced as Shannon poured betadine straight from a bottle onto his open wound. She then applied antiseptic, gauze, tape, and finally wrapped his thigh with an elastic bandage.

"How does it feel?" she asked as she finished.

"Are there enough elastic bandages left to wrap the knee as well? I'm talking tight."

"Why?"

"When I hit the ground outside the window, I landed wrong."

Shannon nodded and rummaged around the stash of supplies until she pulled out what she needed. She peeled off the paper and rolled the bandage around his knee.

"Thanks." Donovan tested the movement of his knee. "We need to get William into the truck and leave this place."

"Where are we going?"

"Anywhere but here. That guy could easily circle back and sneak up on us again." Donovan clenched his teeth against the pain as he managed to stand. When he put weight on his left leg, the knee nearly buckled and the pain took his breath away.

"Are you okay?"

"No, but I think I can function," Donovan said as he limped into position to see if he could lift the chaise. It barely moved.

"Well?" Shannon said as she began to gather up the remaining medical supplies.

Donovan shook his head in frustration. With only one weight-bearing leg, he had little balance and practically zero leverage.

"Let me take this end, and you take the end by his feet. Maybe the two of us can lift him off the ground."

Donovan had his back to the broken picture window and was in the process of repositioning himself when the entire living room filled with light. He turned to see an expanding fireball boil up into the sky and reach across the horizon before it flickered and faded.

Several seconds later, a heavy boom carried through the trees and rattled the house.

"What was that?" Shannon said as she stepped away from the window.

Donovan turned on his good knee as smaller explosions seemed to reverberate through the house.

"What in the hell is happening?" Shannon asked, her arms wrapped protectively across her chest, one hand covering her mouth.

"Something big exploded in the general direction of Carmel." Donovan confirmed his bearings against the still glowing horizon. "Whatever it was is still burning."

"I think we should go," Shannon said.

Donovan went to the shattered picture window and compared the height of the window to the bed of the truck. He turned away as the house and yard were showered with burning debris swirling down from above. Donovan heard something else, like something approaching. He looked upward as the limbs of the trees began to sway and the warm breeze touched his face. A significant wind was starting to blow, and it was as terrifying as anything he'd ever experienced. A moment later, the first gust reached them, and bone-dry leaves glowed brightly as they ignited and rose and fell in the growing wind. The smoke, illuminated by the massive fire, began to gather speed above the trees. Spurred with a fear spawned millions of years ago when man first learned to flee from fire, Donovan limped as fast as he could for the front door.

CHAPTER TWENTY-NINE

"It was Carmel," Ryan said as he handed the powerful binoculars to Lauren.

Lauren had seen the flash and then waited as the sound and shock wave from the heavy explosion finally reached the *Buckley*. When it hit, she felt the vibrations shake her skeleton. Binoculars in hand, she stepped out of the bridge onto the walkway. She pressed her hip against the railing to compensate for the gentle rolling of the ship, and brought up the binoculars. In the highly magnified field of view, she watched as the flames reached higher into the night sky, as if pulling on an unlimited fuel source. She also took in the fact that it appeared as if the fire was oriented along a straight line, not unlike the gas main explosion they'd seen in Seaside. When the tendrils of the fire began to tilt and dance in the sky, and the thick smoke began to billow and tumble northward, Lauren knew that the wind had arrived.

She remembered and hung onto Ernie's earlier words, that nearly everyone in Carmel had been evacuated. She also reasoned that if Donovan had somehow reached Carmel, he would have evacuated as well. The logic was weak and unfounded, but it was all she had, so she held on tightly.

Lauren saw the first gusts ruffle the water, and then the wind finally met the *Buckley*. She watched as the damaged helicopter blades began rising and falling in the breeze, and she also noted that the air was far warmer than she expected, and she frowned.

"Lauren," Ryan said as he stuck his head outside. "Ernie from Cal Fire is on the line."

Lauren took one last look at the fire ashore. She picked up the phone. "Ernie, it's Lauren."

"What's happened?" Ernie dispensed with any pleasantries. "I've got spotty reports about a major explosion."

"I think it was a gas main explosion in Carmel," Lauren said. "From what we can see, the flames look to be in more or less a straight line, like what we saw in Seaside. And, Ernie, the winds have started picking up."

"How big is the fire?" Ernie asked.

"We're miles away, but it's probably at least two miles long, as big as any of the other clusters. It's also the first to be fanned by the escalating winds."

"So, the Carmel burn is our main fire now, the one that's going to join the others and create the vortex situation Adam was telling me about?"

"All of the fires are going to grow with the wind," Lauren said. "Do you think there's a different situation in play?"

"Lauren, I've been out on the front lines. In all my years fighting fires, I've only seen small, momentary versions of fire tornadoes. I can't even begin to process the magnitude of what he's talking about. Adam is my friend, but he sits in a lab in a white coat, and his computer models have been wrong before."

"Ernie, I wear a lab coat," Lauren said flatly. "We're not wrong."

"Look, maybe if I had more information, I'd be on board with this. As it stands right now, I have very few facts to go on. What you're asking me as a firefighter is to sit back and let this thing have its way with California. That goes against everything I stand for, and right this moment, I'm not prepared to give in."

"I'm not asking you to do anything but accept the possibilities of this fire and be prepared to retreat. Those of us on this side of the computer screen are in a position to connect some of the pertinent information so we can present you a worst-case scenario. Ernie, I'm serious, ignore us at great peril."

"Dr. McKenna, I appreciate your efforts, but I have a fire to put out. When you have more meteorological information, please be kind enough to pass it along."

"You know where to find me." Lauren disconnected the call, perplexed that Ernie had completely shifted his attitude. She wondered about the change. Who or what had put enough pressure on him to turn his back on her? As she pondered the implications, she checked her e-mail. There was one new message from Calvin at the DIA, as well as another she didn't recognize.

Lauren opened Calvin's e-mail first—an aerial image of the fire. She switched from her phone to the computer for better viewing. Calvin had sent a solitary infrared shot of the entire peninsula. She glanced at the identification stamp in the lower corner and instantly thanked the Canadians. The image had been sent from RADARSAT-1, one of Canada's polar orbiting platforms, and time stamped only minutes earlier. Carmel already glowed brighter and larger than all the other clusters.

Lauren studied the image, finding the backburns that Cal Fire and the Forest Service had started. They seemed small and paled in comparison to the fires they were designed to stop. She minimized the image and then pulled up and opened the e-mail she didn't recognize. The message was from a common Hotmail account. She smiled as she dialed the phone number provided.

"Thanks for calling me back," Ernie said immediately.

"I was a little confused, wondering why the shift in tone."

"It's turned into a full-scale bureaucratic shit show around here. Adam's warning went straight to Sacramento. The governor went ballistic over theoretical speculation setting off a possible statewide panic. He pulled overall fire command from those of us here in San Jose and is setting up a governmental bunker in Sacramento. Orders have already come down to fight the fire we have, not the science fiction version from the Forest Service. I think Adam had his ass handed to him as well. He's not answering my calls."

"To hell with the governor, I work for the Department of Defense. I'm going to do everything I can to help you fight the fire we have—plus the one we're about to have. What authority do you have?"

"I'm still in charge of the aerial tanker fleet. We have planes and crews ready to fly at first light."

Lauren thought of Michael and Janie's earlier conversation. "Ernie, have your people considered designated rescue helicopter corridors, to help evacuate survivors?"

"Eco-Watch flight ops sent us some preliminary options, but I can't allow anyone in the air until we're absolutely sure where our very large tankers are going to be flying. I'm sorry, but if you'd ever seen a Boeing 747 drop nineteen thousand gallons of water at tree-top level, you'd understand why we can't have anything in their way, especially helicopters. As soon as there is a lull in the aerial bombardment, we'll clear the choppers to fly."

"I understand," Lauren said as she tapped on the keyboard, and forwarded Ernie the latest Canadian image of the fires. "You've got mail. Take a look and tell me what you see."

"Jesus, the Carmel fire is huge," Ernie said. "Two other details jump out at me. In contrast to the total area on fire, our backburns are pathetic. I also see all of the ingredients needed for Adam's theory to become a reality."

"From your professional perspective, tell me what scares you the most about this situation."

"The lawyers and politicians. If in the course of fighting this fire, we kill one person, hell if we kill one pet with the backburn, it'll end careers. If the fire kills a hundred thousand people while the bureaucrats wring their hands, well, it's an act of God. No one is focused on the greater threat, only the possible fallout on their own little fiefdoms."

"Hang on a second, Ernie." Lauren stood and handed Ryan a note with a phone number. "Can you please call my boss, Calvin Reynolds, at the DIA, and ask him when we'll have the Global Hawk overhead? Okay, Ernie, I'm back."

"A Global Hawk is on its way?" Ernie asked. "Can I use it to direct my aerial assault on the fire?"

"Absolutely. It's a DOD asset." Lauren loved Ernie's dedication to fighting this fire. "We'll know shortly when the Global Hawk will arrive. Until then, what's the situation with the ground forces? Have you completed evacuation in the areas you need to use for the backburn?"

"We've done everything humanly possible. We're still evacuating areas in anticipation of larger backfires, and from what I see on this latest infrared image, we need to keep setting the backfires. Though I can tell you the governor has already given the order to suspend those for fear of damaging private property."

"Okay, the governor is a problem. Tell me, what would top your wish list right now?"

"More time," Ernie said without hesitation.

"I can't give you that." Lauren leaned in to her computer monitor and examined the size of the fires raging on the Monterey Peninsula. She compared it to the tiny backfires designed to stop the threat from going north. "How about a much bigger backburn?"

Ryan walked over and slid a piece of paper in front of Lauren. GLOBAL HAWK ETA—ONE HOUR

"The backfires are going to be tricky."

"I don't want to hear that it can't be done." Lauren cut him off midsentence. "All I want from you is a yes or no. Would something like that work, or are we too late?"

"Help, yes, but I don't know if they'd cover enough ground to do us any good. In a high-wind scenario, sparks and burning debris can stay airborne for a mile or more, and reignite whatever's on the other side. If the men and equipment are in exactly the right place, a thousand tiny fires are manageable. If the burns have time to spread, then we have a thousand large fires that are growing. There's a delicate balance to these things. If we don't do everything right, then the cure can be worse than the disease."

"You're talking about large fires on the wrong side of the backburn?" Lauren asked.

"Yes, I once heard Adam call it the Hydra Effect. Put out one fire, create two others."

"Those lab people and all their fancy words," Lauren said. "Ernie, hang in there, you'll have a Global Hawk in one hour, which is just about first light. I need to make some more phone calls. I'll be in touch."

"Lauren," Ernie said. "If we don't change the governor's tactics, this could be the worst fire in history."

"I'm well aware of the stakes," Lauren said. She disconnected with Ernie and massaged her temples as her phone lit up. Expecting it to be Calvin, she frowned when she saw it was General Curtis calling. She'd forgotten she owed him a call and she took a deep breath, blew it out, and answered.

"Dr. McKenna, General Curtis, how nice to finally get to speak with you."

"Sir, I apologize for the delay," Lauren said. "The situation here is in flux, and I wanted to be able to give you solid intelligence despite our dwindling space-based assets."

"Can you?" Curtis asked. "Can you give me any solid intelligence?"

"I believe I can, and unless we implement the correct steps imme-diately, this fire has the distinct possibility of raging out of control all the way up the coast and engulfing San Jose, San Francisco, and probably Oakland as well."

"I'm listening."

"I know it sounds far-fetched, but the worst of the high winds are going to start blowing within the next hour. I have an idea, but if we wait on the governor of California, it might be too late."

"What's the governor doing?"

"He took the job of firefighting away from the people who know what they are doing, and put it in the hands of lawsuit-averse pol-iticians. He and his staff are in reactive mode, covering their asses. General, you're in the Air Force, I'm sure you're aware of operation Thunderclap, the WWII joint British and American operation to destroy Dresden. You've no doubt seen pictures of the aftermath of the incendiary bombings of both Dresden and Tokyo. Imagine those same images, only it's San Francisco."

"I'm familiar with Thunderclap and Dresden—not one of the military's finer moments."

"General, the wind just started blowing here on the Monterey Peninsula, remnants from a Pacific Coast tropical storm, Evangeline. The Forest Service fire lab just ran several models that predict the possibility of a firestorm even bigger than the one that engulfed Dresden in 1945."

"That's a hell of a fire," Curtis said without emotion. "If I'd heard those words from anyone else but you, Dr. McKenna, I'd tell them they were full of crap. What's your idea?"

"My job at the Defense Intelligence Agency is to assess meteo-rological conditions and their impact on the outcome and effec-tiveness of proposed military operations. Once this mechanism triggers, and the flares and rotation begins, it'll be too late to react. You and I have worked on hundreds of missions over the years, and what I'm asking for is an airstrike. Cal Fire and the Forest Service started several backburns in an effort to fight the fire. The governor has stopped them out of fear of destroying private property. General, what we need is one huge backburn to have any hope of stopping this fire."

"Define huge backburn."

"The burn I have in mind is the kind one gets when a great deal of napalm is dropped from airplanes."

"Jesus Christ, Lauren!" Curtis exploded in what sounded like both shock and skepticism. "You want me to use Air Force jets to bomb civilian targets on United States soil?"

"Yes, sir, I do."

"Logistically, it's possible," Curtis answered. "The only way I can get behind something like this is if you can assure me no civilians get hurt."

"We use the Global Hawk to identify and evacuate people beforehand."

"That's the easy part. From a political point of view, do you have any idea what needs to take place first?"

"Sure I do," Lauren replied calmly. "Skip the governor of California. You call the White House and have the President place the entire area under martial law."

CHAPTER THIRTY

DONOVAN FELT THE heat in the room rising. The sight of the roaring flames through the window was something straight from hell. Flaming branches tumbled and blew through the front yard. They didn't have time to roll William through the kitchen and out to the truck before the wall of flames reached them. Donovan limped for the door.

"What are you doing?" Shannon asked.

"Move away from the window. Cover yourself and William with blankets or pillows," Donovan called over his shoulder. He reached the truck and fired up the engine and punched the gas to jump the truck forward before he slammed on the brakes. He selected reverse, turned in the seat, and aimed the still lowered tailgate straight at the shattered picture window and stepped on the gas pedal. The tailgate hit just below the windowsill, and a combination of masonry, wood splinters, and glass exploded from the impact. The tailgate was now only inches above the floor. Donovan slid out of the cab, landing on his good foot, grabbed the pry bar, and using it as a makeshift cane, he limped into the house.

"Help me lift him up into the bed of the truck," Donovan said the instant Shannon raced back into the room with an armful of soaked bedding, which she heaved into the truck.

Lifting together, they managed to rest two wheels of the chaise lounge onto the metal bed of the truck. Donovan moved to the opposite end, and using the pry bar, began to leverage the metal-framed chaise up into the bed while Shannon pulled. Once Donovan positioned the second set of wheels onto the smooth metal, they rolled William as close to the truck's cab as possible. Donovan used the pry bar to clean the broken glass from what was left of the rear window. Now he and Shannon could talk while he drove. Then he jammed the bar behind the rear wheels of the chaise to prevent it from rolling.

"I'll stay with William. Get us out of here!" Shannon called as she opened the first wet blanket and draped it over William's legs. She picked up the second and set it down where it covered William's torso and head, and then she pulled the rest over her head.

Donovan pulled himself up into the cab. He could feel the heat singeing his hair. "Hang on, we're going to go fast!" he called out through the missing rear glass.

"Do it," Shannon said. "But no sharp turns or we'll dump William into the bed of the truck."

The smoke was getting thick, and Donovan lifted the pillowcase tied around his neck and covered his mouth and nose. The wind seemed to start clearing the smoke, and then just as suddenly the visibility dropped to near zero. Donovan powered toward Cyprus Point Golf Course. He hoped from there they could reverse their earlier course and end up in Pacific Grove.

A shower of glowing embers rained down ahead of them. Donovan slowed and swerved smoothly to miss the worst of them. Then he accelerated until he spotted the turn. Following their previous tire tracks, he drove as fast as he could, taking quick glances back at Shannon and William, making sure they seemed okay. As his eyes shifted to the dashboard, he found a red warning light flashing.

He eased off the gas. The engine was overheating. The temperature gauge was nearing the red line. He swore under his breath. If the truck quit in the middle of the golf course, their options would plummet. He swung to the left, crossed another fairway, destroying a decorative wooden fence and manicured shrubbery, coming to a stop in the side yard of a home bordering the golf course.

The block seemed untouched by fire, though the smoke still raced past and the glow to the south told him the fire was coming.

"What's going on?" Shannon asked through the window.

"The engine is overheating," Donovan said. "Hang on. We need to find another vehicle or at least some water. The quickest way to do that is to use the truck and knock down some garage doors."

Shannon resolutely gripped the frame of the chaise lounge with one hand and put her other hand around William.

Satisfied that they were secure, Donovan allowed the truck to roll down the driveway, cross the street, and then slowly climb the driveway until the grill of the Ford was up against the wood of the garage door. He pushed gently on the gas until the door collapsed inward and the steel rails fell to the floor of the empty garage.

He backed out, and spotted the trail of green antifreeze leaking from under the hood of the Ford. "Shannon, there's a faucet on the side of the house. Can you see if there's any water pressure?"

Shannon jumped from the bed. She ran to the valve, twisted, and waited. Nothing. So she hurried back into the truck.

Donovan glanced at the dashboard. The engine temperature was climbing higher. He drove to the next house and repeated the process. This time, as the door caved in, the truck's headlights illuminated a vehicle on one side of the double garage. It was small and wrapped in a greenish tarp.

Donovan used the pry bar as a cane to ease himself down from the cab. He limped to the vehicle, and with one pull, he yanked

off the cover. Underneath sat a bright red early model Chevrolet
Stingray. The two-seat roadster was beautiful, but useless for three
people.

Shannon jumped down from the bed of the truck, flashlight in
hand, but when she saw the car, her shoulders slumped.

"Can you dig in the medical supplies and see if you can find a
scalpel?" Donovan asked as he took the flashlight from her hand
and limped to the door that led into the house. "I'll be right back."

The hallway led through a laundry room and into the kitchen.
Flashlight in hand, Donovan first verified that there was bottled
water in the refrigerator. Then he selected two deep-sided skillets
hanging from a suspended rack. He swept a dozen bottles of water
into the pans, and made his way back to the garage. Grimacing
from pain, he eased himself down until he sat heavily on the concrete and then lay flat on his back and aimed the light under the
Corvette.

"Hand me the scalpel and get ready to slide one of the skillets
under the car." Donovan spotted the lower radiator hose and sliced
the rubber cleanly. He was rewarded as greenish fluid began to pour
onto the floor. An instant later, Shannon placed a pan under the
leak to catch the flow.

"What else?" Shannon asked.

"There's more water in the fridge. Grab as many as you can carry."

Donovan used the light from the truck's headlights to keep an eye
on the process, and when the skillet neared full, he slid out the first
skillet and slid the second one into place. Using his arms, he pulled
himself to his feet and gave the car an affectionate pat. Years ago
he'd owned a Corvette not unlike this one. The transfusion might
not last long, but it would hopefully get them into Pacific Grove
where they had far more options. Shannon came back, her arms full
of bottled water, which she set down near the front of the truck.

"Can you pop the hood?" Donovan asked as he limped to the front of the Ford. His sense of urgency and frustration was growing at how long it took him to accomplish simple tasks. He heard the latch release and lifted the hood. He pulled off his leather jacket and twisted off the cap to the radiator, turning his head as the steam rose. "Hand me one of the pans."

"Here," Shannon said, using two hands to lift the fluid-filled pan from the floor.

"Perfect," Donovan said as he poured the antifreeze into the reservoir. "Take this pan, grab the other one. We'll repeat the process as long as the Corvette antifreeze keeps draining." Shannon handed up the second one, and then started twisting lids off of water bottles. Working in unison, the two of them added water and antifreeze until the reservoir was full. Donovan tightened the cap, slammed the hood shut, and moved toward the driver's side. He cranked the ignition and watched as the engine temperature dropped. Putting the truck in gear, he called over his shoulder, "We're out of here."

Shannon once again did her best to cover William and she gripped the chaise lounge. "Go!"

As he backed away from the house, Donovan could see the fire had drawn much closer. Something caught his eye through the smoke, and he rolled down the window to get a better look.

"Oh my God," Shannon cried out from the bed of the truck. She tapped Donovan on the shoulder and pointed off to their left.

Through a break in the smoke he could see the leading edge of the fire stretch across the horizon. Flames climbed high into the air where they swirled and licked upwards, twirling in the darkness. They spun and joined, collapsed, rejoined again, and intensified until there were three distinct spirals of flame. The wind strengthened and Donovan watched as trees bent, and shrubbery, as well as branches, papers, and other debris were pulled toward the fire.

Explosions went off like staccato reports of thunder as anything flammable succumbed to the blaze. Donovan could hardly believe what he was seeing, how fast the fire was moving. As the F-250 roared down the street, Donovan heard Shannon start screaming for him to go faster.

CHAPTER THIRTY-ONE

LAUREN STOOD ON the bridge as the freshening wind kicked up whitecaps. She could feel the ship begin to roll and pitch beneath her feet. Below her on the flight deck, crewmen were inspecting the chains that secured the helicopter to the deck, as well as clearing the ladders and lights from earlier.

"What in the hell?" Ryan slid out of his chair, hurried to where Lauren stood, and raised his binoculars.

She raised hers as well and scanned the horizon. Lauren glimpsed a tentacle of fire spiral upward in the distance and disappear, then another one appeared. The second one lasted twice as long.

"They've begun, haven't they?" Ryan asked.

Lauren felt her stomach tighten with fear. The bursts were rotating spires of fire, building to the point that they reached above the layer of smoke and broke into the clear air above. The politicians in Sacramento sitting on their hands were about to witness a shocking change in the fire they were assigned to fight. Lauren had no idea what General Curtis had done with her suggestion, but the flares would soon have everyone's attention. There wasn't anyone left for her to reach out to for help. She hoped Donovan was aware of the shifting nature of the fire and was making his escape. As the spiraling monsters leapt higher into the sky, she faced the reality that he may already be lost to her, and her emotions began to undo her.

"Lauren," Michael called out as he came onto the bridge. "What's happening? I was just with Montero and Ethan down in the shop and headed up here when I heard someone on deck say there are flares of some kind on the horizon. What's going on?"

"The flares we can see are from the fire," Lauren said. "The wind is picking up and what we feared most is starting."

"Ryan, with all due respect," Lauren said. "Can we make this ship go any faster? Anyone who's survived this long will be running for the shore."

"Helm, make our speed fifteen knots," Ryan said. "I want all lights forward, extra lookouts posted port and starboard."

"Thank you," Lauren said to Ryan with a respectful nod. She turned toward Michael. "Have you spoken with Janie? Last I heard she was talking with some Cal Fire people about helicopter rescue routes. If we have helicopters to pull out survivors, now is the time to get them in the air."

"I'm on it," Michael said as he spun and went in search of Janie.

Lauren's phone rang. A glance at the screen identified the caller as General Curtis. She took a deep breath and answered. "Dr. McKenna."

"Dr. McKenna, General Curtis here. I've been in contact with the Global Hawk Ground Control Station at Beale Air Force Base. Monterey Peninsula is just now at the far range of the drone's sensor array, but I'm told the phenomena you spoke to me about earlier may have become a reality."

"General, I can see the spires from the *Buckley*, and we're twelve miles offshore. Can you tell me exactly what the drone is seeing?"

"Check your e-mail; I've sent you the link to connect directly to the Global Hawk sensor array. As the on-site liaison under my command, I've given you full authority on this. I've also sent you a secure phone line to Beale so you can communicate directly with the two men controlling the Global Hawk when you and I are finished. Everyone on the Global Hawk team at Beale has been instructed to follow your orders. What I want right this moment is your assessment of what I'm seeing on the live feed from the Global Hawk."

Using her encrypted DIA passwords, she opened a secure link and clicked files until she was looking at a raw infrared image of Monterey Peninsula taken from a long way away. Lauren finally had a real-time view of everything happening around her. "General, stand by, I'm just now getting a visual feed from the Global Hawk." Fully familiar with the sophisticated software, Lauren toggled and manipulated the controls to magnify the area of the screen she'd selected. Seconds later, the expanded area was as crisp as if she were seeing it from a mile away.

"Doctor," General Curtis said. "What do you see?"

"At first glance, it looks like a boiling cluster of thunderstorms. I count as many as seven areas of rotation. They appear to be climbing and twisting as they grow. I can confirm that this is supported by what we've observed visually. The patterns of smoke surrounding each vortex clearly show the powerful suction within the rotation. Each vortex is pulling in massive amounts of oxygen."

"Doctor, I need facts, and what you think is going to happen next."

"The winds inside these firestorms are going to reach a hundred miles per hour. The temperature will probably climb to fifteen hundred degrees centigrade, so everything burns. It will keep going until it runs out of fuel. This fire is currently destroying the Monterey Peninsula. We're seeing multiple funnels in a single burn area. My immediate concern is that with the wind, the burn areas could merge, and the rotation become one massive spinning super-fire. The largest tornado ever recorded was almost three miles in diameter. What we're seeing now has the potential to develop into a similar-sized event. General, this could be our only chance to stop this fire. Once it reaches San Jose, it's doubtful we can do anything to keep it from consuming San Francisco, and perhaps Oakland, as well."

"Thank you, Dr. McKenna, I understand your sense of urgency. Has your boss, Calvin, seen any of this?"

"Unless he has the same Global Hawk feed I'm looking at, no," Lauren answered. "He's next on my list of people to call."

"Don't bother," General Curtis said. "I'll send him the images myself and then he and I will talk. I want you to move forward and discuss this enhanced backburn with your experts. Pull in everyone you need, but do it fast. I need one condition before I even consider asking the president for an order of martial law."

"What's that?"

"First, this needs to work, so pick this backburn area carefully. Second, as I said earlier, I need assurance that no American citizens are going to be killed in the process of Air Force jets delivering their ordinance. From experience, we both know it's hard to drop bombs and not hurt anyone."

"Yes, sir, General." Lauren's mind jump-started to everything she needed to do and the order in which it needed to be done. One more glance at the image from the Global Hawk confirmed she needed to work fast.

"I hope you're wrong about needing to implement this solution," General Curtis said, his voice retaining its firm edge. "Martial law, by definition, is order, implemented by men trained for chaos. It's a demanding and uncomfortable scenario."

"More uncomfortable than watching thousands of people burn?" Lauren replied and, without waiting for the general to answer, she disconnected the call and punched in the number he'd given her for Global Hawk Command at Beale Air Force Base.

"Operations, Colonel Martin speaking."

"Colonel Martin, this is Dr. Lauren McKenna, Defense Intelligence Agency. I believe General Curtis has been in touch with you?"

"Dr. McKenna, yes. I'm transferring you to flight bay eight. You'll be talking with Lieutenant Sebastian Ruiz, the aircraft commander."

Lauren was encouraged by the swift action and glad her call was directed to the individuals in charge of the Global Hawk. She pictured the darkened room with an array of computer screens and flight information. There'd be the pilot; the other person would be a sensor operator. The Global Hawk itself orbited pilotless, at up to sixty thousand feet, and had the range to remain there for hours. Right now, she needed the matter-of-fact approach of a pilot.

"Dr. McKenna, Lieutenant Ruiz here. What can I do for you today?"

Lauren immediately liked his calm, easy manner. "First of all, please call me Lauren. I'm a senior analyst with the DIA, so I'm familiar with the specifications and capabilities of your sensor array, as well as your aircraft, so please, talk to me like one of the guys."

"Okay, Lauren, my name is Sebastian. Let's get to work. General Curtis asked us to give you whatever you want. Where do we start?"

"I want to add the real-time data stream from the Global Hawk to two more recipients."

"Sure, send me their e-mail."

Lauren's fingers quickly pulled up both Ernie's and Adam's contact pages, grouped their e-mail addresses together, and sent them to Sebastian. "Okay, I just sent them to you. The next thing I want to do is plot and project the fire's progress. From what I saw earlier, I'm guessing the drone is still a ways offshore?"

"Yes," Sebastian said. "We're at fifty-five thousand feet, and we'll be at optimum sensor position in twenty minutes. What do you need us to look for specifically?"

"People," Lauren said bluntly. "How long before you're able to locate individuals who might be in danger from the fire?"

"Fifteen minutes," Sebastian said. "Though, I need you to understand that the conditions aren't perfect for picking out specific individuals. With so many hot spots on the ground, we get intermittent images and false negatives. If there's good contrast, as in cooler air surrounding the individuals, then we can spot them. If they're inside a three-story building, and the roof or an upper floor of the building is on fire, sometimes all we'll see is the structure. Also, we've learned that, at some point, if the air above the ground is superheated to a certain point, the sensors only show us heat, no details."

"I understand," Lauren said. "Do the best you can. The good news is I doubt there are very many people still hanging around."

"From what I can see, I hope you're right. Is there a particular area you need us to scan?"

Lauren bit her lip. She wanted to tell him Pebble Beach, but that wasn't the area where the backburn was going to be launched. "You'll be receiving the coordinates shortly from Cal Fire," Lauren said and then closed her eyes and repeated to herself what she'd told Calvin earlier. If she concentrated on helping everyone she could, Donovan, Shannon, and William might be among them. Though at the moment, she ignored the fact that she was conspiring with the Pentagon to increase the burn area, which could close off any chance of escape they might still have.

"Okay, I just received e-mails from someone named Ernie, and someone else named Adam. They want to know who I am, and where I got the image of the fire."

"Can I put you on hold while I talk to them? They have information we'll need," Lauren said.

"Let's leave this link open," Sebastian said. "Lauren, I'm sitting in a comfortable chair, safely on the ground at Beale Air Force Base.

The Global Hawk is on autopilot, and my sensor operator, David, is next to me making sure everything runs smoothly. If you want, we can pick them up on a conference call and have a staff meeting."

Lauren flipped through the charts until she saw where she'd jotted down the phone numbers earlier, and relayed them to Sebastian. First Ernie and then Adam came onto the line.

"Gentleman, you can call me Sebastian. I'm in command of a Global Hawk unmanned aerial platform that I'm bringing into position over the fire. Also with us is Dr. Lauren McKenna, and right this moment, the three of you have my undivided attention."

"Lauren," Ernie spoke first. "The images are terrifying—this thing is exploding faster than I imagined."

"I agree," Adam added. "I count seven separate clusters with distinct signs of rotation. If they join, hell, if even four of them join, we could have the equivalent of an F-3 tornado, only made of high-velocity flames, not clouds and rain."

"Ernie," Lauren said. "We talked about the backfires. You wanted more time, but that's not an option. Do you remember what I told you I might be able to get?"

"A bigger backburn?"

"Exactly. The Pentagon is analyzing this. I need you to designate an area to ignite, one that will be big enough to slow this fire. We'll use the Global Hawk to make sure the area you chose is big enough to work, and it also needs to be completely devoid of people. We can't have any casualties from this plan. Can the two of you work up a map for the Pentagon that gives us a chance of stopping this thing?"

"Yes, well . . . maybe," Adam replied. "It's going to be a pretty big area, and the fire needs time to consume all available fuel."

"Napalm is what we'll be using as an accelerant," Lauren said. "It should provide the coverage you're asking for. In my mind, we start a huge backfire, nestle it up next to the inland flooding of the

Salinas River caused by the tsunami, and hopefully stop this thing. I know that sparks can ride the wind, but if you positioned your ground and aerial units north of the backburn, you could be ready to jump on all of the tiny fires."

"The scale is beyond anything we've ever dealt with before," Ernie said. "Though, when you simplify it like that, it almost makes sense."

"It does make sense," Adam said excitedly. "I just plugged in some preliminary numbers into the computer. You're right, Lauren, we need a huge backburn, but the program says we can create one that could reduce the main fire as much as eighty-five percent."

"Can you send us the map of the projected backburn needed?" Lauren asked as the first rush of an actual solution gave her a chill.

"There," Adam said. "It's sent. I'll admit it's rough, and I will modify it as we get more information, but the initial numbers say if we burn two separate areas in front of the fire, we'll starve it for lack of fuel."

Lauren waited impatiently until the e-mail arrived, and she furiously clicked the icons until the map appeared on her screen. As she pulled in the details and grasped the boundaries of the two areas Adam had drawn, she felt her hopes waver. She saw an irregular rectangle nearly five miles long and a mile wide, as well as a smaller rectangle farther east near Salinas. "Adam, are you serious? This is what it takes?"

"Adam," Ernie cried out. "I see it. This is brilliant. The fires and flooded area in Seaside already act as a block. Highway 68 was always our projected border. You've staggered the boxes around the areas flooded by the tsunami. I can see this working."

"How much time do we have for all of this?" Lauren asked.

"I've only seen the one snapshot from the Global Hawk," Adam said. "Are there sequential shots to predict the speed of the individual clusters?"

"Yes, they're on their way," Sebastian said.

Lauren pulled up the data, and after quickly comparing it to the earlier feeds, she estimated the movement of all of the fires.

"Oh wow," Adam said. "I'll plug all this into the computer in a second to confirm. But right now I estimate that we'd have to have the fuel consumed in the backburn area in one hour and twenty minutes, or it'll be too late."

"Sebastian," Lauren asked. "Are we close enough to the burn area for the sensors to pick up any people who might be at risk?"

"The slant range makes it a little iffy, so the count is probably a little low until we get directly overhead. Right now the computer says there are at least two dozen people inside the boundaries."

"Ernie, do whatever it takes to get those people out of there," Lauren said. "I need to call the Pentagon and relay this information."

"Lauren, you might also want to know that we're picking up hundreds of infrared signatures of other people."

"Where?" Lauren asked, though she already knew the answer.

"All over, but mostly between the main fire and the one you want to set."

CHAPTER THIRTY-TWO

SPEEDING DOWN THE roadway, Donovan glanced over his shoulder at Shannon and William, and saw hundreds of small burns in the fabric from the swirling embers that filled the air. Not far behind was a wall of flames—just glancing at it made the skin on his face grow hot. He turned his attention back to the road, and pulled up the leather collar to protect the exposed flesh on his neck.

Buffeted by swirling winds, the truck skidded and lurched down the winding roads as Donovan left Pebble Beach behind and raced through Pacific Grove. He passed a huge tree being whipped by the gusts. Moments after they passed, he saw the entire tree began to ignite, the burning branches sucked up into the sky toward the rotating inferno. He swerved up a driveway, powered through a yard to avoid downed power lines, then slammed back down to the asphalt as the truck came off of the curb.

Coming down the hill, the smoke was less thick. He pulled the mask away from his mouth and nose, and let it drop loosely around his neck. The engine temperature was slowly creeping upwards again. Highway 68 was straight ahead, and the route looked clear so far. Explosions boomed in the distance as propane tanks or automobile fuel tanks went off, sparked by the fire and intense heat.

Again he glanced over his shoulder at Shannon and William. "Shannon," Donovan called out and waited for her face to appear from under the blanket. "How are you doing?"

"I think William is starting to come around," Shannon said. "He started groaning and jerking and then kind of settled down again. He might need another injection."

"Not unless you can do it while we're driving," Donovan said. "We put a little distance between us and the fire, but it feels like the wind is blowing harder. Highway 68 is up ahead. We're going to try and take it out of the city."

"Just hurry," Shannon said.

Donovan threaded his way through the remains of a five-car pileup in the middle of an intersection. He made a right turn and breathed a small sigh of relief as he powered down Highway 68. The road was clear and he hit sixty miles per hour. When the pavement started to curve, Donovan was forced to slow. Then suddenly, he slammed on the brakes and the truck fishtailed to a halt. Behind him, Shannon popped up to see what was happening. A hundred yards down the road, advancing flames burst from the trees. The blaze quickly leaped all four lanes of the highway, and the truck shook in the growing winds. When the flames reached the opposite side of the road and moved through an open field, Donovan understood the entire wall was rotating.

"Hang on to William," he yelled above the roar of the inferno and made a hard U-turn and headed back the way they came.

"Where are we going?" Shannon called out from the bed of the truck as she tried to keep the flapping blankets in place.

"Down toward the ocean, near the aquarium. I'm hoping the water has retreated enough to give us a narrow area of saturated ground to keep us out of the fire."

"What about a boat?"

"I was thinking about that, too," Donovan said. "If the road is passable, we should be able to get to the marina."

Donovan drove as fast as he could. The closer they got to the ocean, the greater the carnage from the tsunami. Mangled wreckage was stacked against houses and trees, overturned cars combined with dead bodies. Four blocks up the hill from Cannery Row, Donovan made a right turn and slowed. Downed power lines draped the road, and a huge heap of upended trees were piled up in the cross street. Donovan went up the hill and discovered a street that looked more passable. The continuing explosions, invisible through the smoke, gave him a rough estimate of the fire's location. He caught sight of the flames and realized the swirls seemed to last longer and spur the inferno to even greater heights. For the first time, Donovan pictured the fire as a living, breathing entity, moving closer to consume them all.

"Hang on, we're headed for the marina." Donovan spun the wheel and picked his way down the tsunami-littered street. The muted light from the gathering dawn began to illuminate buildings and trees that weren't burning. They were still on what amounted to a side street. The main thoroughfare was several blocks down the hill, and eventually took motorists through a tunnel that would lead them straight to the marina. Donovan blinked at the smoke that seemed to suddenly obscure everything, and then just as quickly lifted to provide a view into the distance. As he sped toward the center of Monterey, he caught glimpses of distinct landmarks and discovered that the bulk of downtown Monterey was burning.

Donovan braked as he reached a street that was marked as a dead end. Beyond an embankment and a fence sat the grounds of the Presidio. Donovan turned downhill, and as he reached the main road, he slowed.

"Are you kidding me!" Shannon said with equal parts despair and anger as she took in the sight straight ahead.

Donovan could see the first anchorage, the Coast Guard pier. Whatever boats had been moored in the breakwater were now splintered and broken into multiple piles that blocked the road. Just beyond sat the pier and marina; the rows of shops and restaurants that lined the wharf had been wiped into oblivion by the tsunami. The boats in the marina were either sunk or lifted far inland where a funeral pyre of burning yachts had ignited whatever structure had stopped their progress. The Portola Hotel, an icon next to the wharf, was burning brightly. A block away, the Marriott was starting to burn, as well as other buildings reaching into the center of town.

Frustrated, Donovan slammed his hand into the steering wheel. He remained silent and spun the truck around, and with a quick check of the slowly rising engine temperature, powered up the hill where he turned into a parking lot. Moments later, they were rumbling across the manicured grounds of the Presidio. Donovan concentrated on the scene ahead. On either side of them were raging fires. He thought at times he could hear the roar of the flames above the Ford's powerful engine. Behind them in the smoke, the twisting, undulating body of flames scared him most. He'd never seen a fire tornado, and he knew very little about them, only that they operated on the same premise as a dust devil. He weaved between rows of trees, turned onto an asphalt path, and drove even faster.

"William's in terrible pain," Shannon called out. "I'm going to inject him again."

"Shannon, straight ahead is Highway 68. It was the evacuation route we heard about earlier. If there's one road they're going to try to keep open it's that one. Wait three minutes and I promise it'll be far smoother than it is right now."

"I'm going to try anyway."

Without taking his eyes from the road, Donovan swung the truck from the narrow path onto a side street. He fought his temptation to floor the truck, but longevity of the engine was paramount. They were past the point of stopping and hunting for water to put in the radiator. The warning light was on again, far sooner than Donovan expected. He could smell the engine getting hot.

"How much further to the highway?" Shannon called over his shoulder. "It's too rough. I can't get the needle into the vial."

"Hang on. We're not going to make it to the highway. I have to get off this road." Donovan swung the truck across the pavement, downward through a ditch, and popped up on the other side. He drove the dying truck down a winding road until he was rewarded by the sight of an eight-foot-high fence topped with barbed wire.

"Oh my God, what are you doing?" Shannon yelled.

"Get down!" Donovan swung the wheel and aimed the Ford at a locked gate. With steam pouring out from under the hood, he pushed the ailing engine and snapped the chain. The gate swung open, and he squealed the tires, cutting around the edge of a building.

"Where are you taking us?"

Rounding the building, Donovan spotted the last thing he expected to find. Silhouetted by the coming sunrise and the raging fires sat the Eco-Watch Gulfstream. Seconds later, he brought the truck to a halt and shut down the tortured engine.

"Donovan, I need some help!" Shannon shouted as she knelt in the bed of the truck and tried to steady William as he began to thrash on the chaise.

As fast as he could, Donovan limped around to the bed of the truck, but instead of helping Shannon, he leaned in, and using all his strength, rolled the chaise toward the tailgate. William reacted instantly and cried out in pain. "William, it's Donovan. Can you hear me?"

"Where are we?" William cried out as he tried to move.

"Give him the injection," Donovan told Shannon. He leaned close to William. "We're going to help you with the pain, okay? Then we're going to move you."

"What the hell are we doing?" Shannon glared at Donovan, confused.

Donovan motioned for her to turn around so she could finally see the Eco-Watch Gulfstream. "We're getting out of here."

CHAPTER THIRTY-THREE

LAUREN WATCHED AS Ryan read a message a crewman handed him. In an instant, she saw his facial expression turn from quiet determination to frustration. He folded the piece of paper and crushed it in his fist.

"Ryan?" Lauren looked up from the computer feed of the fires marching through Pacific Grove. "What's wrong?"

"It's official," Ryan said. "This entire area is now under martial law. We've been ordered to move the *Buckley* twenty-five miles off-shore and let the military do their job."

"What about the survivors? What's being done about them?" Lauren said, knowing the answer. She'd been betrayed. She'd pushed a bold solution based on science, gathered the resources to make it happen, and now the ugly truth was that the people the Global Hawk had spotted were trapped. Possibly, her husband, William, and Shannon were among the people she'd helped condemn.

"Lauren," Janie called out as she and Michael hurried onto the bridge. "We were just told by Cal Fire to bugger off. What's going on?"

Lauren felt what little control she had slipping away. Martial law stripped local government of their power. The laws and rights of the Constitution fell by the wayside, and all that remained was the military. "We just got word that the entire area is now under martial law. We've been ordered to withdraw while the military takes over all operations."

"At everyone else's expense?" Michael asked. "How close is the nearest military ship or helicopter?"

"Not close enough to do any good." Lauren stared at her phone and gathered in her emotions as she tried to decide who to call first, though she already knew what General Curtis would say.

"What are you thinking?" Michael asked Lauren.

"There are hundreds of people that should be rescued, and aren't going to be. The military is focused on the fire. I feel so helpless. William, Donovan, and Shannon are out there somewhere. The Pentagon wanted me to ensure that no civilians were killed in the actual bombing. Those people were evacuated. What's left are the people trapped between the two fires. Acceptable losses are the official term for those people."

Michael went to Lauren as she seemed to deflate and sit heavily in her chair. "Lauren," Michael asked. "What's this on the monitor?"

Lauren swiveled her chair to look. There were four distinct infrared images being broadcast by Sebastian via the Global Hawk. The lower left square was the one that grabbed her attention. A vehicle had just parked on the ramp next to the Eco-Watch Gulfstream. Compared to the surrounding areas, the vehicle glowed nearly white hot. Lauren brought her phone to her ear. "Sebastian?"

"Still here," Sebastian replied. "I figured the activity at the Monterey airport would get your attention. I haven't seen a vehicle move in that area since we arrived. I'm working on bringing everything to bear on what's happening. Hang on."

"It's got to be Donovan. I can see two people outside the vehicle," Michael said. "It's a pickup truck; it could be the one we saw earlier on the television footage. The engine is super-hot—it's glowing big-time in the infrared spectrum. So much so, I can't see what's inside the cab, or even make out what's in the bed."

The image flickered on the screen and the ghostly infrared was replaced by the high-definition feed from the Global Hawk's

Synthetic Aperture Radar. Lauren and Michael both leaned in to study the real-time image.

"It's Donovan," Michael said as he pointed to the man at the tailgate. "Shannon is the one standing in the bed of the truck."

"Is that William?" Lauren said as she moved closer to the screen. "Someone is lying in the bed of the truck next to a stretcher. That's got to be William."

"We have a big problem," Michael said. "The airplane is sitting there in the dark. Donovan can't see the damage. He's expecting the Gulfstream to be flyable."

"Michael," Lauren said. "How long until he realizes it won't work?"

"Not long. When he climbs into the cockpit, he'll see the left engine firewall has been closed, and both fire bottles have been used. He'll know we had an engine fire. Then there's the fuel situation— the fuel quantity is displayed on one of the screens that won't work. We didn't land with very much. My guess is the Gulfstream only has twenty minutes of fuel aboard, and that's not allowing for what's leaked out of the wings since we landed. Let's hope once he sees how messed up the airplane is, he'll try to find a different one, or at least another car, and keep moving."

"Sebastian," Lauren said into the phone. "Listen carefully. Is there any chance we can get a helicopter or a plane into the Monterey airport to rescue our people?"

"None," Sebastian said. "The airspace around this entire area has been listed as restricted. It's now no different than the airspace around the White House. Cal Fire is in the air, but they're working north, operating multiple heavy tankers, dumping water downwind of the burn area. There's no way anyone is close enough to get in there in the time remaining."

Lauren paused for a second and wondered what she'd done, and forced herself to focus on the immediate problem—trying to help

Donovan. "Can you give me an estimate on how long until the leading edge of the fires reaches the Monterey airport?"

"Is it him, your husband?" Sebastian asked.

"Yes."

"I estimate fifteen to twenty minutes," Sebastian said. "The bigger issue might be the incoming airstrike. The first F-18s are inbound. They've been cleared to fly supersonic. They'll make their first bombing run in seven minutes. The second wave will execute sequential bombing runs until both backburn areas have been fully saturated. If you remember Adam's computer chart, the western boundary of his scheduled burn backs up to the airport. The fighters are coming, and we both know that this isn't a precision bombing. This is low, fast, and dirty."

"The Gulfstream is not airworthy," Lauren continued. "From the infrared images, we think the truck he arrived in is compromised. If he finds another vehicle, does he have an escape route?"

"Once the fighters arrive, he'll be cut off."

"Keep me posted," Lauren said to Sebastian. She glanced at Michael. "We're out of options. Is there even the smallest chance Donovan can get the Gulfstream airborne? Then, if he does, what can he do, where can he go?"

"The problem is I'm not sure he'll even try once he's in the cockpit," Michael answered as he rifled through the charts on Lauren's desk.

"What would you do?" Lauren asked.

"I'd try to find a different plane and fly away from the fire and smoke as quickly as possible." Michael glanced at the monitor. "The Gulfstream isn't going to have any electronic flight instruments. They all failed. He's basically going to be flying a five-hundred-mile-per-hour Piper Cub. He'll need to get out of the smoke before he has any chance to land safely. If he can't, then he's going to be flying blind."

"Would he come toward us?" Lauren said. "He knows we're out here. Would he try to get to us and then ditch?"

"I highly doubt it. We both know he's not wired to put himself into the ocean on purpose. Besides, flying a Gulfstream by himself, with William on a stretcher and only Shannon to assist, I think ditching would be the last thing he'd want to do." Michael leaned over the aviation map to study possible options. "All of the navigation is computer generated, but he won't have any help there at all. If anything he'll fly north towards the Bay Area, expecting to have enough fuel to reach San Jose."

"What happens when he realizes he doesn't have enough fuel?" Lauren asked.

"He won't know until the engines start to flame out and shut down. Then it's a flat spot, a field maybe, or a road." Michael pushed himself away from the table. "That's all he has. The Global Hawk will be able to track him. We might be able to watch, but there's no guarantee we'll like what we see."

"What's going on? Is he hurt?" Lauren asked as she looked closer at the computer screen where Donovan began moving erratically from the truck toward the Gulfstream.

"He's limping; his thigh looks like it's wrapped," Michael said. "That's going to slow him down."

Lauren watched her husband favor his damaged leg, make it to the nose of the Gulfstream and struggle to plant himself in an effort to open the cabin door. As the hatch pivoted free from the fuselage, the stairs stretched outward and settled to the concrete. He turned and started toward the truck but stopped. He stood as if studying the airplane and then went to the wing, touched the metal, rubbed his fingers together, then brought them to his nose.

"Kerosene," Michael whispered. "He's noticed the leaks. Come on, Donovan, quit wasting time. Look at the scorched paint running from the engine to the tail. Find another plane."

Donovan limped around the wingtip and stood for a moment as if taking in the entire airplane, before returning to the airstair and struggling up the stairs.

"It won't take him long now," Michael said.

"Sebastian," Lauren said into her phone. "Can you widen the picture to show us the entire airport? We're interested in what other aircraft or structures might be undamaged."

"We took a quick look at this earlier," Sebastian replied. "The only undamaged hangar is the one closest to the Gulfstream. Though we're now picking up a growing heat source. There might be something burning inside the building."

Lauren watched the image zoom outward until the entire airport filled the screen. She could see the outline of the airliner that burned at the gate. Both airplane and terminal had been reduced to rubble as had most of the other buildings. The Gulfstream that Michael had parked in a hurry, away from any other structures, was intact. Other airplanes parked outside were all on fire or had already burned. Even the parking lots that ringed the airport were full of scorched cars. She and Michael scanned for any options that might be obvious to Donovan, and saw nothing.

"He needs to get to that hangar," Michael said. "Whatever's in there, I promise is a better choice than the Gulfstream."

Lauren tilted her head as she heard the beginnings of a high-pitched whine. The sound grew louder and got Michael's attention as well.

"What is that?" Lauren asked.

"What the hell," Michael said and ran to the forward windows.

Lauren followed and saw a shower of sparks whipped by the wind being blown into the sea. Standing next to Michael, she looked down on the helicopter deck. The helicopter was securely tied down. Crewmen were holding sturdy scaffolding in place. Other groups huddled in teams around each damaged rotor tip.

One person hunched over the blade stepped back, a powerful pneumatic saw in hand. A gloved hand raised goggles, and Lauren was surprised to see it was Janie.

"Unbelievable. I think she's trying to remove the damaged tips from the rotor blades," Michael said.

"Can that work?" Lauren asked. Her knowledge of physics and centrifugal force said no.

"Everyone I talked with said that without a doubt those blades were trashed. They said the rest of the rotor system might be junk as well." Michael spun and stormed away from the window as he headed toward the hatchway. As he glanced at the chart table, he stopped midstride, changed course, and walked straight to the computer monitor. "Oh Jesus."

CHAPTER THIRTY-FOUR

DONOVAN SAT IN the captain's seat of the Gulfstream, switched on the battery, and waited for tubes and lights to come to life, but they didn't. In the growing light of the dawn, he noticed all the things that were wrong. There had been an engine fire. Blood stains on the copilot's seat. Holes in the overhead panel along with a myriad of popped circuit breakers. He looked at the hangar to his left. There were, no doubt, perfectly good airplanes stored inside. He started doing the math on how long it would take to open the doors, find one, and escape.

"Donovan, what are we doing?" Shannon called out as she pounded up the stairs. "The wind is getting stronger."

This time when Donovan glanced across the ramp, he saw flames licking out from around the hangar door. The office attached to the side of the larger hangar collapsed in on itself and was instantly consumed by flames. He was out of options. His hands flew to the battery switch and moments later hit the switch that would start the auxiliary power unit. The APU was critical in getting the engines started, and when the small turbine engine in the tail of the Gulfstream lit and began its familiar whine, he let out a small sigh of relief. Seconds later, the APU stabilized. He switched on the generator, but instead of a great many systems springing to life, the instrument panel remained mostly dark. A quick scan of the circuit breaker panel told him a partial story.

There had been a major short somewhere, and he wasn't going to get the power to any of the normal systems. Undaunted, Donovan moved as fast as he could, down the stairs, across the ramp toward William.

"Donovan, the back of this plane is scorched. There's been a fire," Shannon cried out as she came up from behind him.

"I know," Donovan said. "Grab his legs when I lift. William, I need to get you up the stairs into the Gulfstream. I know the drugs haven't fully kicked in yet, but we have to go."

William nodded a vague understanding, his eyes distant and unfocused.

Donovan leaned in, cradled William in his arms, and began limping toward the Gulfstream. With each step, nearly unbearable pain threatened to buckle his knee. The roar of the fire consuming the nearby hangar complex propelled him on.

"Donovan, behind us!" Shannon screamed. "We need to move faster!"

A quick look. Behind them in the distance, a rotating, churning wall of flame reached up into the sky. Near enough for him to hear detonations and see debris circling the funnel. With a single-minded effort, Donovan balanced the weight of William in his arms and limped heavily up the first step. He used the stainless-steel railing of the Gulfstream's airstair for support and took the steps one at a time. Ten steps later, with his brow dripping sweat and the pain in his leg radiating through his entire body, Donovan managed to place William on the carpeted floor of the Gulfstream's aisle. He rolled to the side and pulled himself up while trying to catch his breath.

"What can I do?" Shannon asked as she raced to the top of the stairs.

"In the lavatory area there should be blankets in a closet. Find them and try to secure William. I want to keep him near the door."

Donovan hurried toward the cockpit. He turned, pushed a button, and the main door began to pull itself into the fuselage. When it came to a stop, Donovan locked and sealed the hatch.

"William's secured. The drugs are working. He's out." Shannon looked expectantly at Donovan. "Where do you want me?"

"In the cockpit. Get in the right seat."

When Donovan moved aside, she slid past, and he climbed into the pilot's seat. With a practiced eye, he began to reset everything he could, beginning with the firewall shutoff that Michael had closed fighting the earlier fire. A barrage that sounded like hail rose as the skin of the airplane was pelted by burning debris. "Strap yourself in as tight as you can. The landing gear handle is here, and the flap switch is here. They're both marked. When I call for one or the other, don't hesitate, just do what I say."

Shannon nodded wordlessly.

From memory, reinforced by having done it thousands of times, Donovan pushed the start button for the right engine. He offered a small thank-you up to the heavens as he was rewarded by the low howl that turned into a muffled roar as the big tail-mounted Rolls Royce engine rotated to life. Donovan had no engine instruments, no flight instruments, just blank tubes. There were the three standby primary instruments, but he held little faith that they would function. He tested his injured leg on the rudder pedal and discovered the intense pain he'd feared. Using sounds to guide him, he released the brake, added power, and the Gulfstream began to roll toward the runway on a single engine.

Shannon flinched and let out an involuntary scream as a loud boom seemed to fill the entire atmosphere and rattle everything around them. The first explosion was trailed by three more, and then a different rumble seemed to shake the ground and vibrate the airframe. Donovan felt the concussive wave and searched the sky for the source.

"What's happening?" Shannon cried out in panic.

Donovan leaned forward and caught a quick glimpse of a gray jet, vapor billowing off swept-back wings as it raced past just above the smoke. "Those were sonic booms; an F-18 just passed overhead."

"Why? What are they doing?" Shannon said, trying to locate the fighter in the smoke-filled sky.

"I don't know." Donovan eyed the wind, calculating how the shifting directions and velocities might affect the takeoff roll. "The only time I've ever heard of fighters going supersonic over populated areas is when there's a threat to national security."

"They won't think we're a threat, will they?" Shannon asked, her eyes darting between the panel, the sky above them, and Donovan.

"Shannon, set the flaps at twenty degrees." Donovan listened intently as the flaps made their normal sound and then stopped. He hoped they were where he wanted them. Donovan taxied fast. They reached the end of the taxiway, and he swung the Gulfstream ninety degrees and stopped short of the runway. More of the earlier rumbling shook the airplane, and again Donovan caught sight of the fighters, locked in tight turns as they screamed low overhead.

"Hurry," Shannon said, looking back the way they'd come.

Donovan glanced out the side window. The rotating blaze was nearly to the airport boundary. The intense heat was igniting trees, grass, and the nearest perimeter fence began to soften and sag. He reached up for the button that would start the second engine. Straight off the end of the runway, the raging inferno leapt and danced high into the sky where the flames licked and touched before twisting even higher into the sky. Donovan pushed the button.

CHAPTER THIRTY-FIVE

"THE HANGAR IS gone." Michael slumped and ran his hands through his hair in disbelief.

Lauren's legs were shaking as she and Michael watched the only remaining hangar at the Monterey airport burn. According to Michael, Donovan had no other options, and after the excruciating, time-consuming effort of carrying William up the stairs, she watched as her husband taxied the questionable jet out to the end of the runway for departure and vanish into the thick, billowing smoke.

She repeatedly tried to reach Ernie at Cal Fire, but her calls went to voice mail.

"Here come the fighters," Michael announced as they all heard the sharp thump from the sonic booms roll across the open water and reach the *Buckley*.

Lauren held her breath and felt like she was dying a little each time as the fast-moving F-18s rolled in on the target area and released a sequence of bombs. She'd given operational support to hundreds of military operations in her years with the Defense Intelligence Agency, and watched hours of after-action video. The difference today was she could see the dirty orange blossom of napalm and hear the roar of the fighters herself, and people she loved were in the line of fire. The napalm exploded into a rolling ball of fire that instantly spread, igniting everything it touched. Lauren knew the realities. The latest incarnation of napalm could burn at five thousand degrees for up to ten minutes, and was next to impossible to extinguish. Upon detonation, the fire was so voracious that the air surrounding the blast would race in at speeds of seventy miles per hour. Destruction was almost always total.

Lauren checked her phone, then put it to her ear. "Sebastian, are you still there? Can you give us an infrared image of the Gulfstream?"

"Hang on, I'm a little busy. We've got thirty-six more fighters inbound, and I need to sequence them in over the target area. There, I just switched over. The right engine is running, but he hasn't started the left one yet. You'll be able to see that there are two people in the cockpit, one in the cabin. That's all three of them, right?"

Lauren studied the screen, confirming everything Sebastian was telling her, and she relayed it to the others.

"Come on, Donovan, get it started and go!" Michael whispered with a sense of urgency.

"Michael, why is he waiting?" Lauren felt all of her muscles tighten as she sat powerless.

"He's probably waiting until he gets to the very end of the runway. He knows that engine was on fire. No reason to start the engine until you need it for takeoff."

"Sebastian," Lauren said into the phone. "Other people can see what's happening at the airport, right? Can you see any assets en route to the Monterey airport?"

"Negative, I have no unauthorized traffic inside a hundred-mile radius."

Lauren watched as the Gulfstream reached the end of the taxiway and stopped. The image pulled back until they could all see the length of the runway.

"The fire is almost there," Lauren said, her hand covering her mouth.

"The flaps are down." Michael tapped the table with a clenched fist. "Come on, Donovan, get out of there!"

Lauren saw a bright flash expand out from what was left of the hangar complex. The explosion glowed white and then dimmed as it receded. Afraid to even blink, she studied the infrared depiction and watched what looked like a burning liquid being flung from the epicenter of the blast. Her first thought was an errant bomb filled with napalm had detonated at the airport, and she felt lost.

"Lauren," Sebastian said over the phone. "The explosion you just saw was an underground fuel tank, most likely kerosene."

"A fuel bunker exploded," Lauren said as she looked anxiously at the others.

Michael flung his clenched fists skyward. "Look! The flash of the ignition. He started the left engine! It's turning."

Lauren watched as a growing white glow emanated from the engine nacelle. The Gulfstream began to roll forward and then the feed was lost.

"No!" Michael yelled. "What happened?"

"Sebastian!" Lauren snapped as her eyes swept the computer monitor for answers. The Global Hawk feed was lost, leaving Lauren shocked and bewildered.

Michael dug his fingers against his temples.

"Sebastian!" Lauren cried out again as she checked her phone and saw that the call had ended. She got up and ran for the door. The morning air smelled burnt and stale. In the distance, the shore of Monterey looked like one solid fire topped by a huge column of towering smoke. The explosions from the faraway airstrikes reached her ears, though muted. They sounded like one steady clap of thunder as the dull roar echoed off the surrounding hills.

A new sound filled the air, familiar, yet distinctly out of place. Lauren hurried along the railing until she could see the bow. The whine was one of the helicopter's engines spooling up. The damaged rotor was spinning. She turned and Michael was already sprinting off the bridge. As the second engine started, Lauren spotted Ethan and Montero, each with a grip on a black duffel bag, running across the deck for the helicopter.

Michael burst into view, ran to the helicopter, leaned in, and spoke to Montero. Ethan pushed the duffel bag into the open door and climbed in behind it. Montero nodded, stepped away, and Michael climbed in with Ethan.

The wind whipped Lauren's hair as she watched Janie add power, and a deafening whistle filled the air. Montero, her hands pressed against her ears, turned away.

The helicopter shook and the blades seemed to wobble. Lauren stepped away in fear of flying parts. The shriek grew—the sound coming from the damaged rotor blades as they spun through the air. She watched as the weight on the skids decreased, and in one smooth motion, Janie pulled the helicopter into the air, where it faltered, the blades buffeted with a sickening staccato sound Lauren had never heard before. Janie pivoted the nose, allowing the helicopter to fully clear the deck and the bow of the *Buckley*, and banked toward shore. The helicopter descended dangerously close to the waves, and the horrendous sound of the blades flailing at the air grew as Janie accelerated.

Lauren pulled her eyes away from the helicopter and fixed her gaze on the distant column of smoke. She prayed that somehow a Gulfstream jet would materialize from inside the inferno.

CHAPTER THIRTY-SIX

DONOVAN LISTENED INTENTLY as the second engine began to rotate. He added fuel when he felt the time was right and heard the *whump* that told him he had ignition. He heard the engine begin to spool up. There wasn't even a working radio aboard the Gulfstream. He was completely on his own.

A flash off to his left startled him. He snapped his head around to see the ground near the burning hangar lift itself up in huge burning chunks, followed by a geyser of liquid fire. He felt the shock wave reverberate through the plane, just as the force lifted the Ford F-250 into the air. Consumed by flames, the truck disintegrated. At the departure end of the runway, the fire and heat had reached the asphalt taxiways, and they were starting to burn.

"Oh Jesus," Shannon said. "Donovan, the runway is burning."

Donovan saw the fragments from the underground explosion scattered over the ramp, burning furiously. They could wait no longer. He had no way to know for sure, but the left engine should have stabilized by now. The flames were closing fast, and not far behind, a fiery cyclone writhed and twisted and vanished upward into the smoke.

"Here we go." Donovan gripped the throttles and pushed them up to guide the Gulfstream out onto the runway. He glanced back at William, still unconscious. If they crashed, William wouldn't feel a thing. Shannon looked terrified but determined. Donovan double-checked the flaps and trims, and then pushed up both throttles.

He felt the familiar forces as he was pressed into his seat by the twin Rolls Royce engines. He held on to the controls, ignoring the pain in his leg as he pushed on the rudders to keep the Gulfstream pointed down the runway. He heard and felt the landing gear throw chunks of debris into the belly. The needle on the emergency airspeed indicator sat lifeless, leaving Donovan with no choice but to estimate when the airplane would fly. There was no stopping—he was committed to getting the crippled Gulfstream into the air. As they raced toward burning asphalt, he pulled the nose up, the wings flexed, and pulled the Gulfstream off the ground and ripped through the flames. Donovan instantly cranked the Gulfstream into a steep bank, the right wingtip only feet above the ground. The air rushing toward the vortex slammed into the Gulfstream and bounced them hard. The turbulence grew worse, and Donovan shot a quick glance out at the left wingtip, and watched it flex wildly as they continued to take a beating from the unseen forces. He was fighting the controls just to keep the airplane right side up when the fire bell erupted. Donovan's eyes darted to a red light on the panel and confirmed the left engine was burning.

"What's happening?" Shannon's voice was shrill.

"The engine is on fire."

He called for Shannon to raise the gear. When she did, he heard the reassuring thump as the struts came up, and all three landing gears tucked themselves into their wheel wells. The twisting column of fire undulated off to their left as the flaps came up. The Gulfstream surged forward and Donovan let the engine burn. It might be on fire, but it was producing thrust.

But when Donovan pulled back on the throttles, he recognized a fresh problem. One that startled him. For the airplane to accelerate as it did meant they were light, which meant the wings held very little fuel. And then another problem: As he banked hard to the left, two F-18s flashed past overhead, pylons under their wings fully loaded with bombs. They were so close he could hear the roar of their engines.

With no instruments to feed him flight information, Donovan stayed low enough to see the ground. He leveled the speeding jet a hundred feet off the ground. Through the smoke, he spotted downtown Monterey. As before, half of the buildings were on fire. The Marriott was starting to collapse, and the Portola Hotel was fully consumed by flames. Ahead, he glimpsed the waters of the Pacific, the clear air over the ocean beckoned, and he pushed up the throttles. He had to squint as sheets of flame seemed to reach up and try to snatch them from the sky. Dangerous winds whipped between the buildings, the turbulent air laden with embers. Donovan held on as the violent currents slammed one wing and then the other as the onslaught continued.

He leveled the aircraft as they flashed across the shore and glanced down at what was left of the marina they'd once considered a refuge. The damage looked worse from above, and he knew they would have had no chance down there. In a hole through the last of the smoke, he caught sight of the commercial wharf—the basic structure that served Monterey's working fishing fleet. Instead of gray concrete, Donovan saw a distinctive mosaic of color that could only be a crowd of people. As the Gulfstream raced overhead, scores of faces looked upward, some waved desperately. An instant later the Gulfstream was out over the waves.

"Shannon. There's a crowd of people on the commercial pier with nowhere to go."

"The marina was destroyed. How can anyone be there?"

"There's another pier that reaches out into the bay. We never would have seen them from where we were." Clear of the shore,

Donovan pulled the left throttle back to see if the fire warning would go out as he reduced the fuel.

"The red light means we're still on fire, right?" Shannon asked

"Yes, but it worked when we needed it." Donovan silenced the bell and reluctantly shut the left engine down. Michael had already used both fire extinguishers to fight the same problem, and all Donovan could hope for was that the fire would burn itself out. He compensated for the uneven thrust by pushing on the right rudder. Finally, clear of the worst of the smoke, he banked toward the north shore of Monterey Bay—the only land he could see that wasn't on fire.

In the distance, he spotted a ship under way in the heavy waves. The *Buckley*. Donovan turned his attention to flying, and from memory, pictured the available airports north of Monterey. San Jose would be ideal, though with no flight instruments, he might have to divert somewhere else. San Francisco was an option or even Oakland if the smoke downwind of the fires brought the visibility down. He studied the hills off his nose and calculated that with only one engine, it would still be an easy climb up and over them. San Francisco Bay would be on the other side, and he could take his pick of airports. Donovan pushed up the right throttle and the engine made a muffled sound of protest, and with little fanfare, the turbine began to slow as it shut down.

"What was that? What's happening?" Shannon asked.

"I think we just ran out of fuel." Donovan switched on both igniters and listened for any sound of the right engine restarting. All he could hear were the turbine blades spooling down, then the inside of the Gulfstream became very quiet.

"How far can we glide?" Shannon asked, rigid in her seat.

"Not far enough." Donovan could see that the nearest shore was shrouded in smoke and the land he could see straight ahead was too far away. They'd never get there. The wind-churned waves below made the decision easy. All he could do was turn into the wind and set them down in the ocean close enough for someone to rescue them quickly. He banked the Gulfstream hard to the left and as he completed the one-hundred-and-eighty-degree turn, he spotted a distinct trail of black smoke and knew with certainty it was coming from the left engine.

Shannon stretched for a better view out the side window of the plane. "Is that smoke coming from us?" she managed.

"I think so," Donovan said as the familiar fear of burning returned. Was more of the Gulfstream on fire than the engine? He pushed the controls to start losing as much altitude as possible. If they were still burning, he needed to get the airplane down before the plane came apart or the fire reached the cabin. He searched the ocean until he spotted the white and red dot that was the *Buckley*. "Shannon, we're going to land in the water. Under your seat is a life vest. Put it on now, but don't inflate it yet."

"That's got to be better than burning."

"I agree. All of this is going to happen fast. I want you to slide your seat all the way back and keep your legs tucked in, away from the rudder pedals. When I say brace for impact, lean over and wrap your arms beneath your legs and hang on. It'll be rough, and the airplane will hit the water more than once, but we'll survive the ditching. Don't move until I say it's safe. We'll plan on using the over wing exits. As soon as I say it's safe, you get up and go straight to the first one you find and get it open."

"Got it." Shannon pulled out her life vest, squirmed in her seat, and pulled harder on the straps of her harness.

"I'll carry William to the exit. The directions on how to pop the hatch are clearly marked. I want you to climb out on the wing and hang on. I'll need you to pull William, as I push. Whatever happens, we get him out of the plane. Understood?"

"The waves look big," Shannon said. "Are you going to be okay in the water?"

Donovan didn't answer. He forced himself to fly the airplane, to accomplish each task in order. The final job, and the answer to Shannon's question, would be answered when it was time to climb out of the Gulfstream and jump into the waiting ocean.

Shannon bit her lip. "You didn't answer me. What do I do if you can't help me?"

"Help William as best you can. Float him out of the exit as the water rises. There are life vests under each of the seats. Above all else, save yourself."

CHAPTER THIRTY-SEVEN

LAUREN PRESSED THE rubber eye guards of the binoculars hard against her face. She braced herself against the pitching and rolling of the ship and methodically swept back and forth across the solid wall of smoke. She couldn't tune out the ticks of the clock in her head that told her time was running out. Donovan should have been airborne by now.

"What's that?" Ryan said as he briefly lowered his own binoculars and pointed toward the two o'clock position. "Low, and slightly starboard of the bow."

Lauren held herself steady until she spotted something in the distance. She zeroed in with her binoculars, furiously searching for the correct focus, until her field of view captured the crisp outline of the Eco-Watch Gulfstream flying low and fast. She held her breath as the powerful magnification brought the flames and swirling debris of downtown Monterey into view. Donovan cleared the last tendrils of smoke and banked away from the *Buckley* allowing Lauren to easily spot the flames pouring from the left engine.

Montero rushed onto the bridge and went straight for Lauren. "Can you see them?"

"*Buckley*, we've got them in sight." Janie's voice came over the overhead speaker. "As soon as I get a lock via the camera array, I'll be transmitting live to the bridge monitors."

"Say your position relative to the Gulfstream," Ryan transmitted and then toggled the input on his computer to receive Janie's feed.

"We're just above wave-top level. This helicopter flies, but just barely. I can't climb very well, and our speed has been cut in half."

Ryan handed Montero a pair of powerful binoculars.

"Their left engine is trailing flames," Lauren said and listened as Ryan relayed the news to the helicopter.

"Can you tell if the flames are coming from the tailpipe?" Michael asked. "Engines are built for heat, which means the things can burn for a long time and not affect the airframe."

Lauren tried to hold the binoculars steady in an attempt to carefully examine the airplane. The Gulfstream bounced in and out of her field of view as the ship plowed into the heavy waves. She finally managed to hold everything still for long enough to get the look she needed. Flames were streaming from the exterior of the engine cowling. In that glimpse, she understood that the entire engine pod itself was on fire, and black smoke was beginning to pour from other parts of the tail section. "Fire is coming out of every seam in the metal."

"We've got the feed," Ryan called out.

Lauren hurried to Ryan and steadied herself against the rolling deck by clutching the frame of his chair. On the big monitor a far superior gyro-stabilized picture of the Gulfstream filled the screen.

"He's in trouble." Michael's voice came from the speaker. "The engine is coming apart."

Lauren was terrified. Watching and waiting was crushing her. She felt Montero's arm reach around her shoulders in an effort to comfort her. Donovan was flying away from them, and there wasn't any way to warn him. His only rescuers were miles away and falling far behind the burning Gulfstream. With her eyes locked on the monitor, she felt a distinct jolt of fear as the left wing began to drop.

The Gulfstream started a steep turn to the left. Lauren stiffened, as it looked to her as if they were out of control. After reversing direction, the wings leveled, though the jet was still losing altitude fast. Donovan was now coming toward them.

"He knows he's on fire, and he's doing his best to lose altitude," Michael reported. "He can't make it to shore. He's turned into the wind to ditch."

As the Gulfstream descended, the camera only found water and lost the lock. Lauren ran to the windows and searched the horizon with her binoculars. Trailing smoke, the jet was wings level and low. To Lauren it looked like it was just above the wave tops. Donovan was still flying and fighting, which meant that he was still alive.

The bow of the *Buckley* rose, and then tipped over the top of the wave, before dropping down the backside and plowing through the trough. Then it came up again, water streaming back from the main deck. Lauren raised her binoculars, searched frantically, but found nothing but empty sky.

CHAPTER THIRTY-EIGHT

DONOVAN STUDIED THE foam-streaked waves as the Gulfstream descended, calculating the best angle for touchdown. He forced out the mental image of his airplane on fire and maintained a steady descent. The wind was blowing hard, turbulence rocking the Gulfstream. As he neared the white caps, he leveled off to bleed the remainder of his excess speed.

His eyes danced between the peaks and valleys of the waves, and he corrected his course to touch down in the smoothest water possible. "Shannon, brace for impact."

Donovan eased the jet down the last few feet, and in the silence, he heard the first wave slap the underside of the fuselage. Doing his best at keeping the wings level, Donovan felt the next impact and then another. The left wing clipped a wave and the Gulfstream skipped, then came down again. The wing dug in and slewed the airplane around hard. Donovan fought the controls to keep the airplane from cartwheeling. Shannon screamed as she was thrown hard against the side of the cockpit.

The right wing and nose hit into the water, the impact causing a roar that left Donovan's ears ringing. His shoulders and hips pulled heavily against the harness. Visibility went to zero and he felt himself being shoved back and forth against the side of the plane. He had no idea if the Gulfstream was even right side up.

As the deceleration forces vanished, Donovan released the straps holding him in his seat, threw off his harness, and reached under his seat to yank out the life vest. He tossed it back into the cabin. The nose of the airplane rebounded and popped above the waves. Donovan felt a new surge of fear when he could finally see the sky and surface of the ocean as the Gulfstream rode up and over a big swell.

Shannon's right hand shot to the side of her head and she groaned.

She seemed rattled by the view out the windscreen, and he leaned over and undid her restraints.

"Shannon, let's go!"

Donovan waited as Shannon climbed out of the cockpit and ran straight for the emergency exit on the right side of the fuselage. She jerked the handle, pulled, allowing the hatch to freefall onto the floor, and climbed out of the Gulfstream.

Donovan pushed himself out of the captain's seat. With the floor of the jet pitching in the waves, he lost his balance and fell heavily in the aisle. The pain from his knee was excruciating as he timed the next wave and used his momentum to crawl to William.

His eyes were closed and his heavily bandaged ankle was bleeding. With no real restraints, William had been tumbled in the galley during the ditching. Donovan tried to rouse him but couldn't, and he decided it might be better for William if he was still out from the morphine.

Shannon stuck her head into the cabin. "The airplane is sinking! Hurry, you need to get out."

The water level in the aisle was rising, and Donovan reached under William's arms, leaned back, and lifted. With just enough room to maneuver, Donovan raised William up onto his right shoulder and took all of the weight on his good leg. Using his left arm to steady himself, and timing each wave, Donovan lurched down the aisle toward the exit.

Shannon was crouched out on the wing, her arms outstretched. Just as Donovan reached the hatch, a wave boiled around Shannon and the ocean poured in through the hatch. Drenched by the cold water, Donovan guided William closer to the exit, until Shannon could grasp him under his arms. Pushing as hard as he could, William's limp form slid through the hatch until he lay on the wing.

"Inflate your vest," Donovan called to Shannon, as he grabbed and put on his own vest. He reached under a seat in the cabin and retrieved a third packaged flotation device and handed it out the hatch to Shannon.

"Donovan, get out of the plane!" Shannon yelled as another wave crashed over the wing and almost washed both her and William into the ocean. "I can't hold him and get his vest on."

Donovan leaned out, his eyes fixed on William instead of the roaring waves, and climbed out the exit. The air smelled clean and free of smoke, but as a swell lifted the airplane, he could see nothing but water and the familiar fear began to squeeze him from the inside out. Decades ago, he'd escaped, but this time he felt wounded and vulnerable. He was a target. This time the ocean wouldn't miss.

"Hurry," Shannon said as she ripped the life vest from its pouch and unfurled the straps.

Donovan forced himself to look away from the endless progression of waves as he slid over to William. He locked his hand around William's belt to hold him in place. Together, he and Shannon wrestled the flotation device around William's neck and fastened the strap around his torso. Donovan yanked the handle, which allowed the small CO_2 bottle to inflate the vest.

Shannon pulled the lanyard to inflate her own, and it took shape, and just as quickly deflated.

"There are holes in the fabric," Donovan said. He peeled off his own vest and tossed it to her. "Take it! I'll hang on to William."

They bottomed out in the swell and Donovan felt the wing he was kneeling on tilt away from him. He turned and saw the Gulfstream's T-tail starting to tip on its side. The warped aluminum and charred paint from the fire damage was clearly visible all along the aft fuselage. From what he could see, the Gulfstream probably couldn't have remained airborne much longer. The tail angled steeply, and the last surge of air trapped in the cabin bubbled to the surface. Then the jet quietly slipped beneath the waves. Donovan kept a firm hand on William as the jet sank below them.

The next surge lifted him and William up, and Donovan heard an unfamiliar sound carried in on the wind. He twisted in the water to find the source, but found nothing as he and William were swept down the backside of the swell. As they rose once again on the next wave, a warbling whistle pierced his ears. Then he heard the deep resonant thud of rotor blades. When he swiveled his head, he finally caught sight of a helicopter.

Brushing seawater from his eyes, Donovan saw the Eco-Watch helicopter coming straight for them. He waved his free hand. Elated, he turned to make sure Shannon saw their rescuers, but there was nothing but empty water. He spun around. Couldn't find her. The helicopter was slowing. Donovan let go of William's belt and made sure he floated faceup without any assistance. He took one quick look at the helicopter to ensure they saw him. Someone in a wetsuit wearing a scuba mask waved from the open door. Confident William would be rescued momentarily, Donovan shut out the demons screaming at him to give up. He took two deep breaths, lunged forward, and dove beneath the surface.

CHAPTER THIRTY-NINE

"WE'VE REACQUIRED THE video feed from the helicopter," Ryan called out to Lauren and Montero from across the bridge.

Lauren turned away from the window and hurried to the monitor at the chart table, Montero right behind her. The Gulfstream was down. She could see it floating in the ocean, the water and foam streaming down from the sides and tail from the ditching. The fire, which a moment earlier was a raging concern, had been reduced to a cloud of steam whipped away by the wind.

"Oh man, Donovan did a perfect job!" Michael's excitement radiated from the speaker. "They're down."

Lauren watched the white caps break along the side of the floating airframe. With muscles wire-taut, she was afraid to breathe as she silently pleaded with the universe for those inside to get out. The emergency hatch fell inward, revealing a hole in the side of the Gulfstream. The first figure climbed out on the wing.

"I see Shannon," Michael said. "Janie says we're less than five minutes out."

Lauren watched Shannon turn and reach back inside the airplane. Moments later, she leaned backwards as if pulling a great weight. A torso appeared in the exit and another set of arms pushed William all the way out on the wing. As the helicopter drew closer, the camera provided enough detail so Lauren could see William's arm in a sling, and his lower leg and foot heavily wrapped.

"Oh no, William looks pretty banged up," Montero said.

"I can see someone else in the cabin," Michael transmitted. "Janie is going to maneuver us directly overhead. You may lose the video again due to the angles."

Lauren let out an involuntary gasp as she spotted Donovan in the exit. He pulled himself out on the wing, and in the high-resolution clarity, she could see the tattered fabric of his trousers and the bandage wrapped around his thigh. Lauren lost sight of Donovan as the waves rose and fell, and when she could finally see him again, he was removing his life vest and handing it to Shannon. Lauren couldn't help but imagine what Donovan must be feeling at being out in the ocean. She'd spent countless nights in their years together holding him as he awoke, covered in sweat and gasping at the reoccurring nightmare of losing both parents and being a teenager adrift at sea.

The transmitted image shook badly, and Lauren couldn't see anything. She glanced at Montero, and then Ryan, who sat resolute at the helm of the *Buckley* as they plowed through swell after swell. The image returned but wildly out of focus, and she squinted to try and make sense out of what she was seeing. The chaotic blob on the screen drew together until Lauren realized that there was nothing to see but water. The Gulfstream was gone. She spotted Donovan in the water next to William, but she couldn't find Shannon. The focus moved in and out quickly, as if searching for something to lock on to, and when the picture stabilized, only William was visible. The rotor wash of the helicopter began to ripple and whip the water, and Lauren again couldn't see anything.

When the camera once again projected a workable field of view, Lauren covered her mouth with her hand. She watched Michael and Ethan leap from the helicopter and hit the water. Ethan swam straight for William. Michael tucked and dove straight down, and that was all Lauren could see as tears flooded her vision.

CHAPTER FORTY

DONOVAN IMMEDIATELY FELT the current pulling him sideways as he kicked downward. Bubbles and foam clouded the water as he searched for Shannon. As he swam, he spotted her below him. She was bent at the waist, tumbling in the turbulence created by the big waves. Her legs were kicking fitfully, arms flailing helplessly as she was battered by the force of the sea.

Using powerful arm strokes, Donovan pulled heavily against the water as he swam closer. Shannon was twisting and desperately reaching up for a surface she couldn't touch. Donovan came up from behind her, locked his forearm across her chest, and fought off her final panicked blows just before she went limp. He kicked as hard as he could, his injured leg screaming in pain as he propelled them both upward.

With Shannon in his arms, they broke the surface into the early morning sunshine. Donovan drew in a long breath. Holding Shannon's face above the water, he listened for her to take a breath, but she didn't. They were swept up the side of a swell, when Donovan spotted the helicopter, alarmed at how far he and Shannon had been carried downwind. Keeping Shannon's face above the surface, he used his free arm to wave, and they sank beneath the water. Donovan kicked hard and regained their tenuous position above the surface just as they rode the wave down into the trough between the wave tops. He tried to ignore the cold water, and how quickly he seemed to be losing his strength.

Shannon was wearing a life vest, the one he'd given her. Donovan switched arms, still holding her head up and positioned his mouth over the red inflation tube and started blowing. Bubbles gurgled to the surface between them, and Donovan spotted the holes in the material causing the leak. Identical to the holes in the aluminum skin of the Gulfstream, the vests had been peppered by debris from the meteor. He created enough distance between them for him to gather up the rubberized material, bunch it in his hand, and clamp down. Once again, he blew into the tube, and the yellow fabric began to expand and hold. He blew out a sigh of relief when he realized he didn't need to kick as hard to keep them afloat.

They crested another wave and Donovan saw that the helicopter was even farther away than before. He told himself they were working to get William into the chopper, and once they had him, they'd look for him and Shannon. Clutching the punctured fabric with all his strength, he looked down at Shannon's face. Her eyes were closed. There was a scrape on her temple where she'd hit her head when they'd ditched. A memory of Buck, a fragment from a conversation spoken in a pool years earlier, came to Donovan. He eased Shannon's chin up to keep the water out of her airway, placed his mouth over both her mouth and nose, and began mouth-to-mouth breathing.

With growing frustration and fear, he kept going, only stopping when he needed to blow into the tube to keep it inflated. "Shannon, I need you to breathe!"

He listened for the helicopter and tried to spot it each time the wave crested. Even with the assistance from the partially inflated vest, Donovan could feel the energy drain from his body. He had to concentrate to maintain his kicking as the cold Pacific Ocean robbed the warmth from his body. His teeth started chattering. He closed his eyes, and his entire world became counting each breath. Two for Shannon, three for the vest, two for him, then repeat. The bubbles erupting under his chin told him he was losing his grip on the tear in the vest, and they began to settle lower in the water. Donovan kicked harder, vaguely aware that his leg didn't hurt anymore.

The wind howled as if screaming at him to act, a whistle filled the air, and Donovan felt his grip on Shannon start to slip. He fought to hold her, as well as the rip in the life vest. He blew wildly into the tube and more bubbles surfaced. His hand was mostly numb, but he gripped the material to keep them afloat. As a wave crashed into him, he struggled to keep his grip on Shannon. For so many reasons, he needed her to live. With all of his energy, he focused on saving her.

Donovan felt the hopelessness welling up from within, threatening to paralyze him. It was as if the ocean was toying with his soul, swatting him around, conjuring up the painful images of his past, inexorably linked to bring Donovan to this day, this hour of understanding. He was adrift, being swept out to sea. He continued working on Shannon, trying to save her.

He saw those other waves, the ones from decades ago. The world around him went quiet, and he could picture his mother thrashing to stay afloat, could hear her screaming for him. As Donovan rode up a swell, clutching Shannon, for the first time in his life, he understood he wouldn't have been able to save his mother. She probably would have pulled them both underwater. He had only been fourteen, terrified, and a far cry from the man he was now. He pictured Abigail; the prospect of her growing up without a father created a tangible shudder that snapped him back to reality. Fear and determination rippled through his entire body, and he used thoughts of Abigail to refocus him, until all Donovan had was Shannon and their next breaths together.

An almost unbearable whistle grew louder as Donovan continued breathing into Shannon's mouth and nose. A shadow swept over him, and he looked up and found the Eco-Watch helicopter slowing to a hover above him. A figure jumped out of the passenger door and splashed heavily nearby, followed moments later by a second figure. The noise was deafening, and despite his exhaustion, Donovan leaned in and spoke directly into Shannon's ear. "Keep fighting, we're almost there. Keep fighting."

Michael reached him first, rising up from the water next to them. He pulled up his mask and put his arms around both Donovan and Shannon. "I got you, buddy."

Ethan surfaced next and took Shannon from Donovan. They floated a short distance away with Ethan working to maintain their position.

"We'll get her aboard, and then you and I will be next," Michael said.

"William?" Donovan asked as his teeth continued to chatter.

"He's aboard. Sorry it took us so long to get here."

"How did you find us?" Donovan asked as he surrendered and let Michael keep him afloat.

"Montero spotted you on the helicopter's camera. She and Lauren are onboard the *Buckley*, and they kept us apprised of your position. We were always there, never doubt that, ever."

Donovan watched as Janie brought the helicopter down closer to the tops of the waves. She positioned the helicopter downwind of Ethan and Shannon. Then she turned broadside to the swell. She timed the maneuver perfectly. As the slope of water swept them upward, Janie guided the helicopter so Ethan, holding Shannon, met the helicopter at the apex of the wave. Ethan reached out and hooked an arm around the skid, and then used their combined momentum to leverage Shannon onto the floor of the passenger compartment. As the wave receded, Ethan kicked his legs out in space and climbed inside. Janie maneuvered the ailing helicopter around in a wide circle to move back into position to retrieve Michael and Donovan.

"We're next," Michael said, as he kicked to position the two of them into the trough to catch the next big swell. "I know how you feel about all of this—mixing big waves with helicopters has got to suck."

"I can't kick very well," Donovan said.

"Never mind, just relax. I'll get us to the helicopter. Ethan will be waiting to help pull you inside."

Donovan felt the sea begin to propel them upwards. Downwash from the beating blades churned the surface, and faster than he expected, the sky was filled with helicopter. Ethan's arms joined Michael's as the two of them were propelled into the passenger compartment.

As Janie banked away, Donovan spotted William, who was lying on his back. He felt a surge of relief to see his chest rising and falling. Ethan had already started steady CPR compressions on Shannon. Donovan rested his head, closed his eyes for a second, and then signaled for Michael to lean closer. "We're not done yet. I saw people trapped on the old fishing wharf in Monterey."

"How many?" Michael asked. "Can we pick them up with the helicopter?"

Donovan shook his head. "There's at least a hundred, maybe more."

CHAPTER FORTY-ONE

"WE'VE GOT ALL of them aboard," Janie's voice came through the speaker. "Donovan is injured but seems to be fine. No change for William. Shannon is unresponsive and they're doing CPR."

"This is the *Buckley*," Ryan said into the microphone. "Say your intentions."

"*Buckley*," Janie transmitted. "Prepare to receive the injured. There's no way I can fly this helicopter over any terrain to reach medical help inland."

"*Buckley* copies," Ryan radioed in return.

Lauren closed her eyes and took a moment to collect herself. She and Montero had watched intently via camera as Donovan and Shannon were being swept farther out to sea. When Michael and Ethan finally pulled William aboard the helicopter, Lauren was able to guide them straight to Donovan, unaware that Shannon wasn't breathing. When the helicopter arrived overhead, she realized that her husband was performing mouth-to-mouth on Shannon.

"*Buckley*," Janie said. "Donovan just informed us that there are maybe a hundred or more survivors stranded on the old fishing wharf in Monterey harbor."

Ryan turned and scanned the shore with his binoculars. "Lauren, can we get a real-time picture of what's going on? Are those people still alive?"

"We're cut off." Lauren looked at her phone and confirmed that there were no missed calls or texts. "Martial law has put us in the dark. Even if Cal Air or the Air Force would take my call, the last thing they'd give us is information on the potential collateral damage of civilian lives."

"Helm, set a course for Monterey, and maintain flank speed," Ryan said and then picked up the microphone. "Janie, we're changing course toward the pier, running at twenty-two knots. If needed, we can slow for you when you arrive."

"No worries," Janie said. "Landing isn't a problem. Just have the medical team ready for our arrival."

Lauren felt the ship heel over in the turn. She stood up from the chart table and scanned the horizon for the helicopter. The shoreline was a whirling cauldron of smoke and fire, and the sea between them and the shore roiled with almost solid whitecaps that were still building. Off the port bow, she finally spotted the helicopter, low and slow, flying almost directly into the wind.

Lauren's phone pinged. She quickly read the text and then announced, "I just got a text from the Pentagon. They're ordering us away from shore, said that we're in violation of martial law."

Ryan picked up the microphone, paused a second, and began talking. "This is Captain Pittman. We have a helicopter inbound and we need personnel and stretchers to transport three survivors directly to the infirmary. I want all crew to go to action stations. We're headed at full speed toward Monterey Bay to pull survivors off a pier. I need everyone to be sharp. Pittman out."

Lauren started for the hatch with Montero a step behind. As they stepped out onto the exposed helipad, the wind, which was howling from starboard, hit them full force. Lauren put her hand on the railing for support as the deck tilted. The bow dropped to meet a wave and as the water exploded outward, the noise wasn't unlike the sound of a car wreck. Lauren flexed her legs as the *Buckley*, unscathed, continued toward the shore.

"The hull is ice capable," Montero said. "Four inches of reinforced steel can take a beating. From listening to Ethan, these seas are nothing compared to what they'll encounter up north."

In between the roar of sea and steel, Lauren could hear a distant rumble. The shoreline at this point looked to be only smoke and flames. Somewhere just beyond, the Air Force was still laying down explosives to try to stop the fire.

"Here they come," Montero said, pointing off to the left as crewmen began collecting around the perimeter of the helipad. A single crewman in a bright orange jacket held fluorescent paddles in each outstretched hand and stood tall on the deck.

Low and off the port side, the helicopter drew even with the ship. Janie slowed and was paralleling the *Buckley*. Lauren plugged her ears with her fingers as the shriek from the rotor blades grew painful. Both machine and rotor blades fought the buffeting winds as Janie pivoted the helicopter ninety degrees to the right and moved toward the pad.

Janie brought the struggling helicopter in and hovered briefly above the pitching, rolling deck as the crewman with the paddles gave her instant feedback. The second the skids touched, Janie dumped the collective, killing all the lift as crewmen ran from each side and secured the helicopter to the deck. Janie shut down the engines and the rotor blades screeched to a halt from the rotor brake.

Lauren bolted toward the door.

"Bring the stretchers!" a crewman shouted as he opened the door to the cabin.

Montero pulled open the cockpit door to check on Janie.

Lauren stood on the skid. She spotted Donovan. He had his arms around William, steadying him. He turned when he saw her, tried to smile, but couldn't. Lauren thought he looked more exhausted than she'd ever seen him.

With no wasted motion, crewmen secured William on the first stretcher, and an instant later, he was off the helicopter, being rushed to the infirmary.

On the other side of the cabin, Michael and Ethan were leaning over Shannon performing CPR as a crewman climbed into the cabin with stretcher number two.

"I thought I heard something!" Michael cried out as he leaned down and placed an ear on Shannon's chest. "Ethan, don't stop!"

Lauren could finally see Shannon's face. Her skin was shock white, her wet hair matted to her forehead and neck. She looked small and frail.

"Come on, Shannon!" Michael cried out as once again he leaned down to listen. "You're on the *Buckley*. Open your eyes!"

Shannon sputtered, shook her head back and forth, and heaved seawater onto the floor. Taking one huge gasp after another, she drew in much-needed air. Lauren looked across the cabin and watched as Donovan closed his eyes, knowing a great weight had just been released from her husband.

When Shannon opened her eyes, she momentarily fought against the hands that held her. "Shannon, it's Michael," he said. "Breathe, slow and deep. You're on the *Buckley*."

Her eyes grew wide and she turned her head, confused. Ethan gathered her up in his arms and handed her to several waiting crewmen. They placed Shannon on a stretcher and whisked her below deck.

Montero worked her way from the cockpit to Ethan, where she moved in close and gave him a kiss on the cheek.

As a crewman tried to help Donovan out of the helicopter, Lauren saw him wave him off, and call out to Michael. "I'll catch up with you. Go take care of the others."

As everyone moved off, Lauren went to her husband and wrapped her arms around his neck and hugged him tightly. She felt his arms close around her, and despite his cold, wet clothes, they held each other for what seemed like forever.

"I thought I'd lost you," Lauren whispered as she pulled away and kissed him. Donovan held her face in his hands and returned the embrace.

"I got here as fast as I could," Donovan said.

Lauren wanted to cry in relief as she thought back over everything that had transpired over the last twelve hours.

"I want to hear all about it—later. Right now, I need you to help me out of the helicopter," Donovan said.

Lauren steadied him as he limped to the door. Janie was there and with their help, Donovan slid from the helicopter to the helipad and quickly hugged Janie. "Like I told Lauren, I want to hear everything that happened, but later. What's the helicopter's status? Can you take a team to the wharf?"

"No way," Janie said as she shook her head. "I'm sorry. She's got really messed-up rotor blades. The vibrations finally started shaking important things apart. I was getting a bit nervous those last ten minutes. We're lucky we made it back to the ship."

"Well, you made my day," Donovan said. "I understand you're friends with Shannon. I'd like you to go be with her. She's had a rough go of it. See if you can do anything for her."

"You bet," Janie said.

"Attention on the deck," Captain Pittman's voice sprang from the loudspeakers. "Heads up, we've got two F-18s inbound, twelve o'clock, two miles out, intentions unknown."

Lauren spotted the fighters—they were coming low and fast. Seconds later, they flashed overhead, followed by the excruciatingly loud roar of their jet engines. Lauren felt like the Pentagon had just slapped her across the face, and her anger spiked. The Global Hawk was recording every violation Eco-Watch was committing. Shut out of the loop and told to go away, she stepped away from Donovan and strode out from beneath the helicopter. Exposed, out on the heaving foredeck, Lauren looked up at the sky and raised her arm, offering her middle finger in a hi-resolution statement as to how she was feeling.

CHAPTER FORTY-TWO

THE *BUCKLEY'S* HEAVY bow destroyed waves and exploded them outward as the ship continued its relentless charge toward shore. Limping and leaning on Lauren for support, Donovan walked onto the *Buckley's* bridge and shook Ryan's hand.

"Are you sure you shouldn't be in the infirmary?" Ryan said as he stepped back and noticed Donovan's leg.

"It looks worse than it is," Donovan said then changed the subject. "Lauren just explained to me that the area is under martial law and we've been ordered to withdraw. How far out are we from shore?"

"Fifteen minutes," Ryan said. "I've got an overlay of the harbor. I'd like to know exactly what you saw. Where are those people?"

Donovan followed Ryan to one of the large computer screens used by the helmsman. He stood behind the crewman and studied the screen. He studied the image, a full-color chart of Monterey harbor, with contours denoting depths and clearly marked obstacles. The pier in question was shaped like a twelve-hundred-foot hockey stick, jutting out from the shore and creating the northeast breakwater for the marina. The final section angled thirty degrees from the longer initial portion. Donovan pointed at the spot and turned toward Ryan. "Right here, at the end of the pier, is where I saw the bulk of the people. We were flying low and there was smoke and flames, but I estimate there could be as many as a hundred, probably more."

"Let's hope they're still there," Ryan said. "Helm, what kind of depths are we going to have to work with when we get closer? Also, what's this structure made of?"

"It's mostly wood, though I remember cars driving out at least partway. So, maybe some asphalt as well," Donovan said.

"Captain, from the bend in the pier until the edge, we've got at least twenty fathoms under the keel."

"Okay, my plan is to nudge the starboard side of the ship up to the seaward edge of the pier," Ryan said. "I want to be able to use the entire length of the *Buckley* to bring people aboard. It will take less time that way."

As they drew closer, Donovan watched as rolling clouds of ash and red-hot sparks were lifted into the sky. Through his binoculars, he spotted the aquarium, and to his profound relief, the massive concrete structure, though blackened and windowless, looked mostly intact. All up and down Cannery Row, other buildings were either on fire or had collapsed into the water and were being dismantled wave by wave.

"Ethan," Ryan said into his radio. "I'm putting you in charge deckside. Get everyone you bring aboard straight into the hangar. Alert the medical teams to set up a temporary-aid station in the hangar. They can provide triage, and from there send the more severely injured to the infirmary. All the firefighting stations need to be manned and ready. I've also taken the liberty of assigning the crew of the *Olympia* to work alongside the *Buckley*'s crew. That gives us twice as many crewmen helping to pull the survivors aboard."

"Aye aye, Captain."

"Now, let's pray there are survivors," Ryan said to no one in particular and then raised the handheld radio. "Lookouts, stay sharp. There is a chance people will be in the water. Let's not run over anyone."

"Captain, Monterey wharf number two in sight," the helmsman called out.

Donovan and Lauren swung their binoculars forward. Through gaps in the smoke, Donovan caught sight of the pier and surrounding carnage. He could see the bulk of Monterey's fishing fleet piled up on the shore and burning. He still couldn't see enough of the structure to see if the people he'd spotted earlier were there.

"This is a mess," Ryan muttered as he, too, took in the scene through his binoculars. "Helm, slow to five knots, and stand by for full reverse."

Donovan lowered his binoculars. Lauren continued sweeping the wall of smoke looking for breaks, alleys that might give her a better view of the pier. The wave heights had eased, and shattered debris, sections of ships and buildings bobbed up and down in the murky water. Donovan could smell the heavy fuel oil. A body floated nearby, arms spread and motionless. As the *Buckley* entered thick smoke, Ryan ordered the ship's speed reduced once again.

"Sound the ship's horn," Ryan ordered. "One long blast should suffice."

Donovan stepped closer to the window as the bow of the ship pushed out of the smoke into nearly clear air. A hundred yards straight ahead was the wharf, and just beyond was nothing but a swirling tempest of flames. The wooden pier was burning near the elbow, flames eating away at the oiled wood structure. In the marina, crushed ships and leaking fuel had ignited, and the growing fire was working its way across the water. On the very end of the pier, trapped, were people who began waving their arms as the *Buckley* emerged from the smoke.

"Helm, steer twenty degrees to port, aim for the pier this side of the fire," Ryan called. He reached for the microphone, and his voice boomed ship-wide. "All hands, brace for impact, we're using the *Buckley*'s hull to take out the section of the pier between the fire and the survivors. Again, brace for impact."

Donovan reached for Lauren. As the ship altered course, terrified people on the pier began to stampede toward where they thought the ship was heading.

"Attention," Ryan's voice boomed from the *Buckley*'s loudspeakers. "People on the pier, hold your position. I repeat, stay where you are. We're going to ram the pier to cut off the fire."

"They're not listening," Donovan said as he watched helplessly.

"Fire teams," Ryan said into his handheld. "Make a wall."

Large-diameter jets of water erupted from the nozzles of the high-pressure water cannons mounted at key points on the ship's superstructure. The powerful streams arced out and carpeted the pier, stopping the crowd as the *Buckley* continued forward. The ship vibrated as it ran over floating debris. Donovan held Lauren's hand as they braced.

With a massive lurch, accompanied by the sound of snapping wood, the heavy steel bow came up out of the water. The hull continued across the width of the pier as the massive weight of the ship splintered pilings and ripped apart cross members until it ground to a stop. The water cannons continued to keep the people at bay as the *Buckley* rocked back and forth in the water.

"All astern," Ryan said to the helmsman.

Donovan felt the rumble under his feet ebb and then increase as the *Buckley* began to pull away from the pier. Once the ship eased away from the pilings, Donovan saw that Ryan had created a fifty-foot-wide gap in the structure. Giving a series of deft orders, Ryan and the helmsman used a combination of thrusters and main engines to back the *Buckley* parallel to the pier. With precise applications of power, they nudged the *Buckley* against the wood pilings. The last few feet created a series of grinding and screeching noises as the aging wood of the pier met heavy steel.

"Helm, hold this position," Ryan said. With the handheld radio, he ordered Ethan to begin pulling the survivors off the wharf.

Donovan and Lauren moved to the side of the ship to watch the rescue. Netting was lowered and Ethan and Montero, with several crewmen, went over the side to organize the evacuation at dock level. People on the wharf were met by crewmen of the *Buckley* and the *Olympia*, who calmed them as much as possible for an orderly climb to the deck. Donovan spotted Michael amidships, helping an older man who appeared to be wounded. The streams of people were met by more of the crew and shepherded into the helicopter hangar.

"We need to speed things up," Ryan radioed to Ethan.

Donovan glanced toward the bow. "Ryan, the fire on the pier is growing."

"It's moving this way," Lauren said. "Look, it's being fed by fuel oil bubbling up from that capsized tug. It's going to reach across the gap we made with the ship."

As the fire grew, the wood ripped apart by the *Buckley* ignited and the flames increased. Donovan placed the palm of his hand on the glass. "It's hot."

"Time to go," Ryan said as the water cannons saturated the pier, trying to maintain a barrier between the roaring flames and the ship. "Ethan, we're finished here—we're not going to be able to stop the fire. Helm, sound the horn, one long burst, and get ready to pull us away from the pier."

Donovan and Lauren looked at the survivors still on the dock. People were going to be left behind.

"Captain," Ethan's voice sounded from the radio as the warning blast from the horn came to an end. "We're all headed to the end of the pier. It'll buy us some time."

Donovan watched as Ethan and the other crewmen on the wharf began stopping people, pointing for them to go the other way. Some did as instructed, others panicked, pushing and shoving as they tried to move past. Without hesitation, Michael climbed down to dock level to assist Montero and the others.

"Helm, bow thrusters on my command," Ryan said. "Okay, it's time. Move us away from the wharf."

Donovan heard and felt the particular vibration that came from the propellers mounted on each side of the bow well below the waterline. A muffled screeching emanated from somewhere under their feet and the *Buckley* remained where it was.

"We're not moving." Ryan jumped from his chair and moved behind the helmsman. "We're jammed against the pier by something sturdy. Helm, rock us back and forth just like when we're out on the ice."

Donovan felt the entire ship vibrate beneath his feet as all the engines were put to the task of pushing and pulling the *Buckley*.

"Keep the water cannons on the fire," Ryan said into his radio. "Use one to hose down the ship and keep the exposed crewmen wet."

Lauren touched the glass, and jerked her hand back from the surface.

"Captain," a crewman called out as he burst onto the bridge. "On the VHF radio, I don't know who they are, or what happens when they arrive, but tanker 944 is headed our way."

Lauren pictured the screen saver she'd seen in San Jose. She squeezed Donovan's hand and then looked at Ryan. "Tanker 944 is a 747. Ernie is sending us help. Warn everyone to grab ahold of something."

"Everyone hang on!" Ryan said over the speakers. "There's a 747 inbound to help fight the fire."

A powerful whine began to build until the sound filled the bridge. The massive, low-flying, red-and-white 747 exploded into view and the converted airliner began to disgorge thousands of gallons of water, obliterating the fire on the pier. Seconds later, the 747 roared over the *Buckley*, drenching the ship, before making a sharp bank to the right, the nose pitching up into a steep growling climb.

Donovan felt the power of all four engines as the enormous Boeing thundered upward, and just before the 747 vanished in the smoke, he saw 944 painted on the tail.

"God bless those pilots," Ryan said as the sound of the 747 faded. "Helm, all stop."

Donovan went to the starboard side and watched as the reprieve given to them by the 747 was being used to direct the remaining survivors on the pier back toward the *Buckley*. Michael, Ethan, and Montero, all soaking wet, were urging people to climb aboard the ship. They maneuvered the last civilians off the dock and then climbed aboard the *Buckley* themselves.

"Captain, everyone is aboard," Ethan radioed.

The *Buckley*'s engines began to shake the entire ship. Foam, mud, and debris boiled up from beneath the hull. Ryan ordered the large crane on the starboard side of the *Buckley* to deploy and use the hydraulics like a giant arm to help push the *Buckley* off the pier.

With the added push from the crane, the hull, screeching in protest, began to pull away. The tip of the powerful crane extended into the water next to the ship. The hydraulics snapped wood and other debris, which boiled to the surface as the main engines and thrusters churned the water. With one final lurch, the *Buckley* pulled free and was once again floating.

"Helm." Ryan sat heavily in his seat. "Swing us around and then give me best speed out to sea."

CHAPTER FORTY-THREE

THE *BUCKLEY* CHARGED out into the open ocean, leaving the last of the smoke in its wake. Lauren led Donovan out the door that took them outside. She turned and took in the scene behind them. "Listen."

"For what?" Donovan asked as he scanned the shoreline. Fires were still visible in the blowing smoke, and Monterey and Pacific Grove were smoldering ruins.

"I don't hear the jets, or the constant rumble of explosions." Lauren leaned in, hugged Donovan's shoulder, and kissed him on the cheek. "I think it's a good sign."

"We may have an additional problem," Donovan said as he put his arm around her and pulled her close. "Last night, William, while heavily dosed with morphine, confessed to me, in front of Shannon, that he was sorry he messed up my life by not allowing Robert Huntington to stay and fight."

"Oh no." Lauren hugged her husband. "Did Shannon understand the full implications of what she was hearing?"

"Yes, there was nothing to deny, and she quickly filled in the blanks. She explained that she did graduate-level research on PTSD and used Robert as one of her main examples."

"Have you spoken with her since?"

"No, we've been a little busy." Donovan found a small smile to try to make his wife feel better. "At least for now, she can't go anywhere, and she can't reach the media."

"If she does, we're trapped on this ship," Lauren said. "Our daughter is on the East Coast and there is a no-fly zone in effect. She'll only have my mother as a first line of defense against what we know will be an extremely hostile media. Hell, if they know where to find you, the FBI might step in and detain you until they decide if you've broken any laws."

"We've been over this. I didn't break any laws. Most people who fake their death do it for the life insurance money. I've never had life insurance. I did crash a plane and didn't report it to the FAA—I'll claim amnesia. There are no legal issues at all. I vanished and changed my appearance and my name. People do that all the time. Maybe not as drastically as I did, but everything was legal—William saw to that detail just for this eventuality. The miracle is that my secret has lasted this long."

"If this unravels, we've always foreseen the need to get out of the country fast. It's been a while since we discussed this happening. Is the plan still to get to Austria, and sit out the worst of the fallout?"

"For the moment, I think that works to our advantage."

"We're going to be slowed down getting out of here, plus we have to collect Abigail."

"Within an hour we can have people we trust protecting Abigail. We have friends we can trust in Europe. In the short term, your mom is going to be a little freaked out, but we ran that risk by not telling her who I used to be. All of this, it's going to hurt a great many people. The person I dread most is Michael, and he's here on the ship. I'll have to explain in person why I kept him in the dark all these years."

"God, I hate this. Have you spoken to Montero yet? She'll need to know."

"You're the only one I've told so far," Donovan said. "At this point, as banged up as William is, I'd rather leave Montero with him. If anyone can keep him safe it's her."

"That's probably smart. What about us? You need a doctor, maybe a surgeon. How does all of that play into us needing to leave?"

"I left my briefcase in the SUV we rented. It was stolen. I also lost my wallet, which means I have no documents that allow me to drive a car, let alone leave the country."

"I retrieved your briefcase and handed your things over to Montero for safekeeping."

"That's a miracle. How did you do that?" Donovan said.

"Take a guess."

"I'm going to go with Montero."

"With a little help from Janie."

"I'll need to hear more about that later. Look, we'll figure all this out. We always do. The top story for days is going to be what happened here in California. Plus, Shannon has no vendetta against us. Eco-Watch saved her life a dozen times over the last twelve hours. That should count for something. At the very least she might give us a head start."

"I'll let you handle her. Are you sure she's not angry about Buck's death? You know her better than I, but we'll be in cell phone range soon. Then she'll have access to anyone she wants."

"I'll talk to her."

"I can't believe you were in the ocean for as long as you were. How are you doing?"

"You know, I had some moments where I thought the sea was going to win. There were some insightful flashbacks to when I lost my parents, different than usual, better. We'll talk about it later. Though I need to ask, whose blood was in the cockpit of the Gulfstream?"

"Rick was hit in the initial barrage. We got him to Stanford Medical Center. He's had surgery and is expected to make a complete recovery. How did you get hurt?"

"I was shot fighting a gang of drug thieves."

"You made that up," Lauren said as her phone pinged, alerting her to a text. "It's from Ernie, our friend at Cal Fire."

"What is it?" Donovan leaned in close as she expanded a picture that Ernie had sent. It was infrared, taken from high altitude. Donovan saw the hot spots that depicted the fires burning across the entire peninsula, from Carmel to Seaside, though what struck him was the sharp line of demarcation along an east-west line north of Monterey. "Is that real time?"

"Taken from the Global Hawk fifteen minutes ago," Lauren said. "Look, you can even see the *Buckley* in the harbor. The backburn is working. The main fire reached the one we set. Once the fuel is consumed, it's a stalemate. That's probably the reason Ernie could send the 747 to the harbor to help us. It worked."

Donovan looked at Lauren suspiciously. "The backburn was your idea? The planes dropping napalm, the ones that almost blew me up at the airport, they were your idea?"

"Not all mine; it was an idea we threw together on short notice. I may have suggested a little more horsepower be added to the effort," Lauren said, shrugging it off. "Had we not damaged the helicopter, I'm confident we would have gotten to you earlier."

"Exactly what happened to our helicopter?"

"Oh, that," Lauren said. "It's kind of a big deal. Janie was remarkable. All the rotor tips were messed up after we clipped a container from a sinking ship. Everyone agreed the helicopter was grounded, but when she saw you arrive at the Monterey airport, Janie went into action and was nothing short of heroic. It was extraordinary, really. Apparently, she'd heard some story once, probably in a bar, from an old-timer in Australia, about rotor damage in Vietnam. She grabbed some guys from engineering, and on a pitching deck, they cut off all four of the damaged tips, trying to make them as even as possible. In a matter of minutes, she fired that thing up and it flew."

"Amazing. I've never heard of such a thing," Donovan said as he tried to picture the aerodynamics, but couldn't.

"No one else had either. If it wasn't for Janie, you'd have been in the water way longer than you were."

"Speaking of helicopters." Donovan pointed out across the water. "We've got one headed our way. I hope it's a medevac for William."

"What if they take Shannon?" Lauren said. "We'll lose all containment."

"There's got to be more seriously injured people than her."

"Donovan, Lauren," Ryan said as he stuck his head out of the hatchway. "The inbound Coast Guard helicopter is for William, and the injured sailor from the *Olympia*. Michael just reported that William seems stable and good for transport. We're about to move our helicopter into the hangar, to make room for them to land."

"Let's get down there." Donovan limped toward the elevator that would take them to the helipad. "Ryan, how many people did we pull off the pier?"

"One hundred and twelve," Ryan said. "The story I've heard is that they sought refuge from the tsunami by fleeing to the upper floors of the Marriott. When the power went out, they elected to wait until morning for help to arrive. When fire became a threat, they were forced to evacuate, and the only place they could go was the pier."

"Where are we headed?" Lauren asked.

"We've been asked to bring the survivors to San Francisco," Ryan said. "Then we're headed to the shipyard. I've got a damaged helicopter, as well as a hull that needs to be inspected. We'll probably be there for a while."

"Sounds good," Donovan said as the door to the elevator opened and out charged Ethan. Sidestepping at the last second to avoid a collision, he dropped a hundred-dollar poker chip, which fell on the floor and started to roll away.

"Mr. Nash, Dr. McKenna, excuse me," Ethan said, a towel around his neck. "I was headed to my quarters for dry clothes."

Lauren used the toe of her shoe to stop the chip and reached down to pick it up. "Bellagio? Ethan, are you a gambler?"

"No, not really, it's for good luck," Ethan said.

"I'd say it worked today," Lauren said as she handed him the chip.

"Thank you, Ethan," Donovan said. "Nice work finding us out at sea, and then getting all the survivors on the ship. The *Buckley* is lucky to have you aboard."

"I'm glad it worked. The 747 was a nice touch. Thanks to who-ever made that little miracle happen," Ethan said over his shoulder as he hurried down the passageway.

As the elevator door closed, Lauren looked up at her husband. "He seems nice. Where did Ryan find him, or is Ethan from one of the other Eco-Watch ships?"

"Actually, it was Montero who knew him. They have a history that stretches back to when Montero was living in Florida working for the FBI. Ethan's former Coast Guard, and he reached out to Montero when he heard we were recruiting people for our new ship. Montero didn't want anyone to accuse her of favoritism in helping a friend get hired, so she came to me and gave me a heads-up before we hired him. He's a good guy," Donovan said as the doors opened and he limped into the passageway.

"Slow down and stop right where you are," Lauren ordered. "I can hear your knee popping. You need to be off your feet, or at least on crutches. In fact, you should see if there's room on the Coast Guard helicopter and fly to the hospital with William."

"We'll see." Donovan held out his arm and used Lauren's shoulder for support. The Coast Guard helicopter was hovering off the port bow. The damaged Eco-Watch helicopter was up on a motorized lift that supported the weight of the machine and allowed it to be rolled from the pad into the hangar. Under Janie's watchful eye, the helicopter was maneuvered inside the hangar and dozens of survivors gathered around the helicopter to witness the process. When the helicopter was secured, the survivors gave themselves a round of applause, and then gathered behind a mesh barrier the crew had hastily strung across the hangar entrance to allow the Coast Guard helicopter to land on a secure pad.

Donovan and Lauren made their way to William's stretcher. Michael and Montero were kneeling next to him. As they approached, Donovan was stunned to see that William's eyes were open. At seeing Donovan, he reached out with his good arm. Donovan ignored the pain in his leg, leaned down, and gripped William's hand.

"How much do you remember?" Donovan asked, wondering if William had any memory of revealing their secret, knowing they'd eventually discuss every detail as William recuperated.

"Only bits and pieces."

"I'm going to see if I can get on this helicopter and go with you. We'll have plenty of time to talk."

"Son," William said as the noise from the helicopter grew louder. Donovan leaned down, and the two men held on to each other.

"Thank you for coming to get me."

"If you remember, you came for me once upon a time," Donovan said referring to William's swift actions when Donovan's parents drowned. "You've rescued me more than once."

William smiled weakly and held Donovan's hand as the Coast Guard helicopter touched down. The aft doors slid open and two men wearing orange jumpsuits, helmets, and yellow life vests raced across the deck. They were trailed by a man in a suit, wearing a life jacket. The helicopter crew took the injured crewman from the

Olympia first, and once he was secured in the helicopter, they came back for William.

Above the dull roar from the idling helicopter, Donovan asked one of the jumpsuited men. "Can I go with him?"

"Sorry, no room."

Donovan let go of William's hand as they lifted him and walked to the idling helicopter.

"Dr. McKenna," the man in the suit called out to Lauren.

Donovan heard his wife's name and saw Lauren look up, a flash of worry crossing her face when she spotted the stranger. Donovan turned and limped to intercept the man before he reached Lauren. "Excuse me. Who are you?"

"I'm Coast Guard Special Agent Billings. I've been sent to escort Dr. McKenna back to San Francisco."

"She's not going anywhere with you," Donovan said loud enough for the others around him to hear.

"What's going on here?" Montero said, slipping between Donovan and the man in the suit. "I'm former FBI agent Veronica Montero. State your business."

"I'm well aware who you are, Ms. Montero, but regardless of your standing, I was dispatched to escort Dr. McKenna to San Francisco."

"Under whose authority?" Montero snapped. "Is she under arrest?"

"She can be," Agent Billings replied. "Or I can bring her in under her own recognizance, which is my preference."

"What are the charges?" Montero asked.

"There's a list, and most fall under the heading of treason under martial law."

"It's okay," Lauren said as she stepped forward. "I'll go."

"Don't talk to anyone. I'll try to have an attorney waiting for you when you land," Montero said. "Don't worry. We'll fix this."

Donovan leaned in and kissed Lauren, hugged her, and whispered in her ear. "I'll see you later. Go easy on the government, we may need them later."

Lauren smiled at him over her shoulder as she was escorted to the helicopter. Moments later, it lifted off the helipad, rotated smartly, and powered toward the distant hills and the city beyond.

"I'll arrange a charter to get us to San Francisco as fast as possible," Montero said.

"There's still a no-fly zone in effect." Michael looked at his watch. "We'll probably be at the dock in five hours or so."

"That'll give us enough time." Donovan put his arms around Michael and Montero. "Let's go visit our survivors and see if we can sway some public opinion."

"What are you talking about?" Montero said. "A hundred survivors aren't going to sway the FBI or the Pentagon."

"Probably not directly." Donovan stood in front of the assembled crowd and raised his hands to get their attention. "Ladies and gentlemen, it's been a hell of a day, hasn't it? But we're all alive, which is, in and of itself, a miracle."

Donovan paused as the crowd cheered, and more people packed in to join the throng. "Earlier this morning, at first light, a jet flew over the pier. You probably couldn't see what happened after that, but the jet crashed into the ocean. I was the pilot, and this ship, and the brave crew of the *Buckley*, came to my rescue, and then they came to yours."

More cheers erupted and Donovan waited. Then he held up his hands and continued to talk. "You just watched as the Coast Guard landed and evacuated our more seriously wounded. You also no doubt saw them escort a woman aboard the helicopter. That woman is Dr. Lauren McKenna. It was Lauren's connections that brought in the 747 tanker, and allowed all of you to board this ship.

It was her and the entire crew of the *Buckley* who put their lives on the line to rescue you. The problem is that, to save you, she violated direct orders from the military and breached a restricted area under martial law. Now, mind you, there were no military assets that were going to help you. No, you were an acceptable loss in their eyes, but Dr. McKenna didn't think that was right. She was just taken into custody, and now faces charges of treason."

Boos and jeers echoed in the hangar as the survivors reacted.

Donovan waited until the noise finally died out enough to be heard. "My question to you people is this: How many of you took pictures or video when this ship came out of the smoke into Monterey Harbor to save you?"

Donovan smiled as dozens of people held up their phones. "How many of you have footage of the *Buckley* crashing into the pier to stop the fire from reaching you? Or the 747 saving us all?"

More people held up phones and began cheering.

"We'll be in cell phone range shortly," Montero said so only Donovan could hear.

"All of us on this ship are alive because of Eco-Watch and Dr. Lauren McKenna. In spite of what we endured, the horrors we witnessed, good things happened here today. We'll be in cell phone range shortly, so I urge all of you to post and share what you witnessed this morning. If reporters want to interview you, let them. Tell the world what it felt like to be trapped and about to die, and then tell them how it felt to be saved. Dr. McKenna shouldn't be persecuted by shortsighted military leaders. She's the reason we're alive, and she should be hailed as a hero. Let's all do everything we can to make sure that happens."

Amplified from being inside the metal hangar, the noise from the survivors was deafening. Donovan waved, and with Michael's and Montero's help, he hobbled away.

Michael leaned in. "The crew set up an overflow infirmary down the corridor. On the direct orders of your wife, you're going there right now to get your leg checked out. If you argue, I'm going to turn the situation over to Montero."

"Okay, okay." Donovan held up his hands in surrender. "I'll let Montero take me. Michael, I want you to find out how Shannon is doing."

"I'll get an update," Michael said. "Then you and I need to talk. It's important."

"I can listen now." Donovan could hear the seriousness in his voice.

"No, get your leg fixed up, and after I check on Shannon, I'll find you," Michael said as he peeled off.

"What's up?" Montero asked the moment they were alone.

"Shannon knows the truth about me."

"Oh no," Montero said. "What do you need me to do? Our hands are tied until I can get a helicopter out here to fly us ashore."

"The situation isn't critical, yet. I need to talk to Shannon," Donovan said. "I wanted you in the loop. If Lauren and I need to leave, I'm going to ask you to stay and protect William. He's vulnerable right now."

"Understood," Montero said. "Out of curiosity, how did she find out?"

"William's injuries combined with morphine, shock, and regrets. It wasn't his fault."

CHAPTER FORTY-FOUR

"I WASN'T AWARE that any Eco-Watch personnel were in need of treatment." The surprised crewman looked up to find Donovan and Montero standing in the small room. "I just finished treating the last of the survivors."

"Marcus," Montero said. "Mr. Nash is having leg issues."

"Okay, Mr. Nash, I'm Marcus." He shook Donovan's hand and snapped on a fresh pair of rubber gloves. "Ms. Montero, let's see if we can help Mr. Nash up on the table."

Donovan hadn't yet met all of the crew. If he had, he'd have remembered Marcus. He was probably six foot four, broad-shouldered and fit. He had brown skin, a broad smile, and dense black hair buzzed short on the sides. His intense brown eyes were deep set and serious, though subtle laugh lines softened the effect. Donovan braced himself against the pain as Marcus and Montero helped him up onto the table.

"Ms. Montero, I've got it from here. Maybe you could be so kind as to ask the first mate for some dry clothes for Mr. Nash?" Marcus said. He took his first look at Donovan's blood-stained trouser leg, and removed a pair of scissors from his kit.

"I'll be back." Montero stepped out and closed the door.

"While I cut, why don't you tell me what happened here." Marcus took the scissors and began cutting the fabric high on Donovan's thigh. When he finished, he eased the soaked material from Donovan's leg.

"I was shot," Donovan said. "Though, the worst of my injuries is my knee. I jumped from a window and landed badly. I can hardly put any weight on it at all."

"I see." Marcus continued snipping until all of the earlier dressings Shannon had applied fell away. He dried the skin to finally examine the furrow in Donovan's thigh. "Is this your only gunshot wound?"

"Yes," Donovan said.

"Okay, it's just a nick. You'll have another scar," Marcus said. "Your knee is a problem, I can see the swelling."

Donovan nodded as he felt Marcus gently manipulate the knee in several directions.

"It doesn't feel loose," Marcus said. "You may have some damaged cartilage. I'll get everything wrapped up, but you'll need to get with an orthopedic doctor. Once they MRI your knee, they'll know what's going on."

"Thanks. Sounds like a plan," Donovan said.

"Can I ask how you managed to get shot?"

"I had an unfortunate run-in with some looters," Donovan replied, and then changed the subject. "You're new to Eco-Watch, aren't you?"

"Yes, sir. I'm from Norfolk, Virginia. Ever since I was a little kid, I've always loved ships. I'd ride my bike down to the waterfront and sit and watch the harbor for hours. I still go down and look at the ships. When I saw my first Eco-Watch ship, I thought it looked cool, and it made me curious. I did some research and I knew where I needed to work."

"That's not a southern accent," Donovan said. "Where are you from?"

"All over, actually," Marcus said. "Most people hear the British accent, courtesy of my mother. My father is Egyptian. We traveled a lot when I was a kid, so I've assembled a multicultural collection of accents. I can curse in seven languages."

"That's excellent." Donovan laughed, and was struck by the fact that it felt like it had been forever since he'd even smiled.

"What's your specialty?" Donovan asked, knowing that the two men who doubled as paramedics on board had other special training.

"I was in the Navy for six years as an electrical engineer. I trained as a paramedic in Norfolk after I was out of the Navy."

"Marcus, welcome aboard. It's been a hell of a first cruise for the *Buckley*."

"It's exactly what I signed up for," Marcus said as he finished dressing the wound and then wrapped Donovan's knee tightly. "I'm glad we saved those people. I've followed Eco-Watch Marine since its inception, and helping people is the number one reason I wanted to be a part of the organization."

"I can't tell you how nice it is to hear you say that," Donovan said. "It's what I had in mind when I joined in on the creation of the company. I'm curious, of all the survivors we pulled off the wharf, what were the worst of the injuries?"

"I don't think there were any serious injuries with that group. If there were, they would have been taken to the infirmary. What I saw here were people with bumps and bruises, some cuts and abrasions."

"That's good to hear," Donovan said. "I hope we can sway some public opinion, and get Dr. McKenna released."

"Your speech was excellent. I think you reached them. What struck me today was talking with people who thought they were going to die, and didn't, because of us. They were so thankful, almost apologetic for taking up my time. Even the last guy, who had the worst injury of the morning, was relieved to be alive. He asked me a ton of questions about the ship."

"What was his injury?"

"He said he fell on a section of exposed rebar. I stitched up his arm and sent him to the infirmary for a tetanus shot and something for the pain. How is your pain level? I don't have anything here stronger than Tylenol."

Donovan was about to take Marcus up on some Tylenol when he stopped. "This guy with the rebar injury. What did he look like?"

"He was medium height, muscles, bald with a ton of tattoos, why?"

"Does a rebar injury look anything like a bullet wound?"

"Maybe," Marcus said as his eyes turned serious. "Who is this guy?"

"The one who shot me." Donovan sat up and swept his legs off the side of the table and let himself down to the floor. "Did you get his name?"

"He said everyone just calls him Jake. I can radio the bridge and have security converge on the infirmary." Marcus peeled off his gloves and reached for a handheld radio on a shelf.

"No," Donovan said. "He could have a radio as well. You sent him to the infirmary?"

"Yes, not five minutes before you arrived."

"The woman who nearly drowned—she came in on the Eco-Watch helicopter. Is she still in there? Do you know who I'm talking about?"

"Yes, we were briefed on all the VIPs. You're talking about Shannon, the girlfriend of the man this ship is named after, right?"

"Yes."

"As far as I know, she's still in the infirmary," Marcus said. "Though, as other injuries came in, she may have been moved. I've been working in here, so I just don't know."

"If she's still in there, she's in trouble, and so is Michael Ross." Donovan limped for the door. "I need to take him by surprise. Do you have anything I can use as a weapon?"

"I do." Marcus stepped forward. "Me. He knows I'm a medic; I told him I'd check in on him. I can walk in and he won't suspect a thing."

"Are you sure?" Donovan asked. "This guy is a killer."

"Not on my ship, he's not." Marcus clipped his radio on his belt, put on his Eco-Watch hat, and moved past Donovan out into the passageway. "Follow me."

Donovan ignored his exposed leg and limped as fast as he could but fell behind. Marcus was a man on a mission. As they reached a junction in the corridor, Marcus stopped to wait for Donovan.

"The infirmary is the third door on the left," Marcus whispered, and then snapped his head around as he heard someone opening a nearby hatch.

Donovan watched as Marcus walked toward the sound and waited until a young woman stepped out of the room.

"Teresa," Marcus said quietly as he took her by the arm. "We have a problem. We need your help."

"Marcus, what are you talking about?" The young woman turned toward Donovan. "Mr. Nash? What's going on?"

"We have a potential situation in the infirmary. One of the survivors from the wharf is a suspected criminal. He's bald, tattoos, probably armed and dangerous," Marcus said in a rush. "Don't use the radio. In fact, don't let anyone use a radio. I need you to get to the bridge. Inform the captain what's going on, and we need to find Montero."

To his great relief, Teresa nodded and took off running. Donovan turned toward Marcus. "Ready?"

"Try to keep up," Marcus said as he strode toward the infirmary.

Marcus threw open the door and with Donovan right behind him, they barreled into the room. The four bunks were empty, and on the floor lay a man wearing an Eco-Watch uniform.

"Tim." Marcus knelt next to the man and checked his pulse. Then he stood, opened a locker, and extracted a package.

Marcus snapped a capsule in half, and Donovan instantly smelled the acrid ammonia vapors.

"Tim, time to wake up." Marcus waved the capsule under the downed man's nose and within seconds, Tim began to respond. "Tim, it's Marcus. Are you hurt?"

"That bastard." Tim waved at the capsule to get it out of his face and then touched the growing bump on his forehead. "He held a scalpel to Shannon's neck until I gave him all of our narcotics. Then he slammed my head into the wall."

"He has Shannon. Who else was in here?" Donovan asked.

"Michael Ross came in and was sitting with her when he was called to the bridge," Tim said as he raised himself up with Marcus' help.

"Michael's on the bridge?" Donovan asked.

"I don't know for sure. He left before the guy came in and grabbed Shannon."

"Okay, the tattooed guy wants off this ship," Donovan said to Marcus. "Which way is the boat deck?"

"This is a full-blown hostage situation," Marcus said. "I think we should wait for Montero."

"Attention, helicopter launch crew, this is the Captain. Man your departure stations. We need the helicopter airborne as soon as possible."

"Montero's not coming," Donovan said to Marcus. "She would have been here by now. Our guy is on the bridge, and he's using Shannon to get off the ship via the helicopter. The captain knows the helicopter won't fly. He's trying to buy some time. The guns aboard—are they still locked in the captain's quarters?"

"Yes, the captain and his second-in-command have the only keys, but we'd have to run the risk of trying to get past the bridge to get to them."

"The problem with using a gun is if that jerk is holding a scalpel to Shannon's carotid artery, one involuntary nerve twitch, and she's dead."

Donovan heard the sound of someone running down the corridor.

"It's me." Teresa held up her hands as she stepped into the infirmary. "The tattooed guy, he's up there on the bridge with Shannon. I couldn't tell anyone anything."

"Who all is up there?"

"Captain Pittman, the usual two-man crew seated at the controls, Ethan, Ms. Montero, and Michael Ross."

"Marcus, you bandaged his arm," Donovan said. "I'm trying to find a weakness. How much can he use his injured arm and hand?"

"His hand works fine," Marcus said. "His problems come with strength in his upper arm as well as range of motion. He'll have some limitations, as in it's unlikely he can throw much of a punch."

"Teresa," Donovan said. "When you saw him, how was he positioned in relation to Shannon?"

"He was standing behind her, his left arm across her chest. With his right hand, he was holding something against her neck. I only took one glance and then turned and ran back."

"Okay, here's what I want you to do, and we don't have much time." As Donovan spoke, he remembered Buck always telling him he was impatient and reckless, and this idea wasn't going to be any different. "When he and Shannon go from the bridge to the helipad, I'll ambush him."

"You can barely walk," Marcus said. "Let me take this guy out."

"He's mine. If it doesn't work, I take the responsibility. If we find the right place for the ambush, I won't need to walk." Donovan took a moment and looked at Teresa. "If I remember correctly, you're part of the dive team, right?"

"Yes, sir, assistant dive master."

"Perfect," Donovan said. "As fast as you can, go to the equipment room and bring up three of the bang sticks. I want the four-footers."

Teresa's eyes grew wide, before she smiled at the idea and raced from the infirmary.

"I see now what you're thinking," Marcus said, "but we run into the same problem we have with a gun. Just like with a shark, if you hit him with a bang stick, the bullet goes off, the shark flinches and twists in the water. If this guy jerks with that scalpel, Shannon runs the risk of bleeding out." He started to pace in the small compartment. "There's got to be a better way."

"Hang on. Mr. Nash might be on to something." Tim walked over to Donovan. "Can you feel this?"

"Sure," Donovan said as the tips of Tim's fingers pressed into the flesh at the base of his skull.

"Now, imagine a golf ball–sized sphere positioned where my fingers are. Roughly, that's the area that contains the brain stem. All of the brain's messages to the body are routed through here. If you can position the force from the cartridge in the bang stick here, it's over. The assailant will experience flaccid paralysis—no messages from the brain reach the body. He'll go limp."

"Perfect," Donovan said. "All we need is to set up the ambush."

"There are two completely separate ways for them to get from the bridge to the helipad," Marcus said. "We'll have to set up two different ambush points."

"No, there's one place we know he'll be. Plus, he'll be an easier target if he's stationary."

"The helicopter?" Tim asked.

"Yes, and we need to get out there before he does. Let's plan for the worst. Marcus, is there a portable trauma kit of some kind you guys could bring to use on Shannon if things go south?"

"I'll get the go-kit." Tim opened a locker and grabbed a red duffel bag.

"Find me a roll of white tape," Donovan said as he formed the beginning of an idea.

"I'm ready." Tim looped the go-kit across his back and handed Donovan the roll of tape.

"Can I ask you two for a little help?" With Tim on one side and Marcus on the other, Donovan was whisked out of the infirmary down the passageway that ran alongside the hangar. They stopped at the door that led to the helipad. The ground crew had already pulled the helicopter from the hangar and positioned it on the pad. Donovan was relieved that the large hangar doors were closed in preparation for the launch, which prevented an audience. Janie, a worried frown on her face, had just pulled herself up into the pilot's seat, the door still open.

"I need to step outside and try to talk to Janie without anyone from the bridge seeing me," Donovan said as he opened the hatch and realized it was strangely quiet. The wind was blowing from the stern and blocked by the superstructure of the ship. He steadied himself on his good leg against the pitching of the ship in the following sea and waved his arms until he got Janie's attention.

"Don't look at me, but listen," Donovan called out, hoping that his voice wouldn't carry to the bridge. "Whatever you do, don't take this thing into the air. Sit on the helipad and melt the engines if you need to, but don't fly."

"I wasn't going to," Janie said as she continued running her checklist. "Once I start the engines, the guy is coming down from the bridge with Shannon. Montero whispered to me that once the guy is off the bridge, Ethan is going to break out rifles from the weapons locker. The plan is for Montero to try to take him out before he reaches the helicopter."

Donovan turned as Teresa arrived and handed him the bang sticks.

"They're loaded and ready," Teresa said.

Donovan selected two and gave the remaining one back to Teresa. "Self-defense."

"Mr. Nash," Teresa asked. "Have you ever used one of these before?"

"I have. Buck taught me." Donovan faced the helicopter. "Janie, if you can, radio the bridge, tell Montero to shoot only as a last resort. Once this guy is on his way down here with Shannon, I'm going to climb up on the roof of the helicopter. It'll put me high enough he won't be able to see me from hangar level. Make sure to leave the side doors open. Tell him it's his only way out if you need to ditch or something. I need the doors open. When the rotors reach full speed, I'm making my move. Understand?"

"Got it," Janie said, never once glancing at Donovan. "I'll flash a landing light when they're on their way down."

Donovan handed Marcus the tape and lined up both bang sticks so that the cartridge-filled power tips were side by side. "Tape these together. Two shots are better than one."

Marcus worked quickly, wrapping the tape tightly at both ends.

"Well done." Donovan tested the lightweight weapon. It felt as nimble as a pool cue compared to the steel pry bar that had gotten him through the night. "I'm going to need a boost up to the top of the helicopter when it's time. Once I'm up, I'll need you to toss up the bang sticks."

"No problem," Marcus said as he studied the helicopter. "I'll step up on the skid, and you use my shoulders like a ladder."

Donovan took off his shoes and instead of leaving them to be noticed, he threw them over the railing. "I need to stay quiet until Janie has the engines and rotors making enough noise so the target can't hear me moving on top of the helicopter."

"Is there going to be enough room when the rotors start to turn?" Marcus asked.

"Yes, as long as I don't stand up. What I need from you is a signal to tell me where he's seated. Can you do that?"

"Sure," Marcus said. "Janie is in seat one. Seat two is right next to her. Seat three is behind her. Four is next to it, back and forth. Will that work? Once I get you situated, I'll drop down off the helipad to the main deck. You'll be able to see me, he won't. I'll get a look and hold up some fingers."

"That's perfect," Donovan said.

Janie turned on the red rotating beacon as a warning to the ground crew, and the first turbine engine began a low whine as she began the start sequence. Donovan put his arm around Marcus and waited.

"Go!" Donovan said the instant Janie flashed the helicopter's landing lights. With Marcus taking most of his weight, they quickly made it around the fuselage, and Donovan felt himself being boosted up toward the top of the helicopter. He placed his good foot on Marcus' shoulder, pushed off, and squirmed his way on top of the cabin. Marcus handed up the two bang sticks and then dropped to the pad and slid off to the deck below.

Donovan did his best to make himself as flat as possible. The rotor was spinning just above him, and the hideous whistle from the damaged blades seemed to rip through his entire body, shaking his bones. His eyes locked on Marcus, and the noise grew even louder as Janie started the second engine. As it spooled up, Donovan caught sight of shadows on the deck moving toward the helicopter.

It was too loud to hear anything but the deafening shriek, and the entire helicopter shook to the point that Donovan worried about his ability to deliver an accurate strike.

Marcus held up three fingers. His target was seated directly behind Janie. As the rotor accelerated, Donovan slid to the edge of the roof. Mounted in front of him was the housing for the hoist. The brackets were stressed to suspend nearly seven hundred pounds.

Donovan pictured the interior one last time and wrapped his left hand around the hoist for balance. He clenched the bang stick firmly, and in one fluid motion, he swung his upper body down into the space created by the open door. Hanging upside down, Donovan zeroed in on the side of the bald head, pinpointed his target, and jabbed the twin cartridges as hard as he could.

The noise from the rotor blades masked the simultaneous discharges from the bang sticks. A spray of blood peppered the opposite wall, and the man who had caused Donovan and Shannon so much grief dropped the scalpel and slumped in his seat.

Donovan felt himself sliding. His center of gravity was too far over the edge, and he desperately grabbed for the hoist with his other hand as he reached the edge.

Janie chopped the power to the engines and threw off her harness. Donovan's hand momentarily caught the hoist, jerking him outward, but his fingers slipped off the metal. A yell came from deep inside Donovan's chest as he twisted in an effort to land on his good leg.

The impact rattled him. He rolled onto his shoulder, hit hard, and lay still. On his back, Donovan watched Marcus, gloved up, reach into the cabin and come away with Shannon in his arms. She looked small in his thick arms. Marcus lowered her to the deck.

"Donovan, don't move," Janie called out as she used the rotor brake and brought the whistling blades to an abrupt stop. The only sounds Donovan could hear were the pounding of the *Buckley's* bow against the waves and people running.

Michael knelt at Donovan's side and put his hand on Donovan's chest to keep him from moving. "Stay where you are. Don't try to get up quite yet. Wiggle your hands and toes."

Donovan did as Michael asked. "I'm fine. Everything works. Shannon?"

"They're working on her," Montero said as she joined them. "Donovan! Holy crap. A bang stick? That was genius. I was watching through a scoped rifle—it was going to be a pretty dicey shot with the pitching deck. You nailed him. His entire body went limp the instant you hit him. Can you move?"

Donovan raised his head and looked to where Shannon lay. Marcus, gauze pads in hand, worked to pull her hair away from her blood-covered neck. Donovan saw her eyes wide open with fear.

Tim arrived and knelt next to Marcus. He set the go-kit on the deck next to him and joined in to wipe away the blood on her neck. "Where's she hit?"

Janie swung out of the cockpit and leaned over Shannon. "Come on, Shannon, talk to us."

"I don't think this is her blood," Tim said as he continued searching her neck and head. "She's not injured. I can't find a single laceration."

Shannon's expression changed as the fear slowly left her body, and it began to sink in that she'd survived. "Oh, my God, thank you," she said and began to sob.

"Are you sure you're okay? You're a little old to be doing gymnastics," Michael said to Donovan.

"I'm good." With Michael and Montero's help, Donovan eased himself up until he was standing between them. He tested his joints and his balance. "No worse than before. I might be a little sore in the morning, but I'll live."

"Let's get you up to the bridge," Michael said.

"Janie and I will stay with Shannon," Montero said.

Marcus helped Shannon to her feet. He used his body to block her view of the carnage inside the helicopter. Before she was helped away, Shannon turned and over her shoulder gave Donovan a grateful nod.

"We still need to talk," Michael said as they made their way toward the elevator.

"Can it wait twenty minutes while I clean up and change clothes? If not, we can talk now."

"It'll wait for twenty minutes."

CHAPTER FORTY-FIVE

DONOVAN SAT IN Captain Ryan's ready room, complete with dry clothes, crutches, and an icepack bundled around his knee. He'd wolfed down a breakfast sandwich and a bottle of orange juice. He'd made several phone calls while watching the reports about how the enormous fire on the Monterey Peninsula had been stopped. It would be months before the full extent of the damage and loss of life would be known. What was clear was that California might still be burning without the daring plan initiated by Lauren and an assemblage of government agencies working together.

Precisely twenty minutes elapsed when Michael knocked and let himself into the room. He held two cups of coffee. He handed one to Donovan.

"Thanks for the refill," Donovan said.

Michael took a chair across from Donovan. He placed his hands flat on the table, looked into his lap, then took in a deep breath and let it out slowly.

Donovan felt the little hairs on the back of his neck tingle. Michael was typically easygoing, yet quietly fearless. They'd been close friends for years. In all that time, he'd never seen him have to build up the courage to speak.

"I'm just going to come out and say this. We have a problem. I overheard Shannon trying to talk to William in the infirmary."

"Talking about what?"

"She was whispering—I only heard bits and pieces. William was still kind of out of it, so it was pretty much a one-sided conversation. When I moved closer, she stopped. I heard enough to realize that somehow she knows you used to be Robert Huntington. With William and Lauren ashore, I needed to warn you so we can start making contingency plans."

Donovan reeled from the words. He felt his body deflate, as if all of the air had left him. He searched Michael's eyes, and to his great relief there was no judgment or blame—only concern and urgency. "How did you find out? How long have you known?"

"Oh, God, I've known for years. Before I came to Eco-Watch, I knew of Robert Huntington, hell, everyone did. But all I cared about was he was a rich guy who owned and flew a bunch of cool airplanes. When he died in a crash, I remember thinking it was sad. Years later I started working with you, and one night, we were drinking in Montreal, and the conversation turned to airplane accidents involving celebrities. We talked about Payne Stewart and John Denver. At one point I mentioned Robert Huntington, and at the mention of that name, there was a subtle shift in your eyes, your body language tightened. It had been a normal conversation up until that point, and it made me curious. At first, I thought maybe you were a friend of Huntington's, or in some way connected to the crash itself. Trust me, I wasn't on some sort of quest, but over the course of several months of digging through aviation archives, I ran across a bootleg tape of a speech you gave at the Smithsonian—it was you, your voice. You're Robert Huntington, and I was blown away. I mean, how could I not be?"

"Yet, you didn't say anything."

"I gave it a great deal of thought. Ultimately, I kind of understood. Everyone has a past, and yours has been difficult." Michael shrugged. "I looked back and pieced together what it must have taken to endure everything that had happened to you. Who among us hasn't wished for some kind of do-over? You pulled it off. You re-invented yourself, and that can't be easy. When I was able to calmly process what I'd discovered, and combine it with what I already knew about you, there were several constants. You're a highly in-telligent man, and your loyalty is extraordinary, as is your passion for what we do. That's enough for me, and our friendship has never wavered. You've taken Eco-Watch and turned it into more than a place to work. It's a family. My worst fear was if I ever said some-thing, it might somehow alter our friendship, which was the last thing I wanted."

Donovan remembered dozens of conversations with Michael that seemed to take on a new meaning. "It's the same reason I never told you who I really was. Eco-Watch is what it is because of all the work we've done together, and I can't thank you enough. You're the best friend I've ever had. Robert never really enjoyed that luxury. I thought about telling you hundreds of times, but I was terrified the truth might change everything between us."

"Same here. I wouldn't have said anything today, except Shannon may be a problem, and she's uncontained. I'm assuming you've planned for this possibility? The media, as well as public opinion, weren't very kind to you twenty-five years ago. I can't imagine what today's media storm will look like if you were exposed."

"Thank you," Donovan said. "You've always had my back. If I could get up, I'd give you a hug."

"Let's put a rain check on the hug and figure out what we need to do to keep you and your family safe."

"As for Shannon, Lauren and Montero are already in the loop. I'll talk with her, and see what she's thinking. Montero's been keeping an eye on her. If she gives us any inkling she's going to go to the media, we can slow her down until we reach port. Then you're right, I'm out of here. Lauren and Abigail and I have had plans in place for years to deal with this problem."

"Montero knows?" Michael shook his head in bewilderment. "How many of us are there?"

"As of today, besides you and I, there are ten other people in the world who know the secret—unless you've told someone?"

"No one."

"Thank you for that," Donovan said.

A knock sounded at the door and Montero announced herself.

"Hang on a second," Donovan called out. "For the moment let's not share this discussion with Montero. I need to think about how best to proceed. Are we good?"

"We're good," Michael said.

"You and I will sit down sometime soon and we'll talk at length."

"That works for me." Michael stood.

"Thank you," Donovan said and then called out to Montero.

"Am I bothering you?" Montero said as she poked her head into the room. "Oh, Michael, I didn't know you were here. I can come back."

"Have a seat." Michael stepped toward the door.

"I'm good," Montero said. "I'll stand. This won't take long. I want to bring everyone up to date. One of our survivors is a Monterey County Deputy Sheriff. He's taken full control of the crime scene that is our helicopter. We used several tarps to fully wrap the cabin to conceal the interior. The helicopter has been moved back into the hangar. I told the sheriff you were recovering from injuries, and that you would be happy to give a formal statement later. He agreed."

"What else?" Donovan asked.

"The perp is known to the sheriff. Seems he was a wanted felon. With an entire bridge of witnesses who saw you stop a kidnapping, there won't be any legal issues."

"What about our federal law enforcement issues?" Donovan asked. "Any word on Lauren?"

"I learned she was met at the hospital by more agents and transferred to another helicopter. I've had zero luck chartering a helicopter to fly out and pick us up. Once we make port, I'm headed to San Francisco FBI headquarters. I'll find the answers."

"Keep me posted. Anything else?" Donovan asked.

"I helped Shannon clean up and we found her some clothes. She's tough, I'll give her that much. She's also waiting in the passageway to speak with you."

Donovan's thoughts began to churn. He had no idea what to expect from Shannon. "Let her in. She and I have a lot to talk about."

Montero opened the door, held it for Shannon, and then quietly closed the door behind her as she and Michael left the room.

"Please, sit." Donovan held out his hand.

Shannon sat with her hands folded in her lap.

"We survived," Donovan said.

"We did. Thank you for keeping your promise to me. Janie told me everything that took place after we crashed," Shannon said. "She explained how you left William behind, dived and brought me up, and then you performed mouth-to-mouth resuscitation until we were aboard the helicopter. I know enough to understand how difficult that must have been for you. I remember the expression on your face when we were first out on the wing. You were suffering. When I woke up in the helicopter, I made the assumption that Ethan and Michael were the ones who'd saved me. I'm so thankful for what you did."

"As always, it was a group effort," Donovan said.

"I finally understand. I've been down in the infirmary with Janie and Montero. I can't believe the number of people who stopped by to see how I was doing, to share with me what took place all over the ship when that monster took me hostage. I knew I was going to die, and I was so scared I could barely move. Even after Janie told me how you rescued me, I can hardly believe I'm still here."

"That's what families do," Donovan said, reminded of Michael's earlier words.

"Can we talk about last night?"

"Sure," Donovan said.

"I've been thinking about what I know, and how that might be perceived as a threat to you and your family. You have my word that your secret will stay that way. Buck would never forgive me for doing anything to damage you or Eco-Watch. He thought the world of you and what you've created. He was nothing if not loyal. It was one of the things I loved most about him. I'll never say a word. I do, however, have one small request."

"I'm listening," Donovan said.

"I'd like to be a part of Eco-Watch. It doesn't have to be full-time or anything, but I'd love a chance to be on call if someone in your organization is having problems. I can't express how much it would mean to me to be the therapist in position to move quickly so Eco-Watch personnel get immediate help."

"Starting with me?" Donovan said, and was rewarded by a rare full smile from Shannon.

"That's entirely your choice. Though after what you did saving me, I think you're doing very well. I'm sorry if I crossed any boundaries or offered any unwanted advice last night."

"You meant well, and you weren't wrong. I am a bit of a mess at times, but I'm working on things. I like your idea. I also have to say you handled yourself pretty well under extreme stress. Consider yourself hired. We'll sit down and discuss the details once we get home. How does that sound?"

"Perfect. Thank you. I saw what you and the others did today. I've been around Eco-Watch for less than two days, and I have a clearer vision of why Buck became so attached to your group of people. I think in his heart, Eco-Watch felt like a home to him, and I'll love being a part of that same experience."

"Did he ever tell you the story of the first time he and I met?"

"No, and I'd love to hear."

"It was years ago. We were in the back of a C-17 cargo plane—headed out to sea to intercept a category-five hurricane. He'd volunteered to parachute into the eye of the storm in a last-ditch effort to rescue some people. I remember him being so relaxed and cavalier as he described his plan. Buck picked up on my uneasiness about the mission pretty quickly. In the process of flying out to our destination, he was injured, and couldn't go into the water as planned. He talked me into facing my very worst fear. Through him, I found the courage needed. I ended up taking his place that day and went into the ocean."

"All of that took place before I met him, but I remember his injuries from that day. As tough as he was, he couldn't have swum that day. Did you save the people?"

"I had help, but yes. Thanks to Buck, we saved Michael, Lauren, and others. Everything worked, and he's the one who gave me the strength to do what I did. I often think back to that day, and the unlikely chain of events. I met Buck for the first time, and within hours he'd changed us all. If you can do a fraction of what he did, you'll truly be a gift to the organization."

"I will always try."

"Donovan," Ryan said as he knocked once and opened the door. "Sorry to interrupt, but the flashing light on the phone is a priority call for you from Washington."

"If it's the White House, tell them I'm busy," Donovan said.

"It's the Pentagon."

"I'll go." Shannon started to get up.

"No, stay," Donovan said to Shannon.

"There's also a helicopter inbound asking for permission to land." Ryan checked his watch. "Their ETA is fifteen minutes."

"Do we know who they are?"

"No."

"Grant them permission and inform Montero."

Ryan closed the door and Donovan eyed the phone momentarily. Then he picked up the receiver and pressed the button. "Donovan Nash."

"Mr. Nash, this is General Curtis at the Pentagon."

"General Curtis, what can I do for you?"

"I work with your wife, have for years, and it's come to my attention that we may have a misunderstanding that needs our combined attention."

"What particular misunderstanding might you be talking about?"

"Can we drop all the formalities?" Curtis exhaled heavily. "The last twenty-four hours have been some of the worst this country has faced. In the resulting confusion, some of the people under me may have acted without my approval or knowledge. Lauren, as she does so often, put together a solution to a problem that no one else had. She put the people together who could make it happen, and as usual, her idea worked, and as we both know, she never quits. My people don't understand that gift and acted impulsively after you charged into Monterey Harbor. I'm trying to make this right."

"I'm listening." Donovan smiled as he waited for the rest of the conversation to unfold.

"I have a television, as well as the Internet, Nash. I know what you did. Images of your ship coming through the smoke, ramming the dock, and working in conjunction with a 747 to save those people is the lead story all over the world, as is your wife. The men who ordered Lauren's arrest will be dealt with, I promise, but here's what I need from you. Lauren is en route via helicopter to the *Buckley*. She'll be there in ten minutes. I'd like her to be seen smiling, and for her to explain a few things to the survivors aboard your ship. The story she and I agreed upon was that there was a small, local misunderstanding, and that she was only being brought in for a debriefing, to give her the opportunity for us to bring her up to speed on all of the disaster operations."

"I think I can live with that," Donovan said. "Though there are a few things I'd like in return."

"What might they be?"

"Allow Eco-Watch to operate despite the no-fly order. We've got people who need to return to Washington."

"Done."

"One more thing. There was a former Navy SEAL, Howard Buckley. In fact, this ship is named after him. He was one of the bravest men I ever met, and he died doing the kind of thing we did today. The *Buckley* lived up to its name, and the world needs to know about that man, and the purpose of this ship. Will you help with his story?"

"I knew Buck," General Curtis said. "His uncle was a good friend of mine. It will be an honor and a privilege to honor your wish. Is there anything else I can do?"

"We're good," Donovan said. "I've got a helicopter to meet."

"Take care, Mr. Nash."

Donovan hung up the phone and began to pull himself up. Shannon hurried to his side and helped him stand as he positioned the crutches under his arms.

"That was beautiful." Shannon opened the door. "Thank you."

"I didn't do it for you," Donovan said. "I did it for him, as well as every person who will ever step foot aboard this ship."

CHAPTER FORTY-SIX

LAUREN FELT THE skids of the helicopter touch the helipad. Just outside the spinning arc of the rotor stood Donovan, stocking-footed, wearing borrowed clothes, a blue Eco-Watch hat pulled low. She smiled when she saw he was using crutches.

Donovan waited for her. A crewman opened the door and helped her to the deck, and she hurried to where Donovan stood. They hugged and kissed as the helicopter pilot shut down the engines and the assembled crowd of people began to cheer. Lauren felt her cheeks blush at all the attention and stood close to Donovan.

"I had a conversation with Shannon," Donovan said. "We're all good. She wants to work for Eco-Watch."

"The secret is safe?"

"Yes, though the big surprise of the day is that it turns out Michael knows about my past, and has for years. He came to warn me about Shannon. We had a good talk."

"Really?" Lauren looked at Donovan and waited for him to answer. "You've always dreaded him finding out the truth. Are you sure you're all right?"

"It's all good. I also spoke with General Curtis. I guess you're supposed to say a few words about a misunderstanding, a briefing, you know, government stuff, how you saved the world, and then we'll go up to the bridge for the rest of the trip."

"Actually, we're leaving in the helicopter," Lauren said as she smiled and waved. "It's part of my deal with the people who tried to mess with us."

"You're kidding." Donovan smiled as well. "I talked with the hospital. William is out of surgery. It went well, but they're going to keep him sedated until tomorrow."

"You've been busy," Lauren said as she glanced downward. "I really have to ask. How did you manage to lose your shoes?"

"Long story." Donovan swiveled on his crutches and they moved toward the crowd.

"I want to thank all of you," Lauren said as she shook outstretched hands. "I'm here to tell you that what looked like my arrest was actually a misunderstanding. Turns out I was needed ashore to consult on some after-action reports, and some of the language was misconstrued by the team sent out to the *Buckley* to get me. It's all good, but you guys are the best!

"I wanted to come back and personally thank you for your voice. The world knows what teamwork looks like. It's a good message to send. You all were great today. In the eye of the storm you kept calm, and we were able to pull everyone off the pier. Monterey Peninsula is going to need a great deal of work to be wonderful again, and I hope the camaraderie we all experienced today will motivate us all to work together, and be better neighbors, better people. At some point in the near future, this ship, the Eco-Watch research vessel *Buckley*, is going to be placed on loan to the Monterey Bay Aquarium for a joint mission studying the Arctic. On the day that happens, there is going to be one big party, and we want each and every one of you there to help us celebrate."

The survivors' cheers erupted. Donovan limped over to her side and hugged her.

"Please." Lauren held up her hands. "I'm going to take that applause as each of us applauding each other. We all deserve that today. Now, if you don't mind. I'm going to take my injured husband to San Francisco."

Donovan heard the turbine engine behind them spin to life, and the rotor blades began to turn.

Montero ran across the landing pad with Donovan's briefcase and leaned in so he could hear her. "There's an envelope in there I need you to read. We'll talk later."

Donovan nodded and he and Lauren climbed aboard. They waved to their friends on the bridge as they lifted clear of the *Buckley* and banked toward the Golden Gate Bridge.

"So, I made some phone calls," Donovan said as he put his arms around his wife. "You'll be happy to know I have an MRI scheduled for early tomorrow before we see William. Which means we have the rest of today to ourselves. I say the first thing we do is call our daughter, and tell her we're both fine, and that we'll be home soon. Then I thought we might try and have a nice dinner, relax, and catch up?"

"Are you kidding, you must be exhausted," Lauren said and smiled. "I bet neither one of us has slept in ages."

"Exactly," Donovan said. "Which is why I've reserved us a suite at the Fairmont, and then I called Phillipe."

Lauren spun in her seat, eyes wide. "Can he seat us? What time?"

"Even better," Donovan said. "He has, of course, seen the news. When I called, he didn't hesitate. He told me not to worry about a thing, that he was closing his restaurant tonight. As it turns out, he knows the executive chef at the Fairmont, who in turn has invited Phillipe to be the guest chef cooking for us tonight. We never have to leave our suite."

"Oh my God, does Phillipe remember what I like? Never mind, it doesn't matter, I love anything he cooks."

"He knows," Donovan said. "You'll be having the halibut dish you love. There is one detail I'll need your help with, though. It seems I've misplaced my wallet. You're going to have to buy."

"I think I can manage that," Lauren said as she cuddled up even closer. "Have I told you lately how much I love being married to you?"

"Yes, you have, but I always like hearing you say those words. Before we get to the hotel and open the bottle of champagne I ordered, can you tell me how much trouble you caused today?"

"I learned that General Curtis doesn't like to be flipped off, even if it's from clear across the country via the link from one of his drones. Beyond that little bit of awkwardness, it's all fine. Everyone seems happy with the results. That's enough work-talk. I have to ask again: Where in the world *are* your shoes?"

"I threw them overboard," Donovan said without hesitation.

"Why?"

"They made too much noise. So I kicked them off, but I couldn't leave them on the deck. That would have raised eyebrows, so I tossed them into the ocean. I'll buy a new pair."

"I gather there's a larger explanation coming?"

"Yes, much later," Donovan said. "Before I forget, Montero put a letter in my briefcase. Can you reach it and hand it to me?"

Lauren passed the envelope to Donovan, who opened it, quickly read the contents, and handed it back to her. Lauren began to read.

Donovan,

I know there is a great deal happening right now but I have news. You both saw Ethan with a one hundred dollar Bellagio chip. There's a story behind that chip. It has to do with relationships, leaps of faith, or as I told him, the gamble of allowing someone to get close. The chip was a gift for me, it means he's all in and wants a future together. That said, I'd like to request a partial transfer from Eco-Watch headquarters. For the time being, I'll be taking care of my duties from California, commuting as needed. I am more than happy to discuss more about this at your convenience.

Sincerely,
Montero

"I think it's wonderful." Lauren folded the paper. "Can she do it?"

"Of course." Donovan shrugged. "This is huge for her. I wouldn't dream of getting in her way."

"Let's text her right now." Lauren grabbed her phone. "What do you want to say?"

"Tell her to set up whatever works best for her. Tell her we love her, and we wish her the best."

"Perfect." Lauren punched in the letters and hit send. She pocketed her phone, took his face in both of her hands, and kissed him. "I'm so happy you're still alive."

"Me, too, and I'm married to someone famous now," Donovan said between kisses. "Your picture is attached to lead stories circulating around the world. You saved California. You could be governor if you wanted. I keep thinking about how lucky I am to be the guy who gets to sleep with you tonight."

"That's good, you keep thinking those thoughts. I have a limo waiting for us at the heliport." She snuggled in next to him. "I think we should go visit Rick tomorrow after we see William. We should probably get a car for the entire day," Lauren said, relishing being close to Donovan. When he didn't answer, she glanced over and realized his eyes were shut. He was asleep.

EPILOGUE

"Good morning." Lauren held the door open so Donovan could limp into the hospital room with his crutches. At the center of several monitors and wires lay William.

"This is a pleasant surprise," William said with a smile as he set aside his newspaper.

"Have you been awake long?" Donovan asked William. "How do you feel?"

"It's a hospital. They woke me at five a.m." William and Donovan hugged, and then William opened his arms for Lauren. "I'm a little beat up, but at least there's no pain. Considering all that happened, I feel pretty good."

"That's great news," Lauren said.

"I'll admit, when I was lying on the golf course after the tsunami, I was thinking it was the end." William shook his head as if casting aside the dark thoughts.

"Do you have everything you need?" Lauren asked. "Can we bring you anything?"

"I'm all set, thank you. You know I was just reading about you in the newspaper. You're famous. Besides the military, it seems Cal Fire and the Forest Service are also giving you credit for helping stop the fire. How does it feel?"

"It'll last until the next news cycle," Lauren said with a shrug. "Though the hotel staff were very sweet, as was the limo driver, and everyone else we've met this morning. I'll take my fifteen minutes, and then I plan to go back to my regular life."

"Have you had your leg looked at yet?" William asked Donovan.

"Yes, we got here early, and Donovan had an MRI," Lauren said. "The doctor explained that there are broken pieces of cartilage in his knee, and he'll need surgery to clean it all out. The good news is it'll wait until we're back in Virginia, so Donovan can recover at home. The procedure is minimally invasive, and we're told he'll be back to normal in six weeks."

"That's good news. How is everyone else doing?" William asked. "I only remember bits and pieces. Shannon?"

"Everyone is fine. Michael has a nick on his ear. Rick is recovering from his surgery and expected to make a full recovery," Donovan said. "Shannon is fine, physically, though she endured a great deal of stress. She's tough, and I think she'll be good. At least we'll be able to keep an eye on her—I hired her."

"I do like her." William nodded his head in approval. "Nice move."

"I need to ask you something." Donovan lowered his voice. "When we were in Pebble Beach, we'd just given you morphine, and you said some things. Do you remember anything?"

"Oh no." William's eyes darted from Lauren to Donovan. "Not a thing. What did I say?"

"Everything has been handled. You were swimming in morphine and you happened to mention Robert Huntington in front of Shannon. Now, before you get all concerned, Shannon is one of us now, and she's fine with what she knows. Because she's the new therapist on staff, which was her idea by the way, she can't reveal anything she's been told in confidence. It's a win-win."

"Everything is good," Lauren said. "We're just a little worried about you."

"You said some other things. Again, it could have been the morphine talking, but I need to ask. You said you felt like you ruined my life by helping me end Robert Huntington. That you conspired to help me leave a winnable fight, which in turn robbed me of my life."

William closed his eyes and his body sagged at the words.

"I hope you've never consciously felt that way," Donovan continued. "I've never regretted what we did. I have Lauren, Abigail, Michael, you, and Eco-Watch. I have a wealth that Robert was never going to attain. I have you to thank for all of those things. I wasn't robbed. You gave me the gift of life, as any father would."

"I've always loved you like a son, and I know exactly where my words came from. All day, while I was playing golf, I was reminded of our past together. Pebble Beach brought up so many memories of the two of us, as well as your mother and father. I found myself thinking of your father, who was without a doubt, my closest friend ever. I was remembering the business battles he and I engaged in and won. He was an exceptional man, a fighter, and a brilliant businessman. After the tsunami, I'm sure I was in shock, feeling I was about to die. I knew my only chance at survival was you. If you humanly could, you'd be coming for me. You're a fighter, too, even more so than your father. It was then I began to feel like I'd helped cheat the world out of Robert Huntington the III, who, in the tradition of his father, and his grandfather, is a remarkable individual. I felt as though I'd altered history, altered you—that my actions shortchanged the Huntington legacy."

"We did change a few things, in the best way possible, and I'll always love you for that." Donovan leaned down and kissed William on the forehead. "The truth of the matter is that, one day, Abigail will fully understand her family tree, and she'll evolve into the matriarch of the Huntington family. She'll be free to do with it as she pleases, and if you ask me, she may exceed the accomplishments of all the Huntingtons who've come before."

"We both love you so much. No regrets, ever," Lauren said. "In fact, one of the best things to happen over the course of the last two days we owe to you. It turns out that Michael has known about Donovan's secret for years. On the ship, he overheard Shannon and understood that she'd found out Donovan's past. Worried, because you and I were ashore, Michael took it upon himself to warn Donovan."

"You gave me my closest friend, Michael, who I now never have to lie to again. Thank you," Donovan said. "Look, we'll both have time to discuss this at length as we convalesce. Did the doctor give you any idea how long you'll be in here?"

"I haven't seen him yet today, but that's one of the questions on my list."

"Ask him if you can be discharged tomorrow morning. You'll be flying home on a chartered jet with your friends and family. Tell him he can come if he wants. The jet will be turning around, and he'll fly straight back here. In fact, why don't you plan to come home with Lauren and me, let us look after you until you feel better."

"I think that's a marvelous idea," Lauren said. "In fact, that's what's going to happen. I won't allow you to say no."

"Just think, Abigail will have her father and grandfather to spoil her around the clock."

"Oh, please, God, anything but that." Lauren laughed.

"Knock knock." The door opened partially, and Michael's voice called out. "Feel like more company?"

"Michael, come in, please," William said.

"Hey, guys," Michael said as he walked into the room holding a shopping bag.

Lauren was closest, and she leaned in and wrapped her arms around Michael and squeezed hard, followed by a kiss on the cheek.

Donovan adjusted his crutches with difficulty, reached out, grabbed Michael, and the two friends hugged.

"Michael, we can't tell you how happy we are with how everything turned out," Lauren said.

"Me, too," Michael said and then turned to William. "I've got to say, you look far better than when we plucked you out of the ocean."

"I don't know if I properly thanked you for that," William said. "Thank you."

"Glad to help." Michael reached into the bag and slid out a brand-new electronic tablet. "I borrowed this from the ship. I know for a fact, you didn't check in with very many possessions. I don't know about you, but I'd go crazy if television was the only news outlet I had."

"I refused to even turn it on this morning," William said. "Thank you, Michael. This is perfect."

"I do need to warn you. All that's on the news right now is endless footage of a cool ship and a very smart woman, who seems to have saved the world," Michael said. "The footage of the *Buckley* barging into Monterey Bay and wrecking the pier is almost topped by the low-flying 747 appearing out of the clouds and putting out the fire. We're all famous now, and I think it should be a movie. Matter of fact, we should all be in the movie."

"Not that Eco-Watch needed the press, but I think we did some good things out there this weekend," Lauren said. "A nonprofit can always use more donors."

"Montero, Janie, and Shannon are right behind me," Michael said. "We weren't sure how many visitors you could have, so I came up first while they stopped at the gift shop."

"Really, you guys are amazing," Donovan said as he stood and positioned his crutches to move out of the way to make more room near William. "Wait, you docked the ship in Oakland, spent the night there, and then drove over here this morning?"

"Uh, not exactly." Michael's eyes darted back and forth between Lauren and Donovan. "Lauren sent me a text yesterday saying that we all had rooms at the Fairmont, and dinner was on the house. Lauren's helicopter—that's what we sort of started calling it— landed on the *Buckley* just after we docked and we flew to downtown San Francisco. Thank you so much. We had an incredible dinner, followed by a few drinks at the bar afterwards. Maybe more than a few, but you'll see the rest of that story on my expense account."

"I picked up that tab," Lauren said before Donovan could even open his mouth. "It was an impressive bill. As a group, you do know how to celebrate."

"We're here," Montero said as she swung open the door, flowers in hand, leading Janie and Shannon into the room. "I don't know how long we can stay. The nurses looked at us funny as we walked past their station."

Janie stepped over to where Donovan stood. "I was hoping I'd see you today. I wanted to explain to you in person about the damaged helicopter."

"I've already heard all about it from Lauren," Donovan said with a smile. "She used words like extraordinary and remarkable. Without you, I'm not sure the three of us in the Gulfstream would still be alive. As far as I'm concerned, you're a legend."

"I got lucky," Janie said.

"Whoa." Montero slid into the conversation. "You got lucky?"

"By getting everyone back on the ship in that messed-up chopper."

"That's not luck," Montero said. "That's you, girl. You're the best helicopter pilot who ever lived."

"A legend," Donovan said.

"Exactly," Montero said.

"Janie," Michael called out. "When you get a moment, come tell William how you repaired the helicopter."

"Thank you for the text yesterday," Montero said as Janie walked away. "I wasn't sure how you'd respond to my request, or when I was going to see you again."

"Lauren and I are both thrilled. Ethan is a good guy. You know, I remember back to when you and I first met. You were one of the angriest people I'd ever met, with good reason. We've both come a long way since then, and I'm so happy you've found someone."

"Any advice?"

"We've both lost people we loved. If you're all in—live it the best you can, each and every day. Never take a single moment for granted."

Montero put her arms around Donovan, gave him a quick hug, and whispered, "Thank you."

Donovan smiled as Montero slid past Michael and found Lauren. Donovan adjusted his crutches, centered his weight, and decided he already hated the things. When he looked up, Shannon was standing in front of him.

"How's the leg?" Shannon asked.

"Nothing a little surgery can't fix," Donovan said. "How do you feel today?"

"It's still all a little surreal. Considering everything we went through, it'll take a little while for me to process everything, but I'll be fine. To be honest, I feel like a different person, that the fog I've been living in is gone. The world seems bright again. Anyway, enough about me, how are you doing?"

"If I had it to do over, I might have skipped being adrift in the ocean. Then again, I had you to help me past the worst part. Buck would have been proud of you. I know I am."

"Thank you for everything. I owe you my life, like five times over."

"We don't keep track of those things around here," Donovan said. "Any regrets about decisions you made yesterday?"

"None. Well, maybe one," Shannon whispered to Donovan. "I may have had a little too much to drink last night. I've been out drinking with Navy SEALs, so Michael, even Montero, I could keep up with, but Janie is another story."

"Oh, no, you can't keep up with her," Donovan said. "No one can. The Australians are just built different. Trust me. I know."

"Before all that insanity began last night, I did make something for you." Shannon handed Donovan a small scroll wrapped in a pink ribbon. "I thought you could share it with your daughter, you know, from Buck. You can open it later."

"Alright people!" The nurse opened the door, her voice easily filling the room. "Mr. VanGelder is recovering from surgery. We restrict visitors to family only; everyone else needs to leave."

"We're all family," Donovan said.

"He's right," Lauren added. "We all belong here."

"You've got five minutes, and then visitors will be limited to two at a time." The nurse shook her head and left the room.

"I have some quick announcements before they split us up," Donovan said. "I spoke with Rick this morning, and he, like William, is feeling a bit wrung out, but is doing well and expected to make a full recovery. Lauren and I are headed over to see him next. I've arranged for Eco-Watch to fly under a special waiver. We're going home tomorrow via a chartered Gulfstream. The flight leaves San Francisco at noon. Michael, Shannon, Lauren and I, and hopefully William will be on board. Montero will not. She is staying in the Bay Area to help oversee the repairs to the *Buckley*, as well as work with our friends at the Monterey Bay Aquarium. I also want to announce that Shannon is the newest member of Eco-Watch. It's long overdue that we have a mental health professional in house."

"Finally," Michael said amidst the laughter.

"Okay, last night was a practice run. There will be an encore outing this evening that includes my very famous wife, and her very grateful husband. Everyone meet at the hotel bar at six p.m., so we can celebrate all our good fortunes, this evening, together. Montero, please bring Ethan. We really are all family, and let's never do it any other way."

Everyone took turns talking with William and saying their goodbyes. Donovan and Lauren promised to check in on him later in the day, and then made their way out into the hallway.

"I love those people," Lauren said, walking slowly as Donovan found a rhythm with his crutches. "Montero came over and thanked me for all of my support, and then she told me about the advice you gave her. You're so sweet. Did I see Shannon hand you something?"

"Yes, she said it was for Abigail," Donovan said as he stopped, held his crutches with one hand, and pulled the scroll from his pocket. He handed it to Lauren, who untied the ribbon. Inside he saw Shannon's elegant handwritten script as Lauren unrolled the heavy paper.

As the brightness and clarity of the day fades, we ask you, Lord, to keep us safe until morning. In the depth of night, we pray that you will show us the path with your everlasting light. As always, Lord, we trust in you to protect us from danger, and in your wisdom, we pray that you'll speed the dawn. Amen.

Donovan put his arm around Lauren's shoulder and held her close. "It was the middle of the night in Pebble Beach, and I overheard Shannon saying this prayer. She explained that it was from Buck's mother, told to Buck, who in turn shared it with Shannon. She made this for Abigail, as a gift from Buck, a reminder I guess, that he's still watching over all of us."

"It's so beautiful," Lauren said. "I'd forgotten she's an artist. Abigail will love this."

"Absolutely, we'll have it framed for her room." Donovan carefully rolled up the scroll and Lauren retied the ribbon. "I'm assuming Montero asked you for your relationship advice as well as mine. What did you tell her?"

"I told her I didn't know Ethan very well, but I do know her. I reminded her to be strong, but not always the strongest. Bask in the good, repair the bad, and to be Ethan's biggest cheerleader—and expect the same in return."

"That's perfect advice for Montero. Nicely done." Donovan, balancing himself on his good leg, put his free arm around Lauren, pulled her close, and kissed her.

"What was that for?" Lauren asked after the embrace.

"For a million reasons," Donovan said. "Perhaps the most important is the sheer exhilaration at still being alive, and my eternal good fortune to be married to you."